IN VALHALLA'S SHADOWS

DISCARD

IN VALHALLA'S SHADOWS

W.D. VALGARDSON

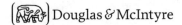 Douglas & McIntyre

DOUGLAS AND MCINTYRE (2013) LTD.
P.O. Box 219, Madeira Park, BC, V0N 2H0
www.douglas-mcintyre.com

Edited by Pam Robertson
Front jacket design by Anna Comfort O'Keeffe
Text design by Shed Simas / Onça Design
Printed and bound in Canada
Printed on paper made from 100% post-consumer waste

Douglas and McIntyre (2013) Ltd. acknowledges the support of the Canada
Council for the Arts, which last year invested $153 million to bring the arts to
Canadians throughout the country. We also gratefully acknowledge financial
support from the Government of Canada and from the Province of British
Columbia through the BC Arts Council and the Book Publishing Tax Credit.

LIBRARY AND ARCHIVES CANADA CATALOGUING IN PUBLICATION
Valgardson, W. D., author
        In Valhalla's shadows / W.D. Valgardson.
Issued in print and electronic formats.
ISBN 978-1-77162-196-0 (hardcover).—ISBN 978-1-77162-197-7 (HTML)
        I. Title.
PS8593.A53158 2018   C813'.54   C2018-901900-X
                                               C2018-901901-8

My thanks to Nina for all her help.

CHAPTER 1

VALHALLA

When Tom nearly tripped over her, the false dawn was just starting. The east side of the lake had lightened with nautical twilight, but there was no sign of the sun. Pools of darkness obscured everything, including the person lying on the ground.

It, he thought, it, he, she, someone, a person, a person was lying there, where no one should be. But on weekends there were often bonfires like a string of small stars on the curve of beach to the north and people partied all night long. If he walked out at night and stood on the water's edge, he could see the dark shapes of people moving in and out of the light cast by the fires, and when they threw a log onto the coals, he could see the shower of sparks rise into the darkness.

He'd slipped out of the house, threaded through the spruce trees at the edge of his property, crossed the road to the harbour area and was heading north across the gravelled space between the government dock on the south and a reef on the north. He was being careful not to stumble over boat trailers or fish boxes that were left scattered about. He'd only moved to Valhalla six weeks ago, but he knew where the commercial fishermen piled their plastic tubs and stored their blue gasoline barrels close to an aluminum-sided shed.

Because of seasonal high water, the store and the six adjacent one-room rental cabins centred on the harbour area were built well back from the lake. The area was low-lying and a strong northeast wind often flooded the ground. The store and cabins were set on concrete blocks, and even the houses farther back were raised so that storm-driven water went beneath them without doing any damage. People just sloshed around in the yards wearing rubber boots for a day or two until the northeast wind fell and the water receded. In place of basements, everyone had a shed. Many of them were in disrepair.

That there'd been high water recently could be seen in the remains of a sandbagged wall at one side of the store. The property just to the south that Tom had bought was opposite the store but on higher ground than the surrounding area. In spite of that, the foundation of his house had settled at one corner, and he was going to have to lift the house and straighten it.

When he realized someone was lying on the ground he was annoyed. *Stupid kids*, he thought. Drinking and drugs and passing out before they made it home. He'd had enough of stupid kids. He was tempted to leave the kid lying there to sleep off whatever he'd taken, but he knew he couldn't. He didn't want to roll him over onto his back. If he vomited, he'd choke. However, he could put him on his side.

Tom put down his rucksack, tackle box and rod, opened the box and took out his penlight. The white shirt was too large and so were the blue jeans, and he thought for a moment that it was a young boy but was shocked when he realized it was a girl. When he pulled her onto her side, one leg stayed in the water-filled rut and the other lay on top of the mud. Her feet were bare. *No socks, no shoes, no service* popped into his mind. It was a sign on the window of the store behind him. Little feet, little hands, a kid, he thought, maybe early high school.

Her long black hair was plastered to the side of her face by the mud. He felt her hand and it was cold and there was no pulse, and he wished that he hadn't been driven out of the house by nightmares. Although he'd brought his fishing tackle, he'd planned to just sit and wait for the sun to come up, for the surface of the lake to turn from slate to silver to pale blue and to listen to the faint lap of the water at the edge of the shore.

He'd seen them dead before, too many of them, in wrecked cars mostly, thrown from motorcycles, stupid tricks gone wrong, kids with their arms or heads out of car windows hitting a sign, diving into shallow water, drinking, drinking, drinking, dealing, stabbed or shot or overdosed, always immortal until the moment they weren't.

He kneeled in the mud and leaned close to her and smelled whisky. He leaned so his nose was nearly touching her and there was no mistaking the smell. He then leaned over the water in the rut and smelled it; it, too, smelled faintly of whisky.

I don't want this, he thought. *I've had too much of it*, and he wondered if he could slip back to his bed and go to sleep and pretend it had never happened. *The dead are dead*, he thought, you can't resurrect them, not unless you're God. And he thought about picking up his minnow net, his rod, his tackle box, his father's World War II rucksack that was an affection, an affectation; his father had brought it home from the war, and when he died it was one of the few things of his that Tom had kept, along with his chess set, his fly-fishing equipment and his music. It was out of date, not nearly as light or efficient as anything he could buy at Walmart, but it suited him.

His father had taken it on every fishing trip. Tom couldn't imagine going fishing without it, without a thermos of coffee with cream and sugar and an egg salad sandwich to eat as he watched the sun rise. He'd moved here for that, for silence, for casting his line over the still surface of the lake, for getting away from all the noise in his head, from all the memories. Away from the grow ops, the meth labs, from young studs shooting each other to save face and territory, from drunken family brawls, from battered wives.

He glanced over the lake at the eastern horizon. Nautical twilight, the best time of day, soon civil twilight, then dawn. There was a thin crimson line that might have been drawn with one stroke of a brush but no sign of the sun. The masts of the sailboats at the dock stood up sharp and threatening like lances against the lightening sky. The powerboats and yachts, though, anchored farther out in the harbour, were still obscured by darkness.

He turned the girl fully onto her back and used the flashlight beam to probe the rut where she'd been lying face down. The sides of the rut had been forced upward and then eroded by the rain. It had maybe four inches of water in it. Not much, but you didn't need much to drown.

She couldn't, Tom thought, have been lying here for long. The ruts were from the sports fishermen pulling up their boats the previous evening. Normally, fishermen, and even the sailboaters, lingered on the water, then crowded in as the light began to fade, but there had been a storm warning, high winds and rain. Everyone had come back early. No one wanted to be caught on the lake during an electrical storm, with squalls that could turn a boat upside down in an instant, then disappear as suddenly as they came. But most dangerous of all were the reefs. The locals knew where every reef was, those that rose above the water, those that lurked beneath the surface. Numerous visiting anglers had wrecked a propeller or holed their craft. The reefs that rose above the surface of the water were hazardous but, unless the sports fishermen were too busy partying, could be seen and avoided. Those that lay just below the surface were the ones that brought visiting anglers and sailboaters to grief. There'd been some discussion of putting markers on the submerged reefs, but nothing had come of it. There was a small but steady business rescuing anglers and repairing their boats.

The rain hadn't come before dark. Off to the north, lightning had woven in and out of a thunderhead, and then there had been bolt lightning. Lying on the couch reading a biography of Churchill, he could hear distant thunder. Normally, he would have waited expectantly for the storm to roll over him, but he'd been so tired that he fell asleep with the book on his chest.

She could, he thought, have passed out in the rut before the rain came. She'd have been in no danger. She'd have slept off whatever mix she'd taken, gotten up and gone home. She'd have been thirsty, with a headache, a sick stomach, maybe puke a few times, but she'd get over it. Unless, of course, she'd taken something laced with fentanyl.

The rain had been hard, a Manitoba summer downpour. A peal of thunder had wakened him and the rain that followed had come all at once like a waterfall, pounding on the roof. He'd listened to it for a minute or two, then got up and lowered the windows until they were nearly shut. It had been hot during the day, muggy at night, and he'd been sleeping with the windows open so the cooler air from the lake would seep in through the screens. During the day he'd been ripping out dry rot, putting in new two-by-fours. Between the work and the heat, he was exhausted, so when he rolled back into bed, he quickly fell asleep. When he woke from his nightmares, the rain was over, but he could smell the heavy mustiness of it, smell and feel the cooler air, the dampness.

This morning, when he'd stepped off the back porch, there'd been puddles. There should have been a story in her footprints, other footprints, but the churned clay was soft and the hard rain had blurred everything.

It was not unusual for people at the beach to walk around barefoot. People walked along the water's edge barefoot. Waded barefoot. Went barefoot up to the store, where there was a galvanized tub filled with flip-flops for people to put on before they entered. Just like in classier restaurants where a jacket was necessary but not necessarily your own jacket. The hostess would bring you a jacket from a nearby closet. Dress codes were one thing. Losing business was another. Of course, if the hostess didn't like the cut of your jib, there would be no jacket brought out of the closet. His father often had said that: the cut of your jib. His father had been in the army not the navy, but he'd picked up a small dictionary of military terms that peppered his speech.

His father had had a moustache that he carefully scrutinized in front of the mirror every morning. If there were an errant hair, he clipped it with a tiny pair of scissors with curved blades. He was a bookkeeper, and his days were taken up with numbers. Every number had to be in its precise place by the end of each day or he couldn't go home.

Tom jerked his attention back to the girl lying in the mud and water. Since his accident, he found it difficult to focus, his mind pulling him away from anything stressful, blocking it out with memories. "Focus," he whispered to himself, "focus, focus."

No jewellery on her ankles or fingers. He stood up and walked toward the lake. He thought whatever she might have been wearing on her feet could have gotten stuck in the mud and might indicate the direction from which she was coming. The pale circle of light revealed nothing in the mud, nothing at the water's edge.

The light was spreading up the sky, the shadows shortening. He went back and forced himself to crouch beside the body.

Where was she from, he wondered, the village, the dock, the cottages, the beach? He hadn't been in Valhalla long enough to know or even guess. Someone was going to be getting bad news. He hated that, when he was on the Force, having to go to a house, knock on the door and when it opened, ask if he could come in and the mother, father, wife, husband would hesitate, uncertain, then their face would tense with worry, and they'd say, "Yes, of course, officer, come in." And he'd go in and ask them to sit down, as he had something to tell them, and they'd sit, usually on a living room couch or, especially in the country, on a kitchen chair, and they might distractedly ask him if he'd like coffee and he'd say, "No, thank you, I have bad news for you." Sometimes, they'd scream or cry, but often they'd just sit stunned, their faces drained of blood, their bodies paralyzed and their eyes not seeing anything. If they were alone, he'd ask if there was a relative they could call and ask to come over. They'd ask him if he was sure, couldn't it be a mistake, couldn't it be a neighbour's house he should be visiting? Or they'd insist it wasn't possible because they had an event planned for the evening. They'd ask what happened and he'd tell them what he knew. As he left, he'd ask them if they were going to be okay and they'd say, "Yes, I'll be fine, I'll be fine," but he knew they wouldn't be.

He heard the faint metallic clank of a coffee pot being put on a stove in one of the boats. An early riser. Unless they were going sailing or motoring to another harbour, most of the boat people slept late. There really was nothing for them to do in Valhalla. That was why they came. Away from the city, away even from the larger towns, to a place where nothing ever happened, where there was nothing to tempt them away from a hammock or a foamy thrown on deck. They would sail out to one of the islands, anchor there, go ashore and wander about. The only wild animals they needed to keep an eye out for were bears. They'd have a picnic, sail back. Occasionally, they'd make friends with a cottager and visit back and forth. Mostly, they visited among themselves, setting up a BBQ on the dock, having drinks on deck, talking, their sudden bursts of laughter like small explosions in the silence.

The clank of the pot was followed by a brief muttering of morning voices. In the silence, every sound carried. The standard poodle on the *Lazy Johanna* barked and the owner told it to be quiet. It was a ritual. It barked every morning and it was told to shut up every morning. Once the sun was above the horizon, a rooster would crow from among the cluster of village houses.

The mud squelched as Tom moved. If he still had his cellphone, he'd have called the local detachment, but he couldn't afford the plan right now. Lumber, nails, wiring, the price of everything had been going up lately. He'd start the plan again in the fall. In any case, the service here was spotty. You had to walk around with your phone, testing for areas where it would work. Mostly, the message on the phones was *No service*. He really didn't need one, though, because there was no one to call. He hadn't talked to Sally in three months. The last time he'd called, the conversation had been short, awkward. He'd wanted to know if the kids had been in touch. "I'm sure if they want to talk to you, they'll call you," she said before she hung up. She took the craziness of their adolescence personally.

He didn't understand why she was angry. It had been her idea to separate. She couldn't, she said, put up with his moping, his being depressed after he came out of the hospital.

"Get a job," she'd said, "any job. Go back to school. Don't just sit there."

If his father had been alive, he'd have said, "Buck up. Don't be like those who got shell shock. Thinking about what you can't change is a waste of time. Pick up your rifle and keep going. Otherwise, an officer will have to shoot you." His father had joined the army as soon as the war had started, had survived six years of war. He was a military buff and had a small library of books on World Wars I and II. Being in the army had been the most important thing in his life. Tom thought that when the war was over every serviceman had cheered, but his father said no, that wasn't the case. Many had fallen into deep depression because they were going back to being shop assistants or cab drivers.

Tom looked east. He liked to have his line in the water just as the sun rose. The fishing was always best first thing in the morning, when the water was cool. He liked to sit as far out on the reef as possible, bait his hook with a minnow, cast, then sit and watch another day begin. His father always said still fishing was lazy man's fishing. He preferred fly-fishing, whipping flies out onto the surface of the water, skipping the fly to tease and trick the fish into biting. More than once he said he wouldn't have been able to fly-fish in England. Not enough money, wrong social class. He would like to have fished for trout but couldn't afford the trips, the rentals, the meals. He made do with fishing the rivers that ran through and near Winnipeg.

There were no trout here, in Valhalla, and if fish came to the surface to feed on insects, it was in the evening, when the water dimpled with overlapping circles. Mornings, Tom stuck to his still fishing, casting his bait out, letting it sink, his finger on the line, waiting for the slight vibration to tell him that he had a nibble and, when it grew stronger, to set the hook. In any case, these weren't really fighting fish, not like the big jacks or the trout in other spots. This was frying pan fishing. Out of the water, into the frying pan: silver fillets—pickerel, sauger and perch.

The north beach was still deep in shadow, but he knew what was there. Weekend tenters, usually in their teens or early twenties, roasting wieners and marshmallows around open fires every night. The kind of tenters that the yacht people kept their kids away from, not wanting them to join in the singing and guitar playing, people dancing around campfires, smoking weed, making love in the bushes or in sleeping bags. They didn't want their kids going over there to have fun with the hoi polloi or, if you believed them, join in the orgies. There was a lot of beer drinking around the campfires, or at least, there were a lot of empty beer bottles stacked in cases behind the store. The local kids scavenged the beach because the store gave them cash for the bottles.

The yachters were people in their fifties with money, who seldom had kids with them and didn't pay any attention to what went on down the beach. In any case, they could hardly complain about the beer bottles. There were a lot of mornings when a flotilla of wine bottles floated in the harbour.

She was dead, dead, dead. There was nothing he could do to help. He didn't want to be involved; he had come here to avoid situations like this. But then he thought of his daughter, Myrna, and how it could be her. But it couldn't be her: this girl was small boned, fragile; Myrna took after him, solidly built. She was attractive but muscular from running, weightlifting, playing hockey, kick-boxing. A broken rib hadn't stopped the kick-boxing. She was proud of her bruises. "Black and blue," she bragged. "It's the colour scheme for a goth."

The girl in the mud was someone's daughter, but he'd had enough of this, too much of this, and he shut his eyes and thought if no one found her body until the sun rose, it would make no difference. He was trying to decide what to do when he realized that a person was standing in the shadows, watching him.

CHAPTER 2

A FALLEN ANGEL

"Who's there?" Tom asked.

"Me. Albert," a high reedy voice replied. "What are you doing? Is everything all right?" He was standing at the end of a sailboat that was up on blocks. Tom wouldn't have known anyone was there except that Albert had moved.

"Oh, shit," Tom said under his breath; it could have been anyone but Albert Scutter. He'd stopped and met him just to say hello, nice to meet you, but he'd seen him drinking a cup of coffee and it had been painful to watch. Albert was a nervous wreck of a man, stoop shouldered, thin as a slat, hands that never stopped trembling. He went out every morning around dawn for his constitutional, thrashing his way around the village three times. He wore an old, battered panama hat, light corduroy pants and a short-sleeved dress shirt without a tie. Although he'd been in Canada a good part of his life, he still had his London accent. He had a habit of taking a deep breath and pursing his lips when he disapproved of something.

The sky was rapidly growing pink and yellow, while the ground was still thick with shadow. The darkness, heavier than light, seemed to be draining from the sky and pooling on the ground before sinking into the earth. Tom stood up and went to where Albert was peering from behind the bow of the boat.

"There's a girl lying on the ground," Tom said.

"One of those drunk kids passed out," Albert said disapprovingly. "Nowadays—" he started.

"She's dead," Tom said, cutting him off. He wasn't interested in hearing a speech about how depraved the younger generation was.

Albert stopped what he was going to say and took a sharp breath; his tremor increased so that his whole body shook. He opened and closed his mouth twice before he managed to say, "Who?"

"I don't know. A young girl. Long dark hair, jeans, a white shirt."

"What were you doing there?" He was gripping the bow of the boat with both hands.

"We'll need to call the police. Do you want to look and see if you recognize her?"

"No." Albert's different parts shook at different speeds and in different directions. He looked like he might fly apart. "Those hippies. It'll be one of them. Them and their commune. They're a bad lot." His voice had risen so high that it reminded Tom of the whistle of a steam kettle.

Sometimes, in the early morning, day fishermen would turn up, but since there were none this morning, Tom thought the road must have turned into a quagmire. The last sixty miles was swamp and muskeg that had no bottom and, in spite of endless loads of crushed rock being dumped on it, constantly threatened to disintegrate. Heavy rain returned the road to the swamp. If a car went down to its axles, it would require a tractor to pull it out. Mud holes would mean that the uniforms might be slow arriving.

A woman from the village appeared, pulling a wagon with a gasoline can and a box of nets on it. She was large, big boned, wearing overalls with a plaid shirt underneath, rubber boots, a cap that said, *Hoger's Nets*. Her grey hair was tied back, caught at the nape of her neck. She had the wagon handle in her left hand and a cane in her right.

"What's up?" she asked Albert. "You're usually making your second circuit by now."

Albert was rattling against the side of the boat. Tom thought he was using it to keep from falling down.

"There's been an accident," Tom said. From where they were standing, the dark outline of the body was just visible. "It's a girl. She's dead. We need some stakes and rope to keep people away."

She stared at him, unspeaking, looked toward the vague outline of the body, back at him, nodded once, then turned on her heel and disappeared behind one of the boats.

The horizon was turning blood red, and although the sun was barely above the edge of the lake, it had the look of a polished copper sphere that threatened the kind of heat that would soon turn the leaves of the trees limp and dry up the water underfoot. People from the boats at the docks were starting to appear, stretch, shout to neighbours. The doors of the rental units beside the café were being opened and shut noisily as the renters went to use the bathrooms and showers. The smell of onions cooking at White's drifted from the café.

A couple of boaters had noticed something was amiss and wandered over. By now, the body was obvious, the arm outflung, the leg akimbo. The face, where it was clear of mud and hair, shining in the morning light. Tom explained the situation once again, and after gawking from where they stood, the boaters hurried back to the dock. It was obvious from the waving of their arms and their pointing that they were telling everyone who was awake that there was a body on the beach, and those people, in turn, were ducking into the cabins of boats and signalling the late risers to come onto the dock to hear the news.

For the next little while it was going to be a matter of crowd control, Tom thought. He'd been good at crowd control. That was when he was still a cop, before his accident, before his career had come to a halt and his marriage fallen apart, before days that disappeared in yelling matches and recriminations, and before Sally finally said enough with his black moods. He'd rented an illegal basement suite in a house that had been divided into six apartments. It had a toilet that plugged up for no particular reason. It had a fridge that never kept the milk from going sour for more than three days. It made his depression worse. He had too many books for the suite. There was no proper closet, just a beat-up cabinet painted white and a broom handle hung from two wires for his clothes. There was a four-drawer dresser that didn't match the cabinet. It was the ugliest dresser he had ever seen, white with raised curlicues painted gold. It was, he guessed, supposed to look French. He stored most of his belongings in a rental locker.

The woman in the overalls came back with a bundle of slats and a tangle of yellow rope. She handed them to Tom and they started to jam the sticks into the clay five feet from the body, but their work drew a crowd that formed a ragged crescent. The clay made a sucking sound as Tom pulled his boots free.

"Here," Overalls said, grabbing Albert's arm. "You take these. I'll be right back."

Albert followed Tom, but he refused to look at the body, kept his head turned away, gazing off into the distance. Anyone watching him would have thought there was something of great importance happening where the spruce trees were reluctantly giving up their morning shadows and light was revealing everything that had been shrouded in darkness. People were coming up and looking and leaving, bending their heads together, whispering. Mothers were shooing kids back to the boats or making them keep to the path to the café. The sun was merciless. It allowed nothing to be hidden, the ruts, the water that now gleamed like dark glass, the one foot, naked on top of the rut in which the body half lay.

There was hardly a sound. The spectators stood around, uncertain, like they were waiting for a miracle, for the body to rise up, declare it was all a joke and walk away laughing. Death could be like that. Especially when there were no signs of violence, no gunshot wounds, no severed limbs, no blood, just a body lying on the ground, the only indication of death the awkwardness of the limbs. There was a camera flash, then another.

The woman in the overalls came back with a blue tarp she'd pulled off a pile of boxes near the shed where the fishermen cleaned and iced their fish. Tom would have told her not to disturb the site, in case a crime has been committed, but he, too, was offended by the people snapping pictures, so he said nothing.

She stood for a moment in the not yet closed gap in the rope, then leaned over to get a better look. "It looks like Ben's kid," she said, and the shock in her voice seemed to hollow out the words, make them crumble before they had gone any distance. She leaned closer to get a better look, then pulled back and spread the tarp over the body.

Ben Finlayson, he thought, with a sudden twinge. Ben in his plaid shirt and wide red suspenders. He drove a beat-up Dodge box truck. He was fat, not sloppy fat but huge around the waist, with big shoulders and arms like hams. He was not a talker. He mostly stuck to facts, saying things like "This here's the key to the front door. This one's the key to the back door. You give me a grocery list for my run and I buy at Superstore." A couple of times he'd stayed to talk about where Tom could get lumber cheap from a local mill, that sort of thing. He said his truck was clean. He swept it out and washed it after every trip.

"It was an accident," Albert said sharply, nearly shouting, to nobody in particular, his voice high, on the verge of breaking. Tom was waiting for Overalls to back up now that she'd covered the body. Albert had a fierce grip on the remaining slats. He had them pressed tightly to his narrow chest. "Some people's kids get drunk. That's all. They're not brought up right. This is a good community."

"This isn't a show," the woman said to the spectators. "Go on. Go about your business." Her voice was harsh, angry. She waved her arms at the crowd standing there. The line broke up and people walked away, muttering to each other and looking back over their shoulders.

Tom finished setting up the sticks and rope. The blue tarp didn't cover the body's left foot, and lying there, naked, it seemed obscene. Tom pulled the tarp over the foot.

He turned to Albert, who was still talking about how safe the town was. He lived by a schedule. After his constitutional, he milked and fed his five goats, had tea and a muffin with jam, worked in his garden until noon, had lunch, walked up to the store to see if any mail had come, bought a Mars bar summer and winter, walked back to his house, finished his chores, and then began carving.

"You're free to go," the woman in overalls said to Albert, before Tom had a chance to say anything, dismissing him as a teacher might a pupil from detention. Albert's Adam's apple jerked up and down, his body vibrated faster. He shoved the remaining slats at her, turned and fled.

Just then Horst and Karla White appeared on the porch of their emporium. "Store" didn't describe it adequately because it was also the post office, a café, an ice cream shop, and it had the six one-room shacks the owners rented out to sports fishermen or tourists. The shacks didn't have toilets, but attached to one end of the emporium were two rooms with multiple toilets and showers. Normally, if there was an incident of any kind, Karla was quick to push her way into it, making certain that her clients paying for space at the dock, or renting a cabin, or hiring a guide were taken care of. Now, she hung back, staying on the front porch, one arm resting on a wooden pillar. Her husband had come out pulling his oxygen tank in a bundle buggy. Horst was shorter than Karla, bald and bad-tempered, heavy-set. His head was moving from side to side like he was smelling the air. He took in the situation, the sticks and rope, the tarp, the people bunched together all looking at the same thing, and he jerked his oxygen tank down the steps and started toward where the blue tarp lay like a stain on the ground. He couldn't manage more than a slow walk, stopping when the wheels stuck in the soft ground, jerking the buggy free. Karla called him back, and when he didn't listen to her, she followed him. She was dressed like a Hollywood cowgirl. Tom had never seen her in anything but Western-style blouses and skirts and cowboy boots. She also kept getting stuck in the mud and had to stop, catch the top of a boot and pull on it to get it loose.

Tom could hear Horst cursing as he once again jerked the buggy free. Karla caught up to him and grabbed his arm to stop him from coming any closer. They didn't join the knot of people who had gathered to one side.

"Ben's kid," Overalls half shouted to Karla. Horst couldn't hear her and had to ask his wife what had been said, and she turned her head sharply and repeated the information. He raised himself to his full height to get a better look at what was under the tarp. He would have started forward again, but his wife tightened her grip on his arm.

"What happened?" Karla demanded. She still had a firm grip on her husband's arm.

Overalls raised both arms halfway with her hands out and shrugged. "Ben's overnight in the city," she said.

A few locals had gathered but stayed back a ways and separate from the summer visitors. Tom recognized some of them, not by name but from having seen them around the village, mostly in the store. Tom realized that they were looking at him. Even though no one said so, it was obvious that they expected him to do something.

Overalls went over to the group of locals. They gathered around her, asking questions for which she had no answers except for the name of the girl hidden from the rising sun by the tarp. The sun, though it was barely above the horizon, was already driving away the last vestiges of cool air created by the storm of the previous night.

From the time he'd moved into the Ford place in mid-May, word had gotten around that Tom was an ex-cop. God knows what rumours went with it. No one had been rude, but no one had gone out of their way to be friendly, either.

Most bachelors moving in merited an apple pie or an invitation to supper. He hadn't had either. He'd been posted to towns like that. Everyone had something they'd just as soon not have the local police know. Usually domestic stuff, a drinking problem, kids doing petty crimes, minor drug dealing, moose meat in the freezer out of season. And if a local got to be known as a friend of the cops, people stopped talking freely around them, too.

He shifted off his game leg. The surgeons did what they could after he was cut out of his car, but now his left leg was slightly shorter than his right. It didn't show much unless he got tired and then his foot dragged a bit, or if he had to stand in one place too long.

Some of the waitresses had crowded onto the porch. Karla turned and shouted, "Go back inside. You've got work to do." Their pale inquisitive faces had clustered just beyond the door. "Back, back," she repeated, more harshly now. They hesitated, looking at each other, looking at Karla, looking at the blue tarp, then fled inside. "The Mounties will be here shortly," Karla said to no one in particular, and her voice was high and sharp. "Accidents happen."

Normally, Karla was noisy, shouting out to people with exaggerated greetings. She had bangles on both arms and large earrings. She was always performing, always onstage, even if you were just buying a litre of milk, but now she stood in the morning light, her makeup harsh, her Western outfit out of place, her shoulders slumped. She stood in one place, but her body twisted back and forth as if she wanted to turn around and flee but couldn't get her feet loose from the mud. Her cowboy boots, Tom thought, were going to be a mess. White and tan, intricately decorated, they weren't made for wading in the mud.

She let go of her husband's arm, said something to him that Tom could not hear and walked away. Her husband jerked his bundle buggy loose and reluctantly followed her, his bald head shining and his fringe of white hair reflecting little points of light.

"What's that about?"

"Bad for business. She takes bad for business things personally."

Studying the woman facing him, he thought she must be in her late seventies. Her skin was heavily wrinkled, wind and sun burned.

"What're you staring at?" she demanded.

He took two steps toward her and stuck out his hand. "Tom Parsons," he said.

She studied his hand for a moment before reaching out and shaking it. Her grip was firm and her hand rough. "Sarah O'Hara," she replied.

Her fingers were stained dark brown. They didn't worry about smoking rules here. People smoked wherever they felt like it, and Tom thought that if a bylaws officer came out to investigate, he would end up being tossed off the dock.

Her red wagon waited with its dull red gasoline can and box of nets. The black handle sat tilted back, pointing at nothing. She leaned on her cane, and Tom noticed it was made from diamond willow. From top to bottom there were the light and dark diamond patterns that gave it its name. She saw him looking at the cane and said, "Bad hip. I'm waiting for a replacement." Her cane had sunk into the mud.

"I've got a couple of nets to lift. After I get back and get my catch cleaned and iced, if you want a cup of tea, you're welcome to drop by. Karla will have called the cops, but twenty people probably beat her to it." She pointed to her house, which was on the other side of the harbour. "The red roof. That's mine. Sort of exciting," she added sarcastically, "being able to call and say somebody's dead."

She was right. He remembered those calls, not the calls of the family or friends in pain but of strangers wanting to be part of the action, part of something they could tell their friends about over a drink.

"An hour?" he asked.

"Two. Lift the nets, bring in the fish, clean it, ice it, pack it, clean me up. Takes time."

He thought he'd get a chair and sit with the body, and Sarah offered to go get him one. A guy in bright yellow swim trunks came to take a video. Tom chased him away by saying that if he took a video, the Mounties would want it as evidence.

Sarah reappeared trailed by a tall thin elderly man with a long white beard. He was carrying a metal chair he had taken from the veranda of White's Emporium in one hand and a Bible with a black cover in the other. Sarah had a piece of scrap plywood that she put down so the legs of the chair wouldn't sink into the soft ground.

"This is Joseph," she said. "He can watch that no one bothers the body." She paused to look at the tarp. She clenched her hand in anger and frustration. "She was fifteen. Her sixteenth birthday would have been in two weeks."

"Have you been saved?" Joseph asked.

Tom was caught by surprise, had to think for a moment, then said, "Probably not."

"We never know from one day to the next what our fate will be," Joseph said with the flat certainty of someone who has found the truth. "The wages of sin is death. Repent and you will be saved."

Tom glanced at Sarah, who had looked away. She wanted no part of the conversation.

"Thank you for watching over—" Tom paused.

"Angel," Sarah interjected.

"Angel," Tom repeated. "For looking after Angel."

He needed to leave. The wide awake nightmares were coming back, the flood of dead and injured that forced their way out of cellars where he tried to keep them locked up. Tom took his rucksack and fishing equipment back to the house.

His strategy was to keep busy, to keep focused, to not let his mind wander, to stay in the moment, to give the memories no place. So he cleaned up debris, old stovepipes, a disintegrating rain barrel, pieces of tin. He worked for nearly two hours, then got cleaned up.

On the way over to Sarah's he stopped to ask Joseph if there'd been any problems. Joseph was reading the Bible he'd been carrying. He stood and with his long white hair and beard he might have been an Old Testament prophet. He raised his Bible in front of him. "Be gone, I've said, and they fled before my wrath."

Tom would have been more impressed if he hadn't noticed that inside the Bible cover, Joseph had a paperback of some sort.

When she answered the door, Sarah was wearing a loose pair of jeans and a clean checked shirt.

"You know this will cause some gossip? They'll be saying that Sarah doesn't waste any time. She's making a move on that new bachelor. Are you a bachelor?"

"Separated. Heading that way. It takes two years."

They sat at a kitchen table Sarah said was made from local birch. She said that her husband had logged the trees, sawed them up, built the table and the chairs. He could, she said, do anything.

"Widow?" he asked.

"That's what they say." In spite of her age, she was square-shouldered and strong-looking, though her fingers were swollen with arthritis. "I heard about you. Moving into Jessie's place. You've got cheek, snapping it up under the noses of people who've been waiting years for her to die so they could get it."

"She didn't give me much choice," he said. "I came to look and the next thing I knew I owned a house."

"A poor helpless male," she replied. "Taken advantage of by an old woman. Outfoxed. You want to sell it, there are buyers. Here, I'll just wet the tea."

Sarah was prepared for his visit. She had a kettle on the stove and a plate of bannock, a dish of butter and a jar of mossberry jam on the table. As Sarah got the tea ready, he looked around the kitchen. The walls were made of squared timbers. The floors were unpainted planks, grey with age.

At one time this house had been filled with people. He could imagine the boisterous family, the constant visitors, travellers making their way north and south, stopping here for shelter and warm food. Everything in the kitchen was homemade. Tabletop and countertops made of thick slabs of wood, cut locally, run through a local sawmill, planed by hand—a kitchen meant to be used, one that wouldn't wear out or collapse. Yet everything was well finished; Sarah's husband had indeed been a good carpenter.

The shelves were of birch, deep, meant to hold large plates and mugs. He put his foot across one of the oiled floor planks. It was around six inches wide and probably six feet long; you didn't see planks like that anymore. In a smaller room, the planks would have looked out of place, but here they were the right size. Along one wall were shelves that held framed photographs and items collected over the years: birch bark and woven baskets, rocks with labels, including some that were encrusted with garnets.

Sarah put a Brown Betty on the table. She put out two china cups and saucers and dessert plates. He was surprised. He'd expected mugs and heavy crockery.

From where he sat, he could look down a long hallway. The house was sturdy, meant to hold back forty below and raging winds. In the kitchen there was an electric stove and, beside it, a wood-burning stove.

Seeing Tom's interest, Sarah patted the top of the wood stove. "Power goes out for three or four days in the winter, you can shut the doors and live in the kitchen. But I'm okay anyway because I've got an oil burner in the living room."

She had the soft lilt of Bungee, the local mix of Scots and Cree, except it wasn't Scots that softened the edges of her words.

"You're not from here," he said.

"Sixty years here, but you're never from here unless you're born here. I'm still from away. Sarah O'Hara, married to a McAra. As he said, our names rhymed, so we were fated for each other. He'd been posted with the air force to Metz and come to see Ireland. I was eighteen, working in my father's pub and McAra came in big as a bull, half Orkney and half Cree. None of that meant anything to me. I couldn't have found Canada on a map. He hung around the bar, telling me stories about the Great White North."

She shook her head at the memory, then added, "I left plumbing and paved streets, art galleries and candy shops. I never dreamt I was going to learn to catch fish, skin muskrats, have six kids without a doctor."

"You could have gone back after your husband died," he said, trying to imagine what Ireland would have been like for kids who'd grown up in northern Manitoba.

"To what?" she asked. "My parents were dead. My relatives good for a weekend before I would have begun to stink like three-day-old fish. And who would want six kids?"

"And that's it. Disowned."

"Not disowned. There are letters, and every Christmas there's plum pudding and Christmas cake and boxes of sweets and knitted sweaters and socks. It's part of the bargain, I expect. We'll keep giving you things if you'll just stay away."

"Never been back?"

"Never could afford it. And who would have looked after the brood?"

He wondered then about his father, his English accent never lost, his impeccable clothes, the Christmas cards and small gifts, the occasional letter, usually because someone had died, the religiously shined shoes, buffed until they reflected the light. That had been Tom's job from the time he was little, making sure that his father never went out of the apartment without shined shoes. Images of his father's shoes floated through his mind. The feel of them, the smell of the polish, the stiffness of the brush, the softness of the cloth.

His parents had no excuse not to go back to England for a visit. No brood. One son who could have been left under the landlady's care. It would, however, have meant breaking established rituals, taken away the utter predictability of their lives.

Sarah's kitchen was orderly, everything in its place. "The brood's gone. Flown the coop. Nothing to keep them here. This place is much too big for me. Lots of bedrooms. When there's work crews in the area, I board and room them. Karla and Horst try to get all of them, but those one-room shacks are freezing in the cold weather. Not properly insulated. And my food's better. Karla's been trying to get Horst to fix up those shacks and really promote ice fishing. Could be work for you, but they drive a hard bargain. Make sure you have a written agreement. I hope they succeed. We already get some sports fishermen in the winter—ice augers, tents and little huts out on the lake. Some ice fishermen have gotten big pickerel and they've spread the word and now we get a few over the winter. I'm sort of like a B & B without being a B & B, if you know what I mean?"

"You told the Whites that it was Ben's kid," he said. "That the Ben who was taking care of Jessie's house?"

"That's him," Sarah said. "Ben Finlayson. You haven't been here long enough to get to know everyone. He's got a daughter who lives in the city. She's got two kids. That's her daughter, Angel, who's died. God help Ben. He's lived for Angel since Betty passed." A silence fell between them. "Albert says it looked like you were fighting with her. Like you picked her up."

"She was lying face down in the water. I had to turn her over."

"The Mounties should be here soon."

"What do you think she was up to?"

Sarah got up and walked to the window, pushed aside the kitchen curtains. He went to see what she was looking at. There were kids in the playground, climbing on a slide, through monkey bars, swinging on swings, riding on a teeter-totter.

"Our kids," she said, "the village kids. Angel isn't the first death. Usually, though, they die somewhere else. It's not as bad as on the reserve but..." she paused in frustration, shook her head, "some people feel the ground itself is poisoned. Not heavy metals. With evil. Biblio Braggi came and sanctified the playground to keep the devil out."

"Was he the local minister?" Tom asked.

"Some people thought he was a minister, but he was just a Bible salesman. His big pitch was if you didn't buy a Bible and get buried with it on your chest, you were going to hell."

If she was looking out the window for an answer, she didn't find it, for when she came back to the table she said, "I don't know what Angel was up to. With my kids gone, I don't hear anything anymore. Kids keep their own secrets."

"That you?" he asked, pointing to a small framed picture that was sitting on top of a cupboard.

She reached it down, handed it to him. She was young, in a long dress and a fancy hat, probably in her father's inn. He wondered what her new in-laws had thought of her and her city clothes, there in the bush. Tom put the picture back, took down another, this one with her husband. They were standing outside a log cabin that was deep in snow. He had his arm around her shoulders. She was wearing slacks, mukluks and a homemade parka with fur trim on the hood. She'd pushed her hood back for the picture. She was resting her right hand on a pair of snowshoes.

"You look like you adjusted pretty quick," he said.

"You ever tried to wash crinolines in a tub?"

That made him smile. The idea of washing crinolines in a tub. He'd heard of crazier things, the kind of things people kept doing after they'd left the old country and come to Canada, trying to live in a soddy as if they were still in London or Glasgow.

"I've still got that dress," she said. "In the trunk I brought from Ireland. I can't get into it anymore, but every so often I take it out and hold it up to remind myself of what I was like then. Do you do that? With your uniform?"

He said he preferred to travel light, except for his books and a few other things. Sally had been nostalgic, though. She still listened to her music from high school, kept her pompoms from being a cheerleader, report cards, clothes she'd never wear again but held memories she didn't want to let go. He envied her that, having memories that made her fall asleep smiling. When things were bad, she fell asleep with her pompoms beside her.

In the picture, Sarah was young; now she was old, her face and body heavy from years of hard physical work. She leaned heavily on her cane and her body inclined slightly forward. If she'd felt any remorse or regret earlier in her life, it had disappeared from her face and been replaced by a granite look she must have developed in confrontation with the endlessly unexpected.

She'd been watching him as he looked at the pictures. "We make our choices," she said, "with no way of knowing the outcome. What will your life be like twenty years from now if you stay here? How won't it be like what it would have been?"

"Hard questions," he replied. Thoughts flitted through his mind, not complete but fragmented, bits of images: his parents' deaths, becoming a Mountie, getting married, not getting married, getting married to someone else. One of his father's friends had offered him an office job, but he'd turned it down. If he'd taken it, he'd have become an accountant.

The questions made him uneasy. There'd been no maliciousness in Sarah's voice, though, no hostility, maybe a touch of sadness, and he wondered how often she had regretted her decision, the decision of a young girl with no warning of what she was getting into.

Sarah didn't sit down or offer to refill his cup, so he thanked her for the tea and bannock and went out into the sunshine. There were kids swinging as high as they could on the swings in the schoolyard. From the look of it, they were competing to see if anyone could go over the top.

CHAPTER 3

THE PAST INTRUDES

The sun was so bright he squinted to shield his eyes and put on his sunglasses. The air was wet, muggy with the evaporating rain. The smell of the ground was thick, and he could feel his chest tighten. His asthma was always there, waiting, ready to squeeze his lungs until he started wheezing and coughing. Summer it was the dust and pollen, and fall it was mould. Winter, in spite of the cold, was his best season.

The Mounties and medical examiner hadn't arrived yet. Joseph was still sitting in his chair, but instead of reading his Bible, he was talking to a young girl holding a baby. Tom avoided him by going around the back of the emporium. He came out on the main road, then walked down it to his driveway. He couldn't escape the image of Angel's foot sticking out from beneath the tarp. Details like that triggered memories, unexpectedly opened doors. *Stop*, he said to himself, *stop*, and he began to hum, "She wheeled her wheelbarrow through streets broad and narrow." Sometimes, when the images wouldn't go away, he sang or played songs, searching for an earworm that would block out everything else.

He wanted to flee, to disappear into the forest, set up a tent on the beach where there was nothing but wilderness; however, since he found the body, there was no avoiding an interview. They'd find him, and his trying to avoid them would make them suspicious.

Why me? he asked himself. Why not Sarah on her way to her boat? Why not an early rising angler? Since leaving the Force, he'd avoided his former colleagues, and when he accidentally bumped into them their conversations were awkward. He was no longer part of the tribe; he was an embarrassment, an awkward reminder of what could happen to them. He was not looking forward to the interview.

That was one of the reasons he picked this place. Quiet, out of the way, nothing to do but take care of daily business. All new people. He would have preferred it if no one had known about his past life. He'd put up a poster at the emporium and on the town bulletin board as someone who could do repairs, drywalling, carpentry, plumbing. He'd be busy in the summer with the cottagers, busy with local people and the farmers to the west all year round, and he'd have time to read in the winter. There'd be plenty of time for fishing. Or so he hoped.

He went back to replacing dry rot. Ben had done chores for Jessie, taken care of the house for her sister after Jessie died. He'd said when Tom got to take a close look he'd find that there was a lot of work to be done. Ben had been right. From a distance, you'd have thought there was nothing wrong with the house. It was when the snow had melted and he'd gotten a close look that he'd been able to see everything that needed fixing, the places where wood crumbled under his hand. There was dry rot in the banisters, in a couple of the floorboards on the porch. The house and roof were covered in cedar shingles. Replacing them would be expensive. It looked like he'd even have to take out part of a wall on the south side where the spruce trees grew too close, blocking out the sun. He'd carefully lift the window frames out, support the roof and then pull out the rotten two-by-fours.

He was cutting some boards with the table saw when he saw two blue and whites pull up beside the blue tarp. Joseph stood up to meet them, talked to them briefly, then pointed to Tom's house. Tom was watching through the screen of trees. One car stayed and the other car backed up, crossed the gravel road down which it had just come, then bumped along the narrow driveway covered in spruce needles and rough with shallow roots and parked behind Oli and Jessie's old Chevy half-ton, which had come with the house. Prince Travis got out and Tom hissed under his breath.

If there was anyone he didn't want to see, it was Travis. They'd worked together a couple of times. Travis was a sharp-creases, smile-a-lot prick, a stuck-on-himself kind of guy. He knew the rule book by heart. He gave people speeding tickets for being two miles over the speed limit. He enjoyed nailing people for rolling stops and constantly watched for seatbelt violations. He was the only person Tom had ever worked with who issued littering citations.

His mother gave him his first two names, Prince Albert, to honour the English royal family and to display the family's loyalty and ambition. But not too much ambition, not overweening ambition; otherwise, as some of their colleagues said, she'd have named him King, like one of the K-9 dogs. His suffering in school with his classmates calling, "Here, Prince. Fetch," must have made him the jerk he was. Those who knew about his middle name tormented him with questions about when he was going to England to claim the throne. He responded by being an insufferable snob. He was, Tom thought, the epitome of good intentions gone wrong.

Travis swivelled his head, looking everything over, and from the look on his face, not approving. A guy who pressed his underwear and socks wouldn't live in an old house that needed fixing, that badly needed a coat of paint. The storage shed with the moss-covered roof. The outhouse. The lumber pile. The yard that was still littered with the previous owner's disintegrating possessions. For a moment, an old tape kicked in and Tom felt he should go inside, shave, whip on a pair of dress pants and a dress shirt, if he could find them in the boxes, and reappear respectable. The moment passed. He turned off the saw.

"What are you doing here?" Travis asked.

"My place," Tom answered, waving his hand at the house. "I just moved in."

"The locals say you found the body."

"I put up the sticks and the rope. Sarah O'Hara put the tarp over it. A nervous wreck called Albert Scutter helped. The tall guy with the beard, Joseph, has been keeping an eye on things"

"We'll need a statement."

"Of course."

Tom thought Travis might ask how Myrna was doing, or Joel, and was relieved when he didn't. He was even more relieved that he never mentioned Sally. Tom had heard that after he moved out, Travis had hit on Sally. Knowing him, he'd have thought he was doing her a favour. He hoped she hadn't slept with him.

"An accident?"

"Probably. No bruises, no blood."

"Your DNA on her?"

"I had to roll her over. I thought maybe CPR."

"Did you?"

"No, she was cold. No pulse."

"Is she cute?"

"It's hard to be cute when you're dead. I've never seen her before. Sara O'Hara says she's Ben the transfer guy's grandkid."

"Mother?"

"Winnipeg, I think. I don't know. I just moved here six weeks ago."

"Mind your own business?" Travis said.

"I'm busy. I've got a house to fix up."

"How old was she?"

"Ask Sarah O'Hara. She knows all the details."

Travis hadn't appreciated that Tom hadn't always dotted his i's and crossed his t's, that he sometimes let people go with a warning or a lecture. Tom always said he didn't want the paperwork, but they both knew it wasn't just that. "Soft," Travis had said, and they all knew that he meant weak.

"Somebody will come over and get a report." They both turned to look as a pickup truck and a hearse arrived at the scene. The truck, Tom assumed, was the local medical examiner, who needed to say she was dead, and then leave.

"Okay," Tom said and turned on the saw.

Travis watched him for a moment longer than necessary, then got back into the car and went to join the new arrivals. Travis once arrested a kid for stealing a donut but gave a warning to the mayor for driving drunk. His rules were flexible at the upper end.

Tom turned off the table saw. A table saw was nothing to be using when he was upset. He liked his fingers and intended to keep them. He went inside and poured himself a rye. He had one drink straight, then took the second one outside and sat in a Muskoka chair that had once been painted green. Now the wood was silver and the nailheads rusted. Green paint still clung in places where the wood was rough. He sipped his drink and watched the routine through the trees. A few people had gathered to watch, but they stayed well back and out of the way.

A female constable came over to take his statement. He didn't know her. They sat facing each other at the picnic table, which had been worn grey by the weather. He wondered what Travis had told her about him, because her questions were sharp, nearly accusatory. She had the grim look of someone wanting to prove she could do her job. Women on the force were always having to try to prove themselves.

The driver of the hearse sat with the back door open, smoking a cigarette, then went over to the café.

The forensic team set up a tent to keep away prying eyes and people with cameras, then checked the body—or he assumed that they checked the body; he knew the ritual—collected anything and everything on the body, around the body, and put it in bags. And when all that was done, put the body into a bag, then put that into another bag for transportation.

There had been no signs of trauma, no wounds, no obvious broken limbs, just a kid face down in a water-filled rut, a kid from the wrong side of the tracks, a kid with a grandfather who didn't know anyone important. They'd make it quick, and curse the paperwork. Drunk probably, drugged maybe, taking god knows what, anything from meth to bath salts, gasoline fumes in a plastic bag, lots of ways to end up face down in a puddle.

They'd cut her chest open, making cuts under her young breasts, then down to her crotch, cut out her insides, take slices for analysis, check her lungs to be sure she drowned, use a Black+Decker saw to cut off the top of her head, take out her brain, take more samples, end up cremating it or putting it back inside and sewing her up. *Dead, dead, dead,* he thought, deader than dead, no magic to breathe life back into her, ask her what she saw before everything went black. Did she float over her body, looking down, watching calmly? Did she walk into a tunnel of light? Did she see her grandmother waiting for her, ready to take her into her arms, saying it was all determined before you were born, fifteen years was all you were given, maybe next time you'll get a long life, get to grow old, have kids and grandkids, have a husband, a house, an education, holidays where there are palm trees, maybe you'll be white, whiter than white, with blonde hair and blue eyes?

He thought of Myrna then. She wasn't handicapped by the colour of her skin, had lived in a decent home, had a doll carriage and three dolls, one of which wet herself and needed to be changed. Her mother loved her, at least at first, certainly until she grew breasts and an attitude and wanted someone to blame for indecipherable crimes. They'd given her birthday parties, skating lessons, dance lessons, piano lessons, French lessons so that later in life, if she wanted, she could have a job in Ottawa, get back some of the tax money her parents had paid. They tried to make up for the overtime they both worked, for the times the house was empty. There were no odd uncles with roving hands. He wondered if they had tried too hard—was that why she painted her lips and fingernails black, dressed in leather, professed to love another woman? Was it to challenge her parents, force them into an admission of guilt? Finally, Sally said, "Enough. I didn't sign on for this." But things might have worked out if he'd agreed to tough love, kicked Myrna out, out there with the feral cat, turning up at the patio door from time to time with crazy eyes, hissing at any approach.

He slipped on his sunglasses. Macular degeneration ran in the family, his mother had said, even though his mother's family had dark hair and dark eyes. Her dark eyes were no protection from the sun's summer glare or its blinding reflection on the snow in Manitoba. She resented the fact that her darkness gave her no benefit, because when she was a girl in Iceland and had been sent to a farm in the summers, she'd been badly treated. A black-haired Icelander among the pale blond.

A slight breeze had sprung up from the lake. It wasn't strong enough to cool him off, but it drove away the mosquitoes. They sheltered behind objects. Later in the summer, if you accidentally brushed against a branch, clouds of them would rise out of the spruce trees. He looked around the property he'd bought from Jessie Olason. There was a time when he'd have rushed at everything that needed to be done with the property, but depression sapped energy and he worked in fits and starts. He had made a list, ranking the tasks. He'd taped the list to the fridge door, but even then, because he was so easily distracted, he sometimes just did whatever caught his attention.

Jessie's husband, Oli, had been dead for five years by the time Tom met her and looked at the house, and she'd obviously not been up to doing much physical work. She'd been gaunt, fragile looking, her clothes too large, like she'd shrunk inside them. She'd left behind a yard filled with wooden planters that were falling apart, full of soil and weeds; two wooden picnic tables; some outdoor chairs that might be salvaged; an ugly, slightly off-kilter bird bath made of beach stone and concrete with a cross in the centre. To one side of the yard there were six small graves with wooden crosses that were rotted at the bottom,

tipped this way and that. They were nearly buried in weeds and the brown needles from the spruce trees. They were the graves of pets that had been company
for a couple without children or, he expected, maybe loyal hunting dogs for the
husband. People left so little of themselves behind, and what they left, unless
they kept diaries or wrote a lot of letters, was unfathomable.

When he looked east, through the brown, scaly trunks of the spruce, the
far shore was a low dark line. Some days it sat above the water, floating in the
sky like some mystical place, a mirage of some sort, and other days it wasn't
there at all. You never knew what to believe, he thought, when what you looked
at was always changing.

CHAPTER 4

THE FORD PLACE

The basement suite Tom moved into after his split with Sally smelled of mould. When he mentioned it, the landlord had shrugged, handed him a spray bottle of Javex and said, "There are no cockroaches, no bedbugs. You wanna go upper class, you gotta pay more."

A previous tenant had left a plaque that said, "May your house never be big enough to hold all your friends." The unit had been too big, because he could have provided seating for four and the only one who ever came to see him was his daughter.

He was in the apartment two months when one day Myrna came pounding down the stairs. She was nineteen and working on a degree at the local university.

"The judge and jury have decided on solitary confinement for the accused," she declared rather dramatically, standing in the doorway. You could tell she was a theatre major. He was lying on the couch in the room the landlord called a living room but was really a rectangular basement space made of two-by-fours and cheap wallboard.

Myrna strode across the room to look at his bedroom, with its four concrete walls. He thought it might have originally been meant to be a cold room for vegetables and preserves. "Shit, why don't you chain yourself to the wall? I can get one of my friends to come in and whip you. Would you like that? She's a very attractive blonde. She wears leather. She's just a little older than me."

"Bugger off. I'm depressed."

"See a shrink. Take Mom with you. You both need help. She's got all these guys hitting on her. They figure she can't go without sex."

"I tried. She wouldn't go. There's no point in going to a marriage counsellor by myself."

She sat down across from him on one of the two chairs with gold plastic seats and gold-coloured legs. She'd dyed her blonde hair black, had shaved the left side, and had so much metal hanging from her face that he hoped she never went too close to a large magnet.

"Have you heard from Joel?" Tom asked.

"Joel's screwed. Forget about him. He's lost in computer game space. He's in Vancouver, pushing boxes out of Best Buy and trying to make it big on the comedy circuit."

"In Vancouver? Why not stay in Winnipeg?"

"He wants to be as far away from his mother as possible." She sighed dramatically. "He took the bus to Vancouver and is surfing couches. The last I heard. With no altruistic goals. You brought up a kid without a social conscience. If it was me, I'd be out there saving the Great Bear Rainforest."

"Hey, I made you two a lot of grilled cheese sandwiches," he said in his own defence. It was true. After Sally said no more catering to any of them, when she made supper, if any of them weren't at the table within five minutes of the food being put out, she threw their share into the garburator. Whenever Myrna or Joel wandered in late, he made them and their friends grilled cheese and bacon sandwiches.

"What do you think of my outfit?" Myrna got up and turned in a circle. Black leather boots to the knee, a three-inch-wide belt with metal spikes, black blouse, black leather vest, black cargo pants. Chains everywhere.

"Gorgeous," he answered.

"Liar," she said. "You hate it. Mom hates it. But it's me. At least right now it's me. Tomorrow I might become a jock. Or a preppie."

"Go preppie and get a job."

"Look who's talking. I've got a job. The tips are good. I'm paying the rent. I didn't come here to talk about me. I'm not living in a mouldy hole. I've got a window in my bedroom."

He shrugged and opened a beer.

"Keep doing that and you're going to get a gut," she said. "Old men with beer bellies aren't sexy. Empty calories. Why don't you go fishing? You used to love fishing. You even forgot my birthday that time because you were going fishing."

She was right. He had. However, her saying so didn't make him feel guilty. She'd used it before.

He told her there was a cold bottle of beer in the fridge, but she sniffed and said she only drank red wine. When she was eighteen, she'd talked regularly about craft beers, the flavours: a hint of chocolate, mint, leather. She'd even worked for a while promoting a small local brewer.

"I may," she said, "follow Joel to BC, but it'd be to the Okanagan. They make great wines there, and artists are appreciated."

With that, she turned, posed for a moment as if getting ready to go on stage and ascended the steps. Others would have just climbed the steps, but she ascended.

After she left, he felt better. She cared enough to come see how he was doing. He knew she was right, of course. He needed to rise out of the darkness of the basement apartment into the sunshine. But his leg, from the hip to the ankle, had been operated on three times. It now had more metal in it than Myrna had on her whole body, and he had developed a morbid fear that the screws and pins and plates would not hold. The surgeon had reassured him that he'd walk again, that his leg would regain its strength. It was the shrink who said that his focus on his leg was irrational, a kind of self-punishment for what had happened. He'd understood that intellectually, but it didn't help.

When Tom was young, the landlady of the apartment block where he lived with his parents befriended him. Anna Kolababa had taken Tom with her to many of her family gatherings, and that's where he'd met her cousin who couldn't stop asking, "Why me, why me, what's special about me?" And he'd name the different members of his platoon who were all killed in a variety of ways, and he'd go outside, away from everyone, and stand smoking one cigarette after the other until his wife would take him home.

In the month following Myrna's visit, as winter closed down the light that came through the one basement window, and there was no solace in watching television or reading, he started to think about what she had said, about fishing,

and about a village he'd gone to five years before because a commercial fisherman's boat had overturned in a squall on the west shore of Lake Winnipeg. It
had taken three days to find the fisherman's body. What had stayed with Tom
was an image of the village, Valhalla. It was nearly at the end of the road, a place
where you had to stop because there was nowhere else to go.

He'd gassed up the truck and put a couple of jerry cans in the back, threw
in a sleeping bag and canned soup and beans, a can of corned beef, bottled
water to make tea, a pot and kettle and a two-burner Coleman stove in case
he got stuck or trapped by a blizzard. He always had an emergency kit with
matches and candles and a collapsible shovel. He checked and double-checked
the weather. The forecast said clear with drifting snow. He had a sack of sand
over each of the rear wheels.

He took the highway north, gassed up twice to keep the tank full. The
paved highway turned to gravel, and after two hours, the gravel turned to frozen mud with a coating of packed snow and ice. The houses became farther and
farther apart, then open fields and clusters of houses and the occasional village
big enough to have a gas station and a grocery store and a main street banked
with plowed snow. The stretches of undisturbed snow became larger, the side
roads narrower, the sections of cleared field fewer until they stopped altogether,
the forest gradually becoming unbroken, darker.

He listened to the CBC and watched for the reflection of ice. The wind was
cold but the sun shining on the snow was blinding at times. He didn't want
to spend his time digging his truck out of a snowbank, the snowbanks that
were growing higher the farther north he went. Eventually, it was like driving
in a tunnel. The day was clear, intense blue sky. If he'd looked at the sky, he
might have thought it was summer, but when he looked down, there were snow
ghosts swirling across the road.

At the crossroad to the village, a red Jeep had missed the turn and was sitting nose down in the snow. The road, having thawed and frozen, was a sheet
of ice. He didn't attempt to stop or turn, but took his foot off the gas and let the
truck slow nearly to a stop before touching the brakes. He leaned out the window and backed up in the centre of the road. Before he stepped out of the truck,
he put on his leather chapka with its fur lining, pulled down the flaps and tied
them under his chin. He pulled on gauntlets that went well up past his wrists
and were meant to keep the snow from filtering inside and wetting his hands

and the leather. The driver of the Jeep was standing beside her vehicle. She was wearing a round black fur hat and had already pulled down the inside flaps. Her red hair fell over her shoulders. She was dressed for the road in a knee-length brown parka and brightly coloured beaded mukluks. Her breath swirled from her mouth in the freezing air and already her cheeks were pink with cold.

He opened up one of the bags of sand, got out his shovel and spread sand behind the Jeep's wheels.

"I don't know you," she said, clearly puzzled to find anyone coming to Valhalla at this time of year.

"It's mutual," he replied. She was young, pretty. He wondered where she was going with the snow drifting, the roads icy, the temperature around twenty below, but it was no time for chit-chat.

He wondered what was under the snow, what would happen if he stepped onto something unstable and his foot twisted and a pin snapped and he couldn't pull himself free. Would she take his truck, bring help before he froze in place like a sculpture marking the turn? He could have asked her if she knew what was under the snow but decided against it, took his shovel and dug down until he found solid footing.

The snow came up to his thighs. He cleared it away from the front of the car, got a good hold on the bumper and, when she reversed, put his weight on his good leg and pushed. The Jeep moved, but the back wheels didn't catch. He signalled her to stop, and then dug packed snow out from under the Jeep. On the second try the back tires caught and the Jeep rolled back.

The driver rolled down her window. "I'm going that way," she said, pointing in the direction he had come from. "I'll buy you a drink the next time I see you." He wished for a moment that she had been going in the same direction as he was.

When she was gone, Tom looked at the hole in the snow where the Jeep had been stuck. She'd just missed a sign that was nearly covered by a snowdrift. It had a picture of a pickerel with a hook in its mouth jumping out of the water, *Valhalla* in blue letters and the words *a fisherman's paradise*. A local humourist had changed the second *a* to an *e* with a black marker so it said *Valhella*. If it snowed much more, the sign would be completely buried.

Because the road was narrow, the surface treacherous with ice and the snowbanks so high that vehicles coming out of driveways wouldn't be seen, he cautiously edged his way into town. The houses were buried in snow. Snow had drifted up to the eaves and over the lower parts of roofs. A forest of tall spruce trees towered over the houses. Dark green spruce, so old that their branches were sparse and ragged against the pale winter sky. The Canadian Pacific Railway hadn't built this town, he thought. Roads wandered haphazardly to create a puzzle. He could smell woodsmoke, and when he stopped to look, he could see smoke that rose for a couple of feet from the chimneys, then was swept sideways by the wind.

The snow, pristine, blown into drifts, made him think of the books he had read as a boy, of families curling up contentedly before a blazing fire. He'd never had that in the city, only an imitation fireplace that provided no heat.

He followed the road until it ended at the lake. Here there was more evidence of activity, for there were snowmobile trails and a Bombardier trail that went down into the harbour and out over the ice until it disappeared in the glare. The fishermen up and down the lake used these enclosed, teardrop-shaped vehicles with skis at the front and metal tracks at the back to travel over the ice in winter. Just in front of the harbour, snow had been scooped away to create an open area. There were boats raised on empty oil drums and wooden blocks— four fishermen's aluminum skiffs covered in tarps to keep out the snow. Three sailboats were mummified in grey plastic. The harbour was empty. The finger docks were nearly invisible under the snow, the main dock was black, abandoned, and to the north a reef shaped like a crooked finger bent back toward the south. White slabs of ice had broken against and overtop it. Beyond the harbour, the lake was a vast field of drifting snow. A yellow Bombardier and three snowmobiles were parked outside a tin-clad shed.

He sat sideways to the wind, the truck engine idling, so the exhaust was blown away from the truck. It was as if the village were frozen in time, but by ice and snow instead of lava. The snow where the pale sun shone on it was white, but in every place where there was a shadow, in the windblown excavations of the drifts, behind the boats and poles and buildings, the snow was blue. Where the shadows crossed, the snow was a deeper blue touched with grey.

When he'd been here for the drowned fisherman, it was mid-September. No ice or snow then, just warm days, cool nights, everything turning gold and red. The gardens aglow with pumpkins and late-ripening tomatoes, an intense red among yellow leaves.

He backed up and turned his truck around to face a two-storey log building with a front porch held up by peeled tree trunks. It had a sign over the porch that declared in faded white letters: *White's Emporium*. He'd stayed for two nights in one of their cabins. The cabin had been spartan, but it was clean. The mattress lumpy and filled with wool or cotton that had been pressed down by fishermen over many years. There had been a hot plate, a toaster and a kettle, plus two cups and saucers and two plates. None of the dishes matched. The sheets were clean, but he was careful to fold the top of the sheet over the comforter. He'd used the toilets and showers at one end of the emporium. Each day he'd gone to the emporium for a breakfast of bacon and eggs, and fried fish for lunch and supper.

He turned the truck around to look back at the town. He thought it looked like a Christmas card, the houses nearly buried by the snow, the tall trees, the smoke from the chimneys. The tangled roads, the snowdrifts that looked like frozen waves, the windows like the openings to caves filled with secrets, but warm and comforting. He turned off the motor. It was the silence that over-whelmed him. Except for the sound of his breathing, the silence was complete. When he moved, he could hear the rasping of his jacket. In the city, the noise had never stopped. Traffic flowed even in the night's darkest hours, and des-perate individuals held up corner stores when the world should have been fast asleep. He smiled to himself. Viking warriors had been promised that if they died honourably in battle, they would be immortal, would go to Valhalla, where they could feast and drink and go into battle for eternity. If they were killed during the day, in the evening they would rise and continue with the feasting and drinking and wenching. He doubted that any Viking warriors would have settled for this Valhalla while they waited for Ragnarök, the end of the world.

A path just wide enough for one person had been shovelled on the three steps leading to the front door. He parked in front of the building. There was a sign in the window that said, *White's has the best bites*. He wasn't sure if it was referring to fish biting or the food that was served. The sign was faded, the edges curled. He thought the emporium might be closed, but when he pressed his face close to the glass of the front door, he saw there was a single light. He tried the door handle, the door opened and a bell jingled sharply. He stamped the snow off his boots and stepped inside.

The room was dark. The front of the building was all windows, but because the porch was wide enough to accommodate tables during the summer and the porch roof had a wide overhang, the windows let in little light. Tom took off his sunglasses and stood unmoving. The change from the brilliant sunlight reflected by the bright snow to the dim interior left him blind until his eyes adjusted. When he could see again, he realized there was a man sitting on a bar stool on the other side of the store counter. He was wearing a wine-coloured cardigan and fingerless gloves. Beside where Tom was standing, there was a wood furnace made from an oil drum set on its side. A flickering light from the open draft reflected off the floor in front of it.

The store's guardian sat unmoving. If he was surprised to see a stranger in the middle of winter, he didn't show it. He had tubes in his nose from an oxygen tank. He furrowed his brows as he studied Tom, but he also kept flicking his eyes to the right. Tom turned to look at what he was watching. A woman in a long blue parka was sorting through vegetables on a slanted shelf that was shoved against the front wall.

"You the real estate White?" Tom asked, indicating the yellow metal sign nailed onto the opposite wall that said, *Horst White, Realtor*.

Horst hesitated before he nodded briefly, as if he were reluctant to admit his identity.

"Are there any places for rent here?"

Horst shifted on his high-backed stool, mulled over the question. "No, nothing for rent now. Places for rent in the spring," he said in a rasping voice. Between each sentence, he paused and took a breath.

The woman in the parka that made her look like a large blue puffball plunked a bundle of limp carrots onto the counter. The carrots had reached the stage where they were flexible. Horst ignored Tom while he weighed the carrots on a scale. He made a notation in a ledger on the counter.

"Your tab is a hundred and fifty-seven dollars," he said in an aggrieved voice.

"End of the month. As soon as the cheque comes in," the blue puffball said, and took the six mangy carrots and stuffed them into one of her pockets. She asked for a package of cigarettes, and when the storekeeper went to a cabinet to get them, she pointed at Tom, then at herself, then at the door. She took her cigarettes and went out.

"Nothing at all for rent?" Tom said. "When should I check back?"

"End of April maybe." Horst wheezed after he said April and was so short of breath every word seemed to be an effort.

"Any chance of getting a hot meal?" Tom asked. "I've come a long way."

Horst looked offended by the question. The emporium was all one room. To Tom's right was an ice cream freezer and a window where orders could be taken in summer. Six round wire-legged tables were set out with flimsy wire chairs. There was a side counter and behind it the kitchen was dark and empty looking. The smell of french fries hung heavy in the air. Because there was so little light, the room seemed cavernous. Shadows filled the corners and every place the weak light from the one light bulb did not reach. There was a small pile of three-foot tamarack logs beside the heater.

"The kitchen is shut down for the winter. If you want to buy groceries off the shelves, you can turn on a light." There were a number of bare light bulbs hanging from the ceiling over the grocery area.

Tom declined and went out onto the porch. The woman in blue was standing at the corner of the building having a cigarette. When he got close to her, she quietly said, as if afraid of being overheard, "I'm Pearl. I think Jessie might want to rent her house." She pointed across the road.

Through a strand of full-grown spruce, he could see there was a house. "She won't hire Horst to rent it for her. They don't get along."

With that, she flicked her cigarette butt into the snow, pulled up her hood and scurried away.

It was cold enough that the snow squeaked under his boots. The surface of the road, in spite of being plowed, was packed, hardened snow. He suddenly felt his feet go out from underneath him, and he tried to catch his balance, spun, then fell back against a snowbank. He pushed himself upright. The dry snow squeaked under his feet, and when a clump of snow fell from a branch, he could hear it land.

He walked along the road down which he'd driven into town. The house Pearl had pointed out to him had an old-fashioned closed-in porch on the front, overlooking the lake. At the rear there was a shed that protected the back door from the weather. He walked all the way to where the road was blocked by a ridge of lake ice. He looked back through the trees and, though it was still early, saw that there were lights on in the interior. From where he stood, the road ran straight west and separated the house from the dock area and behind that the emporium. The fish shed was closer to the shore and to the north side of the harbour.

If it hadn't been so cold, and if he'd had a coin, he'd have been tempted to toss it to decide if he should knock on the back door of the house.

He walked back to the driveway, followed it to the garage, and then stopped on a path between an old half-ton Chevy and a snowbank that reached his armpits. The truck's wooden box was filled with snow. The path was narrow, as if the person digging it had no energy to waste or wanted it to be invisible to all but those who already knew of its existence. On the far side of the snowbank was the garage, its door held shut with a chain and a large padlock. To the side of the garage and farther back among the trees, there was a shed. Because of the protection afforded by the spruce, no more than a foot or so of snow had found its way past the periphery of this private forest. There was a path to an outhouse, and it was obviously being used because the snow had been dug away so the door could be opened and closed. *Cold visits*, he thought. There'd be no lingering.

There was an oil tank on a stand. Smoke was rising from the chimney. His father would have said, "Don't intrude." But Anna, having spent years managing apartment blocks, supporting herself and her daughter, was never one to miss an opportunity. She would have said, "Nothing ventured, nothing gained, huh? Ain't that right?"

He had to shuffle sideways to get past the truck to the enclosed porch. Hanging over the door was a cage filled with suet and seeds. A chickadee was clinging to it, digging the suet out from between the wires.

To knock off the snow he kicked the toes of his boots against the back step, then let himself into the porch. Whoever lived here was burrowed in for the winter. There was no light in the shed, but he could see that there were men's jackets on hooks and a collection of various kinds of boots lined up against the wall. He put his hand out and touched a brown jacket. It was frozen stiff. He opened the storm door, but before he could knock, the inside door opened and an elderly woman with unhealthy, yellowish skin and a narrow face covered in wrinkles faced him.

"Come in, come in. Shut the door behind you. Don't let the cold in." A cloud of white mist enveloped her.

He quickly stepped inside, pulled the storm door shut, then the inside door, then stood on the rubber mat meant to keep snow and water off the floor.

"Turn around," she said, and when he did, she brushed the snow off him with a straw broom. "I saw you slip. Footing is uncertain here. You could have fallen and broken a leg and got covered over with snow. Nobody would have found you until the spring. It's happened before. Bernie Solmundson disappeared in a blizzard. We walked over him all winter and didn't know until the snow melted."

She stood the broom against the wall.

"I'll watch my step," he said.

"Pearl phoned me. I've been expecting you. Take off your things. I've water on for tea."

He hung his jacket on a hook beside the door, pulled off his boots. When he'd finished, he straightened up and said, "I'm Tom Parsons."

"I'm Jessie Olason." She held out her hand. He could feel the looseness of her skin and the bones beneath it. "You sit."

She went to the stove and took the kettle off, poured water into a teapot and brought it to the kitchen table. She put out milk and sugar and cookies. She gave him a small plate and a paper napkin.

"The tea will be ready in a bit," she said as she sat down opposite him. "Pearl says you were asking about a place."

"Mr. White said there were no places for rent."

"Never are. You might get a cottage for a week or two in the summer. You interested in forty acres and an old house?"

"Maybe," he said. "You mean this place? You want to rent out this place?"

"To sell." She snorted. "It's the only place I've got. Unless I'm going to sell you somebody else's place and run off with the money."

"How much?"

"Eighty thousand. You got four acres with the house. Waterfront. Across the side road to the west is thirty-six acres. You crossed that road on your way into town. It's just at the end of my four acres. It runs parallel to the lake. Thirty acres is cleared. It's good for hay. Six acres is underwater in the spring and wet summers. Good fishing in the marsh behind it if you like jackfish and carp. They come right in. Can you afford that?" She said it in a determined fashion, as if she might be enquiring about the state of his soul.

Her insistence on selling unsettled him. "I don't know if I can get a mortgage," he protested. He felt confused. Buying had never crossed his mind. "If I bought, I'd have to start a handyman business. I was just thinking of renting." Depression started to overwhelm him and his head filled with uncountable voices all contradicting each other. "I'd be working for myself here."

"You a Christian?"

"Yes," he said but then felt guilty, for his yes was based on decades before, baptized, confirmed, getting married in the church but, in the years that followed, moving around for different postings, finding an easy excuse not to attend church. Besides, he'd often had to work on Sundays. At first, Sally took the kids to Sunday school, but as they kept moving from place to place, different churches, different ministers, she lost interest.

"Do you come with a mission? Not Lutheran by any chance?"

"No," he said, concerned that she might not want to sell to any other faith. "Anglican."

"It will have to do," she said. "I could give you a mortgage on this place. Ten per cent down. I'll take back the rest at four per cent. You pay six hundred a month. More, if you've got it. Open mortgage. It would give me a steady income."

"Okay," he said. It was only two hundred more than he was paying for the crappy basement apartment. The house, at least, was above ground.

She held out the plate of cookies and he took one. "Peanut butter," she said with pride. "My husband, Oli, loved peanut butter cookies. He drowned."

"When?" He didn't dare refuse a cookie, but he knew he'd regret it. Peanut butter gave him heartburn and, occasionally, a migraine.

"Five years ago last September."

"I came to help find him. I was with the police."

She jerked her head up so hard that she nearly spilled her tea. "You!" she exclaimed. "You found him. And now you've come back and found me."

He wasn't sure where the conversation was going, so he bit into the cookie. Jessie had clenched her hands in front of her and he thought she might be going to pray. She was wearing two sweaters, one pink and one green, and under her light purple dress, she had on men's long underwear. She wore fishermen's grey socks inside beaded moccasins.

"You would have to promise not to sell to those Whites or to those immoral communist Vikings north of here. Do you promise?"

"Whatever you want," Tom said. He hadn't bought the property yet and she was already talking about his selling it. "Why don't you want them to have the property?"

"The greed of Horst White. And those pagans praising false gods. Have you heard of them? The Godi." She spit out the word. "You'll see."

Tom felt he was on dangerous ground. Horst White was so obnoxious, he could see why she wouldn't want to sell to him, but he had no idea who the communist Vikings were. It was an odd combination of characteristics. He knew that the tsar's royal guard at one time had been made up of Scandinavians, but there were no communists in those days. He felt trapped and thought, *This old woman is crazy*, but then thought about life in his crappy basement apartment in a building where its six suites and hallways always smelled of mould and cabbage. "I'd want to live here all year long. I'm looking for a forever home." He'd seen the term "a forever home" in an advertisement for abandoned pets and had empathized with a black lab with sad eyes.

She relaxed. The wrinkles in her face loosened. She had the palest blue eyes he'd ever seen, so pale they seemed nearly colourless.

"You are the answer to my prayers. The Lord does provide if we just have faith. I have prayed long and hard that the Lord would send a buyer for my house. " She clapped her hands together. "Hallelujah, hallelujah." She smiled at an inner truth, then caught herself and said, "Have you come far?"

"Winnipeg," he replied.

"You've come a long way under difficult conditions. You must have a mission. I came out here one summer as a junior missionary. I was just a girl then, eighteen. That's how I met my husband. The Lord brought me here, and I obeyed him, though His work here has fallen by the wayside and I am shamed."

"You've been here a long time?"

"Sixty-two years," she said. "My husband never wanted to leave this place. He was born here. He said I could do the Lord's work here as well as in a foreign place. The people here certainly needed help with their morals." She hesitated, then smiled at a new thought. "I have an older sister in the city and she'd like me to come live with her. We can take care of each other."

"Eighty thousand?" he said.

"I know it needs a new roof and there's wood needs to be replaced. It needs better insulation. It's not a youngster. Dr. Ford built it in 1938. My husband was a good fisherman, but he wasn't handy at fixing things. He could cut down a tree, but he couldn't make anything useful out of it."

He was surprised by her openness about everything that was wrong with the house. *She'd never make a living selling condos in the city*, Tom thought.

The kitchen had a wood stove against the back wall and beside it a white refrigerator and an electric stove that must have been nearly as old as its owner. On the north side there was a window over a counter and under it what must have been the original sink. On either side of the window there were plain wood cupboards painted white. The floor was covered in battleship linoleum. Lino was, he'd read, coming back into fashion.

Everything about the kitchen that was within Jessie's reach was tidy and clean, but around the ceiling light and where the ceiling and walls met there were cobwebs. She showed him the bathroom that was off the kitchen, and Tom was happy to learn that the outhouse wasn't the only toilet. The bathtub had feet. The floor was black-and-white tile. "There's some tile missing," Jessie said, "but I've kept them. They just need putting back. The toilet quit working two weeks ago and I haven't been able to get anyone to fix it. Are you handy?"

He took the lid off the tank at the back of the toilet. The chain that lifted the stopper had broken. He got her to bring him a piece of copper wire and joined the two pieces together. When he pushed the handle down, the toilet flushed.

"I should have taken courses in mechanics, but the Lord had other tasks for me," she said.

"It'll cost quite a bit to fix everything."

"The Lord will provide. His ways are many. The Lord brought you, but he didn't say I had to give away my property," she declared. "It's on the water. It has potential if you live long enough. We bought it as a place to live, not as an investment. People in those days didn't talk about their houses as investments."

She showed him two bedrooms that were surprisingly large. It was obvious that there'd been a third bedroom that had been divided to create a bathroom, plus a laundry room that also included an oil heater.

Jessie saw him looking at the fireplace in the living room. It was large and made of glacial granite and conglomerate. She had a piece of plywood fitted into the fireplace to stop drafts. Someone had painted the plywood white and stenciled, *The Lord is my shepherd* and crudely drawn a herd of sheep. As soon as he could afford it, he'd put in a wood heater insert with a glass front.

A solid four-inch plank had been used to make the mantel. Perhaps she felt she had to excuse the extravagance, saying, "We didn't build this place. We bought it from Mr. Ford's family in Illinois when he died. They weren't interested in keeping it. He had a lot of money, and used to come up here by boat from Selkirk to hunt and fish. Later, he flew up. Used to bring big shots from the US of America." From her tone of voice, she didn't approve. "I was young then. There was just a winter road. We travelled by boat in the summer. Breakup and freeze-up we hunkered down."

There was a set of moose antlers over the fireplace and a bearskin on the floor. A stuffed Canada goose was on a shelf in one corner, along with a mallard and a teal. A stuffed wolf that was missing a few patches of fur and its left eye lurked in one corner.

The floor was covered by a wool carpet. Jessie bent over and pulled one corner back to show him the floorboards. "Maple planks," she said. "The real thing. Never been sanded." Under the winter light, the wood was the colour of buckwheat honey.

She saw him studying the walls. Every room was covered with a different pattern of wallpaper. The living room wallpaper was covered in small pink flowers.

"This place was never meant to be lived in during the winter. It was just for the good weather. May, June, July, August, sometimes September." She counted out the months on her fingers. "When we moved in, there was just studs. No insulation. We couldn't get insulation like nowadays, but Oli brought loads of sawdust in his skiff from a sawmill north of here. Managed to get lumber he could nail over the studs. I put up the wallpaper. You can take it off and put up drywall. Make it modern."

She had plastic taped over the outer door and the windows of the closed-in front porch to keep the frost out of the house. The porch was obviously being used for storage. There was a jumble of furniture and boxes. There was no heat. Part of an animal's leg was hanging from the ceiling. Pieces had been cut off it. From the size, it was probably the thigh of a moose.

The porch, he thought, with added insulation and baseboard heaters, could be turned into a usable room in winter. He could get rid of the wood stove in the kitchen and keep the oil furnace in the small room between the two bedrooms for emergencies when the power lines went down. After he put a wood stove insert into the fireplace, there'd be plenty of heat.

"If you have guests, there are extra chairs," she informed him. There was a stack of old-fashioned wooden chairs with leather seats that had sunk in the centre. "I won't be taking them. I won't be taking much of anything. My sister's got all the furniture she needs. You can throw out anything you don't want."

He realized that as far as she was concerned, the deal was done: she was leaving; he was moving in. She was just explaining the circumstances. His father would have described her as no-nonsense.

"My sister, Josie, goes away in the winter to Arizona. She doesn't come back until April or May. I have things I need to do in May. I'll be gone by the middle of June. You can move in July one."

There was no arguing, no negotiating. He either took it or he didn't. The Lord had sent him or He hadn't. Financially, he could manage. Eight thousand down; pay off the rest as soon as he could. Get a line of credit. He hoped he wouldn't have to ask Sally if she'd co-sign it. She was working full time and she'd got the house, so there was no mortgage to pay there.

"Is that fine?" Jessie asked. She had her hands on her hips and was looking at him as if he might say no. He realized she was asking about leaving her belongings behind. She had to tip her head back to look into his eyes. She had a small pointed chin, a sharp nose and eyeglasses that sat closer to the end of her nose than to her eyebrows. She made him think of a teacher he'd had once. No nonsense in her class.

"Shouldn't we sign something?" he asked.

"Why?" she replied. "You want it. I want to sell it. We've come to terms. I'll be in the city at the end of May. You write down your address and phone number. We'll get the papers signed. This place is paid for. No mortgage. No liens." She looked out the window. "You'd better be going. It's a long drive back and it looks like more snow."

When he left, he could feel it was getting colder. The chickadee had fled the suet and seeds for shelter. The top of the sun was just visible over the trees. Pale yellow, providing fading light but no warmth. Even though the wind had stopped, the cold was sharper, stung his face. He pulled the earflaps of his chapka down tight.

He'd come to inquire and now he owned a place. He could back out of course. There was nothing signed. He stopped and turned around to look at the cottage under its weight of snow. The spruce trees protected it, but even so, snow rose as high as the windows where the house wasn't sheltered by the trees, was deep on the east side of the roof. The shadows that had been light blue when he'd come were now darker, deeper and had shifted toward the east. The kitchen window gleamed like a jewel. As he watched, a rabbit hopped across the drifts.

When he got back to the city and came to his senses, he could back out, but as he watched the smoke rising from the chimney, he realized he wouldn't want to. He was still standing there when the door of the shed opened and Jessie called for him to come back. He slipped and slid his way to her. She thrust a brown paper bag at him. "Here. This will keep you going until you get home."

"Thank you," he said, and for a moment, he felt his throat tighten. He found kindness hard to deal with. If he'd known her better, he'd have hugged her. "Thanks. Thanks." He stopped with one hand on the snowbank, because the snow beneath his feet was sheathed in ice. "Remind me what happened. You said your husband was a good fisherman, but something went wrong."

She pulled her sweaters more tightly around her. "They say a squall came out of nowhere. He was pulling up nets to reset them where there was better fishing and had anchors resting on one of his gunwales. And some of these fools who were jealous and resented that he wouldn't overfish his limit later said that the wind was created by a hand that rose out of the water and turned the boat over. It didn't. But if it did, it would have done no good, because he always wore a silver cross I gave him."

He felt his feet slide on the uncertainty of the ice, so he reached back to rest his hand on the truck fender.

"You have," she suddenly declared, as if she'd discovered a truth and needed to proclaim it, "a hangdog look. It doesn't become you. The Lord has just given you what you wanted. You should smile more." With that, she pulled her sweaters even more tightly around her shoulders, went into the shed and shut the door.

He went straight back to his truck and drove away. Once he was on the road, he used his right hand to reach into the bag. There were a half dozen peanut butter cookies.

CHAPTER 5

A NEW BEGINNING

At the beginning of May, on his two days off work as a security guard, Tom drove out to take a look at Valhalla and the house he was buying. There was still snow in the shadows on the south side of trees, but runoff had made the road soggy, particularly where it passed through muskeg. Mud soon covered the back window of his canopy. The ditches that had been hidden by snowbanks were deep and narrow, the water in them, in spite of the brightness of the day, black and unfathomable. Mallards paddled in them. In marshy areas were piles of branches and reeds, and the mud of muskrat houses rose up in dark domes.

Crushed limestone had been recently poured onto the surface of the road, but it was already sinking. The forest here was nearly all stunted tamarack. Although things could grow, they could not thrive. Where the ground rose up, occasional larger trees stood like beacons over a forest of miniatures. Fire had burned through the area at some time and these larger trees had been reduced to branchless trunks that were blackened and charred.

Just outside of Valhalla, a black raised Dodge Ram 3500 raced toward him. Tom pulled as close to the ditch as possible, but there was no shoulder, and the edges could easily collapse under the weight of a tire. The Ram threw up mud as it nearly brushed him off the road. "Bloody hell!" Tom yelled as a wave of mud and water splashed across his windshield. He braked, stopped and got out. He left the wipers on and got an empty coffee can from behind the seat, scooping water out of the ditch and throwing it over the windshield. He wished for a moment that he was still on the Force.

At the edge of the village he could smell smoke. The snowbanks had disappeared and the sign saying *Valhella* was revealed in all its glory. When he had come the time before, snow had covered the part of the picture showing a fisherman holding a rod.

Like wreckage at low tide, the houses and trailers had reappeared from the snowdrifts. The pristine white had turned to tangled yellow grass, and the yards, once billowing waves of snow, looked dejected, the equipment in them having taken on the dull colour of the yards. Here and there children's plastic toys, forgotten in the fall and now exposed, provided bursts of bright colour.

At the first houses there were large patches of blackened grass and lines of fire where people burned off last year's lawn while the ground was still wet enough that there was no danger of the fire spreading into the trees. Just in case the fire might leap up with a gust of wind, there were people shepherding their ragged flickering orange lines, holding wet gunny sacks so they could beat out any errant flames. They were all wearing heavy jackets and toques because of the bitter breeze from the still-frozen lake.

Spring was the ugliest time of year. In the city, filthy snow that had shrunk to ice still lined the edges of the roads, and the roads were thick with dirt and gravel. Here, the pristine snow of winter was covered with spray from the water that lay on the road.

When he pulled up to the harbour at Valhalla, the Christmas card snow-covered look of the town had changed to shallow ditches filled with water and roads that had melted into rutted trails of mud. The straw bales around the foundations of houses that had been hidden by the snow were black with mould.

He parked at the edge of the lake. The snowpack had disappeared, and the ice was blue and grey. There was a hundred feet of open water. A strong east wind would drive the ice onto shore, grind it hard upon itself, pile it into a ridge. A shift in the wind would drive it back onto the east shore, create more open water. The ice would groan and heave as it ground upon itself. Once the ice was gone, for a time, the water would be so clear that the rippled sand and rock of the bottom would be visible at twenty feet.

Tom wished that he'd already moved into the house so he'd be able to stand on the shore every day and watch as the lake changed. Since returning to Winnipeg, instead of regretting his impulsive deal with Jessie, he'd become aggravated by his apartment, the other renters, the landlord who despised everyone who rented from him. He'd begun to dream about having his own house, started fantasizing about what he would do to modernize it but still retain its lines. The need for more money for the house had driven him out of the apartment and into a night security job. Instead of spending his days sleeping or staring out his one basement window at a brick wall and a peeling fence, he made sketches and floor plans from what he could remember. He wished he'd taken a camera, but he had, he reminded himself, not planned on buying anything.

He left his truck at the foot of the dock and walked to the Ford place, Jessie's place, *his place*, he thought to himself. The half-ton blue Chevy was still sitting in the driveway. The snow in the back had melted. Since there were fish boxes and anchors in the back, he assumed the truck hadn't been used since Jessie's husband drowned.

He had brought a small box of chocolates to repay Jessie for the peanut butter cookies. He knocked on the back door. There was no answer. He opened the storm door and pressed his face close to the window in the inside door. He knocked again. Jessie didn't appear. There weren't many places she could be. At the store or visiting neighbours, he supposed. He walked over to the store. The bell jingled when he opened and closed the door, but no one appeared.

Ice cream hadn't yet been put in the freezer for the summer trade. It held some brown paper packages with the names of various cuts of meat written on them in black pen. Mostly hamburger. The dark wooden counter that separated the kitchen and living quarters from the general store area was old, its solid wood surface scarred and worn. It would have been brought in, he guessed, from a bar or hotel that had been torn down or modernized, because it had a brass rail for patrons to rest one foot on. The shelves in the south corner looked like they held the same potatoes, carrots and onions that had been there in the winter. The grocery shelves contained canned and boxed goods, but the shelves farther back were taken up with sports-fishing items. Cases of soft drinks were stacked in one corner. Beyond that were free-standing shelves filled with a confusing array of goods, from spare outboard motor parts to bear spray.

He went back to the front door and opened and closed it three times, just in case someone was around. The jingling finally got a response; he heard someone moving about in the living quarters. In a minute, Horst White came out, pulling his oxygen tank.

"I was sleeping," he complained irritably. "What do you want?"

"Jessie Olason. Do you know where I might find her?"

"I couldn't say," Horst snapped. "I don't delve into those kind of affairs."

"Affairs?"

"Where people go."

"I bought her place. We had an arrangement. I am supposed to take it over the beginning of July." Horst looked more irritated than ever. He studied Tom like a dog deciding whether to bite. "Has she gone to her sister's?" Tom asked.

"Someone said that was where she resides."

"Olason was her married name. What was her maiden name?" Tom got out the notepad he always carried and the stub of pencil.

"I've never minded her business. I couldn't say what she was called when she came here. She came here long before me. If you're still looking for a place, I've got a cottage north of here that's for sale. If you don't snap it up right away, it'll be gone. I've already got an offer on it. I could take Jessie's old place off your hands." When Tom didn't reply, Horst jerked the buggy with his oxygen tank around and disappeared into the living quarters.

Tom went out onto the porch. What, he wondered, was the name of the woman in the blue parka? A gem, diamond, ruby, emerald, pearl... Pearl.

He went to a nearby house trailer and knocked on the door. As he waited for an answer, he couldn't help but notice the small house next door that was bright blue with green trim and yellow shutters. There were small trees in the yard, and hanging from the branches were bicycle wheels with two-litre pop bottles tied to them. Even with the slight breeze, the wind spun the wheels, some vertically, some horizontally. Some of the small trees looked like they would rise into the heavens.

A girl who couldn't have been more than seventeen or eighteen opened the door. She was holding a baby and a small child was clinging to her leg. Her long face was pale and her brown hair lank.

He asked where Pearl might live and the young woman said two houses over, the one with the white picket fence. She pointed away from the house that was a riot of colour. Tom thought if Anna had seen her, she would have said, "That girl needs six days of perogies and some kubasa."

Pearl remembered him, asked him in, insisted that he have coffee and told him how sorry she was about Jessie's death, a heart attack, totally unexpected, she was so thin, it wasn't like she was fat, it was fat people like her who were supposed to have heart attacks. Then she poured the coffee, thick as the mud on the road outside, urged him to top it up with cream, asked him if he'd like a shot of brandy in it, and when he said no, he was driving, she poured a generous shot into her own cup.

When he brought up the topic of the house, Pearl said, "You bought it fair and square. Jessie told me about it. If I'd known your name, I'd have called you to tell you what happened." She reminded him of a snowman, made up of three round balls. She had a round, pleasant face with pink cheeks from either brandy or rosacea, and a radiant smile.

"How did you find me?" she asked. From the way she asked it, Valhalla might have been the size of New York or London.

"The girl at the trailer," he replied.

"That's Rose," Pearl said. "She married Haldur in a hurry and now she's got two. It never stops, does it?"

Tom thought of the hurried-up way he and Sally had got married and agreed. These things happened if not in a second or even a minute, then so quickly that they might have been nothing and would have no consequences, like eating a hamburger and fries at a drive-in and then thinking no more about it, not even remembering in the next day or two that you had eaten a double cheeseburger. The sin of momentary gratification, his father had called it.

He explained about Horst and his not knowing Jessie's whereabouts or her maiden name, and Pearl snorted. "Bloody liar. He's been after that property for years. He thought he would get it when Oli died. The Godi wanted it, too. That's the sect that has their property north of town. They all figured she'd go back to where she came from. If she had, Jessie still wouldn't of let Horst be the agent. No love lost there. She stuck it out, hoping someone would turn up so that none of them would get it. And you did, and then she goes and kicks the bucket. Horst figured he'd get it off Jessie's sister. He was all set to offer her a deal when she came for the funeral. There was no funeral. She didn't even come here. She had the body shipped to the city and cremated. I think she's got Jessie in a vase in her china cabinet. Then she went back to Arizona to finish her holidays."

"Her last name?"

Pearl ignored his question. She was wound up. She waved her short arms about when she talked. She might have been conducting a choir. "Josie. Josie and Jessie. Twins."

"Jessie said her sister was older."

"One minute older. Josie was born first. Horst had a sales agreement all made up. He was going to make the offer at the reception afterwards. He had all these reasons why she should sell. Couldn't say enough good things about Jessie. But when she was alive, it wasn't that way."

Pearl poured a splash more brandy into her cup. "Davis, J. Davis. She rents a condo in Tucson. I think I've got her address somewhere. Jessie wrote it down for me. Just in case anything happened to her. That's when Horst was hard after her for the property. If she went up in smoke one night, she wanted me to know where to call."

She jumped up and waddled down the hallway. It wasn't just the parka that had made her look big. He could tell she liked blue. Her dress was blue with a white collar, she had on blue earrings and the strap of her watchband was blue. It suited her high complexion.

She returned without the paper. "It's gone," she said. "But she owns an apartment in Fort Garry."

"I'll find her," he said and drained his cup.

He remembered he had the box of chocolates in his pocket. He took it out and put it on the table. "Thank you for the help," he said.

Pearl became flustered at receiving the gift. She picked up the box and rubbed the side of it between her thumb and forefinger and smiled. From the expression on her face, he might have given her a million dollars. She followed him to the door, and when he got into his truck, she stood there, waving goodbye until he was out of sight.

Dead, he thought, *dead and no contract*. He'd rather have had a contract than six peanut butter cookies he couldn't eat. He'd given Jessie's cookies to the small birds that hung around his backyard. He went back to the house and walked around the outside. It looked shabbier than he remembered it. There were flaws, but if he'd had a contract, they would have been his flaws to correct. He felt that something essential had been ripped away from him.

The next day, he'd looked up J. Davis in the phone book. There were twenty-six. He called three Davises before he got a message that said she was in Arizona, but if there was urgent business, here was the phone number to call.

"I'm Tom Parsons," he said when Josie answered the phone. "Jessie and I had an agreement for me to buy her place. She was going to move in with you."

"She told me."

"I thought you might be back from Tucson."

"I can grieve where it's warm."

"I've given my landlord notice."

"What are you going to do in Valhalla? I asked Jessie that. Why would anyone with any brains want to move there? Especially a young man."

"I'm retired."

"That's not an occupation."

"Medical leave," he explained. "I was in an accident."

"You sound fine."

"Maybe I'll go fishing."

"I wouldn't recommend it. Jessie's husband was a fisherman. No fish, big price. Lots of fish, no price. When they don't make much, they sit around and drink because they're unhappy, and some seasons they make money, and then they sit around drinking because they're happy. However, it's your choice, and the place has to be sold. What price did you agree on?"

"Eighty thousand."

"At least you're honest. That's better than most. Jessie told me that. She said you were honest. However, she said you looked like you needed looking after. You married?"

"Separated," he answered. There was silence on the line. He hoped she didn't have something against people who were separated.

"The price seems cheap. A house on the water and forty acres."

"The house needs a lot of work. Not much done to it since it was built. A part of the property is underwater in the spring."

"Have you got the money?" she asked.

He said no, that Jessie said she would give him a mortgage.

"I can't do that. It's too much trouble. You'll need to get financing. It's not a big amount. If Jessie was right and you were chosen by the Lord to own this place, then you'll find a way. How soon can you move in?"

"We agreed on July first."

"That's not what I asked. I asked how soon can you move in? I don't trust those people there. Jessie was always having to chase people off her property. If she was away for a few days, someone would be digging up her yard. With everything that goes on, you never know if someone is going to tear the place apart."

"Was the heat left on?"

"I'm not a fool. I know what needs to be done. There's a man there—Ben. Jessie thought he was reliable. I asked him to look after the place. He's supposed to check it once a day. I pay him five dollars a day, more if anything needs work."

"I didn't mean to imply you don't know what you're doing."

"Men never think a woman has any brains. You've met that dreadful man—I think his name is Horst. He tried to scare my sister into selling. When he called me, butter wouldn't have melted in his mouth. He must have thought my sister never told me what went on. You have to promise that you won't turn around and sell the property to him. Jessie would spin in her grave."

He just about reminded her that she'd had Jessie cremated but then thought better of it.

"I won't sell it to him. I have to give notice to my boss. Two weeks. Is that soon enough?"

"Fine." She said it exactly as Jessie had said it. "It's as is where is. Don't come back after you've been there a while, wanting your money back. I'm going to take your money and go on a cruise, more than one. You don't spend it, you die, just like Jessie, and someone else spends it. Die broke. That's the way to go."

"I'll need a key."

"You ask that Ben for it."

"Don't you want anything from the house?"

"Jessie had packed up some boxes. They're in the kitchen. Ben can bring them to me. I'll probably throw most of it out, but there might be something I'll want to keep. I'm not a sentimental person. My apartment isn't very large. There's another fellow with a truck. I don't know his name, but don't send Jessie's things with him."

"She was looking forward to joining you."

"She shouldn't have married that man. I told her so. More than once. He wouldn't leave that godforsaken place no matter what. Wasted her life working for God and for him. Shiftless men. Never did a lick of work unless he had to. She paid for that house with money she received when our parents died. Plus, I loaned her some. I'll get in touch with you as soon as I've got everything ready. I'm her executor."

When he'd given her his phone number and address, she hung up.

There were corporations, governments, who needed people like her, he thought. She needed to go to Ottawa as prime minister. She'd straighten everybody out and make them fly right. No fooling around.

Tom had a friend who'd quit the Force and become a mortgage broker. He called him and, with a bit of fudging, his friend arranged the financing for the mortgage. Liar loans. If kids working at McDonald's could get them, why not him? When he did it, an image rose up before him of his father looking shocked, appalled, dismayed.

Connections, Tom thought, it was always that way, never straightforward but along a crooked path of who you knew, of favours given and returned. He'd encouraged his former colleague by suggesting that he come out for some fishing. The guy loved fishing. It would be a free holiday. Tom would even pay for his fishing licence.

CHAPTER 6

BANNOCKBURN

Tom gave two weeks' notice, and since he didn't work weekends, it was only twelve days before he could leave. His landlord insisted on thirty days' notice, but Myrna had an actress friend looking for a place to stay who was happy to pay the rent for two weeks. He thought his daughter would be dismayed at his moving away. Instead, she did a little celebratory dance, not, she said, because he was moving away, but because he'd found something that made him smile again.

Tom had called ahead, and Ben met him at Jessie's house with the keys. The house looked neglected, unloved, as if no one had cared about it, but he knew that wasn't true. *This is what old age and not enough money can do to people,* he thought. After his accident, he'd given up on money. Concentrating on his losses, he cared only about the past, not the future. The house, he thought, as they stood at the front, looking at the veranda, was going to take money, and his future wasn't in some great ambition, the shrink had said that, no big ambitions just small ones, plan a meal, ask someone to visit, start looking for a job, any job, it doesn't matter what it is, deliver the local paper, find something that you want to do, that you have to do, and he hadn't been able to do that, but now in buying wood and screws to replace the front steps that were crumbling with dry rot he could focus and he could plan what he had to do to get the wood and screws. He could manage that. He looked up under the wide eaves and saw that there was a small wooden sign that said, *Bannockburn Cottage.*

"Bannockburn," he said to Ben.

"Scots. He made a lot of money in something. Maybe coal. He named it when he was just coming here for the fishing and the duck hunting."

The aura of neglect was partly because of the debris lying around the yard, plus the irregular patches of dead grass among the towering spruce.

They went inside and Ben walked him through the rooms, just so they both could testify that nothing had been removed. The menagerie was still in the living room, the birds looking a little more dusty and the wolf more disintegrated.

"She said I could have that," Ben said, indicating a maple rocking chair. "I didn't want to take it without you agreeing. I don't want nobody saying I stole nothing. If I took it before you came, people would be slipping over here telling you I was a thief."

Tom told him to take it. It was sturdy enough but could have used a touch of sandpaper and a coat of shellac.

Ben looked pleased and, wanting to show he appreciated the gift, said, "On days I'm not making a run, I haul garbage for people. Not smelly stuff but old barrels, wrecked furniture, dry stuff. There's a dump five miles out of here. No tipping fees."

Tom thought about everything lying around in the yard and what might be in the garage and shed. "I'm okay for taking stuff to the dump," Tom said, "but I'd like to hire you to bring what's left in my apartment. It's boxed and ready to go. No furniture. I've got lots to do here. I don't need a trip to the city."

After being shut up, Jessie's house—his house, he reminded himself— smelled musty. Ben took Jessie's three boxes. When Josie returned to Winnipeg, she'd get in touch and he'd take them in to her.

"Not much been done to keep up this place," Ben said. He was studying where plaster had come off the kitchen ceiling.

They went back out into the yard. There was still snow in the deeper shade. There were a wooden picnic table, worn silver by the weather; some flower gardens; and a vegetable garden surrounded by wooden boxes that had come apart at the joints. There were no plants up yet, but Ben said, "Jessie wasn't able to keep things up in the last few years. There's tools in the shed. They might need a little fixing."

Tom doubted he'd have time for gardening. His mother had a pot in the kitchen window with some chives and parsley and a single geranium. She always claimed that Icelanders had black thumbs instead of green ones. In

Iceland, they lived on fish, lamb, milk and potatoes. Even when she was a girl, Icelanders still referred to salad greens as "grass" and refused to eat them. Grass was starvation food, but it wasn't grass they were eating; it was a special lichen. They might not want a bowl of lettuce with cucumber and radishes in Canada, but in Iceland, during times of starvation, they and their cows and sheep went to the seashore and survived on seaweed.

Anna, however, gardened on the roof of the apartment building. She got Tom to carry sacks of soil, fertilizer, trays of plants up the stairs. Tom thought at times that he was being used as a pawn in a struggle between Icelandic and Ukrainian values. Anna's garden was a hodgepodge of containers: old metal tubs, abandoned plastic planters in various colours, wooden boxes, a baby's bathtub, all of which she'd scavenged from the local back lanes. She had runner beans on poles and squash vines winding around chimneys and stacks. She'd gotten him and her daughter, Tanya, to help with planting and watering, and when vegetables were ripe or flowers bloomed, she'd sent some with him for his mother.

"You got yourself a lot of work," Ben said. "Nothing is ever what it looks to be. This place was well built, but you start looking and there's always things wrong. There's a weasel likes to have her kits under your house. You don't bother her; she won't bother you. She keeps the mice down. I'll haul your stuff back when I've got a load for the city. Cheaper that way. I only have to charge you for one direction."

CHAPTER 7

PICTURE PERFECT

Tom had woken up early and lay in bed thinking over the previous day. The constable who had taken his statement had gone over it three times. She'd talked to Albert, then came back to question him again, after Albert told her that he thought he'd seen Angel move and that it looked like she and Tom might even have been fighting, that he'd been leaning over her. Tom explained again about turning Angel over because she was lying face down in the water and added that Albert suffered from an excitable imagination.

Now Tom was a person of interest. He knew how people's minds worked. The person who found the body. Single male. Fifteen-year-old female. Hopefully, the autopsy would straighten that out.

When Tom had come to Valhalla, it was still chilly at night, but the weather had turned at the beginning of June, and with the beginning of July it had become oppressively hot and humid. He discovered that no matter how stifling the house was, once the sun went down a cool breeze would sweep in from the lake, and since the porch was fronted with windows that could be lifted and hooked to the ceiling, it cooled off enough to sleep covered with a light blanket. The porch just had the stack of wooden chairs, the cot with its thin mattress, a white wooden table with thick turned legs and two chairs that matched.

When he'd moved into the house, there was a half-finished game of solitaire on the living room table. A blue cardigan was hanging from the back of the chair. That was where she'd been found, sitting in front of the cards. Her body had been taken away under Ben's supervision. He'd followed her body out the door, then locked it. The kitchen table was still set for supper. Fortunately, she hadn't started cooking.

In Jessie's bedroom, the waterfall dresser still had her hairbrush and comb, a china dish with a city scene on it filled with bobby pins and safety pins. A small plain tin held an assortment of buttons, all set on an embroidered scarf. The drawers were filled with her personal items. She obviously had little money, for there was nothing extravagant, nothing expensive. The drawers of the tall dresser were filled with neatly arranged sweaters and socks. The closet was small, but it was more than adequate because there were just five dresses and three jackets. If she had sold her property and gone to the city, she could have gone shopping at the Salvation Army and had a whole closet full of clothes. Not selling had come with some sacrifice.

No one had thought to take the food out of the fridge. Tom had to throw everything out. He took the inside of the fridge apart, laid the parts out on the ground and washed them with baking soda and vinegar.

His ambitions for a while were going to be as small as his budget. He'd buy building supplies. The stove and fridge, as old as they were, would do for the time being. He'd concentrate on the insulation, the roof and the gutters. During the winter he could work on the inside.

He got up and went to the emporium for some condensed milk for his coffee. He was hoping that there would be a letter from Myrna. She'd said that she might come and visit. If she did, he wondered what the locals would make of her. Especially if one of her girlfriends drove her out. Goths in leather and metal. He just hoped she didn't lead her friend around on a dog collar and leash. They sometimes did that at the Polo Park mall. They loved the attention.

She'd got in with a bad group in high school. They called themselves the Dregs. When she turned eighteen, she started working part time in a tattoo parlour and later at a bar with strobes and heavy metal bands. When he objected, she said, "It's just a job. I'm not shooting up. No pills. I'm not even drinking much."

The final straw was when Myrna turned up with a girlfriend and Sally caught them kissing in the kitchen. She started screaming. Myrna screamed back, "So, I'm a gothic lesbian slut." Sally said she couldn't deal with it anymore. No more kids in chains and leather, no more sneering, no more girls puking in her toilet or bathtub, no more worrying about a son doing no one knows what on the computer.

Myrna and her girlfriend had stormed out of the house yelling, "Homophobia!" at the top of their lungs. Sally was wild eyed, enraged. Tom tried to find something positive in the situation by saying, "There's no danger of her getting pregnant."

The shrink had said, "Change what you can; accept what you can't. Kids go their own way."

"They're not your kids," Tom had replied angrily. The memory stopped him, made him pause at the bottom of the steps into White's Emporium. He closed his eyes for a moment and thought, *Focus, focus. Milk. I came for milk.* "Stay in the present," the shrink had said.

Horst was hunched behind the counter like an angry bird. His face tensed when he saw Tom. "You got a lot of furniture in Ford's place," he said, "that you won't want. It's not good for much. Old stuff. People nowadays want new things. I'll get Frenchie to clear it out for you and haul it away."

The dining room table and chairs were walnut. Tom planned to photograph them and take the pictures with him when he next went into the city. And Jessie had said the furniture came with the house.

Tom picked a can of beans off the shelf, checked the expiry date and set it on the counter.

"I like old stuff," he said. "Some of that furniture must have belonged to Mr. Ford. Oak and walnut. Some mahogany."

Horst took Tom's five-dollar bill and made change from a cash box. Not all transactions went through the cash register, Tom realized.

"It's all just junk," Horst said. "People like new stuff. You buy new, Frenchie will bring it for you."

Horst was so bloody obvious that he annoyed Tom. He was a con man without any con man skills. The best con men were charming, friendly, always put the victim's concerns first, built up trust. They were like elegant figure skaters, their moves practised. They joined church or ethnic groups, displayed their devotion to the common values of the group. They didn't make their move to defraud people until everything was in place and they could make a maximum profit. Tom didn't know if it was Horst's attempted manipulation that annoyed him so much or his incompetence.

When he returned home, he stood looking through the trees at the harbour. There were no buildings to interfere with his view of the lake. To the north side there was a dock and some finger docks. There were even three boathouses.

In June, the boats had started to turn up, but there'd been no rush for moorage. Once July began, the berths had started to fill up. There were a few powerboats, but most were sailboats. There were some cabin cruisers. There was money there, he thought. Nobody bought those on daily wages. Nobody local was buying boats like that.

He walked along the side of the house to the driveway and onto the road that led out of town. On the south side there was just his property, with its trees and bush. On the north side of the road, the village side, the permanent homes that were visible were scattered haphazardly behind and to the north of the emporium. A narrow drainage ditch that was choked with grass divided the road from his property. He'd have to clean it out. Fire would be the easiest way to do it, but now, with the heat of summer, it would be too dangerous. He'd have to wait until the fall rains. There were bottles and cans, bits of sodden cardboard that would have to be cleaned up. He walked west along the road to where a local side road running south dead-ended. This road ran parallel to the lakeshore but well back of it. His property, the other thirty-six acres, continued on the west side of this road. It looked nondescript, with a ragged row of small trees along the edge. From where he stood he could see an old shingle roof some distance away among a grove of trees. He kept walking because the village properties continued for another half mile, with driveways and culverts leading to yards cleared from the bush.

Walking back he took his time so that he could get a good look at the houses. Some of them weren't finished. They were covered with tarpaper but had never had the siding put on. Others had siding but with some boards missing.

Sweat ran down his back. Heatstroke would be the result of vigorous work. He went to the south side of the house because there he could work in the shade. The thick mats of spruce needles were brown and brittle. If a fire started, it would race through the debris. He remembered that Ben had said there were tools in the garage. Ben had left a key for the old-fashioned lock. Tom let himself in and the smell of dry dirt and air that had sat trapped for an unknown time was thick and heavy and made him cough. There was a rake, but when he took it outside, the handle was loose. He went to his truck, took a hammer and a nail from his toolbox. He drove the nail through the metal and the wood, then bent it over and tapped it down. It was a crude solution, but for the moment, it would work.

He started raking the accumulation of spruce needles, small branches and dead weeds into piles. The ground underneath was bare. Raking was good work. Repetitive but not too strenuous. He worked for two hours, then went to the emporium and bought a soft drink from one of the waitresses. His fridge kept drinks moderately cool. The Whites, with their professional coolers, kept drinks ice cold.

When he went back outside, Karla White was sitting in the shade at a table working with some receipts. He could see that she was having a hard time concentrating because she kept picking up a receipt, reading it, putting it down, and then staring into the middle distance.

"What do you want?" she asked sharply. She was challenging him the way a dog might bark at someone for no reason. He thought it must be the heat. It made everyone cranky. Her face was tense, the muscles around her mouth tight and the skin on her forehead pulled into wrinkles. Even though he'd been in Valhalla a short time, already he knew she felt that anything that might scare off customers was an impending disaster.

"The company of a beautiful woman," he replied. "A beautiful woman on a beautiful day."

In spite of herself, she smiled and shifted to face him. She had large dark eyes, and her makeup emphasized them. She batted her dark lashes at him. It made him feel like he had come courting. She was volatile, quickly changing moods. A compliment, a summer customer buying an expensive piece of fishing equipment, a new renter, was enough to make her hum or even sing a few lines from a cheerful song. A problem with a waitress or an ice cream girl, an unhappy boater or sports fisherman, would wind her up, make her rush to fix whatever was wrong. She apologized to fishermen who didn't catch any fish. She apologized for the weather. Now, she put aside what she was doing, stretched her arms out and drew them back. "If you want to know about that girl, she wasn't working here. Didn't ask for her old job back. Last summer she worked at the ice cream counter. I wasn't even sure of her name. I had to get one of the girls to remind me."

She gave him a quick insincere smile. "She came and went. Depended on whether her mother was drinking or not. Depended on whether her mother had a boyfriend. Depended on lots of things."

"I know Ben a little. He's been transporting stuff for me. Dropping off lumber and stuff. It's his granddaughter."

"You'd be better off with Frenchie. He's more dependable."

She hadn't asked him to join her, but he pulled out a chair and sat down anyway. He was sure he'd be welcome. She liked to be looked at.

"You're a puzzle, you know. Men don't usually come to Valhalla to stay. That's what people are saying. Why'd he come to Valhalla? It's not like there are great opportunities here. "

"There seem to be quite a few men around."

She was wearing a low-cut blouse and she leaned her elbows on the table so he could see her breasts better. She had fine breasts, the skin still smooth, and her bra pushed them up. He thought she must never have had children, or if she had, she'd never nursed them.

"Just the summer ones, and they don't count. They're like the butterflies." She waved her left hand and wiggled her fingers to mimic the fleeing butterflies. "They appear and disappear with the sun. They don't hang around to go to a tombola or dance or bingo in the winter. Summers are short; winters are long. Lots of men around here in the summer. Adds a little spice to our lives. Got to keep them happy. Sell them fresh wrigglers, if you know what I mean. Make sure they get their picture taken with their big catch. They're like the geese, though. They fly south for the winter. Their winters are palm trees and rum. Just us local folk here for whist drives or turkey dinners. Maybe some moose and bear hunters drop by. They don't know how to be part of our community. Do you know how to be part of our community?"

"I'll figure it out," he said. "I've lived in a lot of communities. Posted here, posted there. Some good, some bad. I always found my niche."

Up close, he could see that she was older than he'd first thought. Maybe forty. She did her makeup well, but there were crow's feet at the corners of her eyes and the sides of her jaw were starting to soften. A double chin was just starting to form. She had her hair pulled back and a wild daisy pinned over her left ear. Her nails were bright pink and carefully filed. Her thumbnails were painted blue. Nails not so long that they'd interfere with working but long enough to be noticeable. Her white blouse had a frilly edge.

"You're staring," she said.

"Sorry. When I see something new, I do that. An old habit. I'm trying to get over it. You could wear a higher blouse."

"Bigger tips this way," she said, half joking. She didn't quite manage a smile. "Lots of beach parties around here. Kids come out to drink. Most of the time they're not a nuisance unless they get noisy."

"When I saw her lying there, I thought at first she might be a boy. The jeans. The shirt."

"It's a bit of a fad right now. Girls dressing like cute boys," she said. When he looked puzzled, she added, "It's the fashion. Everything is fashion. You want to succeed, you have to follow the trend. Everyone wants to be discovered, to be on TV, in the movies. Nobody wants to think they're going to spend the rest of their life cleaning houses or waiting tables." She waited for a moment to see if he would say something, then added, "She's got a brother—had a brother. I'm not sure how you put it. When you were a cop, you might have been chasing him."

"I chased lots of people," he replied.

"He's lived in the city for a long time with his mother. He must be over twenty now. Dave, Dick, something with a D."

"For someone who didn't remember Angel's name, you know a lot about her family."

"He's trouble. We don't want trouble. You see these people?" She waved her hand toward the harbour. "They come here to relax. Stressful, important jobs in the city. They don't want city problems following them."

Tom stared at the masts of the sailboats. The squealing from kids jumping in the lake was louder for a moment as someone got thrown in. They all looked like they were having a wonderful time. The sky had shifted to a pale green. In the city, he hardly noticed the sky, but here it was impossible not to be aware of the sky's ever-changing moods, the constant shifting of colours. Anna had sometimes said to him as they worked on her roof garden, "Look at the sky." and he'd tip back his head but most of the time it was the contrails from the commercial airliners that interested him.

"It's like a postcard, isn't it?" Karla asked. "Picture perfect. We want to keep it that way. We scare these people away, we've got nothing. We've got to make enough in summer to last the winter. Not just us, me and Horst, but lots of people. They sell them fish, the girls get work with us, get babysitting. Their mothers get cleaning work. Boats need painting and repairing."

"This morning," he said, "a young woman in a long dress, long brown hair came by. She was carrying a wicker basket filled with fresh lettuce, green onions, some radishes. She said she could bring me fresh vegetables and fruit in season." She'd been like a willow wisp, he'd thought. She'd been wearing a large straw hat to keep off the sun.

Karla's face tensed and her body went rigid. "Odin," she said.

"What's that?"

"They're crazy. They think the end of the world, Ragnarök, is coming. Don't get taken in. They know about you. You get discussed. They know you're living alone. I'm sure she'd be happy to make you a salad, help out with light house-work. They go to the cottages, the boats, no business licence."

"Odin," he repeated.

"The god of gods, the holy of holys, the big guy with one eye, with a big hat and a staff."

"That guy," he said. "What does he have to do with selling fresh vegetables?"

"They own land north of town. Ten acres. They grow their own food. They don't do any business in the community. They take money out. They don't put any money in."

"You don't like them?" he said.

She gave him an exasperated look. "We can't compete. We have to buy vegetables from Winnipeg and have them trucked here. They pick wild raspber-ries, blueberries, everything. No cost. They garden big time." It was obviously a sore point for her, her voice was sharp with the unfairness of it all, but Tom remembered the carrots so limp that they bent, the potatoes thick with sprouts, the lettuce like a dishrag.

He'd bought fresh green onions, lettuce and radishes from his cheerful visitor. He'd taken two bundles of radishes. She said they'd soon have cucum-bers and tomatoes. There'd be new potatoes in a while.

Karla was studying him the way she might study a horse she was thinking of buying. She would, he thought, set a price on him and treat him accordingly.

He expected she would see him not as a racehorse, or a dressage horse, or a going-out-riding-on-Sunday horse, but a workhorse, plodding along.

He didn't want to argue with her about fresh vegetables or some weird group living past the houses and cottages to the north.

"Yes," he agreed, "Valhalla is picture perfect." Except for the police tape that was still up.

Some people came out of the café with ice cream cones. Double scoops. He supposed he wanted one and then decided he didn't. He'd been putting on weight since he'd been living alone. When he did up his pants, he had to pull them tight to get the button done up.

"Was Angel pretty?"

"Pert. More cute than pretty. Great eyes. That innocent look. Not the kind who's going to make the catwalk or win any beauty contests. "

"How could someone age fifteen get so drunk or drugged that she'd pass out in the middle of a water-filled rut?"

He was asking it, but he already knew the answer to his own question. He'd done the same around the same age. There'd been a wedding his father had felt obligated to attend. He took Tom and Tom had drunk a glass of wine that had been left at a table, then a glass of orphaned whisky, then a second glass of whisky that had been left on a table when someone went to dance. Everything started spinning, he started staggering and his father had gripped his arm, led him outside and told him to sit there with his back against a tree until he came to get him. Luckily, it was summer. He threw up.

His father had let him share his taxi home but insisted he sit in the front seat with the driver and that he keep his window open.

The next morning he thought he'd get a sermon, but his father never said a word. Finally, over supper, he'd apologized, said he wouldn't do it again.

"You got drunk," Anna said when he came to help her clean an apartment the next day. "You looked green like spinach." She then staggered back and forth to show him how he'd looked. She laughed out loud. Every so often while they were working, she'd look at him and imitate his staggering and laugh.

Because two couples from the dock had sat down at a table, one of the teenage waitresses came onto the porch. She had dark hair caught at the back with a pink bow. Her hair fell between her shoulder blades. She was wearing a frilly, low white top, a red skirt and leather sandals. Tom wondered if Karla had picked out her clothes or if she was just mimicking her boss.

"Hold it there, Tracy," Karla called. "That's it. Just like that." She snatched up her camera and took a quick shot. She looked at the result, then raised one thumb in approval.

"PR shots," Karla explained. "Every girl has a dream. I used to model quite a bit when I was her age, even when I was older. Had my own band for a while. C and W. We drew big crowds. Toured. I like hiring the ones with ambition, the ones that want to go places. I show them how to walk, how to put their best foot forward. It's good for the restaurant, and you never know who might drop by on a fishing trip. Sometimes it's people with connections. Miracles happen. We had one waitress get picked for a part in a movie. Celebrities come for the big walleye. We've had movie stars stay here. You've got to be seen to get a chance."

Karla tried to go back to her files and receipts, but she was too agitated. She picked them up and left.

He hoped there would be a letter from Myrna, but there wasn't any mail except an old phone bill that had caught up with him. It was already past due. It would have to wait some more. He had lumber to pay for.

He absentmindedly bought himself the chocolate cone he wasn't going to have and wandered down to the beach. Earlier, the surface had been roiled by a light wind, but it had died down, and now the water was dead calm.

The owner of the *Lazy Johanna* was throwing a Frisbee for his poodle. The dog missed the Frisbee, and it landed in the muddy ruts close to the shore. The poodle started to chase it, then stopped, dashed into the water and picked up a pink flip-flop. The owner started yelling at his dog to put it down. The dog stood there grinning at him. The man went over, picked up the flip-flop and threw it back into the water. Tom waited until the Frisbee session was over, then picked up the flip-flop.

Off to one side, there were some commercial fishing boats coming in. He went down to the dock to watch them pull up. The plastic boxes were filled with pickerel, perch, some striped bass, a few large sunfish. Most people didn't know what to do with sunfish. They were no good for filleting. His mother stuffed sunfish like a chicken and baked them.

"Good catch," he said, meaning it as a compliment.

A runty guy with a beard who he thought was Frenchie looked up and grunted but didn't say anything. He swung two boxes onto the deck, then slung them into a grey panel truck with the back doors missing. He drove off. The other fishermen were at least polite but didn't have much to say either. They had a lot of fish and they were in a hurry to get their catch packed in ice and sent to the processing plant. They all gathered at the same tin shed. At some time in the past, they'd decided it was better to share a space, to have one ice house instead of each of them having his own.

He was going home when he saw Ben's truck pull up to his place. He ran to meet him. Ben didn't get out of the truck, his hands gripping the wheel. Tom went up to the window and knocked on it. Ben didn't respond, so Tom opened the door.

"Ben," he said. "I'm sorry about your granddaughter."

Ben never turned to look at him but sat staring straight ahead. "She never drank," Ben said. He sounded like he was defending Angel against accusations that someone had made. "She promised me. She'd never drink. She was a good girl. She promised me." He was saying the words, but they seemed to come from someplace else, some place disconnected from him. "Wanda, her mother, drinks. She saw too much of that. She said she'd never do it."

His words were anguished. His face crumpled and he put his hands over eyes that were watery with tears.

Tom thought Ben's face was a kind face, a worn face. His eyes had seen a lot, maybe too much in the fish camps, the lumber camps, in the beer parlours he'd once haunted.

Tom had seen other parents, husbands, wives like this—in shock but still functioning for a time like an automaton until the reality broke through. That's when they collapsed. Now, Ben was still pushing reality away, fighting it, insisting that she couldn't have been drinking and she couldn't have died because of it. He had a pattern to his life and the pattern helped hold him together. For now. Later, Ben wouldn't remember anything about the trip.

There were two-by-fours for Tom on the truck. He went to the back of the truck and started to pull them off and stack them beside the house. Local people, having seen Ben's truck come into town, started to appear, first looking from a distance, then hurrying over. The gathering crowd in Tom's driveway was silent, communicating with a touch or a nod of a head or a hand on a shoulder. Three young girls came but hung back, keeping their distance, and one of the women went over to them and quietly chased them away.

A young woman in pink slippers came up to the truck. She was carrying a baby. "The Lord has collected her to Him," she shouted for everyone to hear. "She was His angel and He called her into his arms. Accept God's will and be at peace."

A large man wearing a bandana over his head caught her by the arm and led her away. "Mary, keep your advice to yourself," he said angrily.

"I believe in Jesus," she shouted. "Everything happens for a reason. God rules our lives. She is going to be a bride of Christ."

She would have continued to lecture Ben, but the man spread out his arms and blocked her. He flapped his arms the way he would to chase away birds, herding her out of the driveway onto the road. "No one saved this Angel," he said. "Leave him be."

Two of the men helped Tom finish unloading, then one of them opened the driver's door and told Ben to move over to the passenger's side. He backed the truck away, then turned it around and drove Ben home. The people who had crowded around the truck followed it in a straggling line. From where he stood, Tom could see others appearing on the road to Ben's.

There had been no invitation for Tom to join them. The moment the lumber was unloaded, they left. Like the summer people, he didn't belong, didn't have an earned place in the community. He followed them but stopped where his driveway met the road and stood there by himself. There was nothing he could do. He didn't know the rituals, didn't have the friendships, felt that if he went to Ben's, he would be seen as an intruder, the stranger in a place he didn't belong. He wondered what he should do. If he worked on the outside of the house, would that be seen as not caring? But he knew that others had work that had to be done—with the summer temperatures of the lake, the fishermen had to lift their nets so their fish wouldn't spoil. The emporium still needed to serve meals, sell groceries. The sports fishermen, even if they knew what was happening, wouldn't stop casting their lines.

Later, while Tom was struggling with a piece of eavestroughing, something kept nagging at him. If Angel had been wearing a swimsuit and had gone for a late-night swim and got a cramp or caught in the current, that would have been one thing. But she was fully dressed, so she probably came along the beach. Or she could have fallen off the dock. But then she should have been lying at the water's edge. If she'd been drinking, that would be easy enough, but local kids didn't hang around the dock. The boaters and the locals mostly kept some distance from each other. Besides, she'd have to have swum from where she fell, then staggered or crawled to where she drowned in the rut. And why would she swim in her clothes? The ruts ran up from the lake. Even sober people slipped on the wet clay. He'd seen people who were pushing a boat slip on the clay, fall to their knees. Maybe she was partying with the beach people and was taking ecstasy, smoking pot; nowadays who knew what kids ingested. He'd shoved the flip-flop into his pocket. Now, he took it out and studied it. It held no answers, so he put it on the picnic table and went to work on the house.

"It's not my problem anymore," he said and yanked the old drainpipe off. With it, a section of eavestroughing came down. Years of rotting spruce needles and leaves showered over him.

CHAPTER 8

THE END OF
THE BEGINNING

Work is our salvation. So Tom's father always said.

The house would give him an opportunity to focus and forget his troubles, he thought wryly. At first, he'd felt overwhelmed when he realized how much the house had been let go, how much had been hidden by snowdrifts, all ignored by his desire to own the house, to have a place here, among the tall spruce slightly bent to the south by the relentless wind from the lake, to wake in the morning to the sound of the waves on the shore, to make coffee, sit on the veranda and look out over the water or the vast field of ice stretching to the horizon.

He was standing in the living room, trying to decide what to do about the wolf. It was a large wolf, black. Whether the taxidermist had intended to give it a snarl or whether time and humidity had created it, the wolf had a curled lip and a glare that if it had been alive, would have sent everyone fleeing. Then he was distracted by some wallpaper that had come away at a seam and curled a bit. The glue on the paper had long ago dried out. He tugged slightly and the paper pulled away, revealing planed boards.

At the time the cottage was built, people were using tongue and groove, but a local sawmill wouldn't have been able to do that. They might have had a planer. The sawdust that Oli had brought from the mill would long ago have sunk down, leaving the top part of the walls uninsulated. At least there was the outer shingle, the wooden boards, the studs, the inside board walls. He could, if he wanted, put drywall right over the boards, but he rejected the idea. He needed to put in proper insulation and replace any old wiring. When he first met Jessie, she was wearing men's long underwear, a dress and two sweaters. She might have been cold because she was old and unwell, but the house would have been hard to heat.

His father had often told him the story of the boy who paid too much for a whistle, and he wondered if in spite of his father's warnings he had let himself be that boy. For a moment, he felt ashamed, but then he realized that, finally, he actually wanted something, which was the first indication that he was still alive, that everything inside him wasn't dead, that on his ruined plain a green shoot had appeared. Wanting. His parents had warned him about wanting. But wanting was life.

His parents had never thought they'd be able to have a child. Tom's father, Henry, was fifty, his mother, Gudrun, forty, when he was born. He was a shock that, at first, left them unbelieving, then perplexed, then uncertain. For a time, they'd kept his crib in the living room as if he were crib surfing, a temporary visitor, but when he needed a bed, his parents emptied the room his father had been using as an office and moved him into it.

Just down the hall from their apartment was a large storage closet that wasn't being used. Tom's father negotiated for it with Mrs. Galecian, Anna's mother. They'd moved Henry's desk and filing cabinets, his office chair, a tri-light and a footstool to this room with no windows. Henry bought an electric heater and put in a telephone. He suffered this exile until Tom was twelve, and then he said, over a full English breakfast one Saturday morning, that Tom was old enough to sleep on his own. In Wales, boys of twelve had worked in the mines and the mills; they did men's work. And after fried eggs, beans, streaky bacon, fried tomatoes, fried bread, sausages and black pudding with their morning tea, they moved Tom's bed, chair, desk and bookshelf down the hall into the large closet-cum-office and moved Henry's belongings back to the room from which he'd been exiled.

More than once, his parents forgot that Tom might need to use the bathroom and they put the inside chain on the door of the apartment. Tom kept a pot under the bed just in case he was caught short. There was no window in the room, but there was a window at the end of the hall, and when he couldn't sleep, he'd creep out and sit there. It looked out over a narrow alleyway. Even when he leaned out, he could only glimpse a sliver of sky. Down in the alley, in the early morning, he could see rats foraging in the garbage and street people huddled in the shelter of a back door.

Until Tom was four Mrs. Galecian took care of two apartment blocks, including the one in which Tom and his parents lived. After her daughter, Anna, had her baby, Mrs. Galecian gave the care of Tom's building to her daughter so she would have an income. Henry had been indignant at Mrs. Galecian's eighteen-year-old daughter having a shotgun wedding, a baby and a divorce within twelve months. "What can you expect of those people?" he asked. Those people he was referring to were the DPs: the Eastern Europeans, the Ukrainians, the Russians, the people with no English manners, thick accents and dubious morals.

"Young girls sometimes make mistakes," Gudrun replied.

Although the Germans had been hard at work trying to seduce the Icelanders with flattery and by providing instructors in skiing and mountain climbing, there'd been no opposition by the Icelanders to the English invasion in 1940. The Icelanders had no armed forces and only a handful of unarmed police. The English had broken a door at the telephone office but promised to replace it. The Icelandic president asked his fellow citizens to treat the troops as guests. American troops replaced the British a year later, but Commonwealth troops plus a few English got to stay.

There were around 120,000 Icelanders. Of those, about 40,000 lived in the capital city, Reykjavik. The country was isolated and rural, predictable. The arrival of the soldiers destroyed predictability. The soldiers, resented by the Icelandic men, were welcomed by the Icelandic women. Why not? Here were young men, well dressed, physically fit, exotic, with loose money in their pockets. The women put on their best dresses, did their hair, put on makeup and went trolling. The locals, unhappy about young women being seduced and seducing the soldiers, sailors and airmen, called this ástandið, the situation. In desperation, families sent girls off to stay on farms in the countryside to get them away from temptation. In 1942, there was an investigation of women's morals and a law was passed that allowed women who consorted with soldiers to be locked up in one of two reformatories.

In 1950 Henry was sent with a small army group to see if there were any British assets that could be repatriated. Henry and Gudrun met at Tjörnin pond in Reykjavik. They dated secretly for three months. When her father found out, he bundled her into a car and took her to a farm to stay with his brother's family. There was no escaping, since the distance was great, the farm isolated, travel difficult. During the time that Gudrun was being held on a farm at Grindavík, Henry was posted back to England. Gudrun eventually managed to get back to Reykjavik. All might have worked out for the best if her mother hadn't said, "Well, if the kanamella hasn't returned." Kanamella meant Yankee whore.

In the meantime, Henry had returned to England and written five letters to Gudrun. Gudrun's mother had hidden the letters in a dresser drawer. She didn't mention them to Gudrun. One day when Gudrun was putting away laundry, she found the letters. In one of them, Henry had proposed. She wrote down Henry's address, put the letters back and said nothing. Humiliation was piled on humiliation.

Gudrun replied to Henry, accepting his proposal. She packed a bag and without saying anything to her family got passage on a fishing boat taking cod to England. By the time the war was over, the boom years had begun in Canada, and Henry had met Canadian soldiers in Iceland and England who had told him about the opportunities in the Dominion. Being English he'd get preference over all the DPs who were coming to work on the frontier and as domestics.

Gudrun did not write home. Her adolescent rage had turned her, in her own mind, into an orphan. If asked about her family, she shrugged and said, "The war." Most people had no idea of what went on in Iceland during the war years, remembered the destruction of Europe, said they were sorry, that was a shame and let the topic drop.

In Iceland, when the Christians and pagans were in danger of going to war, they compromised. The pagans agreed to become Christians in public, but they could practise the old religion in private. Gudrun followed their example.

She made shepherd's pie, Yorkshire pudding, pickled beef tongue, mixed grill, kippers. She served high tea to their new English friends: crustless cucumber sandwiches that had cream cheese, dill and chives on them; chicken sandwiches with horseradish sauce on brown bread. She learned to make scones. She listened to BBC radio and imitated the way the announcers spoke. She got a part-time job at an English tea shop on Portage Avenue and worked among the Irish and English and Scots.

However, she hung on to her Icelandic identity in private. She read the few Icelandic books she could find, followed what little news there was of Iceland in the local papers. Read the Icelandic papers *Lögberg* and *Heimskringla* at the local library. Her husband did not read or speak Icelandic and had no interest in learning.

When Henry was away, as he frequently was, she spoke Icelandic to Tom. She read to him about the sagas. Henry had shown him where England was on the globe that sat in their living room. "I'm your other half," his mother said to him, and when he asked where this other half had come from, she showed him where Iceland was. He learned early that Iceland was their secret, just as the Icelandic treats she made were something shared only between the two of them.

The year Tom was twelve, a letter arrived from one of Gudrun's sisters, who had tracked her down to tell her that their mother had cancer and wanted Gudrun to return home so she could ask forgiveness in person. Gudrun had replied, thanking her for the information, but signed her name, Guðrun Ásta Einarsdóttir, kanamella.

There quickly had been another letter, an apology, an acknowledgement that Gudrun had every right to be angry for the unjust accusation. A token of reconciliation was included. It was fine Icelandic wool, enough to knit an adult sweater against the Canadian cold.

Gudrun felt the wool and knew it was the best that could be had. Her sister said, in her note, "We send this asking for your forgiveness." When the sweater was finished, she wrote to her sister and thanked her for the gift. After that, they wrote twice more.

When Gudrun said that she was going to see her mother before she died, Henry said, "That's very expensive," and she said, "I've got my own money." She'd saved what she could from working.

Three months later, Gudrun flew to Iceland. Before she left, Tom asked her to show him where her plane would be going. She traced her finger across Canada, from Winnipeg to Newfoundland. From there, she took another plane to Iceland. She was to be gone a month. If her mother died before Gudrun was scheduled to leave, she would change her flight so she could attend the funeral.

He thought, at first, when she didn't return on time, that her mother must have died close to the end of the month, then that there must have been a delay caused by the weather or a problem with the airplane. He'd gone to the library to search through the various newspapers for evidence of a crash.

Finally, one Saturday afternoon, while he was helping Anna clear out an apartment in which a renter had died, he said, "I wonder when my mother will come back."

And Anna, believing that life should be met head on and a spade should be called a shovel, said, "She's not coming back."

Tom had been cleaning a cupboard. He was so shocked that he stood up and banged his head. "It's not a big cut," Anna said when she looked at where he'd hit the edge of the metal cupboard. She dabbed at the blood with a tissue. "You'll have a little scar, but it'll heal. Nobody will know. Your hair will hide it. You'll survive."

Tom had protested. "All her belongings are still here. All her porcelain figurines. Her things in the kitchen."

"She took what she wanted," Anna said. "The rest, she left behind."

His whole body became weak. He thought he might fall down and not get up, but automatically, on their own, his hands started cleaning.

Tom felt heartsick, felt he'd been cast off a cliff into an endless void, as if the falling would never stop. And when he thought of his mother's belongings—her Royal Doulton figurines, her Royal Albert china, her crystal—all displayed in her china cabinet for when Henry's relatives came over, he realized there was nothing, not one single thing to indicate that she was Icelandic.

"She can't just leave," he said, refusing to believe that she could have left him behind. She'd said she was his other half. They'd shared all those times reading stories and learning about Vikings. They had secrets.

"Your father thought she was coming back, too. She sent him a letter."

His body ceased to be his body. It went on doing things, cleaning the fridge, the stove, washing the floor, but he was no longer connected to it.

"You can take care of yourself," Anna said. "You need to know anything, you ask me."

At first, he thought that there would be a letter to him or a postcard. When December came, he checked the mail every day for a Christmas card. There was nothing.

He often thought of what Anna had said: "She took what she wanted." She hadn't taken him, hadn't sent for him. His father wrapped himself in a stoic silence. That first Christmas, his father, not remembering it was Christmas until it was upon them, gave Tom one of his chess books and a chess set.

Mrs. Galecian asked them both to Christmas dinner, but his father declined and told Tom to go. Tom accepted immediately, and Anna and her daughter, Tanya; Anna's brother and his wife and two girls; her younger sister and her boyfriend; and an elderly aunt all crammed into Mr. and Mrs. Galecian's two-bedroom bungalow, a bungalow redolent with smells of turkey, cabbage rolls, perogies, onions, beets, pickles, potatoes and strange vegetables Tom had never heard of. The meal was boisterous and noisy, and laughter filled the room. The brother dipped his spoon into the dish of kutya and flipped it against the ceiling. Everyone clapped when a bit of the boiled wheat and honey clung to the ceiling, because it was a sign of good fortune for the coming year. They danced afterwards and Anna showed him how to polka, and then he did the polka with her daughter, who was twelve years old. Everyone clapped in time to the music as Tom and Tanya hopped around the room.

After they walked back to their apartment block, Anna asked him to come in for a moment. She handed him a gift wrapped in Christmas paper with a blue ribbon around it. He hadn't known what to say, and if he had tried to thank her, he would have started crying, so he hugged her, then fled down the hall and up the stairs to his own apartment. Safely behind the shut door of his bedroom, he opened the gift. It was a finely hand-knit sweater of blue wool. He hoped that his mother had sent it but then realized that he had seen Anna knitting it.

"You should make friends," his father said to him. "Pick the kind who will help you get ahead in life. Join some clubs." His father belonged to the Masons.

He'd joined the chess club at school, and Anna had taken him to events with Tanya. He'd celebrated their holidays, their birthdays, their anniversaries. It was at these events that he'd learned about laughter. For a moment, he thought about the tables laden with food and liquor, the noisy, excited talking, the hugs instead of handshakes, and the way the absurdity of life was celebrated.

His father paid for whatever Tom needed but was home less and less. Henry was distracted, as if in a daze a lot of the time, and when he did spend time in the apartment, he tied flies or worked out historical battles with his toy soldiers.

After a time, his father seemed to see things around him once again, and one day they went on the bus to Assiniboine Park, where Henry showed Tom how to use a fly rod on the grass. Once Tom had mastered casting, they walked to the Assiniboine River and fished from the bank. Twice a summer they took the bus to fish at Lockport. They took sandwiches, fruit and dessert with them in his father's rucksack and bought cold drinks from the local concessions. During these all-day excursions they carefully avoided talking about anything personal. Instead, they talked about military history and biographies. His father loved military history. They discussed the conduct of the Napoleonic Wars, the Crimean War, the D-Day landings. They never discussed the chair that sat empty at the dining room table or the place setting that went unused.

Tom often lay in bed and reflected on little things his mother had done as she prepared to leave. She began to encourage him to look for jobs—running errands, carrying groceries, occasionally babysitting, but most of all making himself useful to Anna.

Was it part of her plan when she took him to the bank and helped him open an account? She put $5.00 into it for him, and he deposited $2.50 that he had saved. She said it was their secret and not to mention this account to his father.

She'd explained to Tom that even though most people in Iceland lived on farms, they raised sheep and dairy cows, not vegetables or flowers. After Anna told him his mother wasn't coming back, Tom took his mother's three ceramic pots with their plants from the kitchen windowsill and dropped them one by one three storeys into the alleyway below. He packed his books about Iceland, his pictures of Vikings into a box and shoved it over the top of the Dumpster.

Was she implementing her plan when she asked Anna to hire him to do jobs around the apartment block? Mrs. Kolababa, Anna Kolababa—Anna told him to call her Anna, but Henry said he didn't ever want to hear him calling Mrs. Kolababa by her first name. After all, he said, although she was socially inferior, she had the right to her dignity. After that Tom always referred to her as "Mrs. Kolababa" in front of his father.

When he was sixteen, Tom was cleaning a vacated apartment for Anna and mentioned that he wanted a real job for the summer.

"You wanna work construction?" Anna asked. "You're a skinny kid."

"I want a real job," Tom replied.

"You do a good job on this apartment, I'll talk to my cousin Peter. He's building a house. It's hard work."

That summer he carried lumber, ran errands, gofered for a month but, gradually, was allowed to do more, always watching, listening, writing down everything he'd learned in a scribbler before he went to sleep at night. He kept the job until school started, and the greatest praise he'd ever received was when Peter said, "You come back next summer. There'll be a job."

Toward the middle of grade twelve, Tom mentioned going to university. His teachers had encouraged him to continue his education. Tom believed his father would be opposed because Henry had often expounded on the inferiority of Canadian schools, on the best strategy being to get a job with a good company and stay there until retirement with a good pension. But Henry's world had crumbled around him when he'd been declared redundant after decades of loyalty. Companies that he'd cited as pillars of certainty had disappeared with hardly a trace.

His father, it turned out, was relieved that Tom hadn't decided to take a trade. In Wales, the family had struggled to get out of the mines. After their move to England, they struggled to get out of the trades. His father never suggested a program of study for him. Tom chose history and criminology for no particular reason, except that his father loved history and biographies. Also, Tom liked memorizing dates and names, building frameworks of boxes one on top of the other and then filling the boxes with shelves and, on every shelf, putting a major date and incident. At first, the boxes represented centuries, but gradually, as he learned more, they became decades, each floor filled with people and events.

Tom was just starting his third year examinations when his father was killed. Henry, who thought riding the bus was safer than driving a car, was waiting at a bus stop when a tire came off a gravel truck and struck him.

Tom was studying at the kitchen table when a policeman came to tell him. Chaos. Chaos. He thought of it as suddenly finding that there was no ground beneath his feet. The policeman was very kind, and a social worker came to the apartment to talk to him. The phone rang, and it was a relative, a portly man who always wore a pork-pie hat, the sort that men wore in black-and-white movies. He'd phoned to ask Henry something about his income tax. Tom told him what had happened. He said he'd be right over. He came and said not to worry, he'd talk to the undertaker. He wanted to go into Henry's office, but the door was locked and Tom had no idea where the key was kept. He thought on a chain in his father's pocket. All the doors in the apartment had locks. Tom had a key to the front door, but all the other keys were locked in his father's bedroom. When his mother was still with them, she'd kept the keys in her pocket.

The Anglican minister came. He was a tall sallow-faced man with a lazy eye that wandered disconcertingly as he talked. He patted Tom on the shoulder, talked about the meaning of life and asked did he know if his father wanted a full funeral? Tom had no idea. He kept waiting for his father to come home.

The undertaker gave Tom his father's personal effects, including the office key, and Cousin Donald—his name turned out to be Donald—opened the office door and they went inside. Everything was precise, just the sort of office you'd expect of a man who trimmed his moustache every morning. Not a piece of paper lying around. The filing cabinets were locked, but there were keys for those, too. Tom had the sense that what they were doing was sinful, disrespectful, but Cousin Donald said it all had to be done. He went through the drawers. The files were clearly marked. Will, funeral plan, power of attorney, bank accounts, pension plan, birth certificates. To Tom's shock, there were divorce papers for his parents. His father had never said anything about a divorce. Everything was in its place, purposeful, except one piece of paper. It was torn from a notebook. Printed on it in his father's careful cursive hand was the word Valhalla. If it had been in his mother's writing, he'd have thought nothing of it. But his father cared nothing about Icelandic mythology and, ever since Gudrun had not returned, wanted to hear no mention of Iceland. Tom folded it and put it in his wallet.

The undertaker had been prepaid, and the will said that there was to be a graveside service. The plots—one for Henry, one for Gudrun—were paid for. His father's body was to be cremated, the urn buried. The urn was already chosen and waiting. Nothing left to chance.

There was nothing to do except put on his best clothes and turn up at the gravesite. There were twelve people, including the undertaker and the minister. The undertaker had the urn in a blue cloth bag. Tom thought at first it was a bag from his father's whisky. The minister said a few words, and the urn was placed in the ground. Then they all went back to the apartment, where Anna had tea and coffee and dainties ready. They talked about what a terrible tragedy it was and asked Tom what he wanted to do, but Tom was unable to pay much attention because he was worried that his father's ashes had been brought to the cemetery in a whisky bag.

A sharp-nosed woman in a big hat took him aside. She claimed to be a second cousin and said that his father had always intended for her to have the Royal Doulton figurines in the locked china cabinet. She had a box and wrapping paper in the car, she said, and was prepared to pack them up right then and there so he wouldn't have that responsibility.

"What people says don't count," Anna declared as she thrust a tray of cream cheese and cucumber sandwiches at the woman. "It's only good what's in writing."

Tom went to see his professors. They all offered to defer his exams.

For three months, he lived as if his father would come back at any moment. He never sat in his father's chair.

His mother had been the queen of the kitchen. It was her domain. She wanted no help when she cooked. She said the kitchen was small, and with two people in it there were likely to be accidents. It was Tom's job to wash the dishes, put them away and set the table for the next meal. Tom would have helped in the kitchen, but his mother said that if he got involved, she'd never be able to find anything. It was Anna who let him help her in the kitchen. Her family were used to crowding in together as one person cooked meat, another made a salad, while someone else prepared dessert.

The family lawyer called. His father had a small life insurance policy. Tom asked Cousin Donald why there wasn't much money in the estate.

"Gambling at bridge is high-stakes stuff," Cousin Donald replied.

While Gudrun was still at home, his father had gone out to play bridge one night a week. After she left, he gradually went out more and more, until he was playing bridge three or four times a week.

It had never occurred to Tom that his father was gambling.

When money was finally deposited into his account, he went to Anna's apartment and paid her the amount that was owed for his rent. She hugged him. Tom's parents were the longest residents in the building. "You'll be okay," she said. "You're a good boy. You work hard."

He thought about drinking his father's port and dry sack, but it seemed impossible, forbidden even in death. He wrote his deferred exams and passed them. Anna's cousin was building houses in Thompson and gave Tom a job. They worked long hours. He'd fall into bed, sleep, get up for work again. Six days a week. He was grateful that the work didn't leave him much time to think. When he returned to Winnipeg and moved back into the apartment, that changed.

He didn't know what changed, but the day after he arrived, he went into his parents' bedroom and lay on the pink silk coverlet on his mother's bed. Then he lay on his father's blue cotton quilt. He lay with his hands behind his head, not planning on sleeping but just staring at the ceiling, smelling his father's pipe and aftershave. He thought there'd still be the faint smell of his mother's lavender, but it had faded away, been overwhelmed by Prince Albert pipe tobacco. At last, he got up and went to the grocery store two blocks away. He asked for empty boxes, and Mr. Cohen, the owner, who knew Tom because he had sometimes stocked shelves, immediately went into the stock room and came back with a dozen boxes in a grocery cart.

"I got you tinned-goods boxes so there shouldn't be any bugs in them. You take the cart," he said, "but you bring it back. It's worth a lot of bucks."

Tom promised. He went back to the apartment and began going through his parents' drawers, piling their clothes neatly into the boxes until all the drawers were empty. Then he went through the closet, carefully folding his mother's dresses and his father's suits. He cleaned out the bathroom. He ran out of boxes and realized he would need more. On the way back to the grocery store, he stopped at Anna's apartment and asked how to get rid of stuff. Anna said, "I'll call our church, Saint Nicholas. They'll come and get it. Did you look in all the pockets? Sometimes people leave money in their pockets."

Tom pulled all his father's pockets inside out. Nothing but a dime had escaped detection. It was in a suit jacket. Two days later, two men with grim unshaven faces came to the door and said, "You want to make a donation?" They said it like they were daring him to say no. Tom showed them the boxes.

He went back to Anna and asked how he could get rid of furniture, other household items. "You going to leave? It doesn't cost much. I won't raise the rent." Tom said he couldn't live in the apartment. His parents' ghosts insisted on staying. Anna told him, "I'll call Zeke Solarchuk. I do business with him. He'll make you an offer."

The auctioneer came. He was a thin, stooped man with a straggly beard and tired eyes. He looked at everything. He shook his head and said, "They're old but not old enough to be antiques. They're well taken care of but were never expensive furniture. I will take it to get it off your hands."

Anna shook her finger at him, pressed her lips together in disapproval and said something sharply in Ukrainian.

"Okay," the auctioneer said, "okay. We won't bargain. I'll give you a thousand dollars. I won't make anything on it," he complained.

Tom gave him everything except personal items he wanted to keep. He gave Anna the Royal Doulton figurines.

"You got a place to go?" the auctioneer asked. "People are moving out of an apartment. One bedroom. The furniture is rental. It's clean. You interested?" The auctioneer provided a truck and driver cheaply because the apartment was in a rental building that belonged to his sister.

Tom thought he might become a history teacher, maybe a professor, maybe join the RCMP, maybe apply for the local police force, maybe... he wasn't sure what. He knew he didn't want to be a bookkeeper like his father.

Later, after he'd been accepted by the RCMP, finished his training, been moved about a bit, he went to have his teeth cleaned and the dental technician, Sally, asked him all about himself, was he married, did he have a job, a girlfriend, kids, as she scraped and polished. As he was leaving, she slipped a piece of paper into his hands with her phone number. He was lonely and called her. They went for pizza. Spent time in the back seat of his car. She called him the next weekend, suggested they go to a bar for a few beer, throw darts, watch sports on the big screen. After they'd been going together for four months, she told him she was pregnant, so they got married, and seven months later, Myrna was born.

Tom had never given any thought to being a father. His father had never really accepted being a father. If they could have afforded sending Tom to a boarding school and just had him return home on holidays, he would have opted for that. Tom had never wanted to ship Myrna or Joel off to boarding school. He wasn't sure what it was that he was supposed to do with a daughter and son, but he knew that they didn't belong in a place where rules and structures were all important. Myrna had always been a tomboy. She climbed trees, did cartwheels on the lawn, wanted a mitt so she could play baseball. She

wore dresses reluctantly unless she was playing dress-up, imagining herself
as various characters she'd seen on television or in movies. When Joel arrived,
he defied all their expectations. He'd always been fragile, thin and rather pale.
He preferred solitary activities, reading and playing checkers, then chess, then
computers. Sally hadn't liked that. She wanted a son who was captain of the
local hockey team, a hero she could cheer on from the sidelines.

Tom grabbed the corner of loose wallpaper and pulled it. It came away in a
long awkward strip. He pulled at another edge. It ripped, and he stepped back
and pulled it down. Once he started, he couldn't stop. The wallpaper came
away easily, except in spots where the boards had knots or rough areas. There
the glue had settled into the grooves and held the paper firm. He left them for
later. He kept on until the room was stripped of its tiny pink flowers and the
wallpaper lay in untidy coils. The lumber Oli had used for the walls was spruce.
Tom measured with his hand. Many of the boards were five inches across, six
feet long. He thought he would salvage them, take the nails out carefully. The
boards came from before the loggers cut down everything of value. Cleaning
out the old sawdust would be messy. He wondered if deer mice wintered there.
If they did, he'd have to wear a mask. Their urine sometimes carried hantavirus.
He'd need a spray bottle and a gallon of Javex.

"If you get angry, if you get depressed, get tactile," the shrink had said.
"Feel things. Smell them. Taste them. Listen to them." And his usual passive,
non-judgmental voice sounded angry, and Tom wondered how he managed to
listen to other people's pain day after day. He wondered if the anger was at him,
or if it was from the hour before, or about the hour to come. Later, he heard that
the shrink's marriage was coming apart. He wondered what the shrink smelled,
tasted, felt. Maybe not his wife.

Tom's anger had eased. He closed his eyes and breathed out. He needed
sunshine, he needed to go outside, so he went to look at the southeast corner
of the house. The corner had dropped, maybe three inches. The ground stayed
damp there because of the shade of the big spruce. He'd see who in town had
a chainsaw and knew how to take down large trees. Maybe trade the wood for
the work.

The corner needed to be lifted. Would it have made any difference, he wondered, if he'd known about the problems? He thought not; he'd have bought
the place anyway. Jessie's price was firm. It was like the house was waiting for

him, maybe seen in a dream, or in a picture. Maybe when he came to help find Jessie's husband, he'd made note of it, not consciously but unconsciously, the wide eaves, the narrow panels of stained glass bordering each window, the clean lines from another time.

Tom rubbed his hand over the shingles. Those closer to the bottom were punky. They would have to come off. He'd do it carefully, preserve everything that was good, get rid of everything that was bad, make it better than new. He'd keep the basic structure but redo Oli's slapdash solutions.

CHAPTER 9

EATING RATS

One thing Tom had learned about small towns was that if you want friends, you've got to participate, doesn't matter how you feel about the activity. It's not like there are myriad choices, as there are in the city. If you don't participate, people assume that you think you're too good for them.

One of Tom's colleagues had once said about small-town postings, "If they eat rats, you eat rats with them."

He went for a swim, then put on clean jeans and a short-sleeved shirt with pictures of ducks on it. Joel had given it to him. In the summers Tom had taken the kids to parks in the various places they'd lived and always took a loaf of stale bread to feed to the ducks. When Joel was little, he called Tom Daddy Duck, and that connection had stuck. At least he didn't associate his father with the various brands of stale bread. Daddy Duck was okay, but Daddy Stale Bread would have been difficult to accept.

There was bingo at the community hall. He wasn't sure of the dress code, but underdressing wasn't likely to be a problem. Because it was hot, he wore his shirt untucked. It also covered up the fact that his pants were tight.

He hadn't played bingo since Anna had occasionally taken him to the Ukrainian church. They'd eaten perogies and borshch in the basement. The air was delicious with the smell of frying onions. For dessert there was poppy seed cake with icing. There was no smoking while people were eating, but once the meal was over and the bingo cards came out, people lit up.

The Valhalla community hall was one large room with a stage at the front and high, narrow windows on each side. A kitchen and cloakroom had been added on the east side. On the stage were a folding table and a cage for balls. Two rows of wooden tables had been set up for the players. He bought a set of sheets with bingo cards printed on them and picked a seat close to the door. He barely had a chance to look around before Sarah O'Hara plunked herself down beside him.

"Don't be such a cheapskate," she said. "No one buys just the basics. This is a fundraiser for the school." She called a volunteer over and said to him, "Sell this guy five more."

"I'll take a blue, pink and yellow," Tom said.

"You got a lot to learn," she said.

"Seems like it," he answered. "I saw Ben. He was going to town to pick up a load."

"He needs the money," she said, but she wasn't really paying attention. She was using Scotch Tape to stick three sheets of the same colour together.

People were shuffling through the front door, saying hello, stopping in the aisle to share news and blocking others from getting to seats at the front. There were cries of "Keep moving" and "Sorry" and "I'll talk to you later" and the scraping of chairs, and calls of "More cards here." The caller had taken his seat. He was a young-looking man with a smooth face but a grey beard that dropped from the point of his chin. He wore a blue polyester suit and a yellow tie, making him more formal than everyone else and giving him authority. He turned the handle of the cage and the wooden balls rattled. He kept turning the cage until everyone had quit talking. When the first ball came out, he picked it up and shouted, "Under the B, three." With that, everyone bent to their cards, and from where he sat, Tom thought they all looked like students intent upon their exams.

Tom would have liked to have talked to Sarah more, but it was obviously against the rules, and given the way she gripped her false teeth together and scanned her cards, it would have been a serious criminal offence to distract her. He thought people might have stayed away, given that Angel had only died two days before, but if they were in mourning, it wasn't going to keep them from a chance to win the $175-dollar grand prize.

Sarah gave him the point of her elbow. "You missed number twenty-one." She was playing her cards and keeping an eye on his as well.

Because there were no ashtrays and there were two large red signs saying *No Smoking* in black letters, he hoped people obeyed them, but you never knew.

Some of the women wore makeup and dresses, but most were in loose track pants that looked like long underwear and tops that hung out. The women who were dolled up and had done their hair were by themselves, and he thought it meant that they were single and looking for a man. Those who already had a man didn't need to set bait. The men, in spite of the heat, wore long-sleeved shirts and blue jeans. Some of them had their sleeves rolled up. Parents had brought their children. Babysitters would be in short supply. If the kids wanted to run around, they went outside. Some of them were bingo mavens in training. Their parents bought them an extra sheet and then helped them keep track of the numbers.

A little blonde girl with pigtails and a short pink dress that stuck out like a tutu was walking about, tugging on the legs of people she knew. Each in turn picked her up and held her on their lap until she squirmed away. She kept going back to a very thin young woman holding a baby. Her mother's top was stained, either from feeding the baby or from it throwing up. Her face was shaped like an ellipse and filled with tiredness. He thought he recognized her, and then realized it was Rose. She had given him directions to Pearl's. She ignored the child that kept pulling on her leg, wanting to get onto her lap with the baby. She stared at the bingo card in front of her with the intensity of someone trying not to see some terrible dark fate approaching. Finally, an older girl, prodded by one of the women, took the child's hand and led her outside.

From what he could tell, the people were all locals. No boat or cottage people. There probably wasn't any such thing in their neighbourhoods. They did their gambling for real money in Las Vegas or the local casinos. They had lots of good surprises in their lives. New cars, boats, planes, houses, furniture, clothes, exotic trips, the sorts of things people who lived locally just dreamed about. If any of them did come, it would be self-conscious slumming so they could regale their friends with stories over dinner.

A woman at Tom's table yelled bingo and after her numbers were called out by the fellow who was selling cards and her win was confirmed, the seller went to the front and brought her the picture of a package of pork chops that had been cut from an advertising flyer and glued onto a piece of cardboard. All the prizes except the last one were for meat. Because of the temperature, the prizes were kept in a freezer on the stage and the winners would be able to pick them up after the last game.

There was a break after game ten. People got up for coffee and cold juice. Everyone started talking at once and it was like the roar of the lake in a storm. He was relieved when he saw the smokers head outside. He filled a paper cup with juice that was vaguely lemon, dropped a loonie onto the donation plate. A pretty blonde woman appeared holding up a broomstick with sugared donuts on it. People took a donut and gave her a loonie. Tom dug in his pocket for a dollar.

When he sat back down beside Sarah he said, "No one seems overcome with grief."

She turned sharply in her chair and stared directly into his face. Her eyes were blue, and at the moment, they looked like they could be made of ice. "When my husband died, I ran his trapline and lifted his nets. People helped me for the first couple of weeks, then I was on my own. They got families to feed and take care of. Do you think I should have played Ophelia?"

"Hamlet?" he said.

"Do you think just because we live back of beyond and don't have a lot of money that we don't know how to read? After he's had a few drinks, ask Helgi History over there to recite from the Edda. He'll keep you up all night." She indicated a man whose dark hair and beard resembled a haystack. In spite of the heat, he was wearing a linen sports jacket, a white shirt and a tie. There was obviously an old argument in her head, for she added, "Just because we can't afford big boats doesn't mean we've haven't got big brains."

The skin around Sarah's eyes was taut. He'd obviously stepped into sensitive territory. The relationship between the locals and the summer types wasn't all that good. He'd noticed that when the commercial fishermen came in from their nets, the summer people sometimes went down to look at the catch, but he'd never seen them having an actual conversation with the fishermen.

He half stood up to look for the blonde woman with the donuts, but she had disappeared.

"Dolly's sold out," Sarah said. "It gives her a bit of cash. She also makes donuts for hockey games and any events where she can make a few dollars. She's a good cook. If you want, she'd make you some real meals."

The big prize went to a woman in a bright orange-and-blue dress. When she yelled bingo, she pounded the table with her fist. There was a collective groan. Everyone who had won earlier prizes crowded up to the freezer to collect their bacon, pork chops or steak.

The next day, when he went to check the mail there was a letter from Joel. The envelope just said Tom Parsons, Valhalla, Manitoba. No postal code. Inside, there was one page, one line. It said, "I've got AIDS." It had a drawing of a stick man lying down with Xs over the circles that were his eyes.

Tom stood there staring at it. It might have been a language incomprehensible to him. Swahili maybe, or Russian. Even if someone had yelled fire, he couldn't have moved. There was no return address, and the postmark was two weeks old. Young, white, male, involved in theatre, comedy, in Vancouver. He didn't think Joel was gay—at least, he'd shown no signs of it. However, he'd preferred computer games to girls.

He knew there were people talking, making noise, but he couldn't hear anything. People were clustered at the ice cream counter, the café tables were full, Horst was putting chocolate bars on a shelf on the counter, but there was no sound. Everything slowed down.

"Is anything wrong?" Karla asked. She'd just come in the door from waiting on an outside table. She stood there, her hip thrust out and her hand on it. The voices, the clanking from the kitchen, from the dirty dishes being picked up, Horst's wheezing—all came back in a rush.

"No," he said too abruptly. "No, fine." And he went over to the vegetable stand, where he pretended to look at limp carrots and wilted lettuce.

He stood staring at the printed letters and wondering if this was one of Joel's crazy practical jokes. When he'd been at summer camps, he'd sent them messages saying, "I've been eaten by a bear." Or "I had my leg cut off because the cook ran out of meat for dinner." It was his way of making fun of their fears. He usually embellished his one-line notes with cartoon characters. The notes usually included a plea for another five dollars for treats.

Lost, Tom thought, imagining the vast distances of the prairies, the foothills, the mountains, and then the coast. Myrna had relented and given him a phone number in case he wanted to call her brother, but she couldn't imagine why. *Siblings*, he thought. He'd never had one and didn't understand why they fought. At times he'd had fantasies that his mother or father had secret children he could discover one day. He'd imagined that if he'd had a brother or sister, he wouldn't have always been lonely.

Just then, two men came in. They were wearing white shoes, white pants, short-sleeved shirts with anchors embroidered on the pockets and captain's caps, bright new ones with gold stars that he knew were an affectation. Potbellies. One of them had a dead cigar clenched between his teeth.

The girls who served ice cream were scooping steadily. Absentmindedly, Tom watched the two men watch the girls bend over the ice cream freezer in short skirts. As if from a great distance, he could hear the orders being given to the kitchen. The waitress clipped the orders with clothespins onto a line in front of the kitchen pass-through but also called out the order for the cook.

His son, he thought, the son he piggybacked around the house, taught to ride a bicycle. The son who, before he lost him, used to challenge him to chess every Saturday morning when he wasn't on duty.

The waitresses were coming in and out delivering and taking orders. Their uniform was a pink top and pink skirt with a white apron.

One of the sailors nudged the other when one of the girls bent right into the ice cream freezer to get at the bottom of a bucket. Tom idly thought the girls should wear longer skirts or Karla should put a half wall behind them.

"Cute, aren't they, at that age," Karla said. She'd sidled up beside him without him noticing and pressed her shoulder against him. Startled, he folded over the letter and put it in his pocket.

He gave her a half smile, then walked down to the dock. There were a couple more yachts anchored in the harbour. "Big bastards," the locals called them, the words expressing their envy and admiration.

There hadn't been a woman in his life for two years, and Karla was giving off all the right signals. How much of it was teasing to prove she was still attractive, and how much of it was meant to end in bed? He wondered if her low-cut blouses and short skirts were more responsible for attracting business than the pickerel fillet dinner.

There were six white punts overturned on the beach. A faded sign said it was two dollars an hour to rent them, but there was no one there who looked like he was in the renting business. There were no oars or oarlocks, so Tom took a piece of board to use as a paddle. He tipped over a punt and pushed it into the water. It leaked, so he hunted for a can he could use for bailing. He pushed himself off and paddled around the harbour, looking over the boats. They were mostly middle-class sailboats, the kind your average doctor or dentist owned. Keeping the punt moving while bailing took some effort. No one paid any attention to him.

When he'd finished with the docks, he paddled out to where the bigger sailboats and the yachts were anchored. There were seven of them. Sleek and, from the antennas, they had all the latest gadgets. One of them was obviously a tug that had been remodelled. Here and there wine bottles and liquor bottles were floating in the water.

There was a light sheen on the water from spilled oil. There was no holding tank for the boaters to pump out their sewage, and he wondered if they flushed it into the harbour or if they sailed out into deeper water where there was a current. They got their drinking and washing water from a standpipe at the foot of the dock.

He picked a whisky bottle out of the water. Glenmorangie. *Nothing but the best*, he thought. He took a sniff. This was the closest he'd get to something this expensive. He dropped the bottle back into the water. No Two Buck Chuck here. *Nothing here but the rich at play*, he said to himself. He resented the rich—or maybe just their lifestyle. His colleagues had sometimes kidded him, calling him Commie Tom. He had to admit that he enjoyed stopping a Ferrari or Mercedes going too fast. He knew the cost of the ticket didn't mean anything, though. Travis would have been too obsequious to actually hand out a ticket—maybe a warning, but he'd do it in his sucky voice. It all depended on how expensive the car was and the address on the licence.

When he got back to the beach, he thought about calling Sally from the store's phone. Karla would bill him at the end of the month and add 10 per cent. He couldn't get Joel's letter out of his mind. He wondered if Sally had received an identical note. If she did, she'd have thrown it out. She'd had enough of all of them. He couldn't blame her. All she wanted was a respectable, stable husband, with no hang-ups and no black marks on his record, and kids whom she could brag about when she got together with her girlfriends. Who wants to brag about a daughter with so much metal in her face that it blinds you in sunlight?

He wandered over to where Frenchie was unloading cases of goods for the store. The ground had dried out in the heat, but there was a dark spot at the back corner of the truck. Frenchie was inside unloading a dolly. Tom knelt down to look at the corner under the wet spot. Water was dripping from the truck, but when he put his hand on the bed, it was dry. The water was coming from below the bed. Tom ran his thumb over the spot where the water was seeping out and held it to his nose. It smelled of fish. He wiped the spot again and took another sniff.

Frenchie appeared around the corner of the truck. "Whaddaya think you're doing?" he demanded.

"I'm Tom Parsons." He held out his hand. Frenchie ignored it. "We met on the dock. You were bringing in your fish."

"Good for you. Leave my truck alone. There's always people hanging around, wanting to swipe stuff. Some kid made off with a box of chocolate bars a couple of weeks ago. It comes out of my pocket."

His voice was sharp, but Tom sensed fear in it, or maybe worry. And Frenchie made a point of grabbing a box marked *Beans*, except from the way he picked it up, Tom could see it was light. Tom followed Frenchie inside. The emporium was crowded; the staff were all busy waiting on customers. There was a noisy hum from all the voices. Frenchie had stacked his delivery at the door to the storeroom. The last box, the one marked *Beans*, was on top. Tom rummaged on a grocery shelf and then turned and lifted the box. It was light, so light it obviously didn't contain tinned goods. He ran the tip of his pocketknife across the top of the box. Inside was women's underwear. It looked like stuff out of the Victoria's Secret catalogue. Who in this town, he wondered, wore stuff like that?

"Dirty old man, are we?" Karla said, coming up behind him and closing the lid.

"I was looking for beans. I was hoping you had some Heinz with maple syrup."

"Those are for our lingerie parties. Ladies only. You want to look, find yourself a woman and buy her some."

He backed up and said, "Sorry, sorry. But it did say beans, and the tins on the shelf looked like they'd been left over from the Great War." Karla wasn't amused.

Just after he got home, Ben drove up. When he got out of the truck, Tom could smell beer on his breath and clothes. Ben opened the back of the truck. He began pulling out two-by-fours.

"She drowned," Ben said belligerently. "They said you found her. How can you drown lying on the ground?" His face was angry and red. He stumbled, then braced himself. "What was she doing at your place?" He was asking questions but was too angry to be interested in Tom's answers.

"She wasn't at my place," Tom replied. "She was over there." He pointed to the sticks and tape, then led the way. Ben shuffled after him.

"There was just you and her," Ben insisted stubbornly.

"Yes," Tom agreed, then said, "No. Albert was there. He was there before me. Over by that boat that's propped up with gas barrels."

They both looked toward the dock, toward the boat that was waiting to be scraped and painted.

"Albert," Ben said. "He's good to kids. Kids go there. He makes things for them. Toys. Whistles and things. He's a good guy."

They stopped at the tape. Ben hung back as if he didn't want to get too close to where Angel had been found. "Come here," Tom said. "You want to see where she drowned?" Ben edged closer but still hung back.

"You see this rut," Tom said, pointing at it. There was more than one, so Tom ducked under the tape and went right up to it. The water had evaporated and the sides of the rut had hardened. "It was full of water. She was lying face down."

Ben came closer to study the ruts. He looked like he didn't believe what Tom was saying. His face was swollen and his eyes were red. With the water gone, the ruts seemed harmless. Ben edged right up to the tape so he could see better. "You've got to try hard to drown in something like that," he said, refusing to believe something so inexplicable. "What was she doing here? You tell me that."

"How am I supposed to know?" Tom asked. "I was going to ask you the same thing. What was she doing there? You tell me."

"How am I supposed to know?" Ben said defensively, angrily, as if he'd been accused of a crime. "I had to do an overnight trip. I sometimes have to stay. She's always been okay. She wasn't wild." He was clenching and unclenching his hands. "I done my best. Where are your kids? Do you know where your kids are?" His face had grown darker, angrier as he demanded an answer.

Tom lifted up the tape and came back outside the barrier. "No, I don't know where they are."

It was obvious Ben wanted to fight with someone. To distract him, Tom said, "The red GMC. Is that Frenchie?"

"That prick."

"His truck's got a leak."

"Maybe he's carrying some ice," Ben said bitterly but immediately turned back to the subject of Angel. "She was taking music lessons at school. She was doing good." He stood there as if it was impossible for him to move. He wanted something or someone to rage against, to argue with. He wanted to demand an explanation that made some sense, but there was nothing there that he could attack, nothing he could destroy. Tom waited until Ben turned and made his way back to his truck. After Ben got into his truck, he leaned forward with his head on the steering wheel for a time before he managed to back away.

Ice, Tom mused. He hadn't seen any evidence of ice. Frenchie delivered perishables, but he had a cooler and freezer in the truck. The red truck was now parked at the side of the fish processing shed. Tom went over and saw that there was a difference of about two inches between the top and bottom of the bed.

He knocked on Sarah O'Hara's door. "Trouble and tea," she said. "I can see it in your face."

She stepped aside so he could come into the room. He was familiar with the kitchen now, and he realized how high the counter was, how big the handles on the cupboards were. The plank table was immense and the benches on either side higher than normal. His mother had told him stories about giants living in caves in the lava fields in Iceland.

"Ben just brought a delivery. He's drinking."

"Is he now? He needs to stay away from the drink."

"He could lose his licence. Maybe talk to him. Get him to take a few days off. He's running on shock. I've seen it lots of times. People keep going until they crash."

"Angel may as well have been his kid, he loved her so much." She stood there, her body tensed as if they were having an argument. "The mother's got the habit, you know." She tipped her hand up to her mouth like she was taking a drink. "She stays off for a while, but then a beer or two to celebrate being sober and she isn't sober anymore. Maybe not for weeks."

"He's got a grandson too, I heard."

Sarah had been making bread and her hands were white with flour. She turned back to the counter and punched down the risen bread dough with more force than necessary. She folded it over and put it under a tea towel to rise a second time.

"He does. Derk." Her words were sharp, chopped. "Older than Angel. He's a handful. He makes regular runs up here. Stops at the fish camps. Stops at some of the cottages. He's always welcome. He's got what people want."

"What do people want?"

She looked like she was going to reply but then stopped, uncertain. She looked away from him the way that he'd seen many people do who wanted to avoid answering one of his questions. She put another tea towel over the board where she'd been making bread. She was going to make more bread, and the towel would keep off the flies.

"I don't know any of this. Just idle gossip. Used to be hash, marijuana, magic mushrooms. Now it's other stuff. Chemicals. He's a favourite with the boaters. He delivers right to their door."

"And his sister?"

"I don't know. It's all just moccasin telegraph anyway. There's nothing to do here, so we gossip. Someone sees you having a drink and the next thing you're a raging alcoholic. Look at me. Support my kids fishing, trapping, cooking for hydro crews, road crews, fish camps, and people say I've made a fortune on my back."

"Ben said Frenchie might be transporting ice. He had water running out of his truck. Looks like it might have a false floor."

"Ben used to have that job delivering mail and store goods. Horst helped Frenchie push him out. They're thick as thieves. You like your tea strong or weak? Now, tell me, you ever been to Disneyland? I always wanted to take my kids to Disneyland. Never had the money. Six kids. That's the way it is." She poured him his tea. It was as dark as coffee. "Indian tea. If I'd been making it in the bush for you, I'd have boiled it in a jam tin."

"We took the kids to Disneyland once. It's overrated. We spent a lot of time in lineups."

It was true that they had stood in lines a long time, and he'd been irritated at having to wait instead of doing the things they'd come for, but he'd enjoyed himself and didn't want to say how much.

She went to the window then, pulled aside a lace curtain. She was looking at the harbour. "See all that? All those boats? All the cottages? You know what they've got? Everything. A big house in the city. Cottages better than the houses we live in year round. You've seen their kids come up to the store. They've got all the gadgets. All the toys. Our kids dig ice cream for them and babysit and they see all these things and you can't buy any of it for minimum wage and kids working don't even get minimum wage. You don't think we want things for our kids? You don't think I didn't dream of taking my kids to Disneyland?"

Not taking her kids to Disneyland was obviously a sore point with her, an old sore that broke open anytime it was scratched.

Sarah dropped the curtain. "We live here, you see. If you stay, you're going to feel what it's like. You're going to see the boats and the clothes and the toys. There'll be lots of work for someone who knows what he's doing fixing things. You'll see lots that needs fixing, but that doesn't mean there's the money for fixing it. Someone said you're doing a good job on the Ford place. You've got to learn to be grateful for anything the summer people give you. You need to learn to doff your hat. People here get into fist fights over minimum-wage jobs."

He didn't know what to say, so he said nothing. He'd wanted the best for his kids, same as everybody else. The school trips. The sports. The latest fashion that every kid just had to have. There were a few kids in the school who could afford to have it all and more. They had the latest, the best, the most. Stuff they'd wheedled out of their parents or shoplifted or paid for with after-school jobs or selling drugs. They had followers, but most of the kids ignored them, created their own groups. He wondered if that was why Myrna became a goth, because he and Sally couldn't afford the latest trends, or why Joel retreated into the private fantasy world of computers.

"You look like you've got a black dog on your back," Sarah said.

"Thinking."

"It's a bad pastime. You want to waste your time, take up making bird-houses. That's what Jumpy Albert does. Sells them to the tourists. Go look at them. Buy one. He never bad-mouths a customer."

"Birdhouses," he said skeptically, but he took the hint.

CHAPTER 10

BIRDHOUSES

At Jumpy Albert's, every tree was festooned with whirligigs of every size and colour made from plastic bottles. There was a slight breeze from the lake, but it was enough for the trees to look like they were getting ready to rise into the heavens. The picket fence that enclosed five goats and a few chickens and geese had every post painted a different colour and topped with a birdhouse, and every birdhouse had a brightly painted roof.

Jumpy Albert's house was small, with green trim and open yellow shutters. Flower boxes filled with gaudy blooms sat under the windows. The house, Tom thought, looked like a larger version of the birdhouses. Everything was persnickety, overdone, as if the house were actually a toy. Two life-sized carvings of pelicans perched on the roof.

The goats eyed Tom suspiciously. The chickens and geese ignored him. A turkey came around the corner of the house, scratched aggressively at the ground and glared at him, ready to defend its territory. As Tom locked the gate behind him, the billy goat lowered his horns, as if to protect his harem. Tom moved slowly along the path to the front door, always half turned to face the goat. It had four horns. Two larger ones at the front and two smaller ones behind. Its eyes were large, and the golden slits of its pupils made Tom think of the devil. He wished he'd brought an apple or two. When he got close to the house, he realized that the brightly coloured flowers were wood carvings. The billy goat followed and stood right behind him as he knocked on the door. When there was no answer, Tom followed the limestone walk around the house.

Every limestone pad was painted so that the path resembled the grada-
tions of a rainbow. At the rear of the house was a shanty workshop. The whole
front wall was made from two doors that were swung wide open. Albert was
sitting on a stool, bent over a bench, carving a piece of wood. When the goat
went over to him, he put out one hand to pat its head, then looked up.

"What do you want?" he said. "I told the Mounties what I saw. That's all."
His voice squeaked with anxiety. He looked like he was ready to jump off his
stool and flee.

"Sarah O'Hara said you've got birdhouses for sale." Tom went over to
admire five birdhouses that were lined up on the bench. Purple, orange, green,
yellow, red roofs. "What birds are they for?"

"Different ones," Albert said, giving nothing away. "You going to start
making birdhouses?"

Tom restrained a smile. Albert was worried about competition. His birdhouses were exquisite. Carved and painted in detail, they were more decoration
than birdhouse. More suitable for a mantelpiece than a tree. There also were
carvings of fish. They reminded Tom of the leaping pickerel on the Valhalla
sign. "Nice," he said of a jackfish. "I'm surprised you don't have them up for
sale at the store."

Albert's mouth twisted into a grimace. "Did before. But then Horst sent
pictures of my birdhouses to China and got them made from plastic. Doesn't
matter what's good or not. Buy them cheap; sell them cheap. Give the tourists whatever they want. You'd think he had enough things going for him. He
doesn't need to grab every dollar the tourists bring. Takes away my business,
but he still wants me to pay for my groceries."

Albert had his heels hooked over the lowest rail. His knees shook.

"I saw those plastic fish and birdhouses. They're junk." Tom held up the
jackfish, turned it around. "You need to have a place down by the dock."

"Can't," Albert said. There was a whine in his voice. "That's their property.
They aren't going to let me sell on their property unless they get fifty per cent."

"Greedy."

Albert's cheeks both had red spots on them. "You want a birdhouse or
not?" He climbed down from his stool and picked up the birdhouse with the
yellow roof. "This one's for yellow warblers." His arms and legs were so long

that they gave him the look of a puppet. He put down the yellow-roofed bird-house and picked up the one with the green roof. "This is for juncos."

Tom took the one that was supposed to attract yellow warblers. He thought it unlikely that a bird would move in. Once Tom had paid for the birdhouse, Albert was all smiles. They might have been old friends.

"You must have a lot of money. You never argued about the price."

"Sarah O'Hara said you're honest and can be trusted. She said you don't cheat people."

Albert looked pleased and preened a bit, his prominent Adam's apple bouncing up and down. "Like a tipple?" he asked. He disappeared and came back in a couple of minutes with two chipped china teacups with an ounce of gin in each. "Just like the queen mother," he said. "The sun is over the yardarm."

"To the queen," Tom said and sipped. Albert raised his cup and also took a sip. His hand was shaking.

"You see this?" he said, looking at the way the gin sloshed about in his cup. "I carve, I build birdhouses, and my mind settles and I relax. And when I relax, the shaking goes away. The doctors can't explain it. My mother always said that I was a nervous child."

"You handled things well the other morning. Lots couldn't have helped like you did."

Instead of the compliment calming him, the reminder made Albert's hand shake harder. He grabbed his right wrist with his left hand and, using it as a lever, got the cup to his mouth so he could drain off the gin.

"Doesn't make any sense about Angel," Albert said. "When she was little, she and her friends used to come around to watch me carve. She'd be in the city and she'd come back here and she always wanted to see the new birdhouses. I'd give her a cold glass of goat milk. She liked that."

"Did she come over lately?"

Albert ducked his head and for a moment he looked like a crane standing at the edge of the water. Two long skinny legs, short body, long neck pushed forward, beak of a nose. "No, she'd got too grown up. I heard her singing last summer on Friday nights. Kids get to a certain age and they don't want their friends seeing them with old people."

"You lived in Valhalla long?"

"Came out to the colonies on an adventure. Going to conquer the Great White North. Hunt polar bears. Pan for gold. I was lots of places. Ended up here."

"Were you on your first circuit when you saw me? You usually do three, I think."

"First," Albert said. "Every morning, three circuits. I like to do them in the dark. I've got this disease and people sometimes laugh when they see me jogging."

"You didn't see anyone?"

"Nobody, but I wasn't looking. Sarah's usually the first at the dock. Early riser. Says she doesn't sleep well."

"It was still dark, but did you hear anything?"

Albert shook his head. "I've thought about that lots. You didn't make any sound, walking in the mud. I just saw you because you moved. Somebody stands still, you could walk right past them. How'd you see me?"

"You moved."

"See. I told you. Your eye will catch movement, even if it can't see what's moving." He hesitated. "You think it was an accident?"

"Probably. That was good gin," Tom said, handing the cup back to Albert. "Where's the nearest place I can get a bottle?"

Albert looked like he might not answer the question, but the purchase and the praise had overcome his reticence. "I'll tell you, but we don't want any trouble." As he talked, he began to twitch. First his hands, then his left shoulder, then his feet. He looked like he was getting ready to jig. "Ask at the store. Under the counter. Bring a bag to put the bottle in. It's government stuff. The boaters don't want local. He makes plenty off those people. You don't tell them I told you. You don't want to get on their bad side. You do and they won't sell to you and you've got a long drive to get it."

Tom looked at the old Volvo station wagon that was in the other half of the workshop. No rust on it and spotlessly clean. Even the tires had been washed so well that there was no dirt or gravel between the treads. He hoped Albert didn't shake when he was gripping the steering wheel.

The billy goat followed him to the gate and waited until Tom had put the loop back around the post before returning to its harem. Tom lingered for a moment, studying the whirly trees, the riot of colour. The birdhouses on the fence posts had carved and painted birds entering or leaving. No real bird could get inside.

He went home for his rucksack, then went to the store. Horst was asleep in the overstuffed easy chair behind the counter. His breathing was heavy, laboured. Tom wondered if the store gave him a reason to live, a reason to get out of bed. Without it, what would he do? Lie in bed all day long straining to breathe?

Karla came out of the back. She leaned on the counter and her breasts pushed forward. "Hiya, handsome. Come for another look?"

"A bottle of rye," he said.

She never blinked. "You'd have to drive to town for that. No off-sales here. We're dry. You could get Frenchie to pick up a bottle the next time he's in town."

"I brought my own bag," he said and slipped his rucksack onto the counter.

"You're a cop," she said. She stepped back from the counter and straightened up. It was as if she had been onstage for so long that every move was calculated for its effect.

"Was. Past tense. Besides, even cops get thirsty." He shifted to look at her sleeping husband. Karla was younger than Horst by twenty years or more. She tinted her hair and her lipstick was laid on a bit heavily, but otherwise, she was quite attractive. For a moment, they looked at each other as if they were contemplating more than a purchase, then looked back at Horst.

Behind his back, in soft whispers, the waitresses called Horst the devil. When Horst was awake, he watched the waitresses, noting the time it took for customers to get their menus, to get served, for the dirty dishes to be picked up. He wrote it all down in a black hardcover book. The devil's book, the waitresses called it, a book from which he read them their sins when he paid them at the end of each week. They were relieved when he fell asleep in his big chair. When he was asleep they walked softly, picked up dishes carefully, were as silent as an order of nuns. For them and, Tom thought, for Karla, a good day was a day when Horst's head drooped, his pencil slipped from his fingers and he slept for hours at a time.

"He was my manager. He was going to make me famous. Made a few people nearly famous. That was after he left the asbestos mines and took up promotion."

"Those are nice pictures of you on the board," Tom said.

Behind him on the wall was a corkboard maybe six feet by four feet, covered with photographs and newspaper clippings. In the centre were a dozen framed pictures of Karla. He went over to study them. "You haven't changed much." In the pictures, she was ten years younger and ten pounds lighter, wearing a buckskin outfit. She was holding a microphone and there was a band behind her. They were all wearing cowboy hats. In most of the pictures, she was with different singers he didn't recognize but who had scrawled their names at the bottom. "You still sing?"

She blushed with pleasure. "I get the occasional gig." She turned toward her husband. "I can't leave him for long, and he has a hard time travelling. I just do overnighters, maybe two nights. I still get bigger gigs, but it's not like it used to be." She smiled and preened a bit at the memory.

"Maybe I'll get to hear you this winter when there's dances. There are old dance posters on the bulletin board outside the community hall. It says Cindy Lou, but it looks like you."

Karla left him to sell bread and cheese to a boater. As Tom waited, he studied the pictures that were pinned on the bulletin board with golden-headed tacks. A lot were of fishermen holding up their catch. Big fish pictures. Big smile pictures. Buddy pictures; boat pictures. But there were also a lot of pictures of the waitresses while they were working. Most were snaps, but others were posed. From the way they were posed, he assumed Karla was behind the camera, giving instructions on how to show their best side.

Karla tiptoed back, looked to see that Horst was still asleep, then reached under the counter and pulled out a mickey of rye. Tom opened his rucksack and she slipped the bottle into it. As she did, she leaned close, and he was overwhelmed by her perfume. She whispered, "Sometimes he pretends to be asleep, but he's really watching what goes on." He paid her five dollars over what he'd have paid in town, then gave her a wink and left.

When Tom walked over to Ben's, he was sitting in a metal lawn chair. It had been painted bright orange. There was a three-sided shed with a shanty roof. At one end there were the remains of last winter's woodpile. Beside the woodpile, there was an old stove and an oil burner. A snowmobile. The back wall of the shed was lined with shelves made from lumber that was now grey with age, and on the shelves were paint cans, small tools, an odd assortment of boxes. The grass was cut and the edges had been trimmed neatly. The house had been recently painted white with a yellow trim. Karla had said there was moss covering the roof, and it was true that there was a little moss where a tree overhung one end of the house, but if she thought that was a mossy roof, Tom wondered what she thought of his place.

In front of the remains of the woodpile was a blue plastic tub, upended, and on it was an empty beer bottle with a finger-sized plastic cowboy doll jammed into the top. Brown glass from broken bottles was scattered over the ground. Ben picked up a stone and lobbed it at the bottle. It went wide and glanced off the stove wood.

"Cowboys and Indians," he slurred and laughed. Behind Ben was a garage sheathed in tin. A small maple tree had grown against it and helped provide shelter from the unrelenting sun.

Tom put the mickey of rye on the table. "You want something stronger?" he asked.

"Beer," Ben said. "I don't drink that stuff."

"Is it okay if I get a glass and water?" Tom asked.

Ben pointed toward the door.

Tom went through the screen door and looked around. There was a living room to his right, a kitchen to his left. He got a glass out of the cupboard, poured water into it, got ice out of the freezer, then went back to the door. Ben was slumped in his chair and looked like he might slide out of it onto the ground at any moment. His arms hung like heavy weights. If the earth had suddenly opened up and threatened to swallow him, he wouldn't have tried to escape. Tom went back out, opened the mickey of rye and poured himself a small drink.

"To Angel," he said and held up his glass.

Ben stared at him, shook his head. "She wouldn't want that kind of toast," he said. "We promised each other we wouldn't drink."

"She came back to stay with you."

"Her mother got a new boyfriend. Always a new boyfriend. She didn't like that." He looked to the side for a while, studying the ground. "Angel used to like this song," Ben said, and he began to sing a song Tom didn't recognize. He had a deep baritone. "We sang it together."

There was a swing at one end of the porch. Ben waved at it. "She used to sit there and play my old guitar."

"When did she come back?"

"Lots of times," Ben said.

"A runaway?" Tom had spent time chasing runaways. They would run away time after time, and sometimes they'd say why they were running, but mostly they wouldn't.

"How," Ben asked, "can you be called a runaway when you're running to a place where people love you?"

Tom didn't know how to reply to that. He'd dealt with a case where a girl on a reserve ran away after being raped by a group of guys at a house party. They thought she'd been uppity because she wouldn't have sex with any of them. She made it to Winnipeg and moved in with people she knew from the reservation. The city cops picked her up and a judge sent her back to the reserve, where she was raped again.

"You're still doing deliveries?"

"Not the good stuff," he said. He grabbed his head with both hands, as if to hold in desperate thoughts. "You got to stay in with the right bastards, you know. That's the way it works. You're in and then you're out. She wanted a new guitar. A good one. I couldn't afford it."

"You got a picture of your granddaughter? I never got to see her."

"Inside, in the living room," Ben said. Tom took that as permission. He went back into the house. There was an old-fashioned dining table and four chairs, a matching hutch, a couch with a plaid blanket thrown over it. The room looked like it was seldom used. Everything had been recently dusted, and Tom wondered if it had been Angel who had taken a dustcloth to everything. An Axminster rug in a dark wine colour with an intricate pattern added a touch of elegance. It was worn at the edges, but the fringe had been combed straight. On the dining table there were a dozen pictures of a young girl. He went over to get a better look. Pert, Karla had said. Big smile. There were pictures of individual family members. Tom slipped a small picture of Angel into his pocket. It was in a shiny tin frame.

When he came out, Ben was snoring. Tom put the bottle of rye into his rucksack and spilled the whisky he'd poured for himself onto the ground. He pulled a patio umbrella over and set it so it would keep the sun off Ben when it moved farther east.

Tom went back to the store. While he waited to be served, he studied the pictures on the corkboard. Horst had woken up and Karla had disappeared.

Horst, Tom knew, would make him wait. That was fine with him. The pictures all had names on the bottom. Cindy, Joan, Barbara, Louise. He skipped from picture to picture. There were lots of pictures of Tracy—Tracy with her hip out, her chest out, Tracy bending over. There were multiple pictures of Cindy, Joan and Louise but just one of Barbara. She was holding a tray of dirty dishes. No pictures of Angel.

Not the good stuff, Ben had said. Not the good stuff. That meant Frenchie was hauling the good stuff.

Everybody, Sarah had said, is just trying to make a living. As friendly as she was, he sensed that she didn't want him disrupting the way things worked. He stopped at the ice cream counter for a chocolate ice cream cone and swore it would be his last.

"How's your day going?" he asked the young woman behind the counter.

"Good," she said and attempted a smile. "What'll it be?"

"Chocolate. Single scoop." As she took the scoop out of the water bucket, he said, "Did you know Angel?"

She froze as if he'd given her an electric shock. Her smile disappeared and he thought she might start to cry.

"Sorry," he said. "I didn't mean to upset you." Her name tag said Barbara, and he recognized her from the photo. "I'm sorry."

She quickly wiped a tear off her cheek and looked around.

"It's okay to grieve," Tom said.

She dug at the chocolate barrel and put the ice cream in a cone.

"Miss Karla says no tears, no frowns, only smiles. The show has to go on. Just like when she's performing."

He handed her a toonie and six quarters and she gave him the cone. She took a deep breath and forced a smile at the next customer. He stood to one side and looked at the other employees. They were all smiling, but they made him think of clowns in the circus with their smiles painted on. There wasn't much of a living to be made here. The summer season was short. It would be a struggle to stretch the summer money from the end of August to the next June. Cutting pulp in winter. The guy driving the road grader had a good job. Government pay. The post office would help support the store over the winter. There'd be the hunters in September and October. Commercial fishing was unpredictable. Everybody shot their own meat or got a licence and had a neighbour or friend shoot it for them. When he'd been in Valhalla in the winter, there'd been deer hanging from the trees in two people's yards. When the owners wanted meat, they came out with an axe and chopped a piece off.

Tom went back to his place and started lifting shingles off the northeast corner. The lower ones were held together by nothing but layers of paint. When he pulled them off, they crumbled in his hands. It was none of his business, he told himself. Lots of things go wrong and nothing is ever done about them. If Angel had been the daughter of one of the boaters, the place would be crawling with uniforms.

None of his business, he said to himself, but he took out the picture of Angel and stared at it as if it could reveal her secrets. Kids kill themselves all the time, one way or another. Being young is dangerous. He'd helped haul broken bodies out of wrecked cars. He'd helped pick up what was left after drug overdoses, got young fools to hospitals with stab wounds, broken bottle wounds, broken face bones, helped drag for bodies of kids who fell off things, out of boats. Motorcycles missing curves left few bones unbroken. He and his colleagues all played tough, but no one ever got used to it. They'd all go home after dealing with an accident with dead kids and hug their children.

Pert, cute, beautiful in a way. In the photo her smile lit up her face. Albert had said that when she was little, she had played music on anything. She had rhythm. For people in places like Valhalla, music was a way out. Poor kids, working-class kids had boxing, athletics, hockey scholarships for boys. There were no places waiting for her, or kids like her, at college or university, no daddy lunches where places in medical school or dentistry were allocated and reserved. A way out.

He looked through the trees at the dirt road. It went west, then south, but where did it lead? To River Heights, to Tuxedo, with mansions and money? Or to the North End, Main and Higgins, weekend stairwell parties fuelled by cheap sherry, sniffing gas, sniffing antifreeze, sniffing Pam, anything to keep away the pain of not having a job, not having any money, not having everything you could see on TV? TV made life hard because it showed what life could be like but not how to get it. Extravagant houses, expensive cars, beautiful clothes, wonderful restaurants, famous friends. At least at one time people didn't know about how the rich lived—unless of course they were the hired help and came to cook and wash and clean. Now, the world you couldn't have came right into your crappy apartment on a rented TV.

He kicked an empty coffee can lying on the ground beside his house, and water from past storms splashed up onto him. He wiped it off his clothes and face. His way out had been joining the Mounties. It was that or the army. A place to bring order from chaos, to have money guaranteed, to have structure but, most important, to have a place.

Most of the time, his anger lay quiet, asleep, but when it woke up, and he felt rage, he did things he shouldn't, said things he shouldn't. He'd been warned. It wasn't good for his career. Don't make other people's troubles your troubles. Don't try to solve society's problems. It's not your fault the mentally ill are on the street.

Tom put Angel's picture back in his pocket. He glanced toward the dock. Although it was obscured by his spruce trees, he could see that there was a boat sitting on a trailer where he'd found Angel. The driver of the truck hauling it had run over the sticks and tape. They knew what their priority was. They weren't going to let sticks and tape keep them from getting their boat in the water.

Around him the ground was deeply littered with decaying spruce needles and moss, and a rich earthy smell rose up when his feet disturbed the ground. When he bent over to look under the house, he saw bits and pieces of lumber, old eavestroughing, sheets of tin and rusting cans of various sizes. By the time he pulled all of it out, raked up the yard, rebuilt parts of the house, he'd have truckloads of garbage to haul away.

He felt as if everything was decaying, fragile, losing its integrity, the buildings, the people, disintegrating in a daily battle to hold back the forest that threatened to spread, once more, over everything, over the abandoned car with the tree growing through where the hood had been. He'd been to towns with no reason to exist, once the ore in the mine had run out or a new highway had been built miles away, and those buildings that couldn't be moved were soon engulfed by weeds and decay and dust.

The poor were always associated with dishonesty, but it was the poor who often turned in a lost wallet, because they knew how devastating it was to lose their grocery money. Were they not all angels when they were born, in places where kinship and community should protect them, hold them safe, where they weren't lost among vast throngs of strangers, where every person should know their name and watch over them? He looked at Angel's picture again, studied it, tried to peer into it, expecting her to speak to him, to reveal her secrets, but there was just glare of the light on the glass.

CHAPTER 11

COOKIES AND COCKROACHES

There was a single light bulb in the garage. Light filtered in from two windows. The window ledges held the dried corpses of flies, and dozens were trapped in spider webs that covered the panes. Empty wooden fish boxes and two old soft drink cases, their green and red letters faded, were stacked in one corner. Old books with yellowing pages were piled on unpainted shelves, and when he opened one, dust slid off the cover in a small avalanche. It was a medical book on naturopathy from the 1920s. A book created out of hope and ignorance because there were no real cures for anything. Tom inspected the ceiling. There were no water stains. The garage, he decided, was worth keeping.

He went back outside to look at the storage shed under the spruce trees. No sun reached there. The roof was thick with moss that had eaten away shingles and boards, soft green moss, gentle to the touch but sucking the strength out of the wood underneath.

He used the split end of a crowbar to grab onto the lock. The screws pulled loose. Whatever secrets the lock was supposed to protect were undone. He pulled the door open. An old washing machine, two oil drums, gasoline cans, boxes of nets, the frame and ends for a baby's crib, rusted muskrat traps hanging on spikes driven into uprights, a beat-up silver outboard, boxes of outboard motor parts, two oars with oarlocks, wooden fish boxes.

If the items in the shed held any secrets, they weren't worth keeping, and they had long ago lost any value they might have had. The shed, as far as he could see, had nothing in it but junk. He carried everything outside and stacked it under a tree.

He pulled off the door and threw it onto the ground, then systematically began pulling off the siding.

As he worked, he couldn't shake the image of Karla in her low-cut blouse. She always flirted with the male customers but was careful not to incite the wrath of any wives that were about. He'd seen one husband wave his hand dismissively and say to his wife, "Forget it. That's just Karla." Still, her behaviour was enough to resurrect his mother's voice, ricocheting around inside his head, saying, "Mind you, you do what you think is right, but I think that it would be best if you didn't waste time with that girl I saw you walking with today. You've got studying to do, and chores, and you said you wanted to work for Mrs. Kolababa. She's got people moving out, and that apartment needs a thorough cleaning. If you want her to keep hiring you, and it's because she's friends with your father and me that she's giving you these opportunities, there are lots of other young people who'd grab these opportunities in a moment, and then it will be money in their pocket, and your pocket will be empty, and then see how interested that girl will be in you."

His mother's tirade had been because she had seen him walking past the grocery store with Sally, his first Sally, his high school crush Sally, whom he'd sat across from and snuck looks of desire and longing at, and had, in spite of his being painfully shy, made attempts to talk to. They'd just happened to be going the same way that day.

Why, he wondered, was he thinking about this high school Sally after all these years, her tight white sweater, her swishy plaid skirt, her way of holding her books against her breasts, her brown hair?

Maybe, he thought, it was because of this girl he'd had a crush on in high school that he'd been so quick to call Sally, his Sally, his used-to-be-his Sally, when she'd slipped him her phone number at the dentist's. For when he thought about his Sally, the Sally he'd got pregnant, the Sally he'd married, he thought about the white sweater and the tartan skirt. *Sorry*, he said to himself, startled at the realization, *sorry, sorry*—it hadn't occurred to him that a name could take his life into dangerous places.

His parents had been correct—don't want anything. Wanting leads to trouble, to disaster, to getting a girl pregnant and having two children and getting a divorce, wanting things he couldn't have, wanting the Sally of math class. If he hadn't wanted her, he wouldn't have picked up the phone and called the other Sally.

Sally thought it was amusing that he'd been a virgin. She wasn't. "You get the benefit of experience," she said, not that she was a tramp or anything, but she'd had boyfriends. On their first date, when they were parked, she'd undone his pants and said, "Get a condom out," and when he said he didn't have one, she'd slipped off the seat, knelt down and given him a blow job. When she got back onto the seat, she said, "Tomorrow go buy condoms, unless you want to be a daddy." At first he'd used a condom, but she got a diaphragm so he could go naked.

Not that he minded that she got pregnant. He just didn't know what he was supposed to do as a father. He read books on being a father. He treated it like a math problem. Study it until you know it. When the kids came, he was surprised at how happy it made him to play with them, feed them, take them for walks. He pushed them on swings, rolled a ball with them. Sally suggested they get a dog, but he didn't think so. Cleaning up after dogs that people had snuck into their apartments had been disgusting. He made up for it by taking the kids to the petting zoo. They got to pet sheep and hold rabbits.

He tried not to be like his father, tried not to be withdrawn and silent as his father had been when he listened to music and tied flies. But there were silences, times that he lost his way, fell back into habits learned over his youth, withdrew, and Sally would say, "What's the matter with you, why don't you just act normal, why can't you just relax? You know, relax, laugh, have a good time, dance, sing, have a drink, have ten." She'd shout with frustration, "You're a freak, and our kids are going to turn into freaks."

He wanted to teach them bridge and cribbage, chess. Sally said no, that was not normal for little kids. He could teach them those things when they were old enough to say no if they didn't want to learn. She wasn't going to have her kids being freaks. He wanted Sally to play whist with them, but after a couple of times she said it was a boring waste of time, so he and the kids played three-handed whist, like he had with his parents.

They moved often, and after a while, Myrna would say, "What dumpy town are we going to live in now? Sure glad I didn't bother making any friends in this dump."

The day he'd chased the druggie, he and Sally and Myrna had been in the kitchen yelling, everybody yelling except Joel. Joel just stood in the doorway, watching, shaking his head in disgust, and went to his room to play games on his computer. The argument hadn't finished by the time Tom left for work. He was angry, furious. He'd been trying to be the peacemaker, but he'd never had a sister, didn't know how to make peace between a mother and daughter, didn't want his daughter having purple hair, wearing lipstick like it was war paint, never communicating except by screaming or crying. He thought of his life with his parents, his life with no emotions, no expressions of affection—he'd hated that, felt locked in ice at times, but this was too much like living in a fire.

He was angry with them all, angry with the stupid teenage drug dealers, the shoplifters, the wife abusers, the drunks, and then a whacked-out OxyContin user dragged a young mother out of her car and drove it away with a baby in the back seat.

He woke up in the hospital after they'd operated on him, stitching his leg together with metal pins, keeping him sedated for days, operating on his head and face, repairing his forehead and cheekbone, leaving him with a scar that ran straight down through his eyebrow. He didn't remember anything, not for weeks, and when it came back, all he remembered was seeing the druggie dragging the mother out of the car and pushing her to the ground, then getting into the car and squealing away. He'd stopped beside the mother, was going to tell her it was just a car, the insurance company would pay for any damage, but she was hysterical—"My baby, my baby," she kept screaming—and he'd jumped back in his patrol car and raced through the parking lot onto the road. It all stopped there. The rest was in the reports he read. Weaving in and out of traffic. Racing through red lights. Onto sidewalks. Driving so fast it was a miracle no pedestrians were killed. Then a semi pulled across the street in front of them. All he could say was, "I don't remember."

He wished he couldn't remember the mother's agonized face streaming with tears, twisted with hysteria. He wished the accident had taken his memory completely away. He would wake up soaked in sweat, sit up straight in bed as if ready to fight, the mother's face in front of him in the darkness. He tried not to think about the baby. Six months old. He studied pictures of the accident. There was hardly anything left of the stolen car. It had gone under the truck. He couldn't make himself read the medical examiner's report.

He knew he must have jerked the wheel hard to the left. They said his car had slewed sideways, rolled, lost momentum. It was a write-off. They had to cut him out of it. When he'd gotten out of the hospital and was still using a cane, he went to see his patrol car. He wondered how he was still alive. He took a small fragment of the taillight and kept it in his pocket. The shattered plastic was sharp, and when he clenched it in his hand, he cut himself and then he sucked on his hand, tasting his blood.

He pushed the images away, made them small, shrank them so he could lock them up and forced himself to think of the present, of his feelings and experiences in the present, but an image of Karla in her low-cut blouse and short skirt and her long slow looks rushed in, and he shut his eyes and said to himself, *No more Sallys, no more Sallys*.

He'd keep his life simple, uncomplicated, quiet. He'd be like his parents, uninvolved. He'd read, he'd sit and think, he'd play chess by himself; maybe he could find someone to play with him, the kind of person willing to sit in silence for hours as they studied the moves. He swung the crowbar with one hand and a two-by-four broke loose from the shed. He caught it with the crook and jerked, and it came away and fell to the ground.

"Beating up the world, are we?"

He looked up. Sarah O'Hara was standing there, watching him. "Jaysus, it's quare warm today, isn't it? I thought you might have something cold in your refrigerator. I could do with a Guinness."

They went into the house and he got a jug of iced tea out of the slope-shouldered refrigerator. He went to the chest freezer on the back porch to see what baking Jessie had left. "No Guinness," he said.

"Never is unless I ask Ben to bring some."

"Cold tea is a bit thin, but it keeps me from passing out."

"You got a lot of work ahead of you," Sarah said. "Oli was a good guy. He'd do you a favour if he could, but he wasn't a cabinetmaker."

Tom moved things around in the freezer. Jessie had everything carefully labelled. There were numerous plastic containers marked peanut butter cookies. He found a container that said cinnamon buns, took it out and put it on the table. It was a hot day; they'd defrost quickly enough. "Do you know anyone who would like a year's supply of peanut butter cookies?" he asked Sarah.

"I can make my own," she said. "You can bring them to events. People will gobble them up. I see you've been sleeping with windows out. Don't the mosquitoes bother you?"

He showed her the screened porch, and how he was able to seal it off from the rest of the house and let the breeze, when there was one, waft in from the lake.

"Does it cool off enough for you to get a good night's sleep?" she asked, and he thought of telling her that he never slept through the night anymore, that the figures in his dreams always woke him, their voices angry, accusatory. In his dreams there were the dead, the maimed, the arms and legs, the heads, the burned bodies. He managed it as well as any of his colleagues until the day when he responded to a motorcycle accident. A girl in leather was lying dead in a ditch. She looked so much like Myrna that he stood frozen, immobile, barely able to breathe. When he got home he frantically searched the neighbourhood until he found Myrna at the food court at the mall.

"If I'd brought a tent, I'd sleep on the beach."

Sarah grunted. "Would you now? I remember that. Me and McAra, on the trapline. Sleeping in one of his shacks or in a tent. Forty below. We kept each other warm. In summer, the mosquitoes and blackflies were thick on the netting."

He tried to imagine what it had been like leaving Ireland and family, the warm familiarity of her father's inn, and beginning a series of journeys away from civilization into the wilderness, where there was nothing but trees and water with the occasional cabin. They'd come to Valhalla in the spring, she'd told him, so they were able to live in a tent while McAra built a log cabin. He wondered if she'd had nights of terror when she'd woken up and thought about how far away she was from anything familiar.

"I saw your picture from when you first arrived. Irish girl, prim and proper."

She waved her hands at the wall. "You got no family?" she asked. "I thought I'd see pictures. Kids, family, dogs."

"In a box."

He was waiting for her to tell him what she'd come to say. It was always like that, full of preliminary conversation, settling into the words, getting comfortable with each other. She was used to silences, not chatty, not having to fill up space with talk. He tried to imagine her forty years before, when she was around thirty-five, swinging her way through the bush on snowshoes, dead animals in her packsack or on a toboggan. Life in the bush had lined her face, shaped it. One day when he'd gone to the store, he'd seen her in her yard, splitting stove wood. No fooling around. She swung the splitter back over her head, brought it down, sending the halves of the block flying. "Off with his head," he'd yelled at her and got a wave back in return.

He waited, and the silence stretched out, became taut as she came nearer to what she was going to say. He put the now semi-frozen cinnamon buns on two plates with a worn palm tree pattern.

She leaned closer and quietly said, "There's rumours going around."

"About what?" he asked.

"You and what happened to Angel. Lot of speculation."

"They haven't sent a serious crimes unit out. They must think it was an accident."

"An accident? No drama in that. Nothing to talk about there. Young girl. Stranger in town. Single. Straight out of Hollywood."

He put his glass down, his body suddenly tense. He glanced over his shoulder to see if any of the people in his nightmares had silently gathered to accuse him. There was nothing but the furious sun shining in the windows, making the linoleum shine dully. Dust floated in the light.

She picked up the cinnamon bun as if she hadn't said anything extraordinary and got syrup on her hand. She looked for a napkin and, not seeing one, licked the syrup off her fingers. He got two sheets off a roll of paper towels and handed her one.

"Albert says there was just you with her. Nobody else in sight. Nobody knows anything much about you. You got kicked out of the Mounties." He went to protest, but she waved his protest away. "I'm not saying you did it, but that's what people are saying—he's young, why'd he get kicked out of the Mounties, what'd he do? You're a stranger. Strangers do bad things. That makes everything easy, you get my drift?"

His chest tightened. Slowly, he let his breath out. "My DNA's on her," he said. "I had to touch her to see if she might still be alive. You have to do that. It's hot at night; her body would cool down slowly. Rigor mortis takes time to set in when it's hot."

Sarah studied him over her glass of tea and her face looked large and threatening, the way he thought the faces of the troll wives looked when they were getting ready to eat children.

"She was cute. There are men who like little girls, you know what I mean?" She saw the dark look on his face and held up her hand with the cinnamon bun in it. "I'm not saying. I'm just warning you. You need to know what people are talking about. If anyone gives you a funny look, you'll know why. Don't shoot the messenger."

"Bloody gossip," he said, but he knew she was right. People never wanted to blame uncles and grandfathers and friends for molested children. It unsettled things, made them uncomfortable, forced confrontations, changed relationships. It was safer blaming a stranger. "What should I do?"

"It's not what you should do. It's what you shouldn't do. Like you shouldn't ask questions. Don't go prying into people's lives. You weren't born here. You first come here because of Oli's death, and then you come and his wife dies. Then Angel dies. People think that's peculiar. You make people nervous, and they won't want to do business with you."

He drummed his right thumb on the table. It was an old habit that used to irritate his mother. He put his hand into his pocket and grasped the piece of broken taillight.

"What are people so afraid of?"

"Everything," Sarah said. The cinnamon bun was thawing, but instead of biting into it she began to unwind it, breaking off small pieces and putting them in her mouth. He did the same, and the cold, sweet pastry felt good. "When you haven't got much, you're afraid of everything. A fine for doing some little thing to make a buck and there's not as much for groceries."

"Why would I report anyone?"

"There's a rumour that if you report to the cops, you get a piece of the fine."

"That's crazy. Nobody gets a piece of anything."

"You're tied to three deaths."

"She probably took something she shouldn't. People are taking pills laced with fentanyl every day. "

"I doubt it. Ben has done his best to keep her away from that sort of thing."

"I don't lust after little girls," he said, and he nearly added, "Big girls, either," but that was just the anger, anger at Sarah for bringing the message, anger at Sally, anger at his mother. "I've been trying to stay out of it. It's none of my business. It's like you said, it's not my town. It's not like Ben is a bosom buddy.

I never met Angel." He said it tight voiced, bitter; his perfect retreat was falling apart all around him.

"What people have got, they've got. It's like a wolf gorging on a moose. It doesn't mind others helping themselves, but if all it's got is a bone with a few scraps of meat on it, it won't let any other animal close." Sarah was watching him to see if he understood. There was a quietness about her, an ability to sit still and watch, and he wondered if she'd learned that in the bush, waiting hours on end for animals to appear, for storms to end, for ice to freeze or melt.

He stared at the place in the kitchen ceiling where the plaster had fallen out, let what she said sink in, thought about it and realized he was no different. When Anna had more places than he could clean, he'd had no problem with her giving jobs to other people, but when there weren't many apartments coming vacant, he didn't want to share. Those were his apartments to clean, and she always knew she could keep him from asking for a raise by mentioning that others had come by looking for cleaning work. He knew that when he cleaned Anna only paid him a portion of the fee. She kept the rest for herself. Management expenses, she called them. "You gotta get paid to be the boss," she said.

"Albert was there before me. He told me he'd already done one circuit. Does he groom kids?"

"Groom kids," she repeated, thinking about it. "He's never been married. Kids sometimes go to watch him carve. Sometimes he'll carve a toy for them."

"Treats? Candy? Cold goat's milk?"

Sarah laughed out loud. "He thinks goat's milk is the cure for everything. He makes cheese out of it. Drinks it every day. Sometimes the kids will drink it to be polite. I never heard that any of them like it. You think he's a pervert?"

"I came here to get away from this crap," he said, and he felt pursued, as if all the eyes of the people he'd seen in alleyways, in Dumpsters, under old blankets and plastic sheets sleeping in doorways, were watching him, waiting to see what he would do to their packsack, their grocery carts full of garbage bags holding their worldly possessions, their dogs, dogs as unkempt as their owners, watching him, knowing his secrets, secrets even he didn't know about himself.

Sarah gave a tight smile. "Did you now? You thought it would be better here? Karla won't sell the kids booze, so they sniff gas. People want stuff, they find it. People sell beer out of the trunk of their car. It pays for gas and their own booze. You got something against people showing initiative? It's all about taxes. The government doesn't care if you drink yourself to death, just so they get the taxes. Did you ever think about that? You weren't a law enforcer; you were a tax collector."

"You've got a lot of opinions," he said, and his voice was colder than he intended. Her words hurt because he knew there was some truth in what she was saying.

"I've watched a lot of crap that goes on. Selective enforcement. You know about that?"

He gave a quick nod. He'd seen a lot of it too. If you were Aboriginal and a pain in the ass, you might end up outside the city in the middle of winter without your boots. You didn't even have to be Aboriginal. Just an annoyance who couldn't afford to hire a high-priced lawyer. You could end up in a wagon with a street person known to be violent and by the time you got to the station, have the shit beat out of you. There was ass-kissing for the people from good neighbourhoods and ass-kicking for the others. He shoved the thought away and said, "There's an old crib there. Do you think anyone could use it?"

"It probably isn't legal anymore. Besides, no one would want it. Bad luck. Their baby dying and all that. One last thing," she said as she got up to leave. "Keep your pecker in your pants. Don't make any more enemies. The local boys don't like the competition."

He wondered if she had anyone in particular in mind, and after she left, he wished he'd asked.

～ CHAPTER 12 ～

BEGINNING

From where he stood on the north side of the harbour, he could see the full crescent of the beach that swept to a broken rocky point more than a mile and a half away. At times, the shore was like a string that held together a necklace of brightly coloured tents, but this morning there was just a small red tent, then nothing until almost the end of the beach, where there was a cluster of vans and tents of various sizes and colours. Many of the locals were unsure of him, suspicious, and he thought it would be a good day to see if Angel had gone north, drawn by the fires and the presence of other young people.

Except for a few clouds that looked like small white islands, there was clear blue sky to the horizon. The sun was hot. He walked north on the sand. As he walked, he breathed deeply, slowly in and out. No purposeful striding, no rushing, no being angry. It scared people, made them uptight, uncommunicative.

Two young guys with wild hair were sitting outside the first tent, nothing on but shorts and strings of beads around their necks, each with a bad case of sunburn, pieces of white skin on their arms and backs. They were getting an early start on the beer they'd lined up in the water at the edge of the shore. They had aluminum and canvas loungers with hoods that could be raised to fend off the sun.

"Hey," the blond one said. He'd been reading a paperback. He put it down on his stomach.

"Hey," Tom replied and dragged over a piece of driftwood to sit on. They'd made a fire pit by piling beach stones in a circle. There was grey ash and charred wood in it. They were using a cast-off shelf from a refrigerator as a grill.

"Do I know you?" the dark-haired one asked. He'd been working on a crossword puzzle.

"I live over there," Tom said, pointing back toward the trees obscuring his house. "I'm friends with Ben, the guy who has a freight business. You know him?"

They both shook their heads.

He held out the picture of Angel. They both leaned forward to look at it. "This is his granddaughter. Have you seen her around lately?"

"Cute," the blond said. "Nope."

His dark-haired partner shook his head.

"She died in an accident a couple of days ago."

"Is that what the cops were about?"

Tom nodded.

"Bad stuff," the blond kid said. "What happened?"

"Don't know. I thought maybe she'd had too much of something."

"Not here," the dark-haired one said. He kept peeling off bits of skin as they talked. "We're into beer. Light beer, dark beer, German beer, Mexican beer."

"You a cop?" the blond one asked.

"No. Just a friend of Ben's. She was his granddaughter."

The blond kid sat up, reached over to Tom, took the picture, studied it. Shook his head.

"You don't go to the store for stuff, flirt with the girls working there, chat them up?"

They looked at each other, shook their heads. "We're not exactly welcome there. We don't spend enough money. The owner doesn't want us hanging around. You know, no shirt, no shoes, no service, no long hair. We might offend the big spenders on the yachts." The blond kid sounded annoyed. "The locals aren't exactly friendly." He said it with a sense of injustice, still expecting people to judge him by his innate values instead of the way he looked or how much money he had.

The dark-haired kid took the picture, studied it. "I'm not sure, but maybe I saw her on the beach one night. Hard to tell. It's dark, a campfire. People around the fire; people behind. People in the shadows. Not here. Down there. The Volkswagen and the other vans. Maybe. Maybe not. Don't say I said so. We don't want any trouble."

Tom thanked him. The kid could just as easily have said nothing, played dumb, dismissed Angel as none of his concern. Instead, he had listened to what Tom said and, despite not wanting to be involved, offered what he could. It was more than many would have done.

They weren't very old, Tom thought. Maybe nineteen or twenty. Still a bit scrawny. Young enough to sleep in a tent, wash in the lake, drink beer for breakfast, hope to get laid, mostly just hang out and talk about the world's injustices and how they'd make films or write great novels. Their old Ford pickup was parked in the scrub behind the beach. He envied them, wished he'd had a time in his life like that.

He started down the beach. The water was so still that the line where it met the sand might have been painted in place. There were freshwater clamshells lying on the limestone. Most of them were shattered by the waves that had cast them against the rocky beach. The inside of the shells shimmered with a translucent purple light. The beach was twenty or so feet wide. Mixed forest started at the edge of the high-water mark. Tamarack, moose maple, spruce, high bush cranberry, Saskatoon, the occasional white birch. Below that, the waves had scoured the limestone beach clean.

Behind the beach were crumbling limestone cliffs, no more than two or three feet in places. In other places the cliffs were ten or twelve feet high. Their surface was weathered away, so the layers of limestone were uneven. Grass and bushes grew in places where soil had gathered in the cracks above the reach of the waves.

As he picked his way over the broken limestone slabs that had fallen from the cliffs, dragonflies—some golden, others large blue—flitted around him. Anna had called the blue ones darning needles. The light reflecting from their bodies turned them to lapis lazuli and gold. Here and there, a few red dragonflies darted about. He'd seldom seen dragonflies in the city, except over Anna's rooftop garden. Or where buildings had been torn down long enough ago for flowering weeds to have grown up through and over the rubble. He thought the dragonflies were beautiful and held out his hand, hoping that one would land there so that he could hold it close to his face to study its intricate design.

Out of the corner of his eye he saw a movement on the broken front of the cliff and went to look. There were garter snakes sunning themselves. He'd been told about garter snake dens in the crevices and holes of the rocks, where in dark subterranean lairs they gathered in winter in great balls, hibernating on the edge of life and death as they waited for the sun's return. The garter snakes had yellow stripes along their sides. Many were small, but others were at least three feet long. Some were stretched out on the sun-hot rock, but others were coiled, and as Tom moved closer they could feel the vibrations in the rock, and he could see their heads immediately rise up. One snatched a blue dragonfly out of the air.

Farther down the beach was a driftwood lean-to and the cluster of vehicles the dark-haired kid had pointed out. Most beach campers were couples, or maybe two couples, but this was a larger group than usual. It looked organized, and he wondered if they were part of the Odin group he had heard mentioned. Modern-day Vikings, Asatru maybe, people who believed in the ancient gods. But then he remembered that the movement was started in Iceland in the 1970s and dismissed the idea, because he'd been told there were permanent buildings and the local sect had lived just outside Valhalla since the 1930s. This looked more like a group of drifters and grifters, more like modern-day gypsies.

As he got closer, a woman in a blue shift saw him. She studied him for a moment, then bent over to speak into the lean-to. Heads popped out and people gathered to stand and watch him approach. By the time he reached them, he had a welcoming committee of ten adults. A couple of small kids were running around naked. He hoped they had sunblock on their sensitive parts.

A man with a beard and dark dreadlocks down past his shoulders took the lead. The dreadlocks were threaded with brightly coloured beads, and a seagull's feather was fitted over his left ear. He was tall and thin, wore half-frame glasses, a multicoloured vest and loose white pants that stopped at his knees.

"Is there something we can help you with?" he asked. Although his voice was soft and offered assistance, his eyes were hard and wary.

Tom played it straight. He'd dealt with groups like this before. They were a community; they'd support each other. Everyone outside their little group was the enemy. They lived by their own rules. It was in their expressionless faces, the way they looked him over. He gave them his name, asked the leader his name and managed to get that it was Jason, no last name. Today, Tom thought, it was Jason, tomorrow Robert or Barney or Zacharias.

He showed them Angel's picture. "I'm looking for anyone who has seen her lately." Jason took it, studied it, handed the picture to the woman standing beside him. The picture made the rounds. Everyone glanced at it and said nothing, but the eyes of a couple of people betrayed them. Their eyes opened wider, and they glanced at whoever was beside them before turning their faces into masks once again.

"She's not here," Jason said.

"I know that," Tom answered. "She's dead."

"Cop?"

"Friend of the family."

"Cop."

"Used to be. This is personal. I'm friends with her grandfather. She was living with him. She wanted to be a musician. Liked playing, singing. I heard you guys have a bonfire in the evening and sit around and play and sing. She'd have liked that."

"Accident?"

"Probably."

"When?"

"Two mornings ago."

Jason shook his head. "She wasn't here two nights ago."

"She'd been?"

"I don't remember her." Jason half turned and looked at everyone, but they all remained stone faced. They didn't want any trouble. He hoped he hadn't spooked them. They might just up and leave. There was nothing to stop them. They'd scatter here and there—God knows where. California, Montreal, Mexico. Picking fruit in the Okanagan, selling crafts at fairs. There were dream catchers hanging in the window of one of the vans and prisms in another. A rainbow of light lay over the limestone. One of the little boys peed on the beach.

"She was a good kid."

"That's all?" Jason asked.

Tom shrugged. "Yes. Her grandfather asked me if I could find out what happened, where she'd been. It helps to know. Anyway, thanks. Knowing she wasn't with the two guys in the tent closer to the village and knowing she wasn't here helps shut off this direction."

"You going to live here?"

"Yeah. Retired. Bad leg." He knew they'd have seen his limp as he'd come up the beach. "I had a young woman come to the house to sell me some fresh vegetables. I think she said she was from Odin. Are you Odin?"

The question was met by silence. They all looked at each other, then at Jason.

"I am a member of Odin," Jason said. "Why do you want to know?"

"She said if I wanted, I could come to buy fresh garden produce." He glanced around the campsite. "No garden produce here, but from what she said this looks about the area."

Jason pointed toward the trees. "In there," he said. "If you bought once, they'll come back."

Tom nodded. When he turned and walked away, they never moved. They stayed watching him, none of them saying anything until he was halfway down the beach and they were certain he couldn't hear them.

He didn't believe them. They kept looking at each other. He expected them to be wary. Cops were the enemy. Cops looking into how they made their living, how they lived, always looking for drugs, ready to report them for not taking proper care of their kids. Drifting, drifting, one place to the next; but one or more of them might have a credit card and a rich daddy. He'd seen that before. The group's cash resource. Used in emergencies. Maybe, maybe not. Groups like that scavenged, often stole on the principle that whatever they took, they needed more than the owner. Sold a few drugs. Panhandled. Busked. He stopped with that thought, mulled it over. Busking—that would explain the music around the fire.

Angel would have liked that, been thrilled to be with people who could perform, could teach her how to improve her playing. He tucked the thought away. Kept making his list. Sidewalk art in chalk. It got rougher if the leader was bent, if there was a real shortage of money, then the women could be sent onto the street to make a few dollars. A van parked close by a tourist area would do for tourist quickies.

It looked at first like an easy path. Drop out of school. Find friends who preached freedom and offered a home away from home. Life on the open road.

A new family. He wondered about Joel and Myrna, what he and Sally had done wrong. Why hadn't they had discussions about what they needed to do so their kids would get a degree, get a job, a spouse, a house in the suburbs?

They'd been busy trying to make enough money to pay the bills. A lot of the time, Myrna and Joel had been left to bring themselves up, and for a moment, he felt a hollowness, kids left to raise themselves in an empty house, looking for someone for guidance. For a moment, he regretted all the times no one was home when his kids returned from school. The shrink had said, "Give up on the blame. It's a waste of time unless it gets you to change your behaviour." It had been a challenge, but there was no going back, no making other decisions with the advantage of hindsight. "Let it go," the shrink had said. "There's enough blame in the world." But when he paused to look back down the beach at the human wreckage there and who had taken on the mantle of leadership, he said, "Oh fuck."

CHAPTER 13

RIG PIGS

Tom asked Sarah if there was anyone who made and sold meals besides the emporium. She reminded him of Dolly, the blonde woman who had sugar-coated donuts on a stick at bingo. Tom went to Dolly's to ask her to make meals for him that he could put into the freezer. She opened the screen door a crack and peered out at him like he might be a home invader in the big city. He introduced himself, and she eyed him up and down.

"Sarah said you take orders for freezer meals," he said. "She says you're the best cook in town."

The door opened slightly, but she was in darkness and he was in blinding light, so he could not make out any of her features. Her hand was on the edge of the door, and he could see her fingers. Every fingernail was a different colour.

"How many?" she asked. He wondered if there was a threshold. If he didn't order enough, she might close the aluminum door and lock it. There were, he knew, unspoken rules that he would discover with time.

"Thirty. For September first. Sarah said I needed to get my order in."

"Cash in advance."

"Twenty-five per cent down. The rest on delivery."

As Dolly made up her mind, the door wavered a bit. She pulled open the door with her right hand, held back a little girl with her left hand and shoved a small dog back with her left foot.

Her kitchen smelled of cinnamon and cloves. He took that as a good sign. She was short, blonde, maybe thirty, pretty.

When he was inside, she said, "Sit over there. I'll get my order book and a pen. I use good ingredients. Better than that junk the Whites make. They use the cheapest stuff. Veggies they can't sell and have got wrinkled. Canned food that's after its expiry date."

"Breakfast is sort of greasy," he said, encouraging her. She chased her daughter and the dog away, got her order book and joined him at the table.

"They say they get their stuff from a wholesale. They don't. They get it from a salvage place. Bankruptcies. Train wrecks. Most of it is out of date when it gets here."

"You think they're making a lot of dough?" he asked.

"Ha!" she said, spitting it up like a piece of food caught in her windpipe. "They're rolling in it. They got all the summer business. And the rest of the year, unless you want to make a trip, you buy from them."

"Where do you get your stuff?"

"I go to town with Ben. He makes deliveries and I shop."

"Frenchie goes to town regularly."

"Yeah," she said, "but the Whites, they don't like competition and, like, if you're competition or they're annoyed at you, Frenchie forgets to bring stuff you need, you know, or he wasn't able to get what you want. There's always a reason. You like meat pies?"

"Sure," he said.

"You sure you want thirty meals? I've got to know so I can order. Everything has to be planned."

"Thirty to start. Suppers.

"Fish okay?"

"No," he said. "I'll get my own fish.

"Five bucks, and that includes dessert."

"Four and a quarter."

"Four seventy-five," she said. "You're not exactly dainty. The portions have got to be good size."

"Four fifty," he countered.

"Done," she said, "but you don't get no fruitcake. You've got to buy that separately." Sarah had said that Dolly liked to bargain. If he gave in to her first price, she'd tell everyone he was a pushover. "I don't cheat on the quality, and

I don't cheat on the quantity. I thought the way you hang around the Whites you'd of gone there."

"I ate one of your donuts at bingo." It was all he needed to say to reassure her that he had come for the right reason. It explained everything, including the arrival at her door of a stranger, one she might have heard accused of secret, terrible things. There are those who make vast, convoluted explanations full of ifs and maybes, but he was not one of them. His explanation was simple and honest.

"Those Whites, they're always chiselling. They wanted me to cook for them, wanted me to chisel on the food, wanted to chisel on my wages. They chisel the girls on their tips. Some people know nothing but chisel."

"They sell a lot of different stuff."

"Yah," she said. "They've got the store, the café, those places they rent out. They charge for using the showers, they sell souvenirs. Horst's got real estate; he takes big commissions. They got those little boats they rent out if you want to row around. They're always figuring out how to chisel more money."

"You've got a big garden."

"Yah," she said, putting the eraser end of her pencil in her mouth like it was a cigarette, then realizing what she'd done, taking it out. "You'll get fresh vegetables. That's why I've got to know. Thirty meals for the cop. So many green beans, so many zucchini, so many potatoes. People come with last-minute orders, maybe I'm all used up. Maybe I can get vegetables from somebody else's garden, but maybe not. Then I have to use canned stuff. You order early, you get fresh. You okay with local meat?"

"Beef?" he asked. She shook her head. "Pork?" She shook her head again. "Mutton?" She looked at him in disgust. "Local meat," he said aloud, then the light went on. "Oh, sorry, sure local meat is fine. Whatever, just so long as it's not rabbit."

"You want fresh eggs, you need to talk to Helga. She's got three hundred chickens. You want chickens for freezing in the fall when she kills off most of the layers, you need to get in your order."

"That the rooster that crows every morning?"

"He's a mean bugger. She's kept him for years. I don't know why. He'll come up behind you and peck your leg."

"Anyone else I should know about?"

"Helga's husband, Bolli, has sheep and goats. You want sheep milk, goat milk, he might sell it to you. Depends. Albert has milk for sale but not much."

"Not many men in town."

"Gone," she answered and put her teacup down so hard the tea spilled over the side into the saucer. She picked up the cup, poured the tea from the saucer back into the cup. "Gone working." She sat back in her chair. "And some don't come back. They find a floozie."

"Sounds like it would pay to go north and keep an eye on the guys."

"I did before our daughter was born. Cooked on the tug. No place for a kid."

"Tough to be apart so much."

"Yah," she agreed. "You ever stationed up there?"

"Yes," he admitted. "For two years."

"You know what goes on."

He wasn't sure what she was referring to. There was lots that went on. A wasp had got inside and it started to circle an open jar of honey on the table. She waved the wasp away and put the lid on the jar. "Local," she said. "Fireweed. Wildflowers. Pastor Jon's hives. It's the best."

The wasp returned, settled on the back of Tom's right hand.

"It's okay," he said. "At this time of year they're fine. He'll drink my sweat and then fly away. In the fall they go crazy, unpredictable. They'll stab you for no reason."

"Pearl stabbed her husband when he came back five years ago. You're not a cop anymore, are you?"

He shook his head and smiled. "I saw guys in a 3500 driving around, big tires."

"The rig pigs," Dolly said. "They go, they come back, they go. There's no jobs here. Just welfare and fish. When they're working, the guys live in dormitories. The company feeds them. If they live in town, they're hot bunking because of the rent. Three guys, eight-hour shifts in bed. The rest of the time they're working. They come back when they get a couple of weeks off."

"When I came last winter, I asked Horst if I could get a hot meal. He said the café was closed for the winter. If I'd known about your cooking, I'd have knocked on your door."

She shifted in her chair with pleasure. "Desserts," she said. "Cakes freeze good, slices, cookies. I don't use no sugar. I use honey straight from Pastor Jon."

"No peanut butter cookies," he said. "No peanut butter. I'm allergic."

She wrote peanut butter down in capital letters then drew an X through it. "The rig pigs get big money?"

"Big trucks. Big parties. Big, big, big," she said. "They drop a hundred-dollar bill on the barroom floor, they don't bother to pick it up. They know how to spend money, show a girl a good time." Thinking about hundred-dollar bills on the barroom floor made her smile. She had a generous mouth, and when she smiled, her face lit up.

"You like rhubarb?" she said as she worked out the desserts. "When the rig pigs have money, Siggi calls me up and says, 'Dolly, we're having a party.' Have you met Siggi?" Tom shook his head. "He says, 'We need you to make stuff for us.'"

"Does he drop a hundred dollars on your floor?"

"He don't argue about what I charge. He pays in cash. Right now, he's short. He's got to stay here for a while until stuff gets sorted out. His greenhouse business isn't so good right now. He got a government grant to grow cucumbers, tomatoes, lettuce, but they quit giving the grant."

"Are you here all year?"

"I used to go out places to cook. Can't do that with a kid. There's always people wanting a woman who knows how to cook in difficult situations. You like chili and stew?" She wrote down more items for the meals, and then added, "Then there's them."

He waited, wondering if he should ask who "them" were. She pushed her chair back and caught her daughter as she ran past, hauled her onto her lap and held her close. Her daughter squirmed and slipped under her mother's arms onto the floor and was off again, running into the hallway on pudgy legs, chasing the dog that fled before her.

"Them?" he asked.

"Them." She jabbed her finger toward the north. "Them. Odin. The crazy Vikings. They run around in costume. They got their own place. Them and their stories. Them and how we're all going to be rich one day. Those of us who stay, who had people here when Odin first came and made everybody crazy."

Her daughter came staggering back into the kitchen, her arms around the dog, under its front legs, the dog nearly as long as she was tall. It was, he thought, a patient dog—it didn't struggle or try to bite her but waited until she let go, then bounded away and ran back down the hallway. With a high-pitched squeal, Dolly's daughter ran after it.

"What do they say?"

"They don't say anything. It's the others, the ones that came before. The founders. They're the ones. They're the ones who had the gold, who hid it away in wooden chests. My grandmother saw it, the gold. Glass sealers full of it. They brought lots of money. The Godi wanted it. I don't know why, since he said the world was going to end. The others didn't come for gold. They came because they believed."

"In God?"

"In Odin. In the one-eyed man. After he came, no one would ever get older. They'd get up every morning and drink and dance and feast and have sex."

Instinctively, he reached up and touched the scar that ran from his forehead down his cheek.

Dolly laughed when she saw him touch his scar. "The ravens come onto your picnic table. Everyone's seen that."

Tom felt that he was becoming unhinged, that reality was sliding away, like he'd taken a drug that altered everything. In college he'd gone to a party where someone had slipped LSD into the punch and he'd felt like this; everything had melted, there was no substance to anything, everything became fluid and the desperate faces rose up, saying nothing but watching him with accusatory eyes.

He put his hand into his pocket and grasped the piece of broken taillight. He squeezed and felt the sharp edges cut into his palm. Pain always brought back reality, brought him back to the present, made everything solid and real. For a time in adolescence, when he thought he was going crazy and he couldn't control his thoughts, he had used a razor blade, cutting himself under his armpit where no one could see it. He even tried putting his hand over a burning candle. Anything to keep from drifting away. That craziness had lasted a short while, and now the scars were faded, thin lines, there under his left arm.

She rubbed the right corner of her mouth with her tongue, looked at him speculatively, then took a cigarette out from a silver-coloured cigarette case, tapped it on the table, flicked her purple lighter and took a long drag. She tipped her head back and blew three smoke rings.

She held out the cigarette case. He shook his head. "Quit," he said.

"Goody two-shoes," she replied, as if his quitting was a criticism.

"No. Asthma. Runs in the family."

He could see that she was relieved that he wasn't a puritan, that he wasn't going to be critical of her smoking. She put her tongue against the back of her front teeth and pulled it away so it made a popping sound.

"You know Pearl. She thinks you're okay. I don't think you should be asking her any questions. She's done you a couple of favours. She told you about Jessie wanting to sell her house. Pearl's got lots of her own problems. Bad nerves." And with that, Tom thought about the brandy in her coffee, the little splash that was followed by another little splash. Dolly jerked the cigarette out of her mouth, and even though it was only half smoked, she butted it out in the ashtray.

"Six months is a long time for a man to be away. They've got needs. Short term. Men and dogs, everything's got to be right now. You know what I mean? They were having supper, eight of them, and one of the men made a joke about my stepdad, Ragnar, having a girlfriend at Norman Wells. We all know he has a hard time keeping it in his pants. It shouldn't have been a surprise or anything. It's too bad they weren't having spaghetti. They were eating T-bones. Steak knives. It happened so fast nobody could do anything about it. He was sitting across the table from her. She reached over and stuck her steak knife into his chest. Right between two ribs. She's always been like that. Overreacts. She's gotta have drama. I've never liked that. She thinks she's living in a movie. You know what I mean? The guys got him into a truck and drove like hell for town.

"Good thing the road was passable. He lost a lot of blood, but he was okay in a week. He said it was an accident. She leaned over to try a piece of his steak and slipped. They all said the same thing. What was she gonna do if he decided to stay up north with his floozie?" She picked up the cigarette, straightened it out and relit it.

"Pearl was fifty. Get a job in a camp as cook? He had good life insurance, but if he'd kicked the bucket, I don't know that they'd of said it was an accident." She thought about it as she took another drag and let it out. "Yeah, they'd have said it was an accident. What the hell. What's the point of her rotting in jail while he's rotting in the ground? She pisses me off at times, but she's a good mom. She's taking yellow pills and green pills for her nerves."

Her mother, he thought, was the blue puffball? That was a surprise. "She stabbed him since?"

"No need. He got the message. No country wives when he's away working. No coming home saying I got a kid with someone else. Not like some other men around here."

He leaned away from the cloud of smoke. "Why are you telling me this?"

"Don't go asking Pearl no questions. She's a nervous wreck as it is. She'll think you're digging that up. People got secrets."

"I thought you were criticizing her."

"Criticize, shmiticize. I love her. We play cribbage and she likes to have a drink or two at happy hour. She keeps buying these things she doesn't need. Mail order. She's crazy for mail order. I can't stand that."

"Is Ben a customer of yours?"

"He hasn't got much money. Just getting by. Now and again, I slip him a meal. Stuff that's starting to be in the freezer too long."

"He's been hauling stuff for me."

"He's a good guy. Not many go cold turkey. It's not like he was a moderate drinker, either. Gave his wife, Betty, a bad time. She just kept knitting socks and sweaters, and making bannock and fancy beaded moccasins to sell to the tourists. Shipped quite a few to the Indian store in Winnipeg. Quiet. She'd come to visit Pearl, and she'd knit and Pearl would do housework, and she'd never say a word. Betty straightened Ben out."

"Anybody have anything against Angel?"

"I dunno. Kids keep kids' stuff to themselves. You know what I mean? There could be a chainsaw killer and they wouldn't tell you. It's a code of silence. Nobody's going to be a squealer. We were the same. You think she was killed?"

"I don't think anything. To think something you've got to have information."

"You going to interview people, like on TV? You visited Albert. He gives me the creeps." She started shaking, imitating him. "You think it was him?"

"Her clothes were on. There were no bruises."

"Maybe it was one of those accidents, if you know what I mean? People do stupid things. Like accidents happen and no use wrecking a person's life over it? You can't fix it. That's the way it is here, you know. Things happen, but once they're done, there's nothing you can do about it. Like putting a person in prison is going to make things better? Not that I'm saying anything happened, but since you're asking, maybe you think something happened." She butted out her cigarette. "Kids do stuff. Booze, drugs, sniffing gas. It's just the way it is."

"I've seen lots of it," he said. "Often, they still have a needle sticking in their arm when we find them."

"That's what I mean. Stuff goes on." She picked up the cigarette butt, looked at it and realized she'd broken it when she butted it out. "Pearl thinks you're great. You gave her those chocolates. She's not used to anybody giving her presents. I think that's why she mail orders so much."

CHAPTER 14

THE FUNERAL

Tom had thought the funeral would be in the community hall. Instead, when Sarah asked him to give her a lift, she said they were going to a church south of the village. It was on a rutted dirt road that meandered along the lake. At one time it had been part of a trail that snaked through the swamps to various homesteads, but had become secondary when the harbour at Valhalla was built.

Sarah was all done up. It was the first time he'd seen her in a dress, and he was surprised that she owned one. Usually, it was jeans and a checked shirt and cut-off rubber boots or runners. The pink dress looked like she'd had it a long time, not because it was worn out, but because it was so out of style and still looked new.

"A little tight," she said and tugged at it as if it might stretch.

"Me too." His white shirt was stretched across his stomach. It didn't show when he stood up, but when he was sitting behind the wheel, the cloth strained at the buttonholes at his waist.

The bush on the sides of the road was white with layers of limestone dust. Here and there, where there was higher ground, fields had been cleared and there were crops for cattle feed, but most of the land was good for nothing but grazing. There were frequent piles of rocks, and seeing them he knew where the stone had come from for Dr. Ford's fireplace.

"Hard work," he said, "with a stoneboat."

"Making a living has always been hard here. My husband never farmed, thank God," Sarah said. "Trapping and fishing were hard enough. I've seen them—kids following a sled, picking up rocks, throwing them onto the boat. All day. My kids stayed in school. I wasn't going to have them spend their lives working part time for next to nothing."

"They got good jobs?"

The land had dipped, turned into muskeg. Water gleamed darkly in places, but most of the surface was thick with bulrushes. With the sun beating down on them, they were unable to open the windows because of the dust, so the truck cab became stifling. Although every vent was closed, the fine white dust settled over the dashboard.

He said to Sarah, "Hold the wheel; keep us on the road," and while she steered, he pulled out a red-and-black tartan bandana that he tied around his head so that it covered his nose and mouth. Sarah laughed and said he looked like a bank robber in an old Western.

When he'd taken the steering wheel back, she answered his question. "Good enough. Union work. Trade ticket. One of them went to university. He's a prof now."

There was a slight breeze from the lake, so the dust plume drifted to the west side of the road. The bushes, trees, weeds went by like ghostly images of themselves.

"Any of the kids go back to Ireland?" As he asked it, he wondered about the English streets he'd never visited. There were, after all, still relatives in England, though they were likely to be the descendants of his grandfather, who had never admitted his existence. He doubted he'd be welcome. Tom never followed his mother to Iceland, because he was afraid of what he might find—if she were still alive, would she want no more to do with him than his English relatives? To have her shut the door in his face would be more than he could bear. Anna, after all, had said she'd taken everything with her that she wanted and left behind what she didn't want. Her china and silver, her Royal Doulton figurines, her furniture, her husband and her son.

"Yes, my youngest, the prof. He gets research and travel grants from the university and teaches Irish poetry."

"Does he visit family?"

She turned her head and studied him. He could see her jaw tense. "Once. He wasn't impressed and neither were they. They didn't know anything about Canada and he didn't know anything about Irish manners."

"Sorry."

"No, it's okay. He waits until the evening before he leaves, rings up and asks how everyone is doing. Uncle George and Auntie Flo, Cousin Berty, et cetera. All so he can tell me how they are when he comes back. They say, 'Oh, you should have told us and come to stay,' and they don't mean it. And he says, 'I would love to, but I'm swamped with research,' and he doesn't mean it. It works fine."

"Families," he said, thinking of his father's relatives who came at Christmas and sat straight backed on the couch and dining room chairs and sipped sherry and ate fruitcake. They weren't the kind of people he'd choose to spend time with. He always wondered what they were thinking or what they thought about. The men were nearly all short and stocky, in tweed jackets and grey pants and ties. The men all wore ties, except Cousin Donald, who wore a bow tie. The women wore dresses that were grey and brown and usually came to their ankles. They reminded him of beetles.

"What is that?" Tom asked, slowing down and pointing to a small stone building on the lake side of the road.

"The folly of the past informing the present," Sarah replied, and he thought she might be joking, but she was not. He slowed to a stop. "When the first settlers arrived, there was already a Scotsman here. He was trading furs and wanted to start a lumber mill. Cranky old coot. He was determined to live in a stone house just like in Scotland. This was one room, and he was going to add on more rooms until he had a small castle."

"What happened to him?"

"He was rescued by one of the Icelandic widows, who made him build her a wood house. No hot soup, no hot sex until he had a warm house. She said she hadn't come all this way to live in a house that was colder than in Iceland."

Tom laughed and drove away.

"You went to see Ben, and then you went asking questions," Sarah said in an accusatory tone. "You aren't going to let it go, are you? You're like a dog I had once. There was a skunk living under our shed. Doing no harm. But the dog couldn't let it be. It got sprayed more than once, but it kept going back."

"Did it get the skunk?"

"Yes, but by that time it stunk so much that even washing it in tomato juice did no good. It had to sleep outside instead of on a nice warm bed. And nobody, I mean nobody, would have anything to do with it."

When he didn't reply, she said, "Have you met Pastor Jon yet? He's Unitarian, or was Unitarian. You'll see. He's a bit of everything." When Tom shook his head she said, "He's Icelandic, not like from Iceland, but FBI, full-blooded Icelander. Traces his family on both sides to great-grandparents from Iceland. He'd come to Valhalla on his holidays for years. He'd stay with friends and give summer services. Three years ago, he had some dispute with his parish and quit before he had a stroke. He's got high blood pressure.

"He knew the Lutheran congregation was desperate to get rid of its church property. It was sitting empty because Biblio Braggi, the Bible salesman who had rented it, had up and left in the middle of the night. Biblio Braggi," she repeated and laughed. "He was a lay preacher of sorts. He got himself ten bee-hives, three sheep, a dozen chickens and a cow. He kept the cow in the church. When people objected, he always replied that Christ was born in a manger. He played the fiddle and gave music lessons. He sold his Bibles and gave private lessons to the buyers. If the rumours are true, he gave some of the local farmers' wives personal lessons on sin.

"So here you are, a church that's been turned into a stable, a manse that needs repairs, property that needs tending and animals that need to be fed and watered. Pastor Jon sold his house in the city, bought the church property for next to nothing. His wife had died a few years back. No kids.

"The Lutherans were glad to be shut of it. Many years ago, after the Christmas Eve service, the evangelicals put skids under the church and hauled it five miles to a farm property of one of the elders. The liberals weren't having any of that and they went one night and hauled it back and bolted it to the foundation. For a while it looked like it was going to be gunfight at the OK Corral. Instead, everyone got fed up. They started using the hall in town for events, and the manse and church sat empty until the Bible salesman came." With that, she pointed ahead to where a white spire topped with a cross rose over a grove of maples. When they got closer, he saw that the cross was missing one arm.

"Broke off in a storm," Sarah said, answering his unasked question. "You want to make a friend, get up there and fix it. Pastor Jon can't stand heights. We all have weaknesses."

The driveway and small parking lot were full, so Tom pulled up at the end of a row of vehicles parked on the edge of the road. The four vehicles ahead of him were lifted trucks, big tires, muscle trucks, and one he recognized—a black Dodge Ram. He was sure it was the truck that had nearly forced him off the road when he'd come in the spring to see Jessie. It had a bumper sticker that said, *I Still Miss My Ex, but My Aim Is Improving* and another that said, *Love Me, Love My Gun.* There was a set of truck nuts attached to the trailer hitch.

The road was narrow, so he had to park on the very margin, where the road and ditch met. Sarah let herself down by holding on to the doorframe. The ditch was dry, but the side was steep. When she slammed the door shut, dust flew up.

"Sorry," he said, "I should have dropped you off at the church and come back to park."

"You could," she replied, "lay down your jacket so I can step on it, but there's no accommodating puddle."

Just past the church, the road ended in a tangle of bush. Although it was now overgrown, it was evident from the different height of the saplings that the bush had been cleared in anticipation of the road continuing. Instead, where it now ended was blocked by large limestone rocks. The impression was of a green trench, and he wondered what had happened. An ambitious plan during a time when there was money, an economic plan gone awry, a change in government, all arbitrary, all decisions made in Winnipeg or Ottawa by people who had never been here. Budget cuts at meetings in boardrooms, visions and people abandoned.

Across from the church was a small graveyard. The stone monuments were old, many covered in moss. The grass grew high around the stones. A single pathway had been mown from the wooden footbridge to where there was a fresh pile of black dirt.

A crowd was gathered around the front steps of the church. It was Tom's first time seeing everyone dressed formally. In honour of the occasion, men were wearing suits that were a bit tight and farm caps in various colours, and some of the women were wearing preposterous hats with large brims and artificial fruit or flowers.

The crowd was larger than he had expected. There were more people than for bingo. People had obviously come from around the surrounding countryside. Sarah said hello to everyone, but she didn't let the greetings slow her down. When Tom paused, Sarah gave him a nudge up the stairs. "I'm past standing any length of time—varicose veins. Let's get a seat." He noticed as they went through the crowd around the front steps that there were three women in traditional Icelandic dress.

"Amazing Grace" was playing on a boom box that was set up along the wall nearest the pulpit. There was a painting of Christ looking toward heaven on the front wall. His head was surrounded by light. However, the bottom half of Christ was obscured by a massive papier mâché sculpture of a brain that sat in front of it.

Pastor Jon was already at the front of the church. He was a squarely built man, heavy-set, with a florid face, wearing a white shirt, blue shorts and sandals with socks.

"Pastor Jon, this is Tom Parsons. He bought Jessie's place," Sarah said.

They shook hands and Jon said, "Your reputation has preceded you. A jack of all trades. That's good. There's lots here that needs repairing. Welcome."

"I suggested that he fix the cross. He doesn't mind heights."

"That would be a blessing," Jon said, "It gives a bad impression."

While they were talking, Tom couldn't take his eyes off the six-foot-high papier mâché brain. The different parts were painted different colours and labelled.

Pastor Jon noticed his interest and said, "I believe in intellect over faith, in history over mysticism, in kindness over dogma. When I saw this left over from a school science fair in the city, I got Ben to bring it out."

The brain seemed to float above the stage, since the wooden supports that held it in place could not be seen unless the viewer came close and peered into the space between the floor of the stage and the bottom of the brain. When he purchased the church, Pastor Jon explained, there were angels painted on the ceiling, playing harps, blowing horns, all looking angelically toward heaven. He thought he'd capture the dynamic energy of the brain by having gold-coloured cardboard lightning bolts rise up from its folded surface, but as Sarah had pointed out, it looked like the lightning bolts were shooting the angels out of the sky. He'd taken the lightning bolts down reluctantly.

Sarah and Tom took seats at the extreme left so that she and her large pink hat wouldn't block other people's view. Directly in front of them was an old-fashioned organ. On it were lined up six jars of honey. The light from the window turned them into amber jewels. A white card sat in front of the jars saying, *five dollars*.

"Jessie used to play that organ for God. Nobody else knows how."

"What is with the jars of honey? Is it sacred?"

Sarah dipped her head and suppressed a laugh. "The honey. I'm so used to it that I never noticed. Five dollars a jar. Pastor Jon is proud of his bees. He takes in a few hundred dollars a year, tax free. He makes the rounds in the fall. He'll knock on your door. Buy a jar. Buy two. It's very good honey. Send it to your family and friends."

Because of the heat, the front doors and the side door were open, but it did little good. There was no breeze and the small fan at the front turned without any discernible effect. The leaded glass windows, ablaze with colourful scenes, couldn't be opened. Although the service had not yet begun, women were vigorously fanning themselves with paper programs that had a picture of Angel on the front.

Tom heard a car's tires on the gravel, then a bit of a commotion outside as those having a last drag on their cigarettes were getting ready to come inside. The latecomers slipped into the last seats, and those who saw there were no seats left lined up along both walls. There was shuffling as men who were sitting gave up their seats for women who were standing. Shortly after, two undertakers in black suits came in: one leading the coffin; the other behind. They turned the coffin at the end of the aisle so it was crosswise to the mourners. Tom was relieved to see it would be a closed coffin.

Ben was wearing a white shirt and a grey sports jacket that was a bit too small for him. Tom realized that he'd never seen him in anything but khaki workpants and checked shirts. He probably hadn't worn the shirt and jacket since his wife died. The aisle was narrow, and his daughter and grandson came behind him. Sarah leaned her mouth close to Tom's ear and whispered, "Here's Wanda and Derk."

Wanda was wearing a black dress and black gloves and had on a small black hat that perched on the top of her head at an angle, giving the impression it would fall off at any moment. Derk was taller than her, his dark hair slicked back, and he was dressed all in white. The gold chains around his neck and his gold watch gleamed in the light from the windows. As he walked behind his grandfather, he moved his head slightly from side to side the way a famous entertainer or a member of royalty might do.

To indicate the service was about to begin, Pastor Jon pulled a purple-and-black stole over his shoulders. Sarah told Tom that it was originally Catholic. Pastor Jon had found it in a thrift shop and snapped it up. He had a dozen stoles he'd found in odd places and wore them as the mood suited him. Although the stoles were not Unitarian orthodox, he felt they were reassuring and added dignity. He also said that they were an outward sign of his ecumenical beliefs.

One of the undertakers went to stand beside the boom box. After a nod from Pastor Jon, he turned off the music.

"Friends," Pastor Jon intoned, "friends," he repeated as if to be sure that all were included, drawn in to the tragedy, "there is no explaining the loss of someone just at the beginning of her life. She was named appropriately, an angel with an angel's voice." He tipped his head back to look at the faded angels that had been painted on the curved, bow-shaped ceiling.

Ben sat with his head in his hands and never looked up. Wanda rested her left hand on his back. Derk turned his head to one side then the other, as if to challenge everyone there.

Pastor Jon raised his right index finger and the undertaker beside the boom box turned it on and they all listened to "Abide with Me." The undertakers seemed impatient. It may have been because they were wearing black suits. One of them kept wiping the sweat from his face with a white handkerchief. The other kept glancing at his watch. It was obvious that Ben wasn't paying a lot for the funeral. The coffin was made of plywood and painted white.

Once the music finished, Pastor Jon said, "This was Angel's favourite song," and Tracy and Amanda, waitresses from the café, got up and sang a popular C&W song that didn't seem to have anything to do with death or religion. As he gave the eulogy, Pastor Jon's face gradually turned magenta, and here and there people squeezed out of the pews and went outside to get a breath of air. The eulogy was about loss, about a life with potential unrealized, about what could have been. At the end of the service, they all stood and sang "The Sweet June Days." Song sheets had been left on the pews, but most people didn't know the song, and its rendition, even led by Pastor Jon's baritone, was ragged.

People sat, uncertain what to do next. The minister, seeing the hesitation, said, "The family will follow the coffin to the graveyard. Those who wish may follow them there. Otherwise, go straight to the community hall, where there will be a lunch provided." His face was even more magenta, and Tom, watching its colour intensify, sat there reviewing his CPR training.

Ben and Wanda and Derk followed the coffin up the aisle, and the mourners, starting with the front rows, followed them. The coffin stopped at the front door and four men eased it down the stairs, carried it over the wooden bridge to the road, across the road to the second bridge and into the graveyard.

Sarah followed the coffin and Tom followed her. The smell of the recently cut grass was rich and moist. The path that had been cut had actually been made by two passes of a scythe, one from the bridge to the grave and one back again. A few mourners filed along this path. A woman in a purple dress was scraping her feet against a headstone to get rid of the grass that clung to the soles of her shoes.

The coffin was lowered into the grave. Pastor Jon, in deference to the fact that Ben's wife, Betty, had been a staunch Lutheran, said, "In sure and certain hope of the resurrection to eternal life through our Lord Jesus Christ, we commend to Almighty God: Angel. We commit her body to the ground, earth to earth, ashes to ashes, dust to dust. The Lord bless her and keep her, the Lord maketh his face to shine upon her and be gracious unto her and give her peace. Amen." He threw in a handful of dirt and stepped aside so Ben and Wanda and Derk could do the same. Tom saw one of the undertakers looking at his watch again.

All at once, Ben's knees gave way and he would have fallen into the grave if not for two men who were standing beside him. They caught him under the arms and held him up. They turned him around and helped him to the road.

One of the undertakers went up to Wanda and Derk and said that they were sorry they couldn't attend the reception, but they had another funeral two hours away.

Instead of going directly to Tom's truck, Sarah waded through grass that came to her knees. Tom followed her to a headstone. The stone was a large block of natural red granite with the name McAra in large letters. "Pastor Jon will scythe this hay when it's ready," Sarah said. "He needs it for his sheep and goats. Not much hay land around here. Every spot gets cut."

"Did your husband not have a first name?" Tom asked.

"He took umbrage with anyone who used it," Sarah said. "He made me promise many times to bury him without it."

"What was he like?" Tom asked.

"Big, a good sense of humour, worked hard, smart, popular. Everyone liked him. He went through the ice one winter."

By the time they pulled up to the community hall, nearly everyone except Ben and his family were there. When Tom and Sarah appeared, the roar of conversation faded briefly as everyone looked toward them, but the crowd soon went back to talking.

Sarah said, "You'll know you're starting to fit in when the conversation never skips a beat as you come in the door."

Tom handed her the bag of peanut butter cookies he'd brought. She took it to the kitchen so one of the women there could put the cookies on a plate. Tom didn't see anyone to talk to except Karla and Horst. Karla was wearing a low-cut black dress and was surveying the crowd, looking for an audience. He avoided catching her eye. Horst was already staring at Tom with his mouth pulled tight with disapproval. If he did go over to them, Karla would flirt and Horst, jealous and resentful, would make snarly remarks and sneer at anything Tom said.

"Hi," a woman's voice said from behind his left shoulder. He turned sharply. At first glance he thought she was in her late twenties, but then when he looked more closely he realized that she was in her early thirties. Her hair was nearly copper coloured, natural, pulled to one side so it hung over her left shoulder. "I'm Freyja. You're my Good Samaritan, aren't you?"

"If you were wearing a fur hat and driving a red Jeep this winter, that's me."

She smiled and said, "You don't look like a cop."

So she'd heard about him. It would have been surprising if she hadn't, he thought. The gossip mill never stopped. "I let my hair grow." He'd always had a short military-style haircut, but now his hair reached the back of his neck. It was his way of rebelling—although when he caught a glimpse of himself in the mirror, he was overcome with momentary guilt, certain that his father's voice would tell him to get a haircut, because a good haircut and shined shoes told people you were respectable.

She was shorter than him, maybe five eight. She tipped her head back to look at him better. Green eyes, he realized. Cat's eyes. She was pretty—more than pretty—not quite Rubenesque but lots of curves.

"Do you dance?" she asked.

"Game leg," he said.

"Polka, schottische, waltz, butterfly?"

"I'm out of practice."

"There's a dance on Saturday. Old-time music. You coming?"

"Three days from now?" he said. He looked around the room. People were chatting together as if everything was normal. The only sign that it was a funeral was a small table covered in a white tablecloth. It had on it a group of framed pictures of Angel with two vases filled with local flowers.

Freyja dressed for her red hair and green eyes. A pale green silk blouse, a soft summer skirt that clung to her hips. *More than pretty*, he thought, *gorgeous*.

Their conversation was cut short by Ben and his family coming into the hall. The hall had been raucous with conversation. It stopped. Everyone stood up. There was silence, except for a slight shuffling of feet as everyone turned toward Ben and his daughter and grandson, who stood just inside the door. Ben, with the two men who had held him up at the graveyard walking beside him, went to a small table at the front of the room. His daughter and grandson followed.

The same tables that were used for bingo were set with paper plates, plastic knives and forks, and paper napkins. There were two tables covered with pots, casseroles and plates of food set end to end along the east side of the hall.

Ben stood, waved for people to sit down. There was a rustling of feet and scraping of chairs. Tom and Freyja sat at the end of a bench. When everyone was seated, Ben tried to speak. He stood there for a moment, bent slightly forward, as if he were carrying a great weight on a tumpline. He looked up but looked over the heads of the crowd. After two tries without being able to say anything, he shook his head and sat down. The man who had called the bingo came forward. He was wearing his electric blue suit and a red tie with a hula dancer and a palm tree on it. His shoes were white and brown and had a pattern of pierced holes.

"You all know me, and if anyone doesn't, I'm Barnabas. I'm a friend of Ben's. Ben," he said, "asked me to say a few words for him if he couldn't. We know his story. We know the story of Angel. You know how she grew up. You saw her playing with your kids and grandkids. You saw her when she was staying with Ben, riding in his truck with him. Sometimes, she went to school here. Although she wasn't here all the time, she was one of us. You heard her sing.

More than anything, she liked playing music and singing. She wanted to start a band. She had a lot of talent. She was a good kid. We don't understand why things like this happen. We'll miss her. Ben appreciates everything everyone has done to help in this difficult time." He paused for a moment of silence, then said, "Please help yourselves." With that, people stood up and began to line up at the buffet.

Tom had thought that he and Freyja would sit together while they had lunch, but one of the women working in the kitchen motioned for Freyja to come. He watched her as she disappeared behind the coffee urns.

Sarah suddenly appeared. "Are you drooling because you're hungry or because of Freyja?"

"I pulled her out of the ditch this winter."

"That was you?" Sarah said. "I knew someone had rescued her. She was on her way to some sort of teachers' meeting in the city."

"Yup. The beautiful damsel in distress and Quasimodo rushing to her rescue," he said, exaggerating.

Sarah rolled her eyes. "Oh, the poor cripple demonstrating his beautiful soul. Or something. A lot of people get killed stopping to help rescue strangers."

That had happened to one of his colleagues. He stopped to help a stranded motorist at night and was struck by a vehicle. Tom didn't want to think about it. "There's a lot of food," he said, indicating the overladen table and changing the topic.

"It is. Potluck," Sarah explained. "Ben couldn't afford to feed all these people. He used up every penny he had for the funeral. He got the best he could afford."

Sarah went to see if Ben wanted anything. Tom stood uncertainly, not sure of his place. Having found Angel's body, he seemed to have taken on some of the responsibility for her death. He would, he knew, be referred to for a long time as "the guy who found Angel."

Karla sashayed up to him. Even if she'd come in complete darkness, he'd have known she was there because her perfume was overpowering, cloyingly sweet. He could feel his chest tighten. She hadn't been to the food table yet. She straightened his tie and quietly said, "It's over. It's done. Bad things happen to good people, but the show must go on." Her tone of voice was that of a disciplinarian talking to a recalcitrant student.

Tom was trying to imagine her ten years earlier, onstage, swinging her fringes for the men in the crowd, getting them excited. Showing a bit of leg. He'd seen women like her up on the stage in beer parlours and bars. Egging the men on. Making the tassels over their breasts rotate. If they were really talented, making them rotate in different directions. Fixing their eyes on a guy in the front row and rotating their hips, his buddies hooting and hollering.

Horst was in the lineup, but he was turned to the side, watching Tom and Karla suspiciously.

"It's a tragedy, but tragedies happen all the time. We can't make a fuss about it, raise questions. People don't like trouble. The summer people create opportunities, and we can't risk scaring them off. You've got to let it blow over. You can't take opportunities away from people," she said. She was eyeing a group of fishermen who had gathered beside the coffee urn. They were passing a bottle around and pouring whisky into their coffee. "See that? They must think you're going to be okay. You aren't going to come and arrest them. It's a compliment. You're new here. People have got to figure you out."

"Opportunities." The word filled up his head. When he heard businessmen say there were great opportunities, he immediately thought of scam artists. That was their opening line. The real opportunity was lining their own pockets. It was a word he'd learned not to trust. Selling liquor under the counter was an opportunity. A good markup and no income tax to pay.

When Karla saw Sarah coming back, she went and joined Horst. Sarah was holding two plates of food. "I got Ben this, but he says he doesn't want anything." She handed Tom one of the plates. "Come over here and meet a few people. Show them you're not stuck up."

He followed her to a table. There were two seats in the middle. Sarah climbed over the bench and sat down. He put his plate down, eased one leg over so he was standing astride the bench, turned and, putting his left hand under his knee and lifting, got his other leg over and under.

"Doesn't work as well as it used to," he said to no one in particular.

"This here is Vidar Sigurdsson and his better half, Arlene. Here's Bob and Linda Olafson. And over there," Sarah indicated three women at the end of the table, "these are the daughters of Fridrik Simundson—the twins, Urdh, and Skuld, and this is Verthandi, their older sister."

Tom tried not to stare. The three women might have been painted and shellacked. There was no telling what colour their skin might really be. Their eyes were circles of dark makeup, their lips violent red, their cheeks blossomed with rouge. Their eyes glittered as they momentarily leaned toward him. Their hair—he was not sure it was their hair, for although the twins were obviously over seventy and the elder sister, he suspected, over ninety—all looked the same, as if they all wore wigs bought in bulk. They were thin, thinner than thin, emaciated even, and he looked at their hands, for unless they were hidden inside mittens, hands did not lie.

All three of them had long fingers with no flesh on them, more like birds' claws, with long nails painted pink. Their narrow wrists, he imagined, led up bony arms to birdcage chests that led to skin-covered skeletal frames. All three wore the same brown-rimmed glasses. Bought, he wondered, like the wigs, at a bargain price in bulk. Their dresses he recognized as traditional women's outfits from the time of Icelandic immigration. His mother had had a similar dress that she'd kept hidden in a wooden trunk and didn't take out until after her sister had asked for forgiveness. For the annual celebration on June 17 at the legislative grounds she made alterations so it would fit. When Tom had asked what the occasion was, she said it was to celebrate Iceland's independence.

He thought he'd seen Vidar at the dock, but he didn't recognize Bob. Vidar was big, heavy-set, with a mop of curly hair starting to go grey. Bob was short, with a round head and a goatee.

"How's the fishing?" he said to Vidar.

"All right," Vidar replied. "A box to a net. But it won't last. Good fish, good fishing, then one morning, I'll go lift my nets and I'll be lucky if there's one fish in a net."

"Why's that?" Tom asked.

"You're not going to buy a licence?"

Tom shook his head and took a mouthful of potato salad. When he'd swallowed, he added, "I'm a handyman. Carpentry, plumbing, drywall, even electric if it's not too complicated. Roofing. Jack of all trades."

Vidar looked like he didn't believe him. Finally, Bob said, "Not much construction around here in the winter."

"Lots of interior work," Tom said. "I can drive to jobs on the farms west of here."

"I heard you were going to buy a fishing licence," Vidar said stubbornly. He scowled at a point in the middle of the table, as if there were something there he disapproved of.

Tom had started on a pickerel fillet. "Sports fishing. Ice fishing."

Vidar's wife poked her husband with her elbow and shot him a sideways look that said, "See, I told you." She looked exasperated.

"What do you do?" Tom asked Bob, to stop what looked like a disagreement from starting. "You fish?"

"Long-haul driver," Bob answered. "Here to the West Coast, sometimes Florida, other times California, east to Quebec. I never know what the next job will be. That's my rig in front of our place."

"It's like being married to a sailor," Linda said. "Come and go, come and go. Mostly go."

Bob shrugged. "I take a load to Toronto, say, then pick up a load there, take it to New York, pick up a load and take it to Regina, then back home. I don't want to be running bobtail. No profit in that."

Bobtail, Tom thought. He hadn't heard that in a long time. Running without a trailer. One night he had chased a stolen cab over country roads. It took three cars, but they'd penned it in.

"Linda, do you ever go with him?" Tom asked. He always used people's names in an effort to remember them.

Linda smiled. She was a dumpling of a woman. Short, bursting at the seams, in a short-sleeved dress that showed her fat arms. "Not yet, but when the kids are old enough to look after themselves I will. It'll be nice to see a few of these places he talks about. And," she added playfully, "keep him out of trouble at the truck stops. Lots of stuff goes on there you don't want your husband involved in."

"I tell her," Bob said, "there's no time for hanky-panky. Just rolling along. Sleep when you have to. Eat when you have to. Making a dime is hard."

Bob had a potbelly from sitting in a truck for too long, eating truck-stop food. His kidneys were probably not good. Driving alone on contract, he'd have a case of Red Bull behind the seat.

Tom had seen truckers in the roadside cafés, the truck stops, had helped pull their bodies out of their cabs after they'd fallen asleep at the wheel, pushed too hard in bad weather, put off maintenance because they weren't making enough and the brakes failed. In the last economic downturn, one of the younger truckers he'd got to know a bit had committed suicide because he was going to lose everything he'd worked for.

"A lonely life," Tom said.

"Yeah," Bob agreed. "You've got to like your own company."

The three sisters had been listening, their bodies leaning toward the conversation. They were like glittering birds of prey, their eyes first looking at others, then shifting back to look at each other. When they locked eyes, they half grinned and ducked their heads.

He thought they might be mute, but then one of the sisters, not looking directly at him but at the table and half smiling, said, "Your name... Is it that you had an ancestor who was a parson?"

"Yes," he said. He'd wondered that himself and had been curious enough to look back four generations. "In England. There were a number of divines in the family." Two of his father's uncles had been ministers with country parishes.

"English," one of the twins said slowly, as if she had heard something distasteful, and she tipped her head back in a way that indicated her superiority and his inferiority.

This was, he decided, Skuld. The twins were hard to separate, but the elder sister—though she looked like them because of the makeup—was bonier, her body more drawn in, her back slightly stooped. He'd seen dead people who were more animated. For a second, he wondered if perhaps she was dead and had been freeze dried. Perhaps when the meal was over, they would pick her up and carry her away. Only her eyes glittered. She had no food in front of her.

"England," he repeated, confirming Skuld's suspicions.

"When people come to Valhalla, it is usually because they have Icelandic blood. Do you, by any chance, have any Icelandic blood?" It was said in a superior way that indicated she believed it was impossible. She tipped her head up as she said it and looked down her nose.

"Yes," he said, so irritated by the prissy sneer and implied mockery that he admitted a fact he had not acknowledged since his mother had left and not returned. He'd put anything Icelandic that she'd given him or that he'd purchased in the garbage. "My mother's people were from Snæfellsness. When the war started, they moved into Reykjavik."

He thought he saw the elder sister flinch. Slowly, her head revolved toward him.

Skuld leaned farther over the table and said in little more than a whisper, "An Icelandic mother? How can that be?" She studied his dark hair and dark eyes and, from her look, found him wanting. His mother had told him that where she came from the people were dark, the black Icelanders, probably from Irish ancestors but possibly Portuguese or Spanish. Foreign fishing boats frequently sank in storms or ran onto the rocks. One or two of the fishermen might survive. Leaving was so difficult that they stayed.

"You didn't tell me that," Sarah said, sounding put out at not having been party to his secret.

"You didn't ask."

"Icelandic with a slight English accent. Great camouflage. The undercover Icelander."

They finished what was on their plates and the women from the kitchen brought plates of desserts and filled their coffee cups. There were, he noticed, Icelandic sweets, the kind his mother had made after her sister's letter. He realized that the three sisters were looking at him with disbelief, as if he'd lied, as if he was a commoner making a claim to royal blood.

"Vinarterta," he said to Sarah, who was filling her plate. "I remember the name for that. But what about these?" He picked up what looked like a donut with two pointy ends.

"Kleinur," she replied.

"My mother sometimes made these for Sunday breakfast if my father was away," he said as he picked up two *pönnukökur*, rolled pancakes, and put them on his plate. "Except my mother usually folded them with whipped cream and strawberry jam."

"Here we roll them with brown sugar."

Urdh and Skuld were carefully picking out two pieces of dessert each. They might have been choosing precious jewels from a queen's treasure chest. Their scrawny hands floated over the plates, hesitated, moved on, finally dipped down and plucked a pönnukaka and a piece of vinarterta with its seven biscuit layers and six layers of prune filling. It had white icing.

"You're icers here," he said, remembering his mother telling him that there was an unending dispute between those who iced their vinarterta and those who didn't.

"Hmm," Sarah replied. "Icers and non-icers, you know about that. Maybe you've a few Icelandic genes, after all."

"The truck stops any better than they used to be?" he asked Bob, moving the topic away from his Icelandic background.

Bob nodded, rubbed his bald head. "There are showers most places now, better meals. Still not enough places to park overnight."

"Long runs?"

"A month," Linda interjected with an edge to her voice. "A month at a time. Trucker's widow, that's me. Every time I hear about a truck accident, I check his route. Home for a few days, then he's gone again. I tell him, sell the truck. Drive for a company. Then you can take time off because the bank isn't waiting for your cheque."

Bob rolled his eyes toward the ceiling. It was obviously an old argument.

"The company pays all the expenses," Linda continued, "pays by the mile. But he doesn't want to have a boss. I say the bank is his boss."

Stepped on a land mine, Tom thought, and got up to get another cup of coffee.

When he got back, Verthandi was sitting motionless, staring at her plate. He wondered if she suffered from lockjaw or if her mouth was wired shut. If maybe she was suffering from rigor mortis.

Vidar was concentrating on his food. Whole slices of vinarterta disappeared into his mouth. He'd chew a couple of times, swallow, wash everything down with coffee, then pop another dessert into his mouth. He brushed the crumbs out of his moustache.

"If you want to fish, you have to buy a licence off someone who's got one," he said. "The government isn't selling any new ones."

"My father was a bookkeeper. My mother was a housewife. No fishermen in my family."

Vidar's wife, Arlene, sighed, shook her head slightly. "We can use a man around here who can fix things. Lots of things are broken, and they stay broken because no one knows how to fix them. Or they're too lazy. Like that light in the back bedroom. It hasn't worked for over a year."

There were, Tom realized, land mines everywhere.

Vidar stood up. "I need to talk to Pastor Jon," he said.

"His truck has been running roughly," Arlene said in explanation. "He needs a prayer from Pastor Jon."

Prayer, Tom thought, *to fix a truck*, but then Bob added for Tom's benefit, "Pastor Jon's the only mechanic for a hundred miles. He can't fix new stuff like your truck. You've got to have computers for that."

"Farm equipment, too," Arlene said. She sounded annoyed. "There's no point in trying to have a wedding during harvest time. A tractor breaks down or a threshing machine and he'll leave the bride standing at the altar."

Throughout the meal, Ben's daughter and grandson remained in their seats beside him. If they wanted anything, one of the women who were serving brought it for them. Derk's grief hadn't lessened his appetite. He'd had his dessert plate filled three times. He kept his elbows on the table on either side of his plate as if protecting it from being snatched away. He ate aggressively, defiantly, looking up from time to time and glaring at people in front of him. He didn't quite sneer, but there were no smiles of recognition either from him or to him.

Wanda looked worn. She slumped in her chair. She stared at the table. There was food on her plate, but it was untouched. She had a drinker's face, the kind of face you saw standing outside the liquor commission, waiting for the doors to open in the morning. The kind of face he'd often seen in the back of his patrol car or in the cells. She'd been pretty once, maybe beautiful, but her face was deeply lined, puffy, the skin slightly yellow. Her hands moved nervously on the table, picking up the utensils, putting them down, then disappearing under the table only to reappear. She needed a drink; she probably needed six drinks, vodka straight up. One of the women, seeing her need, brought a cup of coffee, leaned over to whisper. For the first time, Wanda's face looked animated. She grabbed the cup with both hands and drained it. Liquid courage. Liquid mercy. Her daughter's death wasn't going to change her. Give her what she needed to get by. Now, she needed more help than usual.

CHAPTER 15

LONG-HAUL LIVING

When the funeral reception was over, Tom went back to his place but was too restless to settle to anything.

He couldn't shake the image of Ben standing at the family table, trying to speak and not being able to. His daughter managed to get through the reception with three cups of false courage and his grandson managed it with sneering anger.

Because of the spruce trees, there were ragged patches of grass in the front and side yard. The needles were too acidic to let anything but the hardiest weeds grow. The spruce had shallow roots that ran over the surface of the ground, knobby, twisted roots that crossed and re-crossed, spread out like a large irregular puzzle. The trees, when they were this tall, stopped being attractive—instead, they were stately, living monuments rising over everything else. But they were dangerous, because in a high wind the shallow roots would often not hold and the trees would topple. There was one tree in the corner of the yard that had blown over, and with the tree lying on its side, the roots were higher than Tom. He'd take an axe to the branches, but he'd need to buy or borrow a chainsaw to turn the trunk into firewood. The tangled root ball, unearthed, would take a long time for him to gradually cut into useful pieces.

The mat of decaying needles covered the graves. If it weren't for the remains of the small wooden crosses, there'd have been nothing to show that something had been buried on the edge of the yard. The crosses had rotted at the bottom, turned black, and when he'd picked up one of them, the outer shell of paint disintegrated. There were no names on any of the crosses. The uprights and the arms had been notched, fitted together, then screwed in place.

He peeled back the mat of debris and it came up like a carpet. There was nothing to indicate where a grave might have begun or ended. He threw the remnants of the crosses into the growing pile of spruce needles and twigs. He cleared away more of the reddish-brown mat from a concrete pad set with coloured pebbles. Cut into the concrete were the words *Baby Oli*. He cleared the ground around it, but there was nothing more to see. The pad was about three feet by two feet.

He'd seen graves like this before, usually in the yards of isolated farmhouses. No graveyard nearby at the time. Or terrible weather. Perhaps a death during a time when no one could leave off the harvest. Often those graves were right beside the house, and on the Prairies they often had lilacs planted beside them.

He pulled the debris well away from the grave, went for a pail of water and a stiff brush. He poured the water onto the concrete and brushed it clean. There was so little that could be done, nothing but a momentary token of respect possible, even though the grave held so much grief and pain.

After supper, he walked over to see Bob's semi-trailer. Bob was washing the cab. Even though he knew Tom was there, he didn't stop washing the cab and didn't say hello.

"Hard job," Tom said.

"Yeah," Bob agreed. He just turned his head slightly to acknowledge Tom.

"Hard on the wife and kids. I used to deal with a lot of truckers on the highway. Too little sleep, crazy people in cars passing, then pulling in too soon, brakes go, tires blow up."

"You said it. I'm away a month at a time. I just happen to be here for three days before I head out again."

"Good money?"

"Good enough." He stopped hosing down the truck's grill. "Not big time. Not if you want to live in a smart neighbourhood in the city, but here, it's lots. Food on the table, clothes, a car, even a trip every couple of years."

"Ben a friend of yours?"

"You might say that. You might not. I'm not here for the kind of things that make friends. I think he's okay. He thinks I'm okay. I donated to help pay for the funeral."

"You knew Angel?"

"Not much. Cute kid. Always playing a tune. A comb with a piece of wax paper. Beer bottles with water in them. Beating on the bottom of a washtub. Used to sleep over at our place once in a while. Ben's not much company for her, I guess. They'd play cribbage for pennies. He always let her win. He did what he knew. Checkers. She needed a mom and dad."

"You don't approve?"

"Of Ben? Sure, I approve. She was lucky she had him. Her mother's a drunk. She wasn't lucky to have her for a mother. Every time she ties one on, she ends up with a new boyfriend."

"Her brother?"

"For a retired cop, you're acting a lot like you're still working."

"Old habits. You don't want to know what happened to Angel?"

Bob stopped polishing a headlight and stood up. "There are times it's better to leave things be. No good hurting more people." He started polishing the chrome around the light. "You going to perform a miracle? Bring her back? You going to get her mother to sober up? You going to get her brother to quit dealing and become a preacher?"

"If it was one of your kids?"

"Look," Bob said, annoyed. He ran his left hand over his bald head. "I don't live here much. I just visit now and again. You got questions, ask my wife. I'm leaving tonight at midnight. I got a long haul ahead of me. Just don't ask her until after I'm gone. If she gets upset, she's not so affectionate, you know what I mean?"

Bob ended the conversation by going to the other side of the truck.

Tom turned around and went to the store. He was out of bread. Once he was more settled, he'd ask Sarah to show him how to make his own. The stuff that Karla carried was crap. Crush it in your hand and it became the size of a golf ball. She'd order in better bread if you paid in advance. Frenchie would pick up special-order groceries. He had a cooler and a freezer in the truck. Locals didn't use the service much. It was the sailboat and yacht crowd who put in orders for grade AAA steak, lobster, deli products, New York bagels. When the order arrived, Karla checked off everything, put it into cardboard boxes and sent two of the girls to deliver the orders. Local people didn't tip, but the boaters and cottagers were used to giving tips and always added a few dollars when they got a delivery.

Tom felt the first real rise of resentment. It was like a dark fern unfurling inside him. He had a vehicle, he had disability, he was tight for money, but he could afford gas, and when the house was finished, he'd be able to take on more paid work, but, already, the way that Karla and Horst seemed to have their hands in everything, getting a piece of everyone's action, annoyed him. The locals, he thought, had had years to nurture their resentment.

There were a couple of locals waiting at the counter when he came in. There was a ritual about being served, a prescribed order. Karla always smiled harder for the visitors, her eyes never left them, she always remembered their names and preferred to use their titles—Mr., Mrs., Dr., Professor, Your Honour—as if using their title and their last name added dignity to them, recognized their importance, and their importance reflected on her. She was still the star in her own show, and they were the audience sitting in the expensive seats.

Karla was busy taking care of three cottagers. The locals wouldn't get served until the cottagers had everything they wanted. He didn't feel like standing in line waiting for the elite to be waited on. He knew Karla saw him leave, and he knew, as well, that she didn't care. Whatever it was that he came for, he had to get from her. Otherwise, he had to drive ninety miles to the first town with a decent store. When he went to town, he would, he promised himself, load up on anything that could be stored. Maybe even see what others needed and take a shopping list.

CHAPTER 16

THE SPINNERS

That evening there was no breeze and the air felt heavy. For once, he wished he had a window air conditioner. Beads of sweat formed on his arms. Even though the sun had descended below the spruce trees to the east, the heat was smothering. He saw through the trees that the boaters at the dock had put foamies onto the decks of their boats. One of them had set up a portable hammock and hung a mosquito net over it. He must have been a boy scout, Tom thought, with chagrin. Always prepared.

He put on his swim trunks and waded into the lake. The water was like a warm bath. When he got deep enough, he lay back and floated, kicking just enough to push himself farther out from shore. Once in the deeper water, he dove, trying to reach cooler water, but the heat had penetrated to the bottom. There would be no fish caught off the reef, he thought, the water was too warm, too deprived of oxygen. The fish would have moved toward deeper water. To get those, he needed a boat.

When he came out of the lake, he went back to the house and poured himself a cold lemonade, added ice and went to lie down in the porch. The porch had six windows at the front and one at each end. He'd found their screens in the garage, rinsed the dirt off them, and then put them in place. The windows lifted inward and had hooks that fitted into eyes screwed into the ceiling. Jessie had wallpapered the ceiling. Tom found it impossible to lie on his back and stare at it. It was a variegated green background with white dots. It was the same as the paper in her bedroom. When he'd mentioned the ceiling to Ben, Ben had said, "There must have been paper left over. She never wasted anything."

The moon rose, a vast golden orb over the darkening water, and its beams filtered through the spruce trees in front of the house so that the porch was a tangle of light and shadow with bits and pieces of the cot and stacked chairs revealed. The shade on the trilight seemed to float above him in the darkness. The one eye of the wolf reflected faintly. The cot, with its wire springs and thin mattress that had been frozen and thawed for years on end, smelled musty, and he wondered if he should be sleeping on it. He should, he thought, take the mattress out and leave it in the sun.

From where he lay, he could see the ragged outlines of the trees. *Gnarled.* He had tried to think of the word, but it had escaped him. Now that he had it, he felt satisfied and fell into a fitful sleep with the trilight still on.

He woke up slowly to what he thought was a branch knocking against the screen beside his head. He lay there, his eyes shut, waiting for the soft coolness of a breeze, then realized there was no wind, just the oppressive heat. He was lying on his back with one arm over the edge of the cot, and he didn't want to open his eyes. When he put his hand on his chest his skin was clammy.

He heard the knocking again, and then a barely audible girl's voice say, "Mister, hey mister. Wake up. Mister."

He grunted, sat up and saw pressed against the screen a halo of wild orange hair where the moonlight shone through it. With the moon behind her, he couldn't tell what she looked like.

"You awake?" she asked eagerly.

He grunted.

"I want to go home."

"Why tell me?" he groaned. Both their faces were close to the screen and he could smell peppermint on her breath. "What do you want?"

"You're the police. You've got to help me." Her voice sounded more desperate than petulant.

The moon was higher now. It shone down more intensely. He was wearing his shorts. His shirt lay on a chair. It sat there weighed down with shadow so that it looked like it would take more strength than he had to lift it.

"So go." In the back of his head there was a headache waiting for an excuse to appear.

"The others," she whispered, her mouth pressed against the screen. "You met Jason. He won't let me. You came to talk to us. Jason makes all the decisions. He tells you who you'll sleep with, how you'll work. He organizes everything. You go to a store and create a disturbance while someone else steals."

He wanted to be rude, to be brutal, to tell her to go sleep in the bed she had made, but then he thought about Myrna and Joel and he asked, "Are you afraid of him?"

"He's the leader. He thinks God chose him. We have to do as he says because God tells him."

He lifted his shirt off the chair and pulled it on. He thought he would turn on the porch light, then thought it was not a good idea and, instead, fumbled around on the window ledge for his small flashlight. When he shone the light onto the face on the other side of the screen, tears reflected the light. His visitor had a nose ring and an eyebrow ring.

"I need to hide. Let me stay with you so nobody can find me. The woman at the store, she said I could hide there and go with the guy who drives the truck. She said the back door would be open. That's why I left. She forgot. It's locked. I can't go back. They'll hear me and they'll want to know where I've been. It's okay. They won't look here."

He didn't need this. Crazy adults; crazy children. Once, he'd been involved in breaking up a cult. They'd managed to get one adult put away for statutory rape. Even after the leader had been convicted and jailed, the members of the cult were supportive of him, or terrified, believing he channelled God, afraid of what the other members of the cult might do to them.

Home. Exhausted, he sat there thinking of home—for him it had been an apartment. Painted beige. They were lucky because they were three storeys up and had a corner unit. For the kid on the other side of the screen who wanted to go home, it was probably a split-level in the suburbs with a mom and dad both working to pay the mortgage. Maybe, though, there was no home; maybe if she got there, the door would be opened by a stranger.

When he moved out of his house, his and Sally's house, it was not the loss of the money that distressed him the most. Instead, it was an old feeling that came back, a feeling he had from after his mother had left and his father was home less and less, when he'd sat in the silent apartment as the daylight turned to darkness. He'd read until he couldn't see the print. The darkness when it first came weighed hardly anything, but after a while, it became heavier, threatened to smother him, and if he fell asleep, he'd often wake up with a start from dreams that he was out on the street with nowhere to go.

Sometimes, he fled to Anna's, asking if there was anything she needed him to do. Occasionally, she had a job, but other times, even when there was no work, sensing his desperation, she'd invite him in and he'd sit in the bright light of her kitchen, talking to her, playing solitaire with her daughter, Tanya, watching television with them until the light and the conversation would take away his panic.

When he told Anna about his fears, she said, "Think of your blessings. Your father goes to work every day. Many fathers don't. He pays the bills. You have a good place to stay, food, clothes, until you are ready to support yourself. Many others you see around here don't have that. Use the time to get ready to take care of yourself."

The ceiling was in darkness, but the moonlight gilded everything it touched, making it seem falsely valuable.

"Your name? What do they call you?" he asked without looking at her. His voice was thick with sleep and seemed detached from the rest of him. He'd asked this same set of questions many times before, called social workers, arranged safe passage.

"Morning Dawn," she answered.

"Your real name, the one before you met these people."

"Alice Smithers," she said, as if she didn't believe it, as if it was a name so far in the past that she'd nearly forgotten it.

"Where's home?"

"Hamilton."

"Do you remember the address, the phone number?"

"Yes," she said.

"How long have you been away?"

"Twenty-three months."

He sat up, searched the floor for his sandals, found them and slipped them on.

"Don't turn on a light," she pleaded. "They might see."

He stood up and went to the screen door. She scurried sideways and stood expectantly on the bottom step. He could see her better now. She was a scrawny kid with a nose and ears that looked big because her body was so thin. She had dyed frizzy orange hair.

He was tempted to flip up the hook that held the door shut and let her in, but—the shadows, the impossibility of seeing all of her, as if she were a ghost child, her looking back over her shoulder at a frightful monster that would lunge at her from the darkness—something held him back, made him wary, and he felt guilty—so many times he'd imagined himself at a stranger's doorway asking for help and hoping to be let inside.

Anna had told him over suppers of perogies and sour cream about the brutal treatment of the Ukrainian immigrants, of how they'd go from farm to farm in Alberta pleading for work, for milk for their children, and had been driven away time and again by the farmers. He'd started reading accounts of their treatment, and when they'd discussed what he'd read, she'd often say, "Make yourself valuable so everyone wants what you have and opens the door."

The trees now might have been made of iron, crudely wrought, black, rusting, their points meant for impaling people. Beneath them, all was darkness, and even those things he knew existed could not be seen. He looked at his watch. It was nearly midnight.

He pushed up the catch, but instead of inviting her inside, he leaned into the moonlight.

She had turned toward him, and now that they both stood in the full light of the moon, he could see that she was short, slightly built, wearing a short-sleeved dress. She reached up to grab his arm, but he pulled back, and she, rejected, seemed to shrivel.

"Jason decides how much we get to eat." Her voice had a whine to it like that of a small abused child. "It depends on how useful we've been or how happy we've made him. We can't hold anything back, nothing of ourselves. We have to give everything to him. We have truth sessions where we talk about what we are most afraid of. I said I was afraid of snakes and when we were in Alberta, he made me sleep in a tent with a snake. 'Confront your fear,' he says, 'until no fear is left.' I have nightmares."

"Are you hungry?" he asked. She said yes and he went back into the porch and found an Oh Henry. He offered it to her and she said, "Jason says we can't eat chocolate bars or any food like that. It is not pure. We should only eat pure food."

"I'm not Jason," he said. "Eat the chocolate bar."

She ripped the paper off the bar and bit into it. When she'd finished it, she said, "Jason said I was always hiding a part of myself. I'd never completely let go of my ego and become part of the group."

"Angel?" he asked. "The picture of the girl that I brought." The question surprised her and she looked confused, the way she might if he'd asked her an impossible question like who were the tsars of Russia.

"Yes. No. Not with us. She just came twice."

She let the chocolate wrapper fall to the ground, licked her lips as if to get the last speck of chocolate off them and looked, he thought, like nothing so much as a ferret ready to dart past him through the doorway. Instinctively, he shifted to make sure the door was completely blocked.

"She wanted to be a musician. She had a good voice. She sang with us and Jason got her to sing songs by herself. He accompanied her."

"Did he give her drugs?"

"No drugs. That's not allowed. We sold them to others, but no drugs for us. We had to keep our bodies pure. No liquor, no tobacco, just joints."

"But that's a drug."

"It's sanctified. Jason blesses it. It helps us reach another plane. It helps with sharing our bodies. We have rituals."

"Did she smoke joints?"

"No. She just wanted to sing."

"Sex?"

"She went away when the ritual around the fire began, when we began to get sky clad. She wasn't One."

"She was fifteen."

Alice's face went slack. She lifted one hand to her cheek and with her index finger wiped away the remains of a tear. She said, "I'm sixteen."

Tom said she'd have to find a place to sleep and get a ride in the morning, but she started to become hysterical. With him standing on the top step and her on the ground, she fell to her knees and grabbed his leg. "No, no," she said, her voice tight with fear, he'd have to hide her. They'd come searching for her, and if they found her, they'd make her come back, and they'd make her dig a hole, make her crouch in it and fill it with water until there was no room to breathe, or they'd tie a thick towel over her head and pour water over it so she was sure she was drowning. If she were caught trying to run away, when they started travelling again and they got to a truck stop, she'd be sold to a pimp and spend the rest of her life working in the back of a camper truck. Ten guys a day, no days off. She sounded like she already knew from experience what could happen.

As Tom stood there barring her from the house, he felt terrible guilt because of an incident that had occurred when he was fifteen. The relatives who occasionally turned up for tea and sherry were his parents' age, but he guessed that there were younger members of the family in the city, younger members who occasionally made his mother go tsk, tsk and lecture him about behaving himself.

One Sunday, this was after his mother had left, the doorbell rang and he was surprised because no one ever came over without calling first. His father didn't like being interrupted when he was tying dry flies, so Tom went to the door, fully expecting it to be Anna. Instead, it was a young woman carrying a baby.

At first, they stood there staring at each other. Tom's father called, "Who is it?"

"Who are you?" Tom asked.

"Caroline. Your cousin."

"Wait here," Tom said and shut the door. He went into the living room to tell his father.

His father opened the door and the young woman was still standing there. She shifted the baby from her hip to her chest so that it seemed she might hand it to Tom's father. "I'm Caroline Fairweather. You and my father are cousins."

"And?" his father asked, annoyed and perplexed. "Does your father want anything?"

"No," Caroline said. "It's me. My boyfriend kicked me out of our apartment and I have no place to stay."

"What does your boyfriend do?"

"Sells drugs. What does anyone do nowadays?"

His father was so taken aback by the straightforwardness of the answer that, for a time, he said nothing.

"You need to call the welfare. That's what they are for. Tom, bring the phone book, a pen and a piece of paper."

Caroline looked befuddled, as though her need and helplessness were compelling reasons for others to help her. She could not understand why she was being refused. His father wrote down the number, handed the scrap of paper to Caroline, whose face was a mixture of dismay and disbelief, and closed the door.

Torn by the look of the pale-faced baby and the bruise on Caroline's cheek, Tom said, "Could I give her a couple of dollars?"

"And then what?" his father asked. "Give her money and she'll come back for more. How much of that money you earn for your hard work are you prepared to give her? Some of it? All of it? She was stupid enough to live with a drug dealer. Stupid enough to get pregnant. Stupid enough not to have a plan for when she was kicked out. Do you think your two dollars or five dollars is going to do any good?"

In spite of his father's argument, Tom had gone to his room and taken out five dollars. He put it in his pocket and thought if he saw Caroline outside, he'd give it to her, but when he went downstairs there was no sign of her. He didn't see her for two years, and when he did, she was staggering down the street in the middle of the day. She had no child with her, and he wondered if it had been adopted into a good home or ended up in a Dumpster. He and his father had never discussed the intrusion, except for his father to say, "Your job is to take care of yourself and your family when you have one. Do that and it will be plenty."

"Was Angel with you people the night she died?" Tom asked Morning Dawn. They'd been whispering, as if they were secret lovers, but with this question he'd raised his voice slightly.

She shook herself, as if he'd awakened her from a deep sleep. He repeated the question. "No. Not that night," she answered.

That's when he heard Bob's semi start up. There was a roar, then a steady rumble, and Tom grabbed Morning Dawn's hand, pulled her up and urgently said, "Come on, come on, hurry," and dragged her with him into the darkness. Bob was putting food and drinks into the truck. Away from the headlights, Tom explained about Morning Dawn and asked him to take her to a place where she could catch a bus.

Tom asked Morning Dawn if she had any money, and she said, "No, no money."

"Which way are you going?" he asked Bob.

"Calgary."

"I'm good for twenty. I'll give it to your wife."

"Maybe there'll be a rig going east at one of the stops. I'll get her a ride in Winnipeg if I can."

Tom boosted her up into the cab and told her to get behind the seat onto the bed and stay out of sight, then he swung the door shut and Bob got up from the other side. Tom lifted his hand to Bob and the truck rolled away.

The next morning, while Tom was focused on re-glazing a window, a single drumbeat startled him and made him look through the trees. He could see that there was a group standing in front of the emporium. He closed the putty tin and wiped off his putty knife. When he walked out to the road he recognized the people from the beach plus a dozen or so others.

The men were dressed in baggy white trousers and white shirts and the women were dressed in coloured skirts and tops. They all stood facing the front porch of the store. Jason stood at the front of the group. He slowly raised his arms, and as he raised them, the group began to hum. The drummer began to beat steadily on his drum. The voices rose and fell in unison. The hum turned into a chant that intensified. A woman began to sing in a high, keening voice. He thought that the song sounded Russian, like what he had heard when he was posted to Castlegar and listened to a Doukhobor choir.

As the drum beat continued—demanding, insistent—customers were looking out the windows of the café. Others from the town and harbour had come to look. Gradually, a small crowd gathered.

Karla appeared in stages. First, she leaned out a window, then she stood in the front door and then she came out onto the porch. The singers paid her no attention.

"What do you want?" she yelled.

As if in answer to her question, one of the men took a reed flute from his voluminous top; another took out a whistle. Another took out South American panpipes. The rest of the women had joined the first. The men began to play, the music winding around them, weaving in and out of the chanting. The flute was deep and the whistle high, counterpointing each other. The drum beat steadily in the background. They started slowly but, gradually, began to play faster and faster.

Horst came to the front door of the café, but he didn't cross the threshold. The voices were trained, melodious.

"This is private property," Karla said, her voice rising. "You have no business here. You're trespassing. I'll call the police if you don't stop."

One of the women slipped her arms inside her sleeveless blouse and began to spin. She spun in small tight circles, and her bright red blouse spread out. A woman with a bright green blouse, and then one with a blue blouse, spun. Each woman's blouse was a different colour. The men not playing instruments began to sing and clap.

As the women spun, faster and faster, their loose, brightly coloured blouses with weights set in the hem began to lift. The cloth rose up, became whirling discs resting on their shoulders. They weren't wearing anything underneath.

The dancers, Tom thought, were in a trance. The men who were singing began to rock from side to side. The women were now spinning like brightly coloured tops, their bare feet turning on the ground, their golden anklets spinning and glistening in the sun. The men continued singing and swaying.

Karla's face was bright red with indignation. One of the local men laughed and yelled, "Karla, come on. Give us a spin." He did a couple of turns to encourage her.

"There are children here," Karla yelled. "Think of their morals." She stamped her feet, but on the wood it made no sound. "Do something," she yelled at Horst. He quit staring at the dancers and scuttled inside.

Gradually, the chanting slowed, and with it the spinning slowed, the brightly coloured blouses fell down, concealing the dancers' breasts. The dancers slowed and slowed, one of them losing her footing from dizziness.

When the singing and the music stopped, the group stood silent, their eyes open now but staring straight ahead, ignoring all the people who had been watching them.

Jason looked directly at Karla. "We have cast a spell on all who reside here," he proclaimed. "May those who have brought us harm be harmed. May those who have thought ill of us suffer ill. We call upon the spirits of the earth and sky to strike all these asunder."

He had a deep voice. With his long black beard and hair, he looked like a prophet from the Old Testament. It would not have been unreasonable to expect the earth to open, for earthquakes to tumble down the houses, for the lake to rush over everything. But all that happened was that a raven on the top of a spruce tree began its harsh cry.

Jason stepped forward and tacked a piece of paper to one of the veranda posts.

The group, so animated minutes before, now looked exhausted. They turned as one and walked away.

"I never," said one of the women from the boats.

"Me neither," one of her neighbours replied.

One of the local men, Ingvar, said in a hoarse whisper, "Nice tits." He leaned toward Tom and said, "What the hell was that all about?"

"Don't know," Tom said. He'd met Ingvar at the dock when he'd helped Sarah lift some anchors out of her skiff.

Ingvar was heavy-set with a florid face; the swollen, red nose of a heavy drinker; thick eyebrows; and a day's growth of dark beard.

"Nice tits," Ingvar repeated. He was looking longingly after the cacophony of colour retreating down the beach. "Some guys are lucky. Lots of women. Good-looking women. Why don't they come dance for me?"

"I think," Tom said, "they were casting a spell."

"They can cast a spell on me anytime," Ingvar said. He tugged down on his shoulder straps as if his overalls had become too tight in the crotch.

"I'm Larry," the scrawny fellow beside him said. He was short, needed a haircut. He reminded Tom of a scruffy fox terrier.

Tom wondered if he should just say, "I'm the cop." But said instead, "I'm Tom Parsons."

"Never seen anything like that in my life," Ingvar said. "I wonder if they do it every night or if it was just special?"

"I saw some of them on the beach the other day," Tom said.

"The main bunch got Viking buildings and a Viking ship behind the beach," Larry explained. "You gotta go see the longhouse. They got an old schoolhouse they brought in on a barge. They give musical concerts in it."

"Not like that," Ingvar said. He was rubbing his face with his right hand and contemplating the possibility of regular performances by the spinning sisters.

"Do you go?" Tom asked.

"It's free," Larry said. "Why not?"

"Not much to do here," Ingvar added.

"Do people mind their coming here?"

"Some do; some don't," Ingvar said. He was finally able to tear his eyes away from the disappearing cluster of colourful outfits.

"Why not just have them kicked off the property?"

There was silence as Ingvar stroked his chin and Larry continued to watch the disappearing dancers. The silence stretched out. "Can't do that," Ingvar said. "One of them's great-grandmother was one of the people who bought the property and built the place. She used to talk in tongues. Dance and dance until she fell down and people would pick her up and she'd talk in a language nobody understood."

"Russian, maybe," Larry said, "or one of them Chinese languages."

"They were big here at one time. Lots happening. There weren't many strangers came here in those days. No road."

"Just for the summer," Larry added.

"They didn't believe in marriage. It was sort of communist sex. That's the way they worshipped."

"That one in the yellow top was cute," Larry said. "Like cute, cute, like oh-my-God cute."

"Go get her," Tom said.

"They don't mix," Larry said. "You've got to join and give them everything you've got. You can't get girls there."

"All for one and one for all," Ingvar said. He grabbed Larry's arm. "Come on. We've got nets to lift."

The two of them shambled away in their rubber boots, which made a soft whiffling noise as they walked.

The crowd that had gathered to see the spectacle was slowly dispersing. Karla was still standing on the porch, holding on to one of the supports. Her face was white, and her left hand gripped the support so tightly that her fingers were also white.

"What was that about?"

"I don't know," she replied in a harsh whisper. "We don't want people like that here. They aren't worth the little business they bring. They'll drive our respectable customers away."

Tom pulled off the piece of paper Jason had pinned to the post. It was a diagram and had what looked like four lines of verse, but they were in Icelandic, so he couldn't read them. He handed it to Karla. She looked at it, crumpled it up and threw it on the ground. Tom sat down and gestured at an empty chair for her to join him. "They came. They left. Great show. It'll give people lots to talk about when they go back home. Great dinner party stuff. The day of the tits," he said.

She was clenching her jaw when she slid into the chair. "Tracy," she said to one of the waitresses, "get Mr. Parsons a Coke float."

"Why give a performance here?"

"I don't know. They're all crazy. Free love. They're like mink screwing each other and praying. Godi-1, their first prophet, with long white hair and a white robe, at his pulpit ranting, and people humping. All together. On the stage. On the floor. The women were as bad as the men."

"Before your time?"

"Yes, long before my time. But everyone knows about it. They tried to get local people involved. They were knocking on doors, 'Be immortal, be immortal.' Some of the men thought it was a wonderful idea. If they had dared, they would have been there every night, working their way to being immortal along with the big-shot money people, women from New York, hoity-toity, down on their hands and knees for anyone who wanted them as they talked in tongues. They made people crazy."

"And the local women?"

"They clasped their Bibles to their breasts and repeated Matthew 6:13. 'Lead us not into temptation.' They were outraged by this summer camp for sinners."

"A cult?"

"I'd call it that. They came for four months every summer, brought everything they needed with them. Not all at once. A few, then more. Maybe," Karla paused, "I'm not sure. Maybe a hundred people. You could have asked Jessie. They were her enemy." She stopped. "I shouldn't be talking about this. The soda is on me. Leave Tracy a tip."

She got up to greet a family of four who were coming up from the dock.

"Why not?" Tom asked.

She stopped, looked frustrated at his lack of understanding. When she replied, her voice was edged with annoyance. "Don't you see?" she asked. "Do you think these people want to be associated with craziness? They're successful, respectable. They want to feel secure. No stress. It's all about values." With that, she hurried away to meet the approaching family.

Tom picked up the piece of paper Karla had thrown on the ground. He smoothed it out with his fingers, folded it and put it in his pocket, then sat there, staring at the boats and the lake. There was nothing to indicate this day was different from any other day. The people who had been drawn to the performance had drifted away. The sun was high overhead, a large scorching circle in the sky that would burn your eyes to blindness if you presumed to look upon it. Tom could feel that the armpits of his shirt were soaked.

The reflection from the lake was painful. Tom put on his sunglasses. Cataracts, macular degeneration, the ills of age created by carelessness in youth. His mother had lectured him on these things. She would have been horrified by the day's spectacle, not just the nudity but the violence of it, the noise, the intrusion, the presumption, the disorder, the lack of respect, of decorum, except there'd been no disorder in the performance; it was organized, planned, practised, a ritual, like a religious service. What, he wondered, had they been praying for, or to whom? Karla must have an idea of what it meant; otherwise, why would she be so upset? But for others, like Larry, it was all meaningless except for the tits. And even that had meaning because the women of the community hid their breasts behind bras, shirts, blouses, sweaters, layer upon layer of cloth secured with their crossed arms. The dancers' swirling tops rising until they spun from the shoulders created possibilities, other ways that people might be, might behave.

He wondered briefly about that, about the other ways people might behave, and wondered still more if the women who were watching wished they, too, could dance like that, spin and spin for their men, for themselves, for their sisters, for a life filled with colour and sound and passion, for the dance implied passion—no one watching could be satisfied with a quick coupling in a dingy bedroom on a narrow bed in the missionary position. He wondered if the boats in the harbour would rock tonight, might have started to rock already, if the trailers, houses, cottages might rock and if the people having sex were thinking of the dancing, twirling, brightly coloured half-naked young women, were hearing the wild sounds of the pipes and drums.

He thought then of Freyja, of what she would look like dancing like that if she were dancing for him, if he, magically, could play the South American panpipes, high and keening, until she fell exhausted onto the floor and he joined her.

I need, he thought, *a cold shower, two cold showers, a tub full of cold water and ice.* The crotch of his pants was too tight and, like Ingvar, he shifted to loosen his undershorts. Whatever the performance had been about, it had at least created one miracle.

And he could see his mother's disapproving eyes, as if she were dead, magically knowing the thoughts behind his still face. She told him that the dead know everything. Every thought, every fantasy, every sin. Them and Santa Claus. He'd been terrified of Santa Claus.

If it were winter, he'd have chopped a hole in the ice and dropped into the water for a minute or two to get everything under control again, but it wasn't winter, and the plumbing for the bathtub wasn't working, so he couldn't even buy ice from the fishermen to put in a bathtub full of water. Instead, he went home and masturbated.

Later, he went over to the Olafsons' on the chance that Linda might be able to tell him about Angel.

Linda was working in the garden. He asked her if she had time to visit and she said, "Yes, sure. Why not?"

There was a playset in the yard, bright red metal, two swings and a slide, a sandbox made from a large tire. There were two boys and a girl playing in the sandbox with a dump truck, a grader and a tractor. Close to the sandbox there was a large vegetable garden.

"I was weeding," she said, "when I heard the drum."

She was wearing a yellow cotton dress with an apron over it, a white straw hat with a large brim and a yellow ribbon. She was holding a trowel.

They went inside and she poured them both cold lemonade from the fridge, then called the kids to come and get lemonade.

"Quite a show," he said.

"Nothing I haven't seen before, but they were sort of flat chested."

He laughed. No one could say she was flat chested. She was large all over. He thought about Bob and hoped she'd been feeling affectionate before her husband left just after midnight.

The kitchen was chaotic. Friendly, welcoming, a place it was easy to be relaxed, but dishes were piled haphazardly, cupboard doors open, toys scattered about the floor. The kids drank their lemonade and she gave each one a kleinur, then gave one to Tom.

"Go on," she said to the kids. "Go out and play or go have a nap." The three kids tumbled out the door.

She plopped down in a chair. "When Bob's here, I ignore everything but him. I bake stuff for him to take with him. I give him lots of attention. I want him to want to park his truck in front of this house."

"It's a hard life. Not many truckers have a home to go to."

Linda took a kleinur from the basket on the table and bit off a piece. "Gone for nearly a month each time. The kids forget who he is. We have our life. Then he appears. He thinks he needs to bring us gifts to make up for being away." She waved at the toys. "Same with me. Nice things. More than I need. He's been at it nearly ten years. He hits ten years, then it's over."

"And then?"

"I dunno. Maybe move to the city. Get a job as a dispatcher. Or a diesel mechanic. There's a big shortage. Start a business fixing truck beds. Anything so he can come home after work."

"Where are all the other Valhalla men?" he asked. "There don't seem to be many husbands around."

She thought about it for a moment. "Away," she said. "They'll come back in the fall. A lot of them work up on the Mackenzie River from breakup to freeze-up. Away six months. Home six months."

"Like Bob?" he said.

"Other wives at least get a husband full time for six months."

"Bob says Angel used to sleep over here."

Linda's smile faded. "That's right. Pretty hard for Ben at his age to be a mom and a dad."

"Were you her mom?"

Linda's hands tightened into fists. "No, I got enough taking care of my own. Besides, every time her mother dumped her latest boyfriend, she'd come looking for Angel. Angel would start to have a life and then her mother would drag her off to the city to a dump. I think a few of those boyfriends liked little girls. She ran away lots of times. Hitchhiked back here. You can't get involved in other people's grief."

"You got any idea what happened to Angel?"

She shook her head slightly. "Kids. I'm terrified of my kids growing up. Who knows what they'll get into?"

"Yes," he agreed. "There's no predicting how things will work out."

~ CHAPTER 17 ~

THE FAMILY

Tom left Linda's and walked to Ben's to see if he'd tell him something more about Frenchie and the good stuff. When he came around the corner of the garage, Derk was lying on a lounge chair made from aluminum and purple strapping. A matching purple umbrella had been tied to a pole and stuck into the ground so it cast its shadow over him. The air was so thick and heavy that even the leaves on the small tree growing beside the tin garage were limp and lifeless. When he saw Tom, Derk tensed, put one foot on the ground as if he might suddenly spring away. Derk's Dodge Challenger was backed close to the front door, its front pointing toward the road out of town, and Tom thought Derk might be calculating how quickly he could reach it.

"Nice wheels," Tom said. He didn't want Derk fleeing, so he pulled up a lawn chair, sat down and leaned back. Butterflies and bees and the occasional dragonfly flitted about, attracted by the ragged row of hollyhocks that grew against the south side of the house.

"Whaddaya want?" Derk drawled. His dark hair was carefully combed to hang over one side of his face. If he hadn't been so sullen, he would have been handsome. His face was heart shaped, his eyes dark, his nose narrow. Girls who loved bad boys would love him—the sullen look, the styled hair, the gold chains, the gold ring with the diamond that sparkled when he moved his hand.

In deference to the heat he was wearing a white short-sleeved shirt and white cotton pants with a white belt. A pair of white sandals were lying on the ground beside him, and Tom wondered what any locals walking by would think of white sandals and the designer sunglasses sitting on top of his head. Derk rested the book he was reading on his stomach and waited for Tom to say what was on his mind.

"I'm sorry about your sister." It seemed lame, weak, but he hadn't known her, only the cold feel of her body as he'd rolled her over, only the image of her hair in the mud and water.

"Aren't we all?"

"I found her."

"Did you try mouth-to-mouth?" Derk said it contemptuously, insultingly, making it sound like Tom had done something wrong, or hadn't done something right.

"You're dealing. Did you give her anything?"

"I sell spices. Haven't you heard? Your colleagues have a mistaken idea about me. They've stopped me many times. I offer them cinnamon, thyme, oregano. They keep asking me for things I haven't got." He drawled the words, and although he didn't sneer, his hostility was evident in the exaggerated way he spoke.

With a jerk, he sat up, pulled the lounger into an upright position, dragged it around to face Tom and said, "You still a cop or what?" The words were choppy, angry, demanding. He'd lost the exaggerated drawl.

"Just wondering what happened to her."

"You're still a cop. You'll always be a cop. You've got the look. I'd have known you were a cop from a block away. The way you stand, the way you look at people."

"Don't you care what happened?"

Derk leaned forward, his arms on his knees. He waved one arm to take in the village. "You see this? You think this is a sad place? This is good. There are lots worse."

Tom looked out at the buildings, at the boards of the skating rink that now contained nothing but bare ground and scraps of paper. The nets were still in place, waiting for winter to begin again. Two boys were kicking a soccer ball into one of the nets while a third practised being goaltender. The houses, exposed by the relentless sun, were diminished, appeared to have shrunk in the suffocating heat. From where he sat, he could see Rose sitting on the steps of the trailer where she and her husband and two children lived. She was holding her baby and trying to comb her little girl's hair at the same time. *The heat in the trailer*, he thought, *must be suffocating.* Her husband was sitting on a white plastic chair drinking a beer.

"Don't you want to know what happened?" he asked again.

Derk shut his eyes, took a long drag from his cigarette, tipped his head back, pushed out his lower lip and blew smoke into the air. "I'll find out."

"And then what?"'

Derk opened his eyes and gave a half smile. "I'll find out. Before you do. You don't belong here. You don't know the games. You don't know the players."

Derk was right, of course. He might have moved away to the city, but he was still part of the community. He knew how the pieces fitted together. He knew what people had done and with whom, still had a map of events long past, was wound in an intricate pattern of memories. Tom wondered if anything here could be unravelled and understood. He felt the way he had when confronted with his parents' photograph albums and indecipherable conversations. The memory overwhelmed him with such a sense of hopelessness that he wanted to go back to planing wood, but he remembered Angel's clay-smudged face in the circle of light from his flashlight and her cold hand, and he thought, *I won't take the blame for that.* Silence was often more than many people could stand, and confronted with it, they had to fill it up by speaking, so he sat there, half in and half out of the shade, and waited.

Wanda poked her head out the door, disappeared inside, came out with a bottle of beer and plunked herself onto a chair on the other side of her son. She was wearing shorts, and the tattoo of a dragon wound up her right leg. She had three gold anklets on her right ankle. She'd obviously been drinking, for she smiled at nothing, her mouth open, and looked like she might tip sideways. She held the beer bottle upright delicately, making sure that no beer spilled.

"Move over," she said to Derk. "We want some shade, too."

Derk didn't stand up but lifted himself enough to take his weight off the lounger and pushed it back underneath himself. When Wanda was settled, she looked closely at Tom.

"You're the cop," she said. "I'm Wanda." She reached out her hand, but Derk was between them and they were too far apart for their hands to reach. Tom held out his hand and they did a fake shake.

"Yeah," Derk said, answering for Tom. "He's going to bust us for something. Defiling the landscape maybe."

His mother didn't quite get it, but she laughed anyway, tipped up the bottle and took a drink.

"Isn't that right? Defiling. Betcha didn't know I'd know a big word like that. Being a goddamned Indian and all." For a moment, the smiling mask disappeared and his voice was sharp with anger.

"He's smart," his mother said. "He should go to college."

Derk tipped his head back and took a deep breath, pursed his lips as he let it out. When he spoke again, he'd gotten his control and sarcasm back. "Meth one oh one. I'd be a genius in the chem lab."

"How's Ben?" Tom asked, ignoring Derk.

"Sleeping," Wanda said. "I gave him a pill. They knock me out for four hours. He's not used to them. He'll sleep longer."

"You grew up here?"

"Yeah. Right in this house. My mom was alive then. Aboriginal. I've got treaty."

"And Orkney."

"How'd you know? Ben musta told you. We've got relatives in Scotland. Maybe they live in a castle. You never know. You wanna beer or you on duty?"

"I'm on duty."

"That's too bad." She leaned back and looked at the sky for a moment. "You wanting to know about Angel?"

The sun beat down on them. Tom wiped away a trickle of sweat that ran down the scar on his forehead. Bees buzzed, flitted from flower to flower in the remnants of Betty's garden. Derk closed his eyes again. Wanda was lost in thought.

They might have been a family relaxing together in the shade, sharing each other's company out of the harsh glare of the sun. It could have been Sally and him and Joel, except Joel was blond and would have been in shorts and a T-shirt with the name of a band on it.

A bee flew right up to Wanda's face and she swatted at it. The bee startled her into speech and she said, "She was a good kid. No trouble. Except when she'd run away. Then we'd have to go find her."

"She ran away a lot?"

"Just now and again. She'd hitchhike here. She liked the country better than the city."

"She liked country and western music?"

"Yeah." The idea pleased Wanda. Her face lit up. She looked away, into the distance, remembering. "Yeah. She was always listening to C&W on the radio. Watching the big stars on TV. She was going to start a band. We didn't have no money for lessons. But the music teacher at her school gave her lessons. Got her singing other stuff. Said she was talented."

"Hick music," Derk said. "She was better than that." He didn't open his eyes. The book he'd been reading fell off his lap and landed face up. It had a picture of a schooner in a storm on the cover.

"*Moby-Dick?*" Tom said, surprised.

"Yeah. So what? You think I'm too stupid to read?"

Tom, not wanting to get into an argument, turned to Wanda and asked, "You moved around a lot?"

"Yeah. Coming and going. But she didn't want to leave this school. The music teacher was teaching her a lot. She had friends."

Derk lit another cigarette. His face was pale from spending too much time inside. The tension was in his eyes. It was like he was trying to pull all the skin around them tight. Every so often, he'd jerk his head slightly and take a breath.

"Don't tell him anything," Derk said. "He's a cop. He's no friend of ours. He works for the big shots—you know, the ones in the mansions, the judges and lawyers, the ones who like their stuff delivered to their back door. The kind you deal with on the back porch and stand in front of in court."

"It's a rotten system," Tom agreed.

A slight breeze moved the tips of the grass, but the promise of relief was short lived, for the breeze disappeared as suddenly as it had come and the heat pressed down on Tom's skin without mercy. He shifted his chair closer to Derk to take advantage of the shade.

Derk laughed out loud. "You want to work for me, Mr. Copperman? You could have your own route. You'd make a great deliveryman."

"Street dealers. They've got a flat learning curve. They don't understand why they keep getting busted. They end up in the river."

"No law against oregano. You got a goal. You make so much, you quit. Don't be greedy. Make your stash, then start going to church. Start sucking up to the legal crooks."

"People like you end up in a body bag."

Derk laughed, and his voice was high, preadolescent for a moment. "Slipping sideways. A moving target. Don't fight for a crowded corner. Everybody wants to sell in the same place. Out here I ain't got no competition for cardamom."

"If you start making a lot, competition will appear. They'll find what's left of you in your burned-out car."

"You saying I need protection? You want the job?"

Tom smiled at the audacity of the offer, even if it was insincere. "I've got plenty of work."

"Grow spices and you don't need to live in a shack in the bush," Derk said. His eyes had brightened, shone. He ran his tongue over his lips. He was enjoying himself. "You got a piece of property here. You've got an old barn on the other side of the lake road. Jack a little hydro. Use propane. Operate all year. I'll take all you can grow. Fresh herbs. Fresh spices."

"Jail's not a good place for ex-cops. I might meet a con I'd put in there."

Derk laughed out loud. His laugh was high, brittle. He rocked back and forth on his chair. It was the most animated Tom had seen him.

"You staying around?" Tom asked.

"Maybe, maybe not. Maybe a day or two. You never know. Duty calls. Day or night. Like the postal service, through rain, snow or sleet, we keep moving our feet."

Tom stood up, did another fake shake with Wanda and left. *What a bloody disaster*, he thought. Wanda. Derk. The one person who had been staying clear of disaster was Angel, and now she was dead.

When he got home, he turned on the planer and started to pick out wood. *What the hell. What the hell*, he thought, but he wasn't sure what he was helling about. Everything, life. If he called Myrna to ask about Joel, she'd say why hadn't he called to find out about her, that he'd always paid more attention to Joel than her, even though she'd done her best to help him when he was living in that crummy place where the toilet always plugged, and he never appreciated the effort she'd made. For being so young she was amazingly shrewish at times. If he gave her hell back, she'd switch to Mandarin. When she'd buffaloed them with French, he had, in self-defence, taken French classes, and, she, in a fury, had started to learn Mandarin.

At a parents' night, her homeroom teacher had smiled broadly and said, "Myrna has an ear for languages. She's a natural polyglot." Tom wasn't sure what the hell that was, so he looked it up when they got home. He gave up on the French.

AIDS. Joel couldn't have AIDS. He never had much time for girls in high school because he was always on the computer, but he never showed any interest in pink shirts, holding hands with other guys, ballet—whatever the signs were, he didn't show them. He wasn't on any sports teams, but then, he was skinny and had an astigmatism and eye-hand coordination problems. They'd played catch when he was small, but it was never more than underhand lobbing of the ball. They'd gone to the local park in summer. Sally had been back catcher and Tom pitcher. Joel and Myrna had taken turns being batters. Myrna hit the ball most of the time. Joel hardly ever. Joel joined the computer club. Myrna took kick-boxing.

He shut down the memories, forced them back behind doors in hallways, went back into his house and looked through his notepad for Myrna's number. He sat there staring at the pad. If he called, she might think it was an emergency. She had read everything she could on depression and was convinced that one day she was going to come home from school and find him hanging from the living room light fixture. She said that she imagined him dead in various ways— hanged, shot, drowned, immolated—on the way from school to prepare herself for what she might find. He'd promised her that he wasn't going to kill himself, but he promised himself that if he did, it would look like an accident.

Nagging, nagging, like little hooks pulling at his head, what Sarah had said in one of their conversations about his kids. Myrna and Joel—lucky he had them. If he were lucky, they'd be here with him; maybe he wouldn't be here, maybe he'd be someplace else, someplace with them going to college, or starting out in serious jobs, starting a career, something that made him feel secure instead of wondering where they were, who they were with, what they were doing and, at the same time, not wanting to know.

He turned on the planer again, then turned it off and went to the store. He got the phone from Karla. He had Joel's number on a scrap of paper in his wallet. He made the call, but when the phone was answered, it wasn't Joel.

"I'm calling for Joel Parsons," he said, and the voice at the other end said, "Not here, man, he's moved on. You chasing him for money?" Tom explained that he was Joel's father and that he had money for him. "Maybe try the Laugh Tracks. It's hot. Good food. Stand-up. He thought he had a job doing tables there. Maybe not."

"If you see him, tell him to call his father at this number." Tom gave him the number and assured the voice that he had money for Joel. "I'll tell him," the voice said, then hung up.

Once Tom was out of the hospital and at home recovering from his accident, he was lost. Sally had to go back to work full time and resented it. "I didn't sign up for this," she said. He could cook and mash potatoes, fry an egg, make sandwiches. He'd looked up recipes on the Internet. Easy meals. Breakfast and lunch. On schedule. He got the kids to do the laundry. Sally usually made supper. She said she couldn't eat pizza every night. He encouraged Myrna and Joel to bring home friends and bought a half dozen computer games to keep them occupied. He made endless toasted cheese sandwiches, bought cases of soft drinks, thinking that if they were at home with their friends, he knew where they were. Sally said they couldn't afford it. Keep them busy. They didn't have his overtime anymore and his disability wasn't the same as his salary. Even when he and Sally were both working, they'd lived pretty close to the line.

When he asked the shrink about the kids and the disaster of their lives, the shrink had said, "Relax, they'll survive. Kids are amazingly resilient. Get your own head straight. Lots of times kids have problems, their parents get their own problems fixed and the kids' problems go away. They ask for help, give them what you can. You can't give what you haven't got. Right now, you need it for yourself. Capiche?" And Tom had nodded, and his mind, loosened from the constraints of facts, was led into strange paths, wondered if the shrink was Italian, though he didn't look Italian, and he thought about Italian restaurants where he had eaten and Italian shoes and a deli with crescent-shaped cookies. When this happened, he lost touch with where he was and what was going on, so out of touch that time passed without him realizing it. The shrink kept talking, but Tom heard nothing of what he said and was surprised when he finished up the session by saying, "You can't rescue everyone."

CHAPTER 18

MESSAGE FROM THE FOGGY COAST

The agitation had come back. In the city he had walked for hours, sometimes entire nights, stopping in all-night gas stations, cafés, brooding over bitter coffee, avoiding the eyes of other wanderers, people who couldn't bear being with themselves alone. He wondered what nightmares drove them into the empty, darkened streets but did not ask, for each huddled in his or her own cone of silence, not even breaking it when a waitress came by to refill a cup. The impersonal maze of streets and back lanes provided anonymity, but here in Valhalla no one went on casual Sunday strolls over the dirt roads. The boat people seldom ventured onto the roads, because they were afraid of looking like they were prying.

He'd walked for half an hour when he saw a man he recognized from the funeral reception. He was sitting on a woven willow chair in the shade of three birch trees that grew in front of his house. He had on a large grey hat with a wide brim. His upper body was large, out of proportion to his legs, and, where they showed below his short-sleeved shirt, his arms were thick and muscular. Sitting as he was, his chin tilted up, his arms on the armrests of the chair, he might have been a ruined god. He had a cane hooked on each arm of the chair. There were two chairs with a willow table between them. There was a small yellow bungalow with brown trim behind him.

Tom hesitated because there was no acknowledgement, no wave or raised hand. He went over anyway and introduced himself.

"They call me Mindi Miner," he replied and eyed Tom warily. "You came to the funeral with McAra's wife."

"She helped me when I found Angel's body."

"Middle of the night. What were you doing out in the middle of the night?"

"Dawn," Tom said, realizing that there wasn't going to be a handshake or an invitation to sit down. "Bad leg," he said. "I can't stand in one position for long." Without waiting for an invitation, he sat in the chair.

The sky was bleached by the sun until it had hardly any colour.

Mindi snorted. "That's not a bad leg. I'd like to have two of those. These are bad legs. The mine roof fell on them. I guess I was lucky. Three others died. They didn't get us out for two days."

"Bad luck."

"Capitalism at work. They were going cheap on the supports. Not spaced close enough. Keep mining costs down. Profits up. Bonuses for the bosses."

"Same story over and over."

"In the world war they called the farm boys who went into the trenches the Expendables. In the mines, they treat the farm boys the same way."

"You lived here long?"

"Got a job at the Bissett gold mine right out of high school. Came to a dance in Valhalla. Met a girl I fancied. Came back a few times. Married her. It's an old story."

"Any family?" Tom asked, trying to be sociable.

"A son. He's in Alberta."

"Does he ever get home?"

"Not much to come back for," Mindi said.

There was a movement in the grass and Tom turned toward it. The grass had dried to a dull yellow and brown. There was a line of green and Tom saw that it was a small garter snake. Mindi took one of his canes and tapped the ground. The snake darted forward and disappeared into a hole.

"You see that," he said, tapping the cane on the ground. "It all looks solid, like it's here for eternity. You strip off this layer of dirt and you'll find caverns. I think about that often. We're sitting here, kings of the world, we think, and underneath us there are thousands, hundreds of thousands of creatures hunting, eating, dying, breeding." Mindi gave a grimace of a smile. "You think you know what's going on, but then something happens and you find out you don't know nothing."

"Did you know Angel?"

"Did you?" Mindi replied.

"I know Ben."

"Bad Luck Ben."

"Why do you say that?"

"His wife dies. Cancer. His daughter." Mindi shook his head in disapproval. "His granddaughter."

"Bad way to die."

"You know any good ways?" Mindi asked. "I heard she was raped."

"She was fully clothed. Ask Sarah. Or Albert. Where do you hear this crap?"

"Here and there," Mindi said.

There was a transistor radio on the table between them and a book. It was open, face down, and the title said *As Their Natural Resources Fail*.

"A lot of people married into this town," Tom said.

"Getting married gave us a reason to be here. How about you? What are you doing here? There are lots of better places."

"I was here once. I thought I'd come back."

"You think you're going to find Odin's gold?"

"What's that?"

"The wooden chests of gold buried or sunk somewhere by the first Godi?"

Tom shook his head.

"Some people say they've come here to fish. Except they've also got a shovel and a metal detector in with their fishing rods."

"I've heard old stories about farmers who didn't trust the banks and are supposed to have buried their money in glass jars. After the farmer dies, his family spends years digging up every likely spot."

Mindi smiled wryly.

"Do you have a metal detector? Some people think Odin's treasure might be buried on your property. You seen places on your property where there are holes dug?"

"Yes, a few. I thought they were because spruce trees had come down."

"You got that field with the barn. Lots of holes there. Don't fall in one."

"Do you think it's real? The gold?"

"Probably."

"From the Bissett mine?"

"There were rich veins then. I've heard that guys were taking it out in their ass. They were selling it, but there wasn't any need for Godi to buy stolen stuff. In those days, the Godi could buy all they wanted. Just go into a bank and put your money down."

"Chests of gold?"

"Maybe one. Maybe more. Some people think it might be in your walls. They'd like to tear your house down. Burn it down. Sift the ashes. If you smell smoke some night, grab your pants and run."

"What about Jessie?"

"Lots of people hated her. She chased anyone off she caught digging. Got that ox of a McAra to give them a cuffing to make the point. Or his wife. She's got a bad hip now, but you wouldn't want the back of her hand in your face. No one picked a fight with their sons. Some diggers thought Jessie was keeping them from winning the lottery. Lots of resentment."

"What do you think?"

Mindi tipped his head back and grinned widely. He looked at Tom and said, "Lots of places to hide something. The east side of the lake is all volcanic. I used to prospect over there in my spare time. This side is all sedimentary. You take a boat along the shore, you'll see lots of caves, lots of large cracks in the rock that go way back inland. Big enough to walk into."

"What are these Godi like?"

Mindi shrugged. "They sell me produce at a fair price. You want to know more about them, go visit. They're not like the big shots in the city living in a gated community."

"You said Bad Luck Ben. His wife, daughter, granddaughter. Nothing about his grandson."

"His son is a capitalist. He's figured out how the system works."

"You're a Marxist."

"Try working for the mines. Try working for big business. If you aren't a Marxist, you're a fool. Of course, in the Winnipeg General Strike, you guys worked for the bosses. Shot the protestors."

"That was a long time ago. Times change. Even the Force is getting unionized."

"I heard that. It's the biggest miracle since Moses divided the Red Sea."

"What did you think of yesterday's performance?"

"Trouble. Some of those people aren't part of the Godi community. I don't know where they've come from."

"Jessie said the community were communists."

"Maybe. Depends how you define it. They live in a commune. All for one, one for all. They share the work. They share the rewards."

"Karla doesn't like them."

"Of course not. What capitalist would? They aren't good customers."

"You think Russia was better under the communists?"

"It wasn't communism. It wasn't socialism. After the socialists won the revolution, Stalin had them all shot. It was the cult of personality. Stalin was the new tsar. Putin is the latest tsar. Those people don't know anything except tsars."

"Things work pretty well here. In Canada."

Mindi's laugh was a sharp bark. "You got lots to learn, sonny. Open your eyes. You and me? Disposable people. And you think the system works? For who? Washed up, that's you and me." He saw another garter snake and struck the earth with one of his canes. The snake's body flashed in the sun, then disappeared. "Down there," Mindi said. "Think about what's down there. Lots going on you don't know about. Just like in Ottawa, and Washington, and London. People making decisions. No health care for you. More money for me. No sprinkler system for your building. More money for me." Mindi's voice had become angry. "You know what people say about me? That accident was the best thing that ever happened to him. He's got a disability pension. That's what they're going to say about you."

When Mindi described what was happening beneath them, Tom's head filled up with images of dark caves, of long, twisting holes, of fangs and teeth and snarling death, and he shut his eyes for a moment as he tried to shut out the images. It was like his accident had shattered the barrier between the real world and his imagination, as if an image, once it began, would spiral out of control. He had learned to quiet his mind by choosing an object and focusing on it. The second therapist he'd seen had shown him that trick. It was a kind of self-hypnosis, and with it he shrunk the images and locked them up. Before he'd learned that trick, a rush of images would cause the world to lose its solidity and begin to dissolve, and there were times when he felt as if he might be seasick and throw up, the way he had in a ditch outside of Regina when he saw his first dead child. He turned away from the images and the sounds in his head toward the real and immediate.

"Did you go down to the store, down to the dock, the day Angel died?"

"I did go. I wanted some fresh sunfish. I like it boiled. I got some from Ingvar."

"Did you see Angel?"

"I don't think so. I was busy talking with Ingvar while he was cleaning three sunfish for me."

"You went straight home?"

"No. I stopped at the emporium for my mail. I had a soft drink. I talked to Horst. Karla is trying to get him to hire you to drywall and paint two unfinished rooms upstairs. There are three rooms. She sleeps in the finished room. The other two are just used for storage. She says if they get them finished, they can rent them out."

"I could use the work. What's Horst's objection?"

"He doesn't want you up there with his wife. He thinks you might screw more than the drywall."

"She flirts."

Mindi took out a wooden match and stuck it between his teeth. When he talked it went up and down. He smiled and laughed to himself. "You wanna be careful. Horst has friends. Well, maybe that's an exaggeration. Horst has people who will do jobs for him. The Jones boys that live past the end of the road. Horst got mad at Billy Begood because he thought Billy stole a load of homebrew Horst had brought in for a wedding reception. Some people say Horst paid them to feed him to their pigs. The pigs ate him, then they ate the pigs."

"They didn't want to waste anything."

Mindi Miner slapped his knee and laughed. "You got that, sonny. The difference now is they're more sensitive. If they feed someone to the pigs, they'll sell you the pork chops but won't eat them themselves."

"I'll keep that in mind."

"People do crazy things because of jealousy."

He nodded his agreement. He'd called ambulances for a lot of women. Over the years he'd covered a number of domestic murder-suicides.

"You got a rifle?" Mindi asked.

"If I've got the money, I'll buy one for hunting season. If not, I'll try to borrow one. Do you think I need one?"

"Lots of bears around. A gimp isn't going to outrun a bear."

Tom cringed at being called a gimp. "Even two good legs won't outrun a bear."

"No use trying to climb a tree, either. They'll follow you up and eat you like a piece of fruit. There's lots around. Last time I was at the dump, I counted seven." He picked up his book and Tom knew their conversation was over. Mindi held the book up. "All about the lousy way Native peoples have been treated in Manitoba. Capitalism at work."

Tom tried one more time. "If Angel's death wasn't an accident, where would you look for answers?"

"If," Mindi repeated, an edge of annoyance in his voice. "Big word. If. Lots of possibilities. People camping on the beach. Fishermen in Horst's rentals. People on the boats. The cottagers. People from the east shore coming over to party." He shrugged, then looked steadily at Tom. "You don't know what kids are up to today. Maybe she was sniffing gasoline. All you need is a plastic bag and some gas from someone's outboard motor. Used to be the fishermen left their gas cans in their boats. Now, they lock them up. Maybe taking some of those new pills. You're like a dog with a bone. Don't choke on it."

He sat there glaring at Tom. Tom the intruder. Tom the newcomer who didn't know what went on below the surface, just as he didn't know what went on in the dark subterranean world where the snakes went. Tom didn't look away, and he said with his voice edged with his own resentment, "I found her. I turned her over. I felt her cold hand. I didn't ask for that. I didn't want it. I don't want it. I don't need that memory. "

Mindi studied him. "You lie in a dark mine with rock pinning you down, you learn things other people don't know. Like where your mind can travel. You going to walk much?"

"Maybe," Tom replied.

"People are going to say why's he walking so much? Better to take up a hobby—prospecting, cutting wood, hunting. Nothing unusual about walking all day hunting; nobody's going to say why's he going hunting so much. If you don't bring back any game, they'll just say he's not a good hunter. Maybe even, if they like you, they might say, 'Not much game this year.'"

"Okay," Tom said.

"People think they understand darkness. Most of them don't understand anything about darkness." He looked fiercely into Tom's eyes and banged his cane on the ground.

CHAPTER 19

THE DANCE

He had thought he was tough, followed the code of silence in which no matter how horrific the event—charred corpses, heads blown off by shotguns, severed limbs—no one talked about it, unless it was to make a sardonic joke. They all followed the code. Shut it down, shut it out, shut up. Talk about it, shed a few tears, and the next day when you came to work there was a pink towel hanging over the back of your chair.

He knew that with his leg pinned and bolted together, he needed to move into an administrative job, but there were none available in his detachment. There were endless deadline requests and paperwork, too many people involved. Too many files, too many messages, too many. He spent nights sitting in the living room, walking the floor, watching the sun come up, and Sally, outraged at the lack of help from the Force, and their complete lack of concern, railed against the system. There were no answers, and the rage turned to a feeling of being lost and confused.

He went to see a shrink to help him adjust to his new reality. "You weren't just an RCMP officer," the shrink had said. "You were a person who was an RCMP officer. You were a lot more than that. You were a husband and father, a son. You have lots of options. You could go back to university, become a history professor. You like working with your hands. Take up a trade. You can be anything you want."

Tom thought the shrink was full of shit. He said, "I want to be a quarterback for the Blue Bombers."

The shrink was taken aback. "Within current limitations," he said, but it was obvious that having to admit to limitations instead of believing in a future in which everything was possible was painful for him. Tom got the idea that it was a strategy. Starting out with saying anything being possible and working down to adjusting to reality.

One morning Sally had come into the living room just before dawn and said, "Let it go. The Force won't help you. They'd have preferred it if you'd got killed in that accident. Then they could get all dressed up in their dress uniforms and march together, and a politician could have spouted bullshit."

He'd sat at the window all night watching the houses across the street, houses with no lights in the windows because everyone was asleep. He refused to look at her.

"Are you surprised?" she yelled. "Why should you be surprised? There's never been enough guys to cover. All the times we moved. No bloody communication, no housing arrangements, no furniture storage. They wanted everything from you and delivered nothing in return."

He wasn't going to go back to the shrink, but Sally insisted. "Get him to give you something for depression," she'd said. A pill a day to keep the boogers away.

He gave up on the shrink during a session in which the doc launched into a lecture on how adversity helped people throw off their shell and offered an opportunity for growth. He hoped the bastard drove his Ferrari into a tree, became a paraplegic and, given lots of adversity, grew. Tom got up and put on his cap and his jacket, and the shrink, startled out of his lecture, said, "What doesn't kill us makes us stronger." And Tom thought about four years on traffic duty. They averaged one death a week in summer. Blood and guts everywhere. The worst was a family—parents, four kids—running head on into a semitrailer. The Winnebago looked like it had exploded. They thought they had found all the bodies and were cleaning up when a paramedic lifted a piece of plywood and there was a two-year-old under it.

At some point he developed compassion fatigue. Everything he saw was like a movie out there on a screen and nobody was real. The dead and injured were all actors, and after it was over, they'd wash the fake blood and makeup off, reattach the limbs and go home. The problem was that he took it home with him.

He signed up for handyman courses at the local college. He could, he figured, if nothing else, use his experience with Anna to manage an apartment block or two.

He might have gotten over his depression—the shrink said that it would gradually fade as he adjusted to his new condition and developed new goals—if Sally hadn't gotten a boyfriend. The doctor said Tom was fine physically, but after he got home from the hospital and was doing rehab, he had no desire; it was like his testosterone had been drained. Sally had said to him, "Kiss me," "Cuddle me," "Feel me up," "Fuck me," at various times. It was like she was talking about things beyond his understanding, as if she were in another room, behind an invisible glass wall.

The boyfriend was one of her patients. He came in for a cleaning and left with a date for lunch. He was a real estate agent, one of those sly bastards who lie and manipulate their way to a Beemer. He was married and had a high-end bungalow with a pool, a high school cutie who was aging, two kids and a need to conquer new territory. Tom hadn't told his kids that was why he didn't object when Sally said she wanted a trial separation. The real estate wife had called him and poured out her heart. She didn't want to give up her house, her swimming pool, the annual vacation. She'd serve her husband better meals, she said, so he didn't need to go eat in fast food joints, if Tom knew what she meant. More variety, spicier. She'd lose weight. She didn't like to talk directly about these things.

Before he moved out, he confronted Sally. She said, "What do you care? You don't want the goods anymore. For six months you haven't touched me."

He wasn't, he thought, providing good meals, no sexual grocery cart full of goodies, no mango, no papaya, no chili pepper.

It was easier to leave than to fight. He wasn't even certain what he would have fought about. It's not like it was a competition and the other guy had got the gold medal.

No more, he said to himself, *no more*. But now he needed company, needed to join in community events, needed to be connected so that he wasn't lost in the hallways in his head. So he went to the dance at the community hall. By now, he knew a few people by sight, knew them enough to say, "Hello, how are you?" Knew people that he'd done the odd, small job for, not that they included him in the small knots where they were discussing whatever it was that they were discussing. Outsider—he could feel it—not trusted, and he wondered if he'd been a retired teacher or an accountant or construction worker, instead of a used-to-be cop, if he'd have been welcomed, but he doubted it. He surveyed the hall that just three days before had held Angel's funeral reception, but now the tables and benches were along the walls so that the floor was clear for dancing. A portable stage had been pushed into one corner. On it, a group of men were tuning their instruments and a woman was testing out the keys on a piano. One key was dead. She tapped it a number of times, but all it returned was a *thunk*.

The dance ticket included a supper of pickerel fillets donated by some of the fishermen, potato salad and coleslaw made by the Good Neighbours. The profit was to go to sports equipment for the school.

Because all the seats were taken, he was eating standing up. Freyja had been circulating, going from group to group, saying a few words, listening, giving some of the women hugs, leaning in and whispering to them. He was nearly finished his meal when she came to stand beside him.

"Is your leg improved enough to dance?" she asked, and he took that as an invitation.

"Waltzes," he said. "I'm not sure I'd try polkas, or a kolomyika."

"Waltzes are good," she answered. "But polkas are fun. How do you know about kolomyika?"

"A friend's mom. Anna. She was our apartment manager. She taught her daughter and me how to do different dances. Ukrainian." He remembered those lessons, dancing with Anna as she showed him the steps, then practising with Tanya. Good memories of good times. He and Tanya had danced together at parties.

"I don't understand you. You see those guys hanging around the door? Every woman on her own who comes past them gets a proposition. 'Hey, babe, I've got a case of beer in the back of my truck. Wanna share it?' You, you're different. You don't stop to drink beer with them, shake hands, swap stories. You go straight to the food table."

"Pickerel fillets," he said. "Fresh out of the lake. Besides, I'm older than most of them."

"Tom the foodie. No interest in women. I'd believe you except that I've caught you watching me a couple of times. Except when you were loading up your plate."

"Pickerel fillets, fried potatoes and coleslaw are serious competition."

She didn't laugh, but a smile pulled at her lips. "You're going to have to run harder. There's lots of competition."

"I'm out of practice," he said, picking up the last piece of fried pickerel with his fingers and popping it into his mouth.

"You need to wash your hands before dancing with anyone. You'll get grease on her dress."

He turned and looked for a paper napkin to wipe his fingers. The pickerel was excellent, the potatoes crisp. There were homemade desserts on the table. He wasn't having to eat his own cooking. He was trying to focus on something other than Freyja.

"The best pie is Sessilja's. She picks the blueberries herself every summer. Those must be the last from her freezer."

Freyja was standing there, most of her weight on her right foot, her left hip slightly jutted out. She was wearing a skirt the colour of her eyes, a soft fabric that clung to her. Her blouse was covered in a pattern of pale green leaves, open at the throat, showing the top of her breasts.

He distracted himself by looking away, across the crowd. People were standing in small groups, talking. Others were sitting at the tables along the walls. It was the same crowd, or mostly the same crowd, who had come to Angel's funeral. He thought the funeral reception, having been in the same hall, might have weighed on people, but there was no evidence of grief. *Things happen*, he thought. The excited conversation was shot through with laughter.

He looked back at Freyja and felt for a moment that he understood how a fish felt when it took the hook. She was, he could see from her eyes, enjoying the effect she was having, laughing at him trying to throw the hook free. She was beautiful and she stirred feelings he hadn't had for a long time. Beautiful, beautiful, her red hair woven into an intricate braid, her slightly pursed mouth, as if she were suppressing a laugh, the laughing, teasing eyes like a lodestone.

It was time, he told himself, to go to the dessert table, load up on Nanaimo bars, apple pie, an Icelandic pancake or two. Keep his distance, ignore his loneliness, say to himself, *Not for me, not for me, not for the gimp, no more Sallys, no more complications*—he couldn't deal with the ones he had. He thought about his previous life, the one where he had a wife and two kids and a house in the suburbs and a job and he knew who he was. And he thought about putting his arms around Freyja and dancing away, feeling her warmth, smelling her perfume, having her attention all to himself.

The band had been tuning their instruments. In the background there
had been squawks and bits of tunes, but now they were ready and started with
a waltz.

"First dance gets the last dance," she said.

He turned around to put his plate down, picked up a napkin to wipe his
fingers—when Barnabas stepped between them, put his arms around Freyja
and danced away with her. Tom saw Sarah O'Hara watching. She was eating
chocolate cake. She shook her head and rolled her eyes.

It was just as well, he thought. He hadn't danced in a long time; he wasn't
sure that he remembered how—he and Sally had stopped dancing when the
kids came, only occasionally going onto the dance floor at banquets. When they
were courting, they had danced every weekend, rocking away the nights, dancing until they were exhausted and laughing at their own exuberance. When
they got to his apartment, they would throw themselves on the bed and make
love with the same energy with which they'd danced, then fall asleep until the
morning, when, half awake, they'd make love again, but this time slowly, with
little motion, as they held each other close.

He threw his paper plate into the garbage can at the end of the table,
picked up a dessert plate and helped himself to a slice of the blueberry pie that
Freyja had recommended. Barnabas seemed an unlikely dancer. His long beard
dripped from his chin and his electric blue suit flashed like a neon light as he
turned about the floor. The ends of his shoes were flat and went long past his
toes—either that or he had toes he could wrap around branches and hang
upside down. Tom hoped he didn't step on Freyja's feet. She had on open-toed
shoes with high heels. She'd be crippled for weeks.

"He who hesitates is lost," Sarah said from behind. "No quarter given in
this competition. Every man for himself."

"I was eyeing the dessert."

"You were gawking at her as if she was a Nanaimo bar. I kept waiting for
you to bite her."

"You warned me she was trouble. I was taking your advice seriously."

Sarah snorted in disbelief. "Do you want a drop in your coffee for consolation?" she asked, and when he nodded, she pulled a flask out of her dress, opened it and poured an ounce. "This is the best moose milk around. Made from the finest potatoes and raisins in the district."

The band began to play a polka just as Ben, Wanda and Derk came through the front door. Heads turned, and for a second, the music paused, but then the musicians played the polka harder, faster, louder, interspersing it with hollering. The crowd danced faster, joined in the hollering, their yelling and spinning around the floor an affirmation of life, or a refusal to acknowledge death.

As Ben passed through the crowd, people put their hand on his shoulder, said a word or two, patted his arm. A couple of women hugged him and a dozen men shook his hand. His daughter and grandson were barely recognized with brief nods before people turned away. Many just stared at them for a moment. A couple of men went to Wanda and said a word or two, gave her a brief hug. *Old boyfriends maybe*, Tom thought. Maybe guys she'd gone to school with.

The band played a set, then the violinist leaned into the mike and said, "Tonight, folks, we have a special treat. Our own Cindy Lou." The crowd clapped and whistled, the band struck up a tune and Karla White appeared from the left side of the stage, waved to the crowd and without any further introduction, began singing, "Hey, Good Lookin'." She was wearing a full Western outfit: white cowboy boots, a fringed skirt, an embroidered shirt and a Stetson.

Her voice was good, smoky, but her range wasn't great. Still, she was better than many he'd heard. As she belted out Western songs from the past, people shuffled onto the floor to dance. Karla couldn't resist wiggling her hips as she sang. She strutted about the stage, looking coyly over her shoulder at the dancers. He thought even ten years before she must have had the guys howling with desire. She would have been a knockout. Now, she was an attractive woman in a slightly too-tight outfit with a good voice that had lost a bit of its range with age, reliving her years when she still hoped to make it big in C&W and go to Nashville to perform at the Grand Ole Opry. Her and thousands more. Them and their guitars.

Like Angel, he thought, and his festive mood turned sour. That was what Angel wanted—the dream, having an audience, being discovered, being one of the best—her and the thousands of others, naive, innocent, not understanding that it would mean being deflowered on a couch in a bar owner's office, or agent's office, groped by the bar owners, giving a BJ for the chance of being on a good stage. He'd seen them, after their careers disappeared, those who had gotten hooked on drugs working the streets to pay the bills, working as waitresses where they had once held centre stage, living in shabby rooms. A few lucky ones, the ones that had married a customer with a decent job, became moms and gave music lessons in suburbia.

He looked for Freyja, but she was caught up in conversations. She was a popular dance partner. He'd watched her whirling around the dance floor first with one guy, then another. She danced a butterfly with two guys who deliberately swung her off her feet as they made their figure eights.

"Hi," Karla said. She looked good, like a woman ready for action, for dancing, for wrestling, for making love. Her dancing and singing had made her vibrant.

"You were great," he said, and he meant it. Onstage she was a star; she dominated it, dominated her audience, was absolutely confident. She was happy with her performance, and she smiled broadly and reached out to briefly touch people who complimented her as they went by. "Grand Ole Opry was never better."

She put her arms around him to thank him and kissed him on the cheek. She was going to say something, but a guy with a beard and his cap on backwards grabbed her and hauled her onto the dance floor. Tom looked around. Horst was sitting at one of the tables with his oxygen tank. His eyes followed Karla around the room.

Tom was going to go to the washroom when one of the locals came up and put out his hand. Tom shook it. The man standing across from him was an inch shorter than Tom, with blond hair nearly to his shoulders, wearing a T-shirt that showed off his muscles. Handsome in a rugged way. Strong cheekbones and jaw. He'd had his nose broken at some point and it hadn't been set properly, so it veered slightly to the right.

"I'm Siggi Eyolfson. You're new here. You the guy who bought Jessie's place?" Tom admitted it. "Lot of work fixing it up, but you know that. It's good to see that it's going to be fixed. Welcome to Valhalla. You just going to use it for a cottage?"

"Permanent," Tom replied. "I'm a handyman, jack of all trades. I've got a poster on the board outside. Carpentry, plumbing, plaster work, drywall—that sort of thing."

"Just what we need," Siggi said. "Good luck with the business." Then he stepped sideways, shook the hand of the guy standing beside Tom and talked intensely to him, though he didn't say anything that required intensity. Tom had met people like that before. When they spoke to you, no one else existed. When they left, you didn't exist. People with that ability had usually taken courses on how to be successful. They belonged to clubs where they could hand out business cards and make deals. It was totally insincere, but people loved it, loved that moment of being the complete centre of someone's attention.

To get to the washroom he had to open a door below the right side of the stage, go down a narrow stairwell and make a tight turn. There were two urinals, both empty. He was unzipping his pants when Derk came in. He staggered slightly, caught his balance.

Derk went to the other urinal. "You think I'm shit, don't you," he said angrily. It wasn't a question, rather a statement, and the left top corner of his lip lifted a bit in the beginning of a sneer. "You think you're so shit hot, Mr. Retired Mountie, got a pension."

His body was lean, nearly anorexic, catlike, and in a black shirt and pants he reminded Tom of a black feral cat that had started coming to their patio door, its eyes wary, its body ready to leap away or to attack. They'd put food out for it, scraps that it gobbled down quickly before disappearing into the bushes. They had fed it for six months, but it had never let them get close enough to pet it, backing away as Tom approached, even when he had a bit of bacon in his hand or a piece of hamburger. He'd been transferred and the morning they left, they put out a heaping dish of leftovers from the fridge.

"Watch where you're pissing," Tom said.

Derk looked down. He had turned toward Tom and he was missing the urinal.

Derk gave a short, sharp laugh. "Mr. Mountie, Mr. Mountie," he said as if the words might be the beginning of a song. Tom finished and went to the sink. From Derk's tone of voice, high, like a child's, Tom realized, to his surprise, that Derk was on the verge of tears. Tears of rage. If they came, they'd come with smashing furniture, getting into a fight. That, or he'd attack himself, smash himself into things.

"You think I'm shit? You ever have to Dumpster dive because there's no food? You have to shoplift because there's no food, nothing to wear to school?

You ever slept in a Dumpster because your mother's got two drunken friends banging her in the bedroom and they don't want a kid around? You ever had a mother who needs booze so bad she'll fuck for a six-pack?" He stopped and his chest heaved. He started shaking. "All my sister wanted was a good guitar. You hear me, Mr. Copper?"

"Yes," Tom said just above a whisper. "I hear you." Tom realized that when Karla had kissed him on the cheek, her stage makeup had left a smudge of lipstick.

"What are you going to do about it, Mr. Mountie? What're you going to do?"

Tom wet a paper towel and scrubbed at his face. He threw the towel into the garbage can and turned around. "I'm not a Mountie anymore. I'm done. I came here to fish, to mind my own business. I used to be a cop. Past tense."

"You'll fit right in," Derk accused him. "All the losers in this place. But you're all we've got. People like us, we don't count for nothing. Nobody gives a shit about people like us."

Tom wanted to be reassuring, but he'd quit lying, quit making excuses for the system. He knew it was true. He'd seen it all his career. The kowtowing to the rich and powerful, the beating up of the poor and weak. "Yes sir, no sir, I'll kiss your ass, sir,"—when the houses were expensive enough, when the people were connected enough. And then, when it was somebody from one of those neighbourhoods where there was trash in the yard, where the houses weren't kept up because they were rentals and the developers were letting them go to ruin so they could get the city or town to agree to have them torn down, it was "You stupid son of a bitch. Take that." And a boot to the face or a flashlight to the head.

"It's okay," Derk said bitterly. "I'll take care of it. That's always the way, isn't it? People like us, we've got to take care of business ourselves, because that's not what the law is for, is it? It's for keeping shit like us away from people like them." His voice was bitter as black bile.

"You don't know the half of it," Tom said.

Derk wasn't used to anyone agreeing with him, telling him he was right. He put his left hand against the wall to steady himself and stared at Tom. He let out his breath in a whistle, then said, "I'm not using. I just had a few drinks."

"What are you selling?"

"What do you want? I'll find it for you."

"I'll stick to whisky."

Derk laughed, and his laugh was sharp, bitter, high pitched, as if what Tom had said was hurtful but funny, so there was pain and laughter mixed. He rushed out. The music from above pounded, and the dancer's feet sounded like thunder. Tom followed Derk upstairs into the swirling colour and the noise. There was, to Tom, a sense of desperation, of denial, as if the motion and sound could shut out the sorrow and disappointment of daily life. There was a side door that was open to let in some air. He slipped out past a group of smokers and walked home.

He couldn't sleep, so he sat at the dining room table, shuffled Jessie's worn deck of cards and dealt himself a new hand. He kept thinking about Ben saying he didn't get to deliver the good stuff anymore, and Frenchie being so paranoid, and the water dripping from the corner of Frenchie's truck.

Who knew what was going on? Small-town secrets. Small-town conflicts. Small-town jealousies. He'd seen these at work many times. They were usually small insignificant things, but the resentments tore at the people involved, wouldn't leave them alone. Crazy things. A single man shooting a neighbour's wife and child while her husband was away. The shooter admitted what he'd done and justified it by saying that the neighbour's wife wore shorts, so she was a Jezebel leading the shooter into sinful thoughts. He placed all the blame on her. Tom learned to look not for the logical but for the illogical, to ferret out craziness and how it worked.

Ben and Frenchie. Frenchie and Ben. Loose threads. He'd learned to look for loose threads no matter how unlikely. Local secrets. Water where it shouldn't have been. He slipped his pry bar into his pocket and went out. "Roll out the Barrel" was playing at the dance.

There were clouds drifting over the moon. The fish shed was dark, and there were no lights close to it. The back door of the truck wasn't padlocked. He eased the doors open, then felt along the floor until he found a seam. He slipped his pry bar between the two sections and lifted up half the floor. He used his pen flashlight to look. The space was empty, but it was wet and smelled of fish. He eased the section of floor back into place.

The next morning he was replacing siding on the veranda when he heard someone behind him. He glanced back. Freyja was standing there, watching him speculatively.

"You went home early," she said.

"Hard to dance with a bum leg."

"After you pulled me out of the snowbank, I said I'd buy you a drink. It's a hot day. How better could a man spend it than sitting under an umbrella, looking at the view, sharing a cold drink with an attractive woman?"

He put down his hammer. "Okay," he said, "but there'll be gossip."

"There's gossip already. Don't you think people saw me walk over here?"

He looked at her, in capris and a blouse, with flip-flops, her hair done in a long ponytail to get it off the back of her neck in the heat. She might, from a distance, have been fifteen, like Angel.

They walked to the café without saying anything. She had freckles, not many, but a spray of them across her nose, onto her cheeks. A piece of hair had come loose. She took off her cap, undid the elastic band, shook out her hair, gathered it up, put it back into a ponytail.

"You burn easily," he said.

"That's why I'm wearing this hat." It was a washed-out brown, paler than her freckles. She turned so her back was to him. She undid the metal snap at the back at the bottom of a hole where her hair would fit through. She put the cap back on and said, "Fit my hair through the slot and click the snap. It's hard to do myself."

He hesitated because he had not touched her yet, and as innocent as it was, he felt that a divide was being crossed. He felt the silkiness of her hair, saw how its redness shone with light and saw the vulnerable curve of her neck. The weight of her hair made him pause; then he took the two ends of the narrow strap and clipped them together.

The sun filled up the sky, shining so intensely that it made the umbrella nearly transparent, but the shade, as little as it was, was a relief—beyond the shade, the sun burned like a fire that was too close. The boats in the harbour were still, and no one was moving about. Tarps had been set up on the dock, foamies thrown under them, and people slept or read lying down or sitting in lawn chairs.

They ordered Coke floats and then fell into an uncertain silence. *Is this a date?* he wondered, and felt a momentary rush of his adolescent insecurity.

Freyja turned back toward him and studied his face as if looking for something hidden. Quietly, she said, "You haven't been here long. There are storms in Valhalla. We get snowed in. Sometimes for a week or more. Few people come here in winter. We forgive each other our trespasses for good conversation. Unless you think slasher movies are art and debates about trucks and how getting stuck and unstuck and how shooting or not shooting a moose are intellectual conversation, you'll need some of us and some of us will need you."

He remembered what the town had been like when he'd come the winter before. Buried in snow. Picture perfect but silent, without anyone outdoors, only a rabbit and a chickadee. And Pearl. He remembered Pearl scuttling away through the drifts. "What do you do in the winter?" he asked, thinking of the long silence to come.

"When I'm not teaching? In the evenings and on weekends?"

Her voice had an edge to it. He was, he thought, on dangerous ground, the kind of ground where a misstep could make someone an enemy instead of a friend.

"I read a lot. DVDs. I used to watch Siggi's big TV. Not anymore. Ben said you had boxes of books. Maybe you could lend me a book. Maybe we could discuss it. Would that be all right? Or would that be too risky?"

He was admiring the way her cheek turned under her eye and her pale lashes. "That would be fine. What do you like to read?"

"Hospital romances," she answered sarcastically, and her jaw was tight. When he didn't rise to the bait, she added, "Novels. Poetry. Short stories. A bit of drama even. How about you?"

"Mostly non-fiction. Essays. Biographies. History."

She rolled her eyes. "You probably eat porridge every morning. Oatmeal every day." She obviously had a bone to pick, and he wondered what it was. Him, or her ex, or men in general?

"Sally—" he stopped, surprised that he'd said her name. He was going to say that Sally thought he should read more popular fiction. "My mother liked fiction, drama, poetry. My father loved history and biographies."

She ignored his comment about his father. "Sally," she said. "Who is this Sally? Have I got competition?"

"My ex," he replied, not certain what to say, because it seemed the moment something was said, the entire village knew about it. "She's not quite my ex. There's a two-year waiting period for mutual consent divorces."

"We're both waiting for the judge to say you're free. How long were you married?"

"Twenty-one years. You?"

"Nine months. Siggi Eyolfson. You shook hands with him at the dance. You'll see him around. Sometimes he brings his pet bear Bruno in the back of his truck. Is your wife contesting the divorce?"

"No. She already had a boyfriend waiting to move in." He didn't want to talk about it, so he tried to distract her by talking about the dance. "Did your boyfriend in the blue suit get the last dance? Did he walk you home?" He meant for it to be playful, but as he said it, he could feel his anger surfacing. There had been the edge of an accusation in his voice.

"When you get angry, breathe deeply," his shrink had said and given him a large pillow to punch. "Don't direct anger at those that don't deserve it." Once, he'd smashed a teapot on the floor, and in a rage when he and Sally had a fight over money, he'd punched a hole in the rec room wall. He'd repaired it, but Sally had said, "I'm afraid of you," and the shrink, the next time he saw him, said, "Better the wall than your wife." Once he was on his own, the anger became less intense. He didn't have Sally sneering at him. He didn't blame her. She'd had hopes of his rising through the ranks, giving her bragging rights with her family. One of her sisters was married to a dentist. The other to a stockbroker. He'd failed her in a lot of ways.

"You heard Barnabas at Angel's reception. He has the road grading and snowplowing contracts. He works full time. He kissed me when we were in grade one. Are you jealous?"

He was, but he couldn't admit it. Not because Barnabas had kissed her in grade one but because of the ease with which he danced away with her.

"Nine months isn't very long to be married," he said.

"I was married for a shorter time than that when I was sixteen," she said. "Six months."

"Impetuous?" he asked.

"Maybe," she answered. "But your hanging around for twenty-one years didn't work either."

"We have kids. We tried to keep it together for the kids."

"I've heard that before," she said. "People haven't got the guts to leave."

"Do you have kids?"

"No. Just a miscarriage. Three months after I got married the first time."

"Your husband," he corrected himself. "The latest. You said he's still around?"

"Siggi. He's got a business here."

"The blond guy with the broken nose?"

"That's him," she said. "He usually introduces himself to everyone he sees. He's got a filing cabinet in his head. He never forgets a face."

He expected her to elaborate and when she didn't, he asked, "What business?"

"The greenhouse business." She said it quickly, as if it had been rehearsed, but she ran her tongue over her lips. It was a habit he'd often seen when he was questioning someone and they were lying.

"Greenhouse," he said, genuinely surprised. "Up here?"

"The government gave a lot of people grants to have greenhouses and grow fresh food. A lot of people's diets aren't very good. You'll see greenhouses in some people's yards. Most people did it just to get the grant. He made a business out of it."

He wasn't surprised that people's diets were bad. He'd seen the limp vegetables at the emporium. However, she wasn't telling him the truth. He wondered what it was about her husband's business that she didn't want to talk about. But he wasn't going to push her. It wasn't any of his business.

"You were a cop," she said.

"RCMP," and he didn't wait for her next question. "I was in a car accident. Made a mess of my leg. Some people think it made a mess of my head."

"Are you taking some time off?"

He shook his head. "I'm done. Retired. Disability. Mindi Miner says that people will be envious of me."

"She left you before or after your accident?"

"After," he said. "Did your first husband leave you before or after your miscarriage?"

"I left him."

He thought she was beautiful, but he wasn't sure what to make of her. If they kept talking, he'd find out what she didn't want to tell him. Secrets, there were always secrets, stored in containers like Russian dolls, the easy ones in the first doll, harder ones in the next doll, all the way back to the smallest doll that held the darkest, most painful secrets.

"Barnabas," she said, smiling at him, "is light on his feet. He doesn't look like it, but he is."

"He has two good legs," he said.

"Before your accident, were you light on your feet?"

"I don't know. I didn't step on my wife's toes. We took ballroom dance lessons."

"You should have stayed and danced. The ladies would have appreciated it. People will think you're shy. Are you shy? Do women make you blush easily?"

"Yes," he said and shifted uncomfortably.

"Shy," she said as if she could not believe it. "A shy man in Valhalla."

"Are there no other shy men?"

"Albert Scutter. But he doesn't blush. He stutters. I'll have to think of ways to make you blush."

He knew she was teasing him, but he didn't know how to respond. Sally never teased; his mother never teased. They were very different, but in that way they were the same: direct. He searched for the words, all denotation and no connotation. A cigar was just a cigar. He thought Freyja might have liked him to have teased back, but he wasn't sure how.

"Thanks for shovelling out my car. It would have been a cold walk back to Valhalla." She put the money down for the sodas.

When she had gone, he thought she was a tease, but there was nothing mean about it. He wasn't sure what to think. After he left Sally, he made up his mind never to have another relationship. He thought it would be easy. He hadn't counted on the loneliness, not having someone to talk to about the day. Not that he wasn't lonely when he was married. He wished that Sally had done crossword puzzles with him, played chess, bridge, even whist. He had enough macho stuff at work. When he got home, he needed quiet, a chance to do something that required his complete attention. She wanted to spend her time going to sports bars, having a drink or two or three. She wanted the kids in hockey, soccer, baseball, even tried to get Joel to play lacrosse. He wasn't interested. He referred to lacrosse players as "louts." Myrna got penalties for cross-checking.

As he sat there sipping his soda through a straw, he wondered if Freyja did crossword puzzles, then thought that wasn't something he could ask. What kind of a nerd wanted to know if a woman did crossword puzzles?

He finished his soda, then went home, back to pulling nails out of the boards in the living room.

CHAPTER 20

UNFINISHED BUSINESS

Two days later, as he was cleaning out rotten wood, Sarah drove up in her Ford. When she climbed down from the truck, Tom saw that instead of wearing coveralls and a man's shirt, she was dressed in black slacks and a pink frilly blouse. Her clothes made him feel that she was going to a foreign and dangerous place and was ill prepared.

"Going travelling?" he asked.

"I am. The big city. You need anything?"

"Shopping trip?"

"Anders needs a couple of teeth pulled. I'm taking him in. He'll have two teeth out tomorrow morning, then I'll bring him back."

It was an unsettled day. Clouds seemed to form and disappear so there was no telling what the weather would be like. Now Sarah looked like a stranger. If he'd seen her on a city street, he wouldn't have been sure he should say hello. She'd curled her hair so it turned in at the edges. In her normal Valhalla clothes, in spite of her diamond willow cane, she seemed ageless, solid, like her house, made of sturdy beams, but now, wearing black shoes with raised heels, she seemed old and vulnerable.

He went inside, quickly made out a list of things he could think of on the spur of the moment, made out a cheque for two hundred dollars and gave it to her.

"Ten per cent," she informed him. "If the bill comes to two hundred, you owe me twenty."

"Fair enough," he said. "You got lots of orders?" He looked into the cab and saw Anders, a narrow-faced man with a shock of brown hair holding his hand against his jaw.

"Longer than my arm. Ten per cent will pay the gas, and Anders has a sister in town. We can stay there. I'll shop tonight and tomorrow while he's being worked on." She leaned toward him. "It's Friday. Those yahoos from the embassy may turn up tonight. They get drunk, make a lot of noise. They're always looking for trouble. There's a couple of them are bad actors."

"Embassy?" he said.

"Siggi's fortress along the lakeshore road."

"Siggi," he immediately repeated. "Freyja's ex?"

"Him and his Freemen on the Land buddies. They've declared his place an embassy. You must have come across these kind of guys. They declare a place an embassy, and then no one has any right to come on their property. They believe they don't have to pay taxes."

"Edmonton," he said, a memory jumping out at him. "The guy painted the inside of the house black. Took out walls. The owner never got a penny rent. Crazy as hell."

"These guys at Siggi's are all about not paying taxes."

"Have I seen them?"

"Maybe at the dance. They were hanging around the door, drinking. They're not into dancing."

When she mentioned it, he vaguely remembered three or four guys at the door—work boots, most of the time talking to each other, raising a bottle, and razzing women and teenage girls going in and out of the hall. They weren't wearing colours, so he hadn't paid much attention to them. They'd seemed noisy but harmless enough.

"Watch out for Siggi. He's very aggressive when he drinks. He hangs around with Jason. Alan and Rudy are often with them. They go looking for trouble. Most men go to a dance to dance. Their idea of a good time is to get into a fight."

"Freyja's mentioned Siggi. He doesn't seem to be her favourite person."

"Hot romance turned cold. She likes to think of herself as a sensitive intellectual. Wordsworth and Yeats. I think she secretly writes poetry. He's into *The Texas Chain Saw Massacre*. When he was hot after her, he even got his hair cut and bought a sports jacket. He's very jealous. He beat up a couple of guys just for flirting with her."

"Do I need your thirty-thirty?" he said, half joking.

"I don't think so, but if you do, it's just inside the door. There are bullets in the cutlery drawer."

"They're supposed to be locked up."

"So report me. A bear walks through town like last year and I'm not going to unlock my rifle, unlock my shells, and by the time I make it out the door, it's grabbed a kid off a swing or out of the sandbox or ripped open a screen door to get at the bacon it can smell inside. City rules for city people. I'm just being prepared. In season, moose have been known to stroll through town." With that, she climbed back into her truck. She read his list. "This'll come to more than two hundred dollars. Payment on delivery. No returns."

"Don't spend more than two hundred," he said. "Just leave stuff out."

That afternoon, Freyja stopped by. "You get those walls insulated and this place will be snug. I see you've got the screens up."

"They were under the porch."

"Ben always put her storm windows on in the fall, took them down in the spring, put on the screens." She lifted her hair up and held it against the back of her head and fanned her neck with her other hand. "If I invited you for supper, would you come?"

"Something cold?"

"Ice cubes à la sliced ham, ice cubes à la potato salad, that sort of menu."

He said yes and she said seven thirty, and he thought that was great because he'd have time to do more work, have a swim and get cleaned up without rushing. He'd polish his good shoes and iron a short-sleeved shirt. He could find a pair of decent trousers in one of the boxes stacked in the guest bedroom.

He wondered, though, if he were any better than the locals. When he and Freyja were talking he'd been thinking about putting his hand on her ass. Wanted to. But wanting always brought trouble; better to not want anything. If she were agreeable and he did put his hand on her ass, felt her breasts, kissed her, if they made love, then what? It wasn't like he was a sports fisherman who was staying for a few days and going to have a quickie affair then leave.

Everything would change, there'd be expectations, the community would observe, gossip, judge. Did he want to date? Whatever that meant in a place like Valhalla. Did he want her to move in with him? Did he want another kid? And he saw it all turning inward the way it had with Sally: the conversations turned to brittle silences, the promises to resentment. The divorce rate was around 50 per cent, second marriage split-ups over 70 per cent. *Think*, he heard his father's voice say. *Think of the consequences before you do anything. Use your imagination. The world is full of fools who do things and never think about the outcome.*

He took the want that had surged up, folded and refolded it like a piece of delicate origami, and put it away deep in his chest where it would stay hidden.

Freyja's house surprised him. He had noticed it but thought it must be owned by one of the yacht people. It had a blue-shingled roof. There was a three-car garage with white doors, but the driveway wasn't finished. The wooden forms for the cement were in place. They looked like they'd been there for quite a while.

The front steps were concrete, and on either side there were concrete planters with pansies among yellowish-green shrubs. The sidewalk, like the garage driveway, was laid out, but the concrete hadn't been poured there either. Even though it wasn't finished, it looked out of place among yards littered with garbage, boats and old cars. Most of the houses were small and many had jerry-built additions of one sort or other, obviously added on as the need arose. A few were more decorated than others, with bits of brick or wrought iron, but that just made the houses look ridiculous, as if bits and pieces of other buildings from more hospitable climates had been stolen and transported and attached willy-nilly to houses that should have been made of nothing but wood.

It would have helped the look of the village if it been had laid out as a grid. It was obvious that houses had been thrown up wherever it was convenient at the time, so there was no road that did not cross another road, frequently more than once. The ditches were shallow, narrow, and local people never called them ditches but cuts, meant simply to carry storm water to the large ditches that ran along both sides of the main road.

Tom admired the fill that had been brought in to raise the house up out of the boggy land.

He went around to the back, climbed the steps and knocked on the door.

"Come in. I'm busy," Freyja called.

Freyja was working at the kitchen counter. There was a table with a white cloth and three settings. The lock on the screen door wouldn't, he thought, keep out anyone but the most honest of men, certainly not any intent on intimidation or rape, or fuelled by jealous rage. However, in the closet next to the door, there was a twenty-two rifle propped up, partially hidden by coats and jackets. The butt was resting on a sandal.

"Nice house. Did you win the lottery?" he asked.

"Don't I wish," Freyja replied.

She suggested he take a look around, so he explored the rest of the house. The living room had a leather couch and chair, and the dining room had a table and six chairs, but the trim wasn't done and the living room only had subflooring. He went down the hallway. The doors to the three bedrooms were open. The first, obviously Freyja's, was complete with ivory drapes, a British India rug over a maple floor and a king-sized bed with a patterned ivory-and-green bedspread and what seemed like an excess of pillows. From what he could see there was an ensuite and a walk-in closet. The second bedroom had a futon on the floor, and the third bedroom had a desk and a chair and a filing cabinet. Neither room was finished.

"A work in progress," he said when he came back into the kitchen.

"You might say that," Freyja replied. She was putting food onto the table.

Freyja offered him a glass of wine, and when he said no, she poured him iced tea.

He thought with satisfaction, *She is not a knick-knack queen.* There were carvings of a bear and a wolf on a window ledge. They looked like Albert Scutter's work. He was relieved that there were no plaques with hokey religious sayings or pictures of Jesus's head surrounded by a crown of thorns. He mistrusted plaques. His parents had none, but Anna had her walls covered with them. Most of her plaques had pictures of the suffering Jesus. Others said things like "Home is where the heart is."

He sat astride a kitchen chair. The table was set for three.

"You need two watchdogs?" he asked.

Freyja was taking a plate of sliced ham out of the fridge. "I've asked Ben over. I owe him a favour or two."

"Sarah says Siggi and friends might be coming to town tonight."

"Yes," she said, putting potato salad on the table. Her voice was cautious. "If they're drunk and ugly, they'll just push him out of the way. They've known him too long."

"Guys on a drunk. Looking for action. Angry, aggressive. Sometimes these guys were bad dates. They didn't want to pay the rates they agreed on. It was easier to get a bad date to pay up and include a good tip than have to spend all day filling out forms and appearing in court."

She stopped, turned and stared at him. "Is this the guy who's too shy to ask me to dance?"

He shifted uncomfortably. "There's business, and then there's personal. They were business. You're personal."

"You're blushing," she said. "You really do blush. I haven't seen a guy who blushes in years."

"I blushed so much in school it was like I had permanent sunburn."

He got up and took the twenty-two out of the closet. He pushed the bolt up and pulled it back. The chamber was empty. "You're making sure you're ready if a bear walks through here?"

"Could be. Or a moose. Last winter a moose walked through town. John Anders got him. One shot. He kept a quarter, gave the rest away. Fed a lot of people. Quite a few of us owe him a favour. He provides meat for Dolly."

He put the rifle back. "No one wants to miss an opportunity like that, that's for sure. Don't have to spend all day cold and wet in the bush, then cutting it up and hauling the parts all the way back to wherever your vehicle is parked. Killing them is the easy part. Hauling is the hard part." In one corner of the kitchen there was a large white freezer. "If a moose came by, you could just ask it to climb into your freezer. Save you the trouble of killing it, cutting it up, packaging it."

"Do you hunt?"

"I'm a city boy, but I went with the guys for deer or a moose. We also hunted geese. I did fine. They teach us how to shoot when we're being trained."

"Rats are like that. Always around. Even here. Local lore is they came on the freight boats. Got off and stayed. That's why there's so many cats. That's why I've got Ramses." She said it as a large black-and-white cat wandered into the room, sniffed at Tom disapprovingly, then went over to Freyja and rubbed against her leg.

"Ramses is my first love. About three years ago, he appeared at my back door one day and cried to come in. He was so small. He must have been recently born. I asked around. Nobody claimed him. I rescued him and he rescued me." Ramses got up on a chair and stared at the ham. She picked up a piece and put it in his dish on the floor. "He sleeps on my bed." She paused, then added, "Are you allergic to cats?"

"I take antihistamines," he said, and he wondered if she meant allergic now, in the kitchen, or allergic in her bed. He went to look at a barometer on the wall. It had an oak case and was made of brass.

"My father's," she said. "He was a lake captain. He left it to me."

"How's Ben?"

"Nothing's working for him. He'll quit drinking when his family goes back to the city."

"You like him?"

"He was always good to me when I was growing up. Took me with him in the truck. Out on his boat."

He turned to her, surprised. "You grew up here?"

"Yes. And I came back. Does that surprise you?"

"Yes. Why?"

"Lots of reasons. Aren't there times when you want to go back to where you came from?"

"No." It sounded sharper than he had meant it to. The question had brought back the hallways with their stale smell of cooking, the rows of closed doors, the strangers who came and went, often sullen, resentful, sometimes dangerous, and the warnings of his mother to never accept an invitation into anyone's apartment no matter what they offered him. It was an apartment block where a lot of cabbage was cooked, and he felt slightly ill remembering the smell. "No, there's nothing there, nothing personal. Just an apartment someone else is living in. You don't make friends in the city like you do in a small town. Strangers come and go."

"You must have been lonely." She went to the window and when she saw no sign of Ben, she put wire mesh baskets over the food to keep flies and wasps off, then went to look for him. When she came back, she said, "He'll come later."

She took off her apron, spread her fingers and ran her hands through her hair, pulling it back over her shoulders, and he wanted, for a moment, to lean

toward her and do the same. She got a bottle of white wine out of the fridge.
"An expensive habit," he said.

"Not much. We get the labels made. Make the wine. There's six of us brew
up a batch. We use nothing but the best ingredients. Rhubarb. Wild raspberries.
Chokecherries. Blueberries. This is dandelion. Crisp, dry, tastes of apples and
leather," she said, mocking herself. "I'm not into it, but a few people run a small
still and make vodka from potatoes. Are you shocked?"

"Not much," he replied, imitating her tone. "As long as no one is cooking
up meth."

"Funny, isn't it?" she said. "How what was serious law-breaking at one
time becomes accepted, and then made legal. We're not there yet with distilling,
but if the government could figure out a way to tax homebrew, they'd okay it.
Like gambling. Used to be a big crime, but now the government promotes it."

"I guess," he said.

"Crime is mostly what we don't approve of. If we approve of something,
even if it's illegal, we ignore it," she said.

"Why ask me over?" he asked. "You don't sound like you're a champion
of the law."

"Why not? Who else? You're an unknown quantity. You'll be tested, and
then people will know who and what you are. It's always that way. Strangers
come. Things happen. People draw conclusions. Brave. Cowardly. Smart. Dumb.
Honest. Dishonest. Gradually, gradually the community builds a profile, an
image. They see if you keep your promises, see how careful you are about your
work, see how you take care of your belongings and your family. That's who
you are. They see the work you're doing on your house. You've already done a
few small jobs for people. Everyone knows how well you've done them. How
reliable you are. That'll be who you become."

"But I'm watching them also," he said a bit defensively. "I'm making judg-
ments about them as individuals and as a community."

"Yes, and you've got to decide where you fit in, if you fit in, whether you'll
stay or leave. You've run away once."

He said nothing for a while. Now he didn't like where the conversation
was going, now the tension was in his hands, in the muscles that had tightened in his stomach. Carefully, he said, "I never ran away." But he knew that
wasn't the way others saw it. PTSD, shell shock, compassion fatigue—no one

wanted to admit they existed. He wondered if he tried to tell her, if she would understand. At first there's the shock and the horror, the shattered bodies, the crying, screaming family and friends, and your heart goes out to them, but after a while, you've seen it before, many times, and you don't have any compassion left. You forget how to care.

"From your job. From your wife. From your kids."

"Should I ask for my job back? A gimpy cop? Should I ask my ex," his voice rose as he emphasized the ex, "to leave her boyfriend? Make that sacrifice for me?"

For a second, anger rushed into his head, black, dark anger, anger that he'd bottled up for a long time, anger that could burst out like infection from a wound, and he nearly said, "It's no wonder that Siggi kicked you in the head," but instead, he stood up and filled his glass with cold tea. There were things that never should be said, never could be forgiven—he'd learned that—things he'd said to Sally because she hadn't been in the car with him and didn't understand. There were wounds that never healed. It wasn't, he told himself as he stared to one side of Freyja, her fault; no one had driven the car but him, no one was depressed but him, no one had moved out but him.

In the small world exposed by the window, there were children playing on the swings, then jumping off and chasing each other up the slide, then squealing as they slid down. Why, he wondered, couldn't we stay like that? Happy with small things, being playmates. But, of course, that meant that there had to be adults in the background, out of sight, cooking and cleaning and earning a living, watching for bears.

"Maybe," he said, still refusing to look at her, "maybe there are things worth being sorry about. A career, an identity, an income, a marriage, a family, a future."

"It happens all the time," she said. "Football players who pop a knee, baseball players who throw out a shoulder. Gymnasts are done before they're twenty. Siggi was the town hockey hero. He was going to the NHL. He got picked to try out for the farm team in Winnipeg. He didn't make it."

"You should have been a shrink," he said, resenting the truth of what she said. "I feel like I want to have a tantrum. I want to scream and yell and smash things. I want to be unreasonable. That was never allowed. No one ever raised their voice."

"Is that so bad?"

"Yes," he said. "We're not robots. We're not machines playing chess. We have feelings. We need to be unreasonable so we can be reasonable." His chest felt as if it were being squeezed in a giant bear hug. It was like he wouldn't be able to take another breath. He put his hands on the table and pressed down. He took a deep breath and sat back. "My father said reason would always prevail. If you could just explain consequences to people, they would stop doing self-destructive, foolish things. He thought people should run their lives like a chess game."

"Why don't you chop wood for me? When I've been upset, I've chopped wood. It helps."

"What does it mean if you chop a woman's wood in Valhalla?"

"It means that you're trying to work your way into her bed by doing her favours." She pulled her chair back from the table and the corner of her mouth twitched a bit. He realized she was laughing at him again. His anger rose up again, but now it was confused—he understood that she wasn't mocking him, that she was gently teasing him, while at the same time telling him something about the town and its values. He'd asked the question and she'd answered it in a wry way that he didn't fully understand. His mother would have been disapproving of the question. Anna would have been more blunt.

"You're constantly worrying about what people might think about your being here, about your chopping wood. You're on the edge of a freak-out, but you know what? It's great. Because I know that I don't have to be afraid of you. I'm not afraid that you're going to treat me like a piece of furniture. That's another part of you falling into place."

He got up and barged out of the house, went over to the woodpile, found an axe and the chopping block, and began splitting wood. He sent the straight-grained pieces flying. The pieces that were twisted and knotted he attacked furiously, pounding them into submission, chipping off chunks that would do for kindling. He worked for half an hour. By the time he quit, his shirt was dark with sweat and stuck to his skin. He sank the axe into the chopping block and went back to the house.

Ben was sitting on the front steps with Freyja. He had his plate on his knees. "Did you know Wanda in the city?" he asked.

"No," Tom replied.

"You never seen Derk before? You could have with his business."

"I wasn't on the drug squad."

"You ever see Angel? Did you go visit schools?"

"No."

"She had plans," Ben said, and he couldn't say any more for a minute. "She was going to make something of herself. She was going to make her grandmother proud." He put his head in his hands, and they waited in silence, for it was obvious that he had something more to say. He looked up and wiped at his cheeks. "Maybe you could help us," he said. "I don't know what to do."

There was a pitcher of lemonade and ice and an extra glass. Freyja carefully filled a glass and handed it to Tom. He drank it all at once and took an ice cube into his mouth and cracked it with his teeth.

The chopping had flushed out Tom's anger. He didn't shout, but his voice was determined, insistent. "I found your granddaughter. She was lying on the ground. There wasn't anything I could do." He was still angry with the unreasonableness of everything, and his words came out short, chopped, like the wood.

Ben was looking older, his shoulders were rounder and he sat with them forward, as if he might, in an unguarded moment, topple over. His checked shirt looked like it needed to be washed.

"She was a good kid," Ben said defensively.

"And I'm a good man," Tom replied. "I'm not interested in little girls."

"She came here because her mother was drinking again. She gets crazy when she drinks. She says things she doesn't mean. She does things." Ben shook his head slowly. His eyes were focused on the ground. Tom wondered what he was seeing, what he was reviewing, if he was wondering how it all came to this, where it had started, where it would end.

Then, to Tom's surprise, Ben said strongly, as if he were making a public declaration, "We were good people. Betty never drank. I drank too much, but I quit. When you're young you do stupid things." He stopped and Tom could see the anguish, the self-accusation, and wondered if this was why he had started to drink again, an anesthetic that hadn't been needed when he and his wife were raising Angel and things were working, the past was laid to rest, the craziness was neutered, forgotten, a second chance to get things right. And then it went horribly wrong, and maybe he lay awake at night replaying everything, like a movie in a loop, in a perpetual motion machine—was this what I did wrong, was it this, this, this, was it this I neglected to do?—and wishing and wishing that he could go back and redo whatever it was that ended with his granddaughter lying face down in a water-filled rut.

"They haven't sent anyone to investigate. They must figure it was an accident."

Ben shook his head. "Nothing makes sense."

"When did she come back?"

"A week ago. She took a bus, then she hitchhiked. I told her don't hitchhike, but she hitchhiked."

"Something could have happened to her if she hitchhiked."

"No," Ben said. "She shut herself in her bedroom. I asked her if anything happened. She got good rides."

"Did she apply for a job at the emporium?"

"Maybe. I don't know. I've been really busy. Lots of jobs. She never played her music."

"Events," Tom said, "sometimes have nothing to do with us. It's just the way things work out."

They made a sad sort of trio. If they'd been playing music, it would have been doleful, filled with sadness, a cello and a violin and maybe an oboe. Gimpy Tom, abused Freyja, shattered Ben. Suddenly a painting by Picasso filled Tom's head, a painting from Picasso's cubist days, of people all broken into sharp cornered sections.

Freyja's back steps were concrete with metal rails on each side. The screen door was aluminum and didn't quite fit at the bottom. She had put a piece of weather stripping in the corner so the mosquitoes couldn't sneak in. The siding was white and the trim was blue like the roof. There was a blue-and-white dream catcher in one window. The beads sparkled in the sun.

Ben heaved himself up with the help of the banister and shambled away.

Freyja patted the cement where Ben had been sitting. Tom moved there, his shoulder touching hers.

"Ben just told me Angel was pregnant," Freyja said. "The autopsy confirmed it."

For a moment Tom's mind went blank, and then he asked, "How long?"

"Two months. Maybe she missed two periods."

"The father?"

"Ben doesn't know. He's in a state of shock."

"Boyfriend? Fifteen-year-olds have boyfriends. My GP told me that he's got twelve-year-olds coming in wanting birth control pills."

"She didn't have a boyfriend here. If she had a boyfriend around Valhalla, everyone would know."

"Where was she two months ago?"

"She's been living with her mother. I hear things, naturally, but I don't pry. Unless they're being home-schooled or taking correspondence, the kids from grade nine up go to school in the city. They come back when school ends in June. They're here July and August. There's a lot of wailing and gnashing of teeth when they have to go back to school at the beginning of September. Some refuse to go back. Some run away. Some can't wait to get back. Lots to do in the big city."

"Good things? Bad things?"

"Both. There's shopping and movies and dances and sports and, and, and... And there are parties in stairwells of parkades with lots of booze and drugs. Depends what you want, I guess. There's lots of choice in the big city."

"I know about the bad things. We kept getting reports about girls going missing." He remembered the alerts, the easy dismissal, everyone too busy taking care of more important complaints.

"One of our girls was hitchhiking home," Freyja said. "Got picked up by a father and a teenage son in a motorhome. Over a week, the father used her to teach his son about sex. She might have been a blow-up plastic doll. She was lucky—when they were returning to the US, they dropped her off with twenty dollars at a gas station. She didn't end up dead in a ditch."

"We're not very nice."

"We?"

"Men."

"Some are. Some aren't. Are you nice?"

"I try." It seemed impossible to continue the conversation, so he said, "You must have planted your garden early."

Freyja's garden was large. The soil was dark and the rows were tidily laid out; she'd used bits of lath to mark the ends of rows, and there were empty seed packets on the sticks. At the far end there were raspberry canes. "You've seen the vegetables and fruit at White's," she said.

As they sat there in the dwindling light, he told her about Anna's garden, about police work, funny things that had happened, the weird and wonderful people that turned up, a bearded man dressed in a nun's outfit certain that he'd heard a call from God, a woman who went to a store every day and stole a donut, a robber who wore a paper bag over his head with eyeholes, but the bag kept moving around, so he had to lift it up to see and was recognized.

Freyja was laughing at his goofy stories when a Dodge Ram on outsized wheels came racing down the lane and cut across the backyard. Its windows were down and men were leaning out, yelling and waving their arms. The emergency lights were flashing. Tom jumped up just as one of the passengers threw a partially full beer bottle at the house. The bottle shattered on the bottom step, and the truck turned wide and disappeared around the house. They listened to it race away.

"What the hell?" Tom said.

"Siggi and friends," Freyja said. "If they get wound up enough, they'll do crazy things. They wreck trucks regularly."

Freyja went into the house and came back with a cardboard soft drink box. Together, they picked up broken glass. When they had that done, they went to the backyard. The tires had made deep indentations through the corner rows of lettuce and onions.

"It's okay," Freyja said. "I'll water them in the morning. Most of them will come back up. It could have been worse."

"You shouldn't have to put up with this."

"What would you suggest I do? Call the RCMP? When there are problems here, we have to fix them ourselves."

"Will they come back?"

"I don't know. I don't think so. Not tonight, if that's what you mean."

"Are you afraid?"

"I try not to be. I tell myself that they'll go away one of these days. They don't usually have long attention spans. Siggi's father used to beat up his mother and he believes that's the way relationships are supposed to work."

"Domestic disputes?"

Her laugh was short and brittle, and she looked at him as if he were a stranger. "That's what your colleagues called it. A trip to the hospital, cracked ribs, fourteen stitches in my scalp. They didn't want to get involved. That man-and-woman thing."

"Here? In your house?"

"His house. It was his house. Even after we got married, I told him it was his house. I didn't want half of anything. I've taken care of myself all my life."

He reached over and pushed back her hair. He'd seen the beginning of a scar just past her hairline. The scar ran back for three inches. "I jerked out of the way. Otherwise it would have been my cheek and my eye. You and I could have had matching scars."

"Get a job somewhere else."

"No," she said, and the way she said it, he knew she had thought about it, over and over, and deep inside had decided to give no quarter. "I have friends here who look out for me. He'd find me and I'd have no friends to help me. It's not just about the house anymore. He says if a boyfriend moves in with me, into his house—" she paused, then said, "his house, he'll kill me."

"Let him have the house. No house is worth dying for."

"It wouldn't do any good, don't you see? In his eyes I belong to him. He owns me. Like the truck, the house, his hunting rifle, his dog, his beer. He owns me. I can move, but he'd find me, and I can't live like that, every day going to work, every day coming home, every night going to sleep. Here, everyone knows who did it if anything happens to me. He might figure that if I'm living among strangers, no one would know who killed me."

He realized that her hands were shaking. She took a deep breath and let it out through pursed lips. The light had faded and they were sitting in semi-darkness. Nearby there were frogs croaking. The air was soft, still warm from the day, but the oppressive heat had gone, and as they sat in silence, a slight breeze sprang up from the lake.

"Why didn't Ben come for supper earlier?"

"Johnny Armstrong was shooting his mouth off again, saying maybe you had something to do with Angel's death. You know what people are like. They haven't got much to do, so they gossip." The injustice of the accusation was like acid, and it found old pathways of guilt from all the implied but never spoken accusations of his father, who, even though he was not particularly religious, believed that everyone was born in sin.

She didn't say anything to absolve him of his guilt, so he got up. "I hope they don't come back," he said. "Your ex sounds like bad news. But you aren't going to make it better by having a murderer of a young girl hanging around your house at night."

"I didn't mean that," she said, but it was too late. If he stayed, he was afraid he would sweep everything on the table onto the floor, he would tip over the table; once his anger started, he lost control. He felt panic and wanted to get away before it took over. It wasn't directed at Freyja. It was a rage that burst out, like a volcano. The shrink had said, "When it happens, exhaust yourself, go to the gym, pump iron, walk, walk all night and all day if necessary. Let it exhaust itself. Don't go to bars looking for a fight. Eventually, it will wear itself out."

He went to the garage and let himself in. Ben had brought and piled up the last of Tom's belongings. There was a set of weights. In the dim light of the single bulb that hung down from the ceiling, he did reps until he was soaked in sweat, until he couldn't lift weights anymore. At this moment, he missed the city, missed the lanes and alleyways where he had sometimes walked all night, walked until the city street lamps turned off.

When he went into his house, he drank water from the tap until he couldn't hold any more, then had a shower. When he was drying himself off, mosquitoes were filling the bathroom and he wondered if he'd left a window open. The windows were all closed, but when he went into the porch and turned on the lamp, he saw that his screens had been slashed. *What a way for an evening to end*, he thought. *Son of a bitch, son of a bitch, son of a bitch.* Whoever had done it hadn't missed a single screen, and the mosquitoes had come out in full force the last few days, large grey mosquitoes and little black ones, the little black ones' bite sharp and painful, leaving itchy lumps. He remembered what Sarah had said about the local boys not liking competition and he wondered who thought he was competing for Freyja—or Karla. He remembered Mindi Miner's warning.

He found a roll of duct tape, taped up the screens, and then got undressed. Angry as he was, he couldn't just let his clothes lie on the table or the floor. He carefully hung everything up, folding his socks together. He spent an hour killing the little buggers as they landed on him looking for blood.

CHAPTER 21

A STORM

The next morning he was opening a package of cedar shingles when he saw Freyja coming from the direction of the dock. She was wearing a halter top, shorts and sandals, and a large straw hat with frayed ends. She was swinging a white plastic bag. Anyone watching her would have thought she didn't have a care in the world. She saw him and changed her path. "No vinarterta," she said. "I can't compete with Sarah." She held up the bag. "A fresh pickerel from Ingvar. He even cleaned and scaled it for me."

"There's more to life than dessert," Tom answered.

"Really?" she said. "I wouldn't expect to hear that from you." It was her usual teasing, but the sparkle wasn't in it. She added, more seriously, "You didn't need to go away angry last night."

"Sometimes, when I can't deal with things that stir up a lot of feelings, I have to leave. I'm better than I was, but I know when I need time out. When that happens, I haven't got time to go into a lengthy explanation. I came back here and lifted weights until I couldn't do it anymore."

"I don't think you had anything to do with Angel's death. Sarah doesn't. I don't think Mrs. White does either." She put the emphasis on the Mrs. "Ben still isn't sure. Her death makes no sense to him." She lifted her sunglasses onto her forehead and stood pensively, one foot flat on the ground, the other raised with just her toes pressed against the dirt. Usually, she exuded confidence, but now, waiting for him to reply, she seemed uncertain.

"There's a storm coming," he said, pointing to the sky. There was a thunder-head to the northeast. It rose up in a threatening peak, but the sun still blazed in a kind of fury, like an angry god, making it seem like nothing could interfere with the light that flooded everything, making it impossible to look upon the white limestones scattered about. It all seemed so far away from them, the thunderhead far to the north and sun so high above, that their lives could not be touched.

But Freyja, having experience of these things, studied the black, tumultu-ous clouds and said, "I'd better be on my way."

He would have taken that moment to apologize, that brief moment when she was going to turn and flee to the safety of her house, that moment between light and dark, to explain that he was sorry for being bad-tempered, that it was stress and heat and worry about his kids, and the injustice of being wrongly accused and his inexplicable past, but just then Ben swung his truck beside them. He turned off the motor and climbed down.

"I've got a load for you," he said. "There's drywall. We'd better get it under cover." And Tom, aware of the ritual of delivery and receipt, of unloading goods together, felt uncertain of what he should or should not do.

"In the house," Tom said. He was keeping nearly everything stacked in the living room. Away from the weather and from people who might see an item they could use and take it. Sarah had warned him of this, saying that no one would deliberately steal, but noticing a thing they needed, they might take it home for their own use and, if confronted, would be confused, would apologize profusely and offer to return it or replace it but would likely forget. She thought it was a habit left over from times when they were all related, all family, all in need. "Valhalla people are good people," Sarah had said, "but lock up things you don't want to go astray."

The three of them stood together in the brilliant sunlight as the thunder-head raced toward them. On the dock, a woman in a yellow bikini was hurriedly gathering up a foam mattress and an umbrella. On the boats tied to the finger docks, the owners were testing their moorings.

At the emporium, Karla and two waitresses were taking down the umbrel-las and stacking the chairs tight against the building.

They should have been moving the construction materials off the truck into the house, but there was unfinished business that couldn't be put off. It was evident in the way they were standing. They formed a slightly askew triangle, with Tom and Freyja facing each other, angled toward Ben, and Ben, though close, by himself, facing the two of them.

"Ben," Freyja said. She grabbed the sleeve of his shirt to make him stand and listen. Her voice was intense, low, not much more than an insistent whisper. "People gossip. You know that. They say terrible things. They've said terrible things about you. About me. About everybody. That doesn't make them true."

Ben shifted uncomfortably. He could have been a student once again, being made to stand and listen to a teacher lecture him, and his face pulled together as he waited for a reprimand. And Freyja, being a teacher, could not help but demand that he listen to reason, that he see what was before him, that he look at the evidence and agree with her.

"Ben," she continued insistently. "We've been friends a long time. If I thought that Tom had anything to do with Angel dying, do you think I'd invite him into my house?"

Ben had on a duck-billed baseball cap as a shield against the sun. He took it off and used his thumb to wipe the sweat off the inside. He put the cap back on. Instead of his usual work shirt, he was wearing a T-shirt that didn't reach his belt. A slash of his stomach showed.

"Derk says he's no friend of ours. You ever known the cops to do us any favours?" He had a stubborn look about him, the posture of a person who found it difficult, if not impossible, to change his mind.

"Mindi Miner used to work in the mine. He doesn't anymore. He's not a miner now. Tom used to be a Mountie. Not anymore. It was just his job."

"Going to storm," Ben said. The three of them turned to the north and the growing, rising thunderhead, masses of clouds behind it, clear blue sky in front. "You can smell it." As they watched, jagged lightning bolts drove down into the lake in the distance and sheet lightning flashed among the clouds.

They could hear the thunder rumbling in the distance. Nearby, the sun still held dominion, people shouted to each other on the dock, squealing children jumped into the lake. The day was bright, the sky pale blue, the water barely rippling. Day fishermen were coming into the harbour, though, their outboards shut off and the boats sliding silently through the water. A car backed up with a trailer, and the driver revved his motor more than necessary.

Ben ducked his head sharply, looked sideways at Tom and said, "We'd better get this stuff inside."

"Ben, don't listen to gossip. Be fair to Tom." With that, Freyja hurried away before the storm could hit, and Tom and Ben carried everything into the house, set it down in the living room, then headed back outside. As they reached Ben's truck, Tom made out a cheque.

"Angel," Tom said. "I never had a chance to meet her. I'd like to have heard her sing."

"We loved her," Ben said, as he took the cheque and studied it before he folded it and put it into his pocket. "Me and my Betty. We wanted her. We'd have adopted her. Wanda wouldn't let us. I heard you got kids. You gotta know what that's like when you love your kids. You make them a promise, you gotta keep it. I promised her I wouldn't drink. She promised me she wouldn't. They were telling lies about her right away, right away. They said she must have been drunk. There was no liquor in her blood."

As soon as Ben said there was no liquor in her blood, Tom remembered the smell of whisky on her clothes and skin. Once again, he was kneeling over her, his face close to her muddy face, her blank eyes.

Ben leaned against the fender of his truck and shut his eyes for a moment. Tom thought he might collapse. He'd seen that before, people's legs giving way when they were overwhelmed with grief. Ben took two deep breaths, then opened his eyes.

"I asked you to help the other day. I shouldn't have done that. You don't owe us nothing. I'm sorry. I'm sorry." He shook his head. "I've been blaming you. I wanted it to be you. You don't come from here. If it's not you, then who is it? You never knew her in the city?"

"No," Tom said. "I never knew her in the city."

"She wasn't drinking. She kept her promise and I didn't keep mine. I started drinking." He shook his head in pain at his betrayal of his grand-daughter's trust. "I've quit. I went to her grave and I said, 'Please forgive me.' I shouldn't have asked for your help. You don't..." He paused, as if uncertain how to finish saying what he was going to say, and took a deep breath.

Tom finished the sentence for him, not out loud but in the echo chamber that his skull had become. *Belong.* You don't *belong.*

"Maybe you should take a couple of days off," Tom said.

Ben shook his head. "No money coming in. We live close to the bone here. You'll see. No jobs with big money. You wanna eat, you gotta make wages every day. No credit from Horst for me. Betty was from the reserve. Him and Karla, they don't like Indians."

"There's a false floor in Frenchie's truck. You said you never got the good stuff anymore. What is the good stuff he hides under the floor?"

"Pickerel fillets," Ben replied bitterly, his anger now having a safe focus. "I used to take a few pounds to sell off the back of the truck. It was just a few bucks. Maybe twenty, thirty dollars for each guy. But then the Whites got involved. They wanted to go big time. They always want to go big time. I didn't want to, so they gave their contract to Frenchie. He had the restaurants and butcher shops all lined up. They'd take all he could supply. All back-door stuff. Cash money. Cheaper than retail. No record. The taxman never sees any of it. You keep your mouth shut about it. Everyone would have years of income tax to pay if the government ever found out. Besides, it's not like anybody is getting rich. It just means they get to live like normal people. They've got to be careful, though. They can't put it in the bank. A lot of them sleep uneasy on their mattresses. Think of it as their private retirement plan. Their kids' college education plan."

"You're not in it?"

"Not anymore. I had a few old customers for a while, but I lost those. Every dollar. Frenchie wants every dollar. The Whites know buyers. I could have bought Angel a guitar if I was still hauling the fillets. I don't blame the guys. They're getting bigger money. They're not hurting anybody except the taxman, and that's not hurting anybody except the pricks in Ottawa."

"Nothing to do with Angel?" Tom asked.

Ben shook his head. "She had nothing to do with fish. She had planned on getting an ice cream job at White's. She kept her money in a big glass pickle jar. Wages aren't good, but the tips are."

"That's the waitresses," Tom said. "Not the ice cream girls."

The thunderhead was moving toward them more quickly now. It was close enough that they could see the white line on the surface of the water where the rain was hammering down from the clouds. Where they stood, it was still calm, hardly a ripple, hardly a breeze, the trees motionless, the sunshine sparkling on the water. Lightning bolts made jagged lines and sheet lightning raced through the clouds. The first sudden blasts of wind struck them and Ben raised his hand, then climbed into his truck and backed away. Tom waited for another minute, his eye on the approaching lightning, then went into his house, pulled the door tight and lowered the windows. He hoped, as the first squall of rain struck, that there were no boaters, deceived by the sunlight, who had lingered too long on the lake.

The thunderhead passed over, a dark mass of churning clouds, and a lightning bolt struck so close that thunder shook the house. The sharp smell of ozone filled the air. With the lightning came the rain, sudden, hard, driving straight down, ripping the tips off the spruce trees and flinging them into puddles. The rain slammed against the roof, so loud that if anyone had been with him they couldn't have heard each other shout. Lightning struck all around, and then the wind appeared, jerking, twisting gusts of it, and he felt the house shudder.

Darkness had engulfed Valhalla, and then with each lightning strike, everything lit up for a moment, bleached white.

Anything left loose was flying through the air. He was glad his supplies were in the house. He wished he'd picked up bits of sawed-off ends. They'd end up in the swamp, in the forest, on the lake, maybe in Oz. He hoped they wouldn't end up through anyone's window.

It had become so dark that he switched on the lights in the kitchen. He put water on for coffee, but before the water could boil, the electricity went off. He rummaged in a drawer for a flashlight and went to the shed at the back door. There was a wooden box. He looked in and saw kindling and a few sticks of wood left over from the winter. He found a paper bag with more paper bags stuffed into it, took one, crumpled it and put it into the wood stove. He added a few pieces of kindling and two small pieces of split wood. He knew that the electricity would come back after the storm was over. He waited in the kitchen, turning on his flashlight every so often to see if the water was boiling, and when it was ready he carefully poured the water as the kitchen filled with light, then was plunged into darkness.

His favourite place in the house was the front porch. From there he could watch the sun rise, watch the surface of the water change from silver to azure, watch the night gradually steal away the horizon. The shutters were partially up, and he closed all but one that looked out onto the lake. It had become so dark that he couldn't see the nearest trees. Then lightning flashed, showing the tall spruce thrashing about in the wind, beyond them waves breaking as far as he could see, their white edges threatening as knives, then total darkness, but the image remained on his eyes like the afterimage from a strobe. He was blind, then suddenly, without warning, was given sight and could see everything in exquisite detail.

He felt a kind of nervous excitement about the storm, like the house was a ship in a gale, with the rain beating on it, the wind making it shudder. His coffee was strong and sweet with condensed milk. Then all at once a terrible loneliness crept over him, a loneliness like he'd felt in his parents' apartment as he watched the street from the corner window on nights when the rain swirled, or the snow whipped along the street, and he saw people hurrying by and wished he could go with them, wherever they were going, for he imagined that there was always a family waiting for them, expecting them, glad to see them safely home. His face felt sunken, as though it had lost most of its flesh, and his body felt weak, the way it had felt when he'd been ill with the flu and his mother had let him stay home from school. He wished now that he had a partner, a friend, a lover to sit beside, to share the storm with, to marvel at the imprinted images of the trees and waves, to comfort and reassure each other under a blanket.

The storm was from the northeast, and that meant that the waves would pile up on the shore, batter the north dock, surge over top of it. Experienced boaters knew to anchor close to the centre of the harbour because when the waves broke over the dock, they would send heavy spray flying through the air, enough spray that it could fill a boat and sink it. He went to the living room and was rewarded with thunder and lightning so close he didn't have time to count the seconds between them and saw the waves breaking high over the reef in great white crests. There was a steady roar of waves breaking on the shore. With the intermittent shrieking of the wind under the eaves, the pounding of the waves, the thrashing of the trees, no cries for help could be heard, not from a sinking ship or from a house. The gods of thunder and lightning, of wind, made rescue impossible and everyone had to ride out their own storm in their own way.

Lightning flashed again and he saw a garbage can from the dock flying through the air, frozen in time. When the lightning flashed again, the garbage can was gone. The tenters on the beach would have been driven off. If they were inexperienced and hadn't folded their tents and retreated to their vehicles before the storm reached them, their chances of rescuing their equipment had quickly passed. If they had realized the danger soon enough, they'd have everything packed inside their vehicles.

The rain and wind pounded the house for two hours, then the wind eased and the rain fell straight down like a waterfall. The drumming of the rain on the roof gradually slackened, then diminished to a quick swish of sudden gusts. The lightning and thunder had been swept southwest. The crack of lightning and the roll of thunder were gradually fading. When sheet lightning flashed, he could see the ground covered in large puddles.

The lights in the kitchen flickered on, then off, paused, and then turned on again.

The dark, low clouds brought night earlier than usual. He searched for a pair of rubber boots. When he went out, there were lights in one of the four dormers of White's Emporium, but the store and café were dark.

The windows of the one-room cabins were lit, and vehicles hunched in front of them like dark beasts. Valhalla was a long way from the city for a day's fishing trip. Better to overnight it. Drive there, get a boat into the water, maybe get a few hours fishing in, fish all the next day, fish the following morning. Most fishermen came for more than that, for five days, maybe a week if they had the time. Fishermen were always leaving and others arriving.

The fishermen were nearly all male. Two to a cabin. Father and son. Brothers. Fishing buddies. Occasionally, a husband and wife, the sort of wife who could drink a beer with the boys, gut her own fish, handle a boat and trailer.

As he stood there, in the middle of a puddle, he wondered if Travis had asked for the names and addresses of everyone staying in the cabins on the night Angel died. Men on their own, boozing, bored, looking for local action maybe. If he were in charge, it would have been the first place he looked.

It wasn't his problem anymore. The Whites were supposed to keep the names and addresses, the licence plate numbers of their renters. He wondered then, for an instant, how far back the Whites' records went. There were places that kept them for decades, back to their beginnings, particularly if anyone important had stayed. It was a source of pride, and usually promotion. A prince or a movie star, a wealthy businessman, a politician slept and fished here.

He waded through puddles until he was close enough to Freyja's house to see that there were no vehicles in her yard except her Jeep. He felt relieved, then foolish, for how would he explain what he was doing if he were seen— that he had been worried, that against his best intentions, he'd allowed himself to care. Still, he waited there in the shadow of a birch until he saw Freyja pass a kitchen window. He thought he would go back to his house, and then that he wouldn't.

It was a good time for exploring, because people shunned the outdoors when everything they touched was water laden. The air was still damp, and the temperature had dropped, but soon it would be warm again.

He thought about what Mindi Miner had said, the classifications he'd made of who could have killed Angel, if she'd been killed. Some of the new drugs were hard to detect, maybe were undetectable. Cults were always strange, led by one or more people who thought they had divine connections. They attracted the weird and the desperate. If they were like the group on the beach, the group Morning Dawn was so afraid of, anything was possible.

He went past the store, walked on the grass because the surface of the road had turned to mud, followed the road as it curled away among trailers and houses to the path that led north through the bush. The path was little used and overgrown with grass. Branches crowded each side and grass grew high in the centre. Vehicles had pushed down the grass to form two tracks. The rain had brought silence, for the wet muted everything, made the air heavy. In the distance, lightning cracked and thunder rolled. Because of the clouds, the trees were deep in darkness.

There were few cottages between the village and the Odin group's settlement. Or so Sarah had said. The cottages started north of the settlement. Not many, maybe twenty, tucked among the trees, fronting on the water.

The clouds were breaking up. Intermittently, moonlight would light up the ground. The first thing he saw was an outline of a series of peaked roofs set one against the other. The roofs made a row of six sharp angles. Then there was a space and six more. He stood still as a cloud obscured the moon. When moonlight flooded the open ground, Tom made out the upper edge of a Viking ship. The high prow with the dragon head, the long curved line of the gunwale were fierce against the sky. He bent down to look at the keel, but it was obscured by shadow. The ship was set on wooden cradles. He reached out and felt the clinker-built sides. He stepped back to get a broader view. The mast was not up. It would not be raised until the ship was on the water.

"May I help you," a voice said from behind him. Startled, he turned to face a small gnarled man, a dwarf. Not quite a dwarf, he thought, maybe five feet tall.

"Sorry," Tom said. "Just curious. A Viking longship?"

"We built it here. It would have taken the Vikings six weeks. It took us more than a year."

"Is it just decorative or is it functional?"

"We sail it every season."

The dwarf turned on his flashlight and played it over Tom's face and upper body. The sound of rain dripping into puddles was loud in the silence. Finally, he said, "Constable Parsons, I am Brokkr. Would you like a tour?"

"Yes," Tom said, surprised that he was known. He wasn't surprised at the constable title, though, a generic term that people frequently used. "I'd like a tour."

The rain dripping from the trees and bushes, the early darkness that pooled around everything, seemed to weigh against talking, against making any noise as he followed Brokkr past one, then another hut. "How many huts?" he asked.

"Twenty. At the moment there are ten in use. Plus our longhouse."

Brokkr opened the door to one hut, turned on a light, and Tom realized that he had expected not electricity but a flaming torch or, at least, a lamp with a candle in it. There was nothing exceptional about the hut except that three beds were built as benches against three walls. The bed frames had been made of slender tree trunks. The bark had been peeled off and the varnished wood reflecting the electric light gleamed dully. There were two tables and a desk and chairs, a metal stove with a wood box to one side.

"All built by our people," Brokkr explained. "They were accountants, teachers, housewives, bankers, librarians, but they learned crafts, learned to use the materials around them, to be in touch with their natural soul."

"Sounds like an educated group."

"In the beginning they were sophisticates. Mostly from the United States, a few from the British Isles. They learned to touch their true, primitive selves, to commune with nature."

"All in praise of Odin," Tom said.

Brokkr paused, turned off the light, led the way down two steps to the grass. "We await his return."

Outside, a large dark mound loomed before them. Brokkr led him along a stone path that ran parallel to the building to a heavy wooden door. The inside was lit by recessed electric light. Brokkr led the way, but the passageway was low, and he said, "Be careful. People sometimes bang their heads on the beams." Tom ducked down.

They entered a long room with people sitting on benches and stools on both sides. The room was divided into thirds lengthwise, with the centre third being a walkway. Halfway down the walkway was a narrow fire pit made of stone and sand. A woman in a loose white gown was sitting on a stool and playing a sitar.

Tom recognized the sweet smell of marijuana. Everyone in the room seemed busy. Women were weaving on upright looms, others knitting or spinning. A number of men were carving. Others were working with leather. Everyone was doing a quiet task. Even the children were busy knitting.

Tom and Brokkr waited in the entrance until the sitar player had finished, then Brokkr motioned Tom to come forward and sit on a bench. In the light, Tom could see that Brokkr's body was twisted to one side and his head was abnormally large for his body. The young man beside Tom was braiding strands of leather into a rope. He nodded and smiled. Beside him a young woman was spinning wool. She caught Tom's eye, nodded and smiled, then turned her attention back to the sitar player as the music began again.

When the sitar player finished and went to sit to one side, a woman began to chant in a high-pitched voice in a language Tom didn't recognize, then another voice and another joined in. Once all the women were chanting, the men began to join in, not all at once but one at a time. They didn't stop their work to chant. They were wrapped in silence until the music entered them, caught them up. What had been one person chanting for others was, finally, all, except for Tom, chanting as one. As the music filled the room, Tom wished he knew the words, and he shut his eyes so nothing would distract him from the sound.

When the singing stopped, everyone sat in silence, mesmerized, and then began to stand up and stretch and move toward a large silver samovar that sat on a wooden table. They made themselves tea.

Brokkr led Tom to a handsome older man with white hair. He was medium height and had the confident look of someone who was used to being in charge. Brokkr introduced Tom, then stepped back.

"I am Godi-4," the man said and held out his hand. "I am the spiritual leader of Odin. Welcome to our great hall. Will you share tea with us?"

Tom followed him. One of the young women, wearing a modest white shift with blue trim, put a metal ball into his cup, and then filled it with boiling water from the samovar. The smell reminded Tom of tanned deerskin. She lifted out the ball, then handed him the cup.

"You have purchased Doctor Ford's property?" Godi-4 said.

"Jessie Olason's property."

"We think of it as the Ford property. He was one of the founders of Odin. You have chosen to join the Valhalla community. That is a significant event. Valhalla seldom has people move to it. Usually, they move away."

"I visited Valhalla a few years ago. I imagined living here."

"Yes," Godi-4 agreed. "First we must imagine things before we can do them. You have to imagine the pyramids before you can build them."

"I have smaller ambitions," Tom answered.

Godi-4 smiled at Tom's response. "This is not an exact duplicate of an Icelandic longhouse. The Vikings were early adoptors. They travelled to America and to the depths of Russia. They would have used whatever materials were available. In Iceland, they built with layered lava rocks and turf. Here, we use limestone slabs for our foundation. In Iceland, there is no limestone. Here, there is an abundance of wood, so we use wood. As you can see, we've incorporated electricity. When you come in the daylight, you'll see that we have used turf to insulate our outer walls and we have a grass roof."

Jason and his small group from the beach came into the hall. Godi-4 quickly excused himself and went to intercept them. From the way they were standing, it seemed that a confrontation was taking place. Jason's followers had gathered behind him. Godi-4 stood by himself, facing them the way a prophet or a proselytizer might face a mob.

There seemed to be more than fifty people in the hall before Jason and his group appeared. Many of the women wore the same style of shift with shoulder straps as did the young woman who had served him tea. The men wore loose trousers and tops that came past their hips, tied with brightly coloured woven belts. They were standing around in groups quietly talking, and he realized that every so often a member of the group would turn to glance at him, but only briefly, never catching his eye. Tom sipped his tea and smiled at anyone who looked toward him, but no one came to join him until a young woman offered to refill his cup. Tom thanked her and said, "No thanks, one cup was fine."

Brokkr had come back. He touched Tom's elbow to get his attention and nodded toward the door. Tom put his cup down and Brokkr led him out.

"You knew my name though we hadn't met. You were expecting me?"

"Yes," Brokkr replied. "Not at the exact moment you arrived but perhaps the moment before or the moment after."

"Why is that?"

"Take this flashlight. It will help you find your way. It is easy to get lost when you have no light to guide you. Even though it seems quite safe here, there are wild beasts about. You can return it when you next visit." He handed Tom the flashlight, and as clouds now obscured the moon, Tom was pleased to have it. Brokkr hesitated, as if to prolong the moment, then said, "Your life is now linked with ours. We believe that every act has meaning. Kill a butterfly and alter history. Dr. Ford, Jessie Olason, Tom Parsons, each forming a link in an unpredictable but meaningful chain. Is it a surprise that we are curious about you? Why you? Why here? What does it mean for us?"

With that, he turned and slipped into the darkness, a small misshapen figure disappearing among the trees. Tom wondered if he made it a habit of prowling the woods at night, and if so, was it to catch nosy neighbours, or was it to keep track of the members of Odin?

CHAPTER 22

THE DISAPPEARANCE

"They sing," Tom said. "Beautiful voices. All together, in different groups. Four-part harmony." He was leaning against the store counter. "I need a pound of butter."

"No one needs a pound of butter. Why don't you try margarine?" Karla said. She got a pound of butter from the cooler. Because of the heat, Horst was lying down in their living quarters. Without him there, Karla looked more relaxed. "You'd be better to use margarine."

"How much do you charge for pickerel fillets?" He knew there were fresh fillets in the cooler and frozen fillets in the freezer. The fillets were the most popular meal.

"Six dollars a pound. It's a bargain. Do you know what you'd pay in the city?"

"The fishermen have a quota?" he said.

"Nine thousand pounds per licence. Not enough to live on unless they have the money to buy more than one licence."

The café side of the emporium had customers at three tables. The rest were empty. There was the soft murmur of voices and the clink of cutlery on plates.

When he paid her for the butter, Karla asked, "Did they explain what that hysterical performance out front was about?"

"It never came up," he said. "I see that some of the sailboats left this morning."

"There's a regatta down south. It always takes business away from us. I think some people were offended by the performance and left the next day. I explained that it's never happened before."

"I'll bet nine months from now there's going to be a cluster of babies born. All those guys watching the spinning."

Karla wasn't amused. She stared at him the way his teachers had stared at him when confronted with his sarcastic humour. Sweat formed on her face. She pulled at her blouse and flapped it.

"You'd think a storm would cool things off. All we get here are extremes. A hundred above in the summer and forty below in the winter."

"You sang like a bluebird the other night. Some of us squawk like ravens." He knew that a compliment about her singing always made her easier to deal with.

"Have you had any music lessons? Any music in the family?"

"My father had a good voice, but outside of the church choir he wouldn't sing."

"People should use the talent God has given them," she said with a bit of a sniff.

He realized that her ability, whatever it was, had given her a belief in her own superiority in the same way that ex–hockey players, even when reduced to selling cars, carried a physical arrogance about them the rest of their lives.

"Tin ear," he said, then realizing that she might have thought he was referring to his father, added, "Me. No talent."

"I can teach you. You'd have to pay, of course." She winked at him. "Now, Freyja there, she might provide lessons for free. She has a nice voice. Not much range but pleasant. I've got much better range than her, more experience. I can show you tricks that she can't."

"I'll bet," he said.

She studied him as if she didn't understand him, as if there was a mystery about him yet to be unlocked.

"You like looking, but you're not an action man. None of this grab a girl by her hair and drag her off into the bush. The local boys are action men, or at least they like to think so. Unless, of course, you ask them if that's a wedding ring they've got in their pocket."

Tom took out his wallet and the picture of his father. He handed it to Karla. "This was my father," he said. "He used to be a big fly fisherman. Did he ever come here to fish? It was a long time ago."

She studied the picture. "We've been here fourteen years. My mom died, we came to help my dad. He couldn't manage on his own. Sacrificed my career. Had to pass up big opportunities. Now, he's in a nursing home in the city. Alzheimer's."

"Have you kept your guest records from long ago?"

"My father never threw anything away. There are boxes of paper upstairs. Does it matter?"

"Only to me," Tom replied.

Just then Horst came out, dragging his oxygen canister behind him. Karla handed the photo back to Tom, straightened up and went to check on the waitresses.

"You want something?" Horst demanded with a hint of irritation in his voice. Tom wondered if he'd always been so irritable or whether it came about because of his daily struggle to breathe. *Asbestos mines*, he thought, killing people slowly, making money for the owners but destroying the workers' lungs.

"Information about Jessie," Tom said.

"She's dead."

"I know she's dead. Was she connected to Odin?"

"How would I know? I don't mind other people's business." He settled into his chair, touched the plastic lines that led into his nose and scowled at no one in particular.

"You've lived here for how long? Fourteen years and you buy and sell real estate and have the only store, and you don't know?" Although Tom tried to control it, irritation had crept into his voice, and he immediately regretted it because he knew that Horst would think Tom's irritation was a triumph.

"I could find out," Horst replied. "It would take time and effort. How much is it worth to you?"

Tom just about said, "Fuck you." Instead, he took the pound of butter and left.

Instead of going home, he dropped by Sarah's. He put his pound of butter in her fridge and handed her the picture of his father.

"He is," Tom ranted to Sarah, "the most obnoxious person I've ever met."

"Who?" She put on her reading glasses to see the picture better. "This guy?"

"No," Tom said. "Horst White. That's my father. Did you ever see him around Valhalla?"

When he said the picture was of his father, she moved it back and forth until she had it at exactly the right distance. She looked at the picture, then at Tom.

"I got these glasses at Walmart for ten bucks. They may not be the right strength." She held the picture up beside his left ear. "I'm trying to imagine you with a moustache."

"I look more like my mother," he replied.

She handed him the picture. "How long ago?"

"He died when I was twenty."

"A lot of people come and go. Not us, but the summer people. Some come once, never come back. Others come back a few times. The ones who come back year after year get known, at least enough for people to say that's Herb from the *Pelican II*. We're just the quaint villagers to them." She paused. "You're agitated," she said. "You're doing that thing with your thumbnail. You need a cup of tea."

He looked at his hands. When he was stressed, he had a habit of locking them together and scraping his left thumbnail with his right. It had driven Sally crazy. He unlocked his fingers and put his hands at his side.

"So what's your problem with Horst?" she asked, going back to his earlier comment.

"He's the most obnoxious person I've ever known."

"Including the murderers you dealt with?"

"They were nuts."

"And he isn't?"

"He's just greedy, acquisitive. He's got a house. He doesn't need another one. Jessie sold me hers. Get over it, people."

"For less than he was willing to pay."

That brought him up short. "Less? How much less?"

"She was waiting for the right buyer. She could have sold years ago."

"That's crazy."

"The Odin group thought Ford's land was theirs. They were wrong. It was Ford's. His relatives didn't like the Odin group. They thought the Odin leaders had been milking Ford for his money. The Kerrs, Karla's parents, were interested in the land, but Jessie's husband, Oli, had been Ford's fishing guide. Jessie knew all Ford's business. She had the names and addresses. No flies on her. Jessie beat them all to the punch. She tried to get the Odin property too, but Ford had turned it over to the group. They've been waiting ever since. Christians have been waiting for millennia. People wait for the end of the world. People get a fixed idea and they wait."

Tom slumped in his chair. "I don't want to get involved in whatever craziness is here. I came for a simple life. Like Thoreau. I just want to fix things that are broken."

Sarah smiled widely. "Lots of broken things around here. That Karla been showing you her tits? Are you going to fix whatever's broken there? She sleeps upstairs. Horst can't manage the steps. He sleeps downstairs. Maybe that's why he's grouchy."

"She's inclined to lean over."

"She's got a husband who's got one foot in the grave and is sinking fast. He kicks the bucket, you want to move into her bedroom and run a store the rest of your life? You know why he's got nearly everything valuable behind the counter? Because people steal stuff. You want to deal with shoplifters? With unpaid bills? He's got a ledger with pages of people who buy on credit when their welfare runs out."

"There's no harm in looking."

"It all starts with looking."

"You sound like my mother," he said testily. "If you don't get to practise as a teenager, you make mistakes when you're older."

"Practise?"

"Falling in love. All that kind of stuff."

"You're cute," she said. "And uptight. You know there are bets in town about who's going to get you into the sack first?"

"Nobody's been climbing into my bed at night."

"You have a penchant for women who are trouble," she said. "That Freyja. She's trouble. That won't keep you away, will it? Men like trouble, a little bit of excitement. It's sort of like HP on their steak. You want her reading your future and telling your children-to-come about trolls and giants?"

"Some men."

"You any different?

"I'm in no shape to handle trouble. I came here to avoid it. Besides, I'm not having any more children."

Sarah laughed out loud. "You poor laddie," she said. "Life is full of surprises, and it isn't always a black bear coming through the kitchen door looking for bacon fat."

He felt disgruntled, irritated, as if everyone else in the world knew things he didn't, shared things that weren't shared with him, secrets, always secrets. His family was full of secrets, everything under lock and key, especially their feelings—his father's office, his parents' bedroom door, the food cupboard, the china cabinet, as if a stranger might sneak in and drink from his mother's precious china or sully her sterling silver. The family photo albums were kept in the oak cabinets, each glass door kept closed to keep out the dust, each glass door locked to keep family secrets secret.

When his father's relatives came to visit, they all spoke in code, in an adult language he didn't understand: short, abbreviated sentences, intermingled with knowing looks, nodding heads, looking into space, pressed lips, barely audible laughter. A cousin might say, "Emma." And they all would glance at each other, look away, restrain a smile, nod, shake their heads, not quite restrain their growing grin. Another cousin might add, "Oxford." Still another would add, "Christmas." Then there'd be silence as they sipped their tea, nibbled their Christmas cake, drank their port, and were overcome with all their shared thoughts about Emma, who might or might not be in one of the black-and-white photos in one of the family albums. Women in big hats and men in suit jackets that looked too small. But all was a mystery, a secret, for there were no names, locations, dates, just the photos of strangers from a past life. After his mother had left and his father had died, Tom had the keys to the various locks in the apartment, the keys found in his father's office, and he opened the cabinets, took out the photo albums and searched them for clues about who he might be.

When Cousin Donald in the pork-pie hat had come to help him go through his father's papers, Tom had shown him the albums and asked him about the people in the pictures. He'd named some, was not sure of others.

"We're not a close family," he said. "It was our upbringing.

"Nobody told me anything," Tom said.

Cousin Donald was rifling through Henry's files, making notes. "There's nothing to tell that's worth telling," he said. "We were grubby and hungry, and did no job as well as filling up the local graveyards."

"No lords or dukes or people like that in our family?" Tom asked.

Cousin Donald showed his teeth as he laughed silently. "Not unless one of our girls working as maidservant got caught bending over making a bed. Then we might have had a lord in the family for a while, you might say."

Tom had been shocked. He had never heard either of his parents talk like that. He couldn't imagine his father saying such a thing about the women in his family. Or about any woman. Decorum was his byword, and how could you be decorous bent over a bed with a lord having sex with you? He wondered if the women it happened to kept doing whatever they were doing or if they paused, waited until it was over, then continued as if nothing had happened.

"You're a good lad," Cousin Donald said, "but you've got a lot to learn. Your folks were brittle and a bit tight with the port, but they were all right. They made do and never borrowed a dollar from anyone." Tom wasn't sure what to say to that.

"You've drifted away," Sarah said, startling him. "You do that at times. You're here and then you're not here. It wouldn't be a good thing to do when you're in a skiff or out on the ice. Where were you?"

"Thinking," he replied. "Remembering a man in a pork-pie hat. A cousin of sorts. He helped me with my parents' estate and helped himself to part of it."

"There are lots of those around."

Sarah filled up the room. Her husband, she'd said, had been a huge man, six foot six, broad shouldered, able to walk all day in the bush, sleep on spruce branches outdoors in winter, pull a sleigh loaded with supplies. Together, they must have been formidable, intimidating, but she'd said that her husband was gentle, well liked, enjoyed telling stories.

Tom had grown familiar with Sarah's kitchen. Everything in it was big, made by hand by big people for big people. The table was made from birch planks. It now sat six but with all the leaves in it would seat twelve. According to Sarah, there was a matching piece that, when added, accommodated twenty. There was an old-fashioned clock enclosed in an intricately carved case. A sports fisherman who had once stayed with them sent it as an anniversary gift.

Who, he wondered, would make bread and pies on these too-high counters after she was dead? What good was a house of giants to a race of pygmies?

Sarah asked him how the house was coming, and he said, "It'll be livable by the fall. Jessie managed. I can manage. It would be good to have proper insulation and the drywall up."

"People say you look like you know what you are doing. It's a good advertisement. A craftsman is known by the quality of his work. I hear you've been getting some jobs."

"Here and there. Bits and pieces. Nothing big." She gave him a cup and saucer, a teaspoon and a bowl of sugar cubes. He wondered how many people she had served tea to since she'd arrived here, back of beyond, the Irish girl in the middle of nowhere. She had told him that when they first arrived there'd been no dock. She and her trunk had been lowered into a skiff and rowed to shore. She'd lived in a tent until McAra got their log cabin built. "Why did you leave Ireland?" he asked. "Was your family poor?"

"They had a good living," Sarah replied. "My father had an inn. But I had an older brother. He would have gotten everything. None of the local boys had asked me to marry. I was taller than all of them. Then McAra turned up at the pub one day with friends. They were on leave. A man my size. He hung around for two weeks, and then said he had to go back to his base in France and was I interested in coming with him? I packed up my belongings, shipped a couple of trunks. We got married on the fly, as it were; kiss the bride and she's gone forever, never to return. Spent two years in France. Saved a lot of people a lot of trouble. They were already discussing, 'What are we going to do with Sarah?' I was a problem. I left and the problem was solved."

"Did your parents not love you?"

"Oh, they loved me. They fed me and clothed me and educated me. They just didn't know what to do with me. If I'd have been five foot four and ninety-eight pounds, I'd have fitted right in. One of the boys at the pub would have been keen to get his hands on me. I'd have gotten married, had a couple of kids, and we'd have kept doing what people do if they come from families that have a bit of money. No inherited money but trade money, money earned over the counter. The other solution, of course, the convenient one, would have been if I'd died. The trouble is dying isn't often convenient."

"No," Tom agreed and he thought of his father. He'd died at a terrible time. Tom was immersed in his studies, trying for grades that would bring him a scholarship, maybe lead to graduate school and a fellowship. "Sometimes," he said, referring to death, "it comes when you least expect it. Other times, it won't come no matter how much you wish for it."

"It's never what you expect," Sarah said. "That's like Mindi Miner. Two canes. Legs that don't work. Lying three days with the roof of the mine on his legs."

"A town of cripples," Tom said. "I fit right in."

"You're not Mindi. Don't feel sorry for yourself."

"Do I look like I feel sorry for myself?"

"Mournful, like you've got the weight of the world on your shoulders. Cheer up. Everybody likes a smile. They've got their own problems. They don't need anybody else's."

"And you? What about you?"

Sarah stared at him as he if were a prosecutor who might convict her of an indefinable failing. He thought he might have crossed a barrier into a dark swamp. "My parents are dead, my brother is dead, my husband is dead. My kids have gone. They write. They've done well for themselves. They send me pictures."

Sarah took a deep breath. Her chest rose and fell. Her face was soft with regret. "How old are your kids?" she asked.

"Nineteen and eighteen. Myrna and Joel. As different as chalk and cheese."

"You're lucky. One of each. Good planning. I've all sons. Nothing wrong with sons, but I'd like to have had a daughter. They want me to move to the city. I say to them, 'If I did that, who would I be? Just an old woman living alone in an apartment.' You move, you leave yourself behind."

Her comment shook him for a moment as he thought about everything he'd left behind: his career, his wife, his kids, his house, his coffee shops, the places where he'd found refuge when he'd walked entire winter nights because staying in his apartment was too dangerous.

"I got transferred a lot. My kids were like air force brats. No place became home."

"Maybe every place became home."

"I don't think that works." The shrink had said about his sense of not belonging, "You're a citizen of the world." And he'd replied, "Bullshit." When you belong everywhere, you belong nowhere. No roots. Like the scruff he'd seen on the beach, pretending they had a life. He wished he'd found a job that meant they could have lived in one town. He wondered if he should have taken the job his father's friend had offered him. Become an accountant, had the same office, in the same building, on the same street. "My kids have no place to call home."

"Maybe they'll join you."

"Maybe," he replied, but there was no conviction in his voice. "We don't communicate much."

She looked at the clock. "I'd better get ready to go to the knitting group. We do more talking than knitting, but nice sweaters still get made. They'll be for sale at the Christmas bazaar. You can buy one."

He was walking back home when he saw Mindi Miner struggling along with a black canvas bag over one shoulder. He was coming from White's, and the bag had groceries in it. He used both canes, swung his legs forward in short crescents. Tom would have offered to carry the grocery bag for him, but Freyja had warned him never, under any circumstances, to offer to help him. He accepted no favours. His model was an early pioneer who had frozen both feet, had them amputated and cleared his land on his knees.

"I'd shake your hand," Mindi said, "but if I do, I'll topple over, and you'll have to set me right side up."

"I'd offer to carry your groceries, but I was warned not to offer. You don't accept favours."

"Sarah told you that, I expect." Tom didn't reply. "She and I don't see eye to eye on a lot of things, but she's right about that. You have to do everything you can for yourself or you start to be dependent."

"I've just come from Sarah's. She makes a good cup of tea."

"She has her own way of seeing things. I wouldn't take everything she says as gospel. She's got it in for the Odin group. I wouldn't pay much attention to what she has to say about them. They sell me fresh food all summer. If Brokkr, their blacksmith, stays over the winter, he sells me root crops. They don't overcharge. Good quality."

"She thinks they don't have any morals."

"Different morals. She's got a bone to pick with them. You got a grudge, you see everything that way. Ask me about McAra. I haven't got anything good to say about him."

"What's the grudge?"

"Standing is hard for me. If we're going to talk, let's go sit over there." They went to where a large spruce stump had been cut off at chair height. Mindi shuffled his way around and sat down with a sigh.

"When McAra disappeared, what we wanted to know was, where was his dog? Big bastard. Half-wolf. When he growled, everybody froze. He never bit no one, but nobody wanted to be the first. He followed McAra everywhere. He raised him. When McAra didn't turn up when he should have, Sarah went to look for him. When she didn't find him, she got a gang to go looking for him. We found a spot where there was broken ice. It was frozen over again, but the ice was thin and clear. It was in a spot where there's strong current, and it eats away the ice from underneath. Strange place for him to be."

"The dog?"

"In the spring, they found him washed up on the shore still attached to the toboggan. Bones and fur. The toboggan had held him down. A storm had washed him onto shore."

"No sign of McAra?"

"Sarah searched the shoreline for years. No sign of him. We thought he might turn up in someone's nets. Nothing."

"I've seen his headstone at the graveyard."

"There's no one in that grave."

Tom remembered the smell of newly cut grass, the headstone with the name McAra cut deep into it. There'd even been an overturned plastic flowerpot with dead stems. Who knew how long ago it had been placed there, or by whom? Sarah had leaned with both hands on her cane and stared at the stone as if waiting for it to speak to her. Then she'd stepped back, dissatisfied. He'd thought the grave contained long-held grief.

"It's rocky bottom in places. He could have gotten jammed up against a reef. His clothes could have snagged," Tom said.

"Maybe. Maybe not. There was a ski plane in the area around that time. Maybe sports hunters after wolves. Could have landed. Some of the Odin women were smoking hot for McAra. They liked how big he was. There was one especially. Older, lots of money. She never came back after he disappeared. Maybe just coincidence."

"There'd have been tracks."

"I was out there looking for him. No tracks. Not much snow that winter. Lots of bare ice. Windy. An hour after you made tracks, they were gone."

"Where was she supposed to have taken him?"

"Vancouver. San Diego. There were rumours. More than one person who went to the West Coast for a holiday said they thought they had seen him clean-shaven, dressed up fancy. They weren't sure. He's not the only big man in the world."

"She took over his fishing and trapping licences?"

"Didn't have much choice, did she? Six kids to feed."

"She shot her own meat?"

"And set her own traps. And lifted her own nets. And decked more than one guy who set his nets too close and his traps on top of hers. Some guys are like that, you know. They take advantage of a situation."

"She seems okay now. Not rich but not hand to mouth."

"It was all hand to mouth until ten years ago. She got a bit of an inheritance. Family member died. Maybe a brother. She hasn't run traps for a long time. No money in it anyway. She just fishes one licence. More out of habit."

"Nothing more than that?"

"No," Mindi said. "Just gossip. How about you? What if you were tied down with a wife and six kids and a woman with no kids and lots of money says, 'Come with me'? You're divorced, I heard. Left a wife and kids behind. You just weren't lucky. No rich broad wanting to keep you."

"No rich broad," Tom agreed.

"I can't say I was sorry when he disappeared. Nor were a lot of other people. We were scared of him. One time at a dance, I was talking to a girl I fancied and he came up behind me, lifted me up like I was a small child and set me down to one side. I've never forgiven him for that."

Mindi struggled to his feet, got a good hold on his canes. He was going to start off when he paused and said, "You asked if I'd heard anything that night when Ben's granddaughter died. I've been thinking about that. I didn't. But I saw her getting into Siggi's truck. Not that night, maybe the night before, maybe it was the day before that. I don't pay much attention to what day it is. They're all the same now."

"Siggi. We shook hands at the dance. He was making the rounds."

"Local hero," Mindi said. "Boy wonder. Chamber-of-commerce kind of guy. He'll always lend you a fiver. When my son got picked up for DUI, Siggi loaned me the money to pay his fine. He's the kind of guy you want on your side."

CHAPTER 23

ICE CREAM

"You think it's fun being an attractive woman in Valhalla?" Freyja asked.

She was sitting at Tom's picnic table, looking like the heat didn't bother her. "Cool as a cucumber," his mother would have said. She was swinging her feet back and forth. He was trying to focus on picking out bits of lumber, but she was wearing short blue shorts and a nautical striped top.

"Everyone likes being popular," he said. As he said it he was thinking back to high school, where he stood uncertainly in corners with his back against the wall while others were gathered in small groups, talking and laughing. He had wondered then what it would be like to be popular, to have people calling out his name, inviting him to join them, putting their arms around his shoulders.

"You'd like to have women knocking at your window at night, trying to get your attention? A couple of drunks doing figure eights in your yard, yelling, 'Come out and fuck. We're horny'?"

He thought about the towns where he had worked and said, "Small-town courting behaviour. Goes on everywhere in the boonies."

She stopped swinging her feet and glared at him. "You think it's flattering when a guy comes up behind you and pushes his cock against you?"

"Have I done that? It sounds like you're blaming me."

"Are you different?"

He shrugged. "Maybe. Maybe not. I don't know. I never had a girlfriend until I met Sally and she—" He wasn't sure how to put it, finally settled on, "She wasn't shy."

"If you wanted to pick me up, what would you do?"

"Put my arms around you and lift."

Freyja rolled her eyes. "Adolescent humour. You know what I mean."

He smiled. He liked his own jokes. "I don't know. I didn't make the moves."

"Your wife made all the advances?"

"Yes," he said. The second time they'd gone out, she'd taken him to the apartment she was sharing with two other girls. They were conveniently out for the evening. She had gone into her bedroom and waltzed out in a pair of pyjamas that didn't leave much to the imagination.

"How did you meet?"

"She was cleaning my teeth."

"Good God," Freyja said. "Now that's romantic. At least she wasn't giving you an enema."

He could feel his face flush. She was stirring up too many embarrassing intimate moments. "She was a dental hygienist, not a nurse."

"Are you thick?"

"I don't know. I got good grades in school. I was good at my job. My reading comprehension is above average."

"Thick about women?"

"I don't know. Yes, I guess so. I haven't got much experience."

"You never dated?"

"When I was in grade eleven a girl in grade ten asked me out for Sadie Hawkins. I had to wear a silly corsage."

"Why did she ask you out?"

"I think she needed help with math. I tutored in my spare periods."

"Oh, God," Freyja said, and put her palm against his chest. "I clearly don't need to worry about you grabbing my ass and saying, 'Hey baby, I've got a case of beer in the back of my truck. Wanna come and share it?'"

"I don't drink beer."

Freyja broke into laughter. She still had her palm against his chest, and he could feel the heat from it through his shirt. She leaned close and put her forehead against his chest, and he could smell the sweet, warm smell of her hair. He wanted to drop the piece of wood he was holding and put his arms around her but kept his arms at his sides. He hadn't been this close to a woman since he'd left Sally.

"Will you be my champion?"

"What do you mean?"

"I get hit on a lot. Horny guys with no place to put it. Men in packs are dangerous. Rejected suitors have been known to get together to teach an uppity woman a lesson. You know the kind of lesson I mean?"

This is crazy, he thought. The dock had people sitting on it, sunning themselves, fishing, kids squealing and jumping into the water then thrashing back to climb out and do it again. The sun was high and hot. He could feel a bead of sweat run down the side of his neck. The smell of the spruce needles, bruised by their feet, enveloped them in a rich sweetness. Freyja had her sunglasses set on the top of her head. She looked like she might be going to play tennis. She'd been very animated when she'd been teasing him, but now she was still, watchful, waiting for his reply.

"What do you want me to do?"

"Come if I call. Drop by to say hi. Come and visit when the yahoos are in from Fort McMurray. Or Siggi and his crew are in town. Do you play games?"

"Yes. Checkers. Chess. Whist. Bridge. My parents enjoyed card games. Have they tried to break into your house?"

"They know I've got a rifle. I know how to use it. But I don't know if I'd have the nerve."

"Better not. Lawyers, courts. You end up bankrupt even if you don't get convicted of anything."

"You get raped, nobody does anything about it."

"Treat women with respect," his mother had always said. He wondered if playing Sir Galahad was a form of respect.

"When I'm scared I sleep with the rifle beside me."

He would have told her to call the Mounties, but he knew better. There was nothing they could do, and they were two to three hours away, depending on the weather. There wasn't much that would make them slog over sloppy road, eat dust if it was dry, plow through snow. Her saying somebody was doing wheelies in her yard wasn't going to get a visit. Not even if someone threw a beer bottle through her window. She was right. Order and justice were local.

"Nobody is going to believe we're playing checkers," he said.

"Do you care? Will it damage your reputation? Are you going in for the ministry?" She was, he realized, on the verge of being offended.

"It wasn't my reputation I was thinking about," he blurted out.

She smiled with the left side of her mouth, but her eyes didn't warm up. "I'll ask Albert," she said. "Do you think he'd be a help?"

He looked at her in her sailor's outfit and wanted to say, "Come with me and be my love," but instead said, "I'd love to come and visit. I'm flattered that you've asked me. I'll do my best to be good company."

"If I were bigger, I'd punch you," she said, then did it, punching him in the chest. Just once, as hard as she could. She turned on her heel and stalked away. He could see how stiffly she was holding herself. *Women*, he thought. *I'll never understand them.* In spite of what he'd said about Kelly asking him to the Sadie Hawkins dance because she'd wanted help with her math, he thought that she'd wanted him to kiss her. They'd lingered outside her parents' apartment door, both shuffling a bit, uncomfortable, then her mother had opened the door, and he'd said hello to her mom and good night to Kelly.

His father had lectured him on staying focused, on doing nothing that would interfere with his career. An education, a job, financial security come first, then you can think about marriage. As if, years in the future, he was supposed to come up to a woman and say, "I've got my education, a job and financial security, would you like to marry me?"

His shirt, where Freyja had rested her head, still smelled of her. He put his hand on his shirt, held it up to his face and breathed in. Freyja had gone to White's Emporium. If Karla was there, there'd be tension, maybe a few sparks. Karla resented Freyja's being younger and prettier. Freyja resented Karla's attitude that she was superior because she could sing. When the two of them were in the same room, even if they didn't say anything, they competed.

He was cutting boards with the ripsaw when Freyja returned with vanilla and chocolate ice cream cones. She walked over to him and handed him the chocolate cone. "Here. I'm sorry I hit you."

"It's okay," he said. Freyja was turning her cone around, running the tip of her tongue over the dripping ice cream. "If there's a problem, you can always come over. The door is always unlocked."

"Karla might be over teaching you how to yodel. I wouldn't want to intrude."

He ignored the suggestion. "Nobody who has hit me has ever bought me a treat afterwards."

"You got hit a lot?"

"It was part of the job. Picking up drunks and druggies, stopping fights. Domestic ones were the most dangerous. Husband and wife beating on each other. You get between them and they both start beating on you. Cops get killed on domestic calls."

"Me and Siggi?"

"Maybe," he replied. "I guess we'll find out." Her face clouded and she twisted on her heels. She didn't say anything, so he asked her about something that had been nagging at him. "Do you know anything about Icelandic sorcery? My mother said Icelanders were very superstitious. At Christmas, she told me stories of the thirteen Yule Lads, and sometimes if I misbehaved she threatened me with Grýla."

"Grýla," Freyja repeated. "She carried away many children and ate them. If you want to know about these things, come over after work. I have a book about Icelandic superstitions. In English. You may borrow it."

She left and he stood there admiring her: the long curly red hair, the way her shorts fitted around her hips, the long line of her legs, not at all voluptuous, not like Sally, all tits and ass, but still very feminine. He'd heard about and seen the anger of rejected suitors before, boys who were going to teach a girl a lesson, teach her to keep her place, bring her down a notch or two, teach her to be scared, obedient. It didn't even seem to have much to do with sex for its own sake; it was sex as a weapon, sex as intimidation. In many cases the girl hadn't done anything except have an attitude, maybe teased a bit, flirted. So who were the guys getting even with? Mom? A female teacher? Or maybe it wasn't that at all, maybe it was about being young and having a hard-on all the time and having nowhere to put it.

But here, with the sun shining against his back, the sound of children playing, the low rumble of outboard motors, people talking, people resting, relaxing, reading, fishing, where everyone knew everyone else, where no one was a total stranger, how, he wondered, could it be that anyone needed protection? But then he glanced toward where he had found Angel and the broken sticks on the ground, then back to Freyja's retreating figure.

After he'd finished his work for the day, he took Freyja up on her invitation. She was hanging out clothes.

"Just how superstitious are Icelanders?" Tom asked. They were standing on either side of the clothesline in Freyja's backyard. "I read an article that said they still believe in huldufolk. They build highways around rocks so as to not disturb the hidden people. Do you know anything about that?"

She handed him two wooden clothespins. "Do you know how to use these?"

He helped her peg a sheet to the line. "I'm impressed," she said. "You're definitely husband material. Next thing you're going to tell me you can cook."

"I can." He was going to qualify it by saying he made great toasted bacon and cheese open-face sandwiches, but before he could, Freyja said, "One special recipe. BBQ in the summer. Live off that all year."

His pride hurt, he said, "I'll make you a meal. But it'll have to wait until Ben goes into town and I can get an order for a recipe. Will curry do?"

Curry was safe. He had learned how to make it from a classmate from Trinidad when he was in college. She was right. It was his once-a-year BBQ meal. His mother had been the queen of the kitchen. He was allowed to set the table, wash the dishes, but no cooking. Before she left for what was supposed to be a month, she'd shown him where she kept everything. She taped lists of the contents on the cupboard doors.

Freyja was on the other side of the clothesline. She pulled it down and smiled at him. "I appreciate you scaring off those hoodlums the other night."

"He's not a hoodlum. He's your ex-husband."

"He's not ex yet. We're legally separated. It was a moment of madness, desperation, stupidity. A mistake," she said. "Anyway, it doesn't sound like your marriage was any great success either."

"She was determined."

"Was she now?" She handed him three tea towels and some more wooden pegs. "Hang these up. And you were just a helpless waif? Putty in her hands? Unable to say no?" He hung up the towels. "Was she older than you?"

"Three years."

"Were you, how shall we put this delicately, a virgin, a naïf, a guy who, presented with an opportunity, didn't have the common sense to say no?"

"I don't want to fight."

"We're not even dating. How can we have a fight? We can't fight when we haven't kissed yet. We're just exploring the reason for your knowing how to hang up laundry and cook."

She held up a pair of pink panties with lace on the edges and put them back into the basket. "I'd better hang these up inside. I don't want to inflame the local males."

"I came to ask about superstition. Rituals. The kind of things that people do behind closed doors."

"If you're serious about this, save up your money and go to the Museum of Icelandic Sorcery and Witchcraft in Hólmavik. You're half-Icelandic. You probably have lots of relatives there. They'll feed you puffin."

"No," he said, and the fear of meeting his mother's relatives made his stomach clench. "I don't need to see what they do there. I just need to know what people might do here."

"We sometimes use Ouija boards for fun. I sometimes give tarot readings at the spring fundraiser and dance. I've got an old fishbowl that, turned upside down with a light inside, gives a pretty good impression of a crystal ball."

"Freyja," he said, "is the most beautiful of the goddesses. The powerful practitioner of the art of seiðr. If people are unhappy, they can get her to change their destiny."

"No one believes that stuff anymore."

"Did Siggi think you could change his destiny, make things work better for him?"

"Yes. Sometimes with spells and runes, sometimes with white magic. I bought some books. I didn't take it seriously. Sometimes he wanted me to read the cards. He's superstitious. He's always talking about his luck. He says the Vikings believed that a man not only had to be brave and smart but had to have luck. I always said to him, 'A wise man makes his luck.'"

"And the Godi? Do they practise magic and spells?"

"Yes, but it's just in fun. I've been there when someone has read the fire. It's like telling ghost stories. There's an old tradition of the baðstofa, telling stories in the evening in the main room while people knit or did other small chores. Sometimes they read the Bible. Sometimes they sang rímur. On some farms, everyone had a quota of knitting. They used wake-pics, little wooden sticks, to hold their eyelids open until the knitting was finished. What is this all about?"

"Angel."

"You think she died because someone cast a spell?"

"People who believe weird things do weird things."

"No one has recently been burnt at the stake as far as I know."

She picked up the clothes basket. "The rest of these things need to be hung up inside. We can talk while you're helping me do that."

They went inside and she hung a cord across the living room, but it was obvious that she wanted to avoid talking about Angel and sorcery. "When things are dry, I take the line down. I don't have laundry hanging inside all the time. When we're married will that bother you?"

"We are not getting married. Why do you do this? I don't know anything about you. You don't know anything about me. We're strangers."

"You've eaten at my table. You've chased away my enemies. You've spent the night in my bed."

"I have not. I went home. My screens were slashed."

"People think you stayed. They can't imagine you not staying to reap the rewards of playing Sir Galahad. I could say that you slept across my door with a sword at your side that night, but they wouldn't believe that for one minute. That's not nearly as exciting as thinking that we spent the night making passionate love."

She held up a black bra. "Isn't this sexy?" she asked. She held it across her chest. "So you hate women, but you can't look at them without getting a hard-on."

He instinctively looked down at his crotch to see if his erection was showing. She laughed and he blushed.

"I don't hate women," he said. He was angry, angry with his mother, angry with Sally, angry about what had happened to him, but he didn't hate anyone—maybe, he thought, the druggie who had stolen the car. Trying not to get involved again, not get hurt, wasn't hatred. There was his clumsiness, his fear, his world that had crashed into a thousand pieces, but he didn't know how to explain it.

She held up a pair of baby doll pyjamas. They looked like they were meant for a kid. "How long do you think it would take you to get these off?"

"About thirty seconds," he answered.

"Now, we're being honest. Sarah O'Hara says that you're wound so tight that if you don't unwind, you're going to explode. She tries to talk sense to you. I tease you. Do you know how to laugh? Are you serious because you're religious?"

He was amused and flattered by her teasing, but he couldn't shake the image of Angel, and of Ben with tears streaming down his cheeks. "A lot of magic and sorcery is ugly. People use it to try to get ahead, to try to control the weather or other people. They use poetry to wish others harm. My father thought it was mumbo-jumbo. He was a bookkeeper. He thought in numbers and columns, but my mother believed in it."

"Did she stick pins in dolls?"

"That's voodoo, from the Caribbean. Icelanders have lots of their own superstitions. They don't need to borrow others. When she was angry with her mother, she wrote a poem and drew a diagram that was meant to make her mother ill. I think that's why she felt so guilty when, years later, her mother did become ill."

Freyja studied him as if she was uncertain how to respond. "Isn't this rather far-fetched?"

"Probably. But people believed it enough that they had others killed because they thought their wife or their cows were ill because of some- one else's magic. It doesn't matter what is real. What matters is what people believe."

"Godi-4 is a good man. He's kind. He looks after his flock."

"But what about Jason, the tall guy with the black beard? He looks after his flock, but I don't think you could say he's kind." He thought of Morning Dawn's frightened face outside the porch screen. "They have rituals, punishments."

"I don't know," Freyja replied. "He turns up for a month in the summer. He brings people with him. They don't mix much."

"The music and chanting in front of White's Emporium wasn't entertain- ment. It was putting a curse on the Whites."

"People pray," Freyja said. "They bow down. They drink wine that turns to blood. They eat bread that turns to flesh. They ask for forgiveness. Read your psalms. I don't remember them exactly, but I think one says let the arms of the wicked be broken."

He thought about his parents and their straight backs in the pews at the Anglican church, rigid, looking straight ahead, knowing the ritual by heart like a mathematics lesson. And Mrs. Galecian, Anna's mother, with her walls cov- ered with crucifixion scenes with purple blood and religious mottos on pieces of wood and manger scenes set inside large seashells from exotic places.

"And here, in Valhalla, are any people practising old rituals, Christian or otherwise?"

"Hardly anyone goes to church anymore. Pastor Jon has a hard time shepherding people to his services. I've heard a fisherman say, 'I hope to hell another fisherman doesn't get any fish.' Does that count?"

She meant it lightly, but she had become serious and quiet. Her eyes had darkened to jade, and there was a wistfulness about her; her face seemed fragile and she was hesitant. "You're very serious, even depressed. If you don't want me to tease you, I won't. I'll be serious. Are you sure that's what you want?"

He didn't know how to reply. To want, to want, to want, that was the question, to risk wanting and disappointment, and the emptiness that went with it. And his father saying, "If a girl starts to flirt with you, ask yourself what she wants, what have you got that she wants, what is she going to take away from you?" as if no one could want him for himself. He needed someone, something. He needed people to laugh with. Everything seemed not here but there, out of reach.

"I don't know what I want," he said, and he wondered if his voice sounded as anguished as he felt. "I've got to find out about Angel. I can't live here with people thinking I killed her."

"I don't think that. Sarah doesn't think that."

"I wake up at night and I've been dreaming that I did."

"Angel? In your dreams?"

He hesitated, then looked into her eyes and said, "No, not Angel."

In his dreams, the girl he killed over and over had red hair, and she kept coming alive, and he kept killing her and burying her. He'd never told anyone that, and he wondered if he told her would she hate him for it, for this inexplicable dream world where he lived in terror and committed crimes against a dream woman for no reason. He woke in fear, struggling to escape from a world he didn't understand.

The shrink said that when he quit killing and burying the sensitive side of himself, his anima, the dreams would go away. There was no place for anima in the Force. No place for feelings. No place for tears. Just pick up the pieces and put them into bags. After his accident, Tom was talking to one of the guys he'd last worked with. He asked Tom what he was doing and Tom said, half-jokingly, "I'm working on my anima."

"Enema?" his former colleague said. "If you're constipated, take Ex-Lax."

"They are just dreams," Freyja said. "I ride elephants. I fly through space."

"Maybe she was doing drugs?"

"No," Freyja replied.

"Was there water in her lungs?"

"Yes. Wanda says she drowned. She didn't die of an overdose."

"No fentanyl," he said. "No alcohol, and yet she lay on the ground with her face in a rut full of water."

"Maybe she hit her head on a rock. There was a bruise on her forehead. Nothing serious. Not like somebody had hit her with a baseball bat."

"Blunt force trauma?

"Not from what Wanda says."

"Her face was partly covered with mud. I never saw a bruise. There weren't any rocks where she was lying. I'd have noticed. You don't get bruises from clay." There was something unfinished about the way they stood, facing each other but not touching, unfinished the way the room was unfinished, the subfloor planks with the screw heads that glistened silver where the sun touched them and the lack of trim revealing where the floor and drywall didn't meet. Over them, instead of a chandelier, there was an open hole in the ceiling with wires tied in a knot and fitted into a red plastic cup. Tom felt that it was all hopeless, that no matter how hard he worked, no matter how carefully he reasoned, nothing would come to a conclusion, and he would be left with the shattered pieces of his life never made whole. He thought in his mastering of how to assemble, to fit, to build he had found a way to take the pieces of his life, the lives of others, and give them if not perfection, then the possibility of comfort and safety.

Tom felt depression settling over him. He hadn't wanted this conversation, would now have preferred that she'd kept teasing him.

Seeing his face darken, Freyja tried to change the topic by saying, "I read the tarot cards and the coffee grounds for fun. If you want to know your future, you need to ask the Norns."

"The Norns?" he repeated. He vaguely remembered the name.

"They're the fates. Three sisters. One tells the future, one tells the present, one tells the past. They weave our fate. We have our own version here in Valhalla. You met them. The three weird sisters you sat across from at Angel's funeral. They know everything about Iceland's history."

"Three weird sisters," he replied, not remembering because when Freyja mentioned the funeral, what loomed was Ben trying to speak but being unable to, and how he struggled and then sat down.

"I will foretell the future," Freyja said in a slightly exaggerated manner, trying to lighten his mood. There was a plastic cup on the table beside her. She picked it up, peered into it and said, "You need to work on your house now. The summer will go, and then it'll be fall, and everything has to be done before the weather turns cold. Get your house in order."

"Yes," he answered, but her attempt at humour didn't drive away the image of Ben, his hands shaking, his lips trembling, tears sliding down his cheeks, and when he sat down, Wanda reaching over with a napkin and blotting away the tears. Tom turned on his heel and went out into the blinding sun, and his head ached and he knew that he mustn't use any power tools. He was starting to have a migraine, and when that happened, he lost all sense of where his hands and feet were, and he could cut a finger or a hand off in a moment. He'd work at a task where if he got it wrong, it wouldn't do too much harm. The watery corrugated circle that came before the pain had started, and he knew he needed coffee, double strength to try to keep it away. In the city he would have hurried to the nearest shop where he could get an espresso, but now he'd brew it himself, clumsy from the flashing light and disorientation. The light expanded, became coloured, and he knew there'd be no work done. He needed the espresso, two of them, then to lie down with his eyes shut. And he hoped there were no flies on the porch, for the sound of their buzzing would be like an airplane flying right overhead.

THE NORNS'
INVITATION

When he woke the next morning, the migraine still lingered, still made his head feel distant, but the flashing light was gone. He lay on the couch and stared at the one blue eye and one vacant eye socket of the wolf and thought that he should buy it a new eye or throw it out.

As he lay there, he thought about the house and how strange a turn his life had taken. At least no one had cut the screens again, and soon he'd have all the windows installed. A couple of them needed the entire frame replaced. Slow work—measure, measure again; always measure twice, cut once. The saw, the saw, the sharp whine of the saw as it cut through the wood, the whine of the planer, the sound of the drill as he inserted the screws. He tried to use nails as little as possible. Screws were more forgiving and only took a reversing of the drill to have them miraculously rise out of the wood. It allowed him to go back and fix errors. He wished he could have done the same with his life: reverse the drill, remove the mistakes. Make it right with hindsight.

He'd have to get Ben to bring him more two-inch screws, some two and a half inch. The house, the house, his thoughts like driftwood moving in the current. He thought he'd just move in, there'd be little to do, a few minor adjustments; he'd spend his time sitting on the reef, letting the sound of the waves wash away his memories, leaving his mind clean and clear. He took his wallet and pinched out the piece of paper he'd found in his father's study, unfolded it. He'd hoped it might reveal answers to mysteries, but there was just the one word. He refolded the paper and put it back in his wallet.

He put on his bathing suit and went for a swim, washed himself in the lake and rinsed off the soap by diving and swimming underwater as long as he was able to hold his breath. The city swimming pool had been near their apartment, and his mother had been willing to pay for a yearly pass. He went often and practised his diving and swimming and liked it because swimming laps was something he could do by himself, always working against his personal best.

Now he dove a number of times, pulling himself to the bottom, feeling about for stones, finding one and bringing it to the surface, treading water as he looked at it, hoping it might tell him about its secret life.

His father had seemed so rigid, so set in his ways, living on so narrow a worn path, that it had come as a shock when Tom discovered that he gambled. It would have been no more surprising if it turned out that he robbed banks or paraglided. He wondered if his father had a secret life, somewhere beneath the surface, if he might have had other feelings, a life beyond his tailored, always slightly out-of-date brown suits, the endless calculating of other people's numbers. As he studied the stone, he heard someone calling, shook his hair back off his face and swam to shore. Freyja was standing there waiting for him.

"The Norns have sent a message," she said. "They request our presence."

"The mythological ones?"

"No, the three sisters you met at the funeral reception are asking us over. Skuld, Urdh and Verthandi. How do you like them monikers?"

"Why would anyone do that to their kids?"

"Their father was a descendent of a famous wizard who was burnt for sorcery in Iceland. He wanted to keep up the family tradition. When they got old enough to realize what he'd done to them, they rebelled, but he retaliated by sending them to Iceland to go to school and work in a fish plant."

"Why the invitation?"

"I saw Dolly at the store and mentioned you were interested in magic and Icelandic history. She works for them a couple of days a week. They're expecting us at seven."

The rocks were sharp, and as they talked, he carefully picked his way through them in his bare feet. Grey and black rocks covered with green slime that waved back and forth with the rippling water. "It's sandy farther out," he said. "Good bottom."

"Me, too," she said. "Don't you think?"

"I thought you were going to be serious?"

"I'm doing my best. I've brought you a serious message. Don't you think I deserve a reward?"

"Such as?"

"Breakfast. You said you could cook."

"White's?"

"Their eggs and hash browns are greasy."

They went into the house and he changed into jeans and a T-shirt. He brought out eggs and bacon and bread.

"I think there are twenty outlets hooked up to one line. It's a wonder the place hasn't burned down. Nothing is to code," he complained. "Not all the rings work." He glared at the stove in an accusatory manner.

"You're making excuses. Let's see how good a chef you are."

He found an onion and some boiled potatoes and a tomato, a piece of cheese. "A frittata," he said. "Will that be all right? And coffee. I'm afraid I don't have any juice." When he was cooking for Sally and the kids he often made frittatas. They were easy and there wasn't much cleanup afterwards. He was good at bacon sandwiches. Fried cheese sandwiches. Pancakes from a mix. He wished he hadn't said he could cook. She probably thought that meant he could make a soufflé or something with an exotic sauce. He had made lots of pies using ready-made pastry.

"I'll go get us some orange juice from my freezer." She looked happy then, as though their doing something together mattered to her.

He realized he was out of canned milk, so he ran over to the store. He remembered Dolly's warning and checked the cans of condensed milk. Most of them were past their best-before date. Some had labels that showed smoke damage. Some were dented. He chose the least out-of-date can and vowed to make a trip to the city for cases of canned goods.

He reached into his pocket and realized he didn't have his wallet. He checked his other pocket for change. It was empty.

"You've got a visitor," Karla said.

"Yes," he said. He'd checked his back pocket and shirt pocket. "I'm making breakfast for us. I forgot my wallet. Can I take the milk and come back after breakfast and pay you?"

"You want credit," Karla said.

He stopped and stared at her. "I don't want credit. What difference does it make if I pay you now or an hour from now?"

"You take a product and don't pay for it, that's asking for credit."

"Oh, for cripes' sake," he said and thought about running back, grabbing his wallet, running back to the store, back to the house. "Fine. Yes, I want credit."

Karla smiled at him, opened the ledger that sat on the counter. She entered, *Canned milk, 3.30.* "There'll be a ten per cent charge for thirty days credit."

"Fine," he said. "I'll be back after I have breakfast with Freyja." He saw Karla's mouth tighten and knew it wasn't the thing to say, but he was annoyed.

When he got back to the house, Freyja had returned. She had taken the cast-iron frying pan off the stove and put a pot lid over it so the top of the frittata would finish cooking.

"You can't go off flirting and leave something cooking," she said.

"She was being a bitch," he replied.

"That's either because I'm having breakfast with you, or maybe she's heard you ordered meals from Dolly."

He cut thick slices off a loaf of bread that Sarah had given him, heavy white bread that she said had potato in it. He fried bacon in a large cast-iron pan. He put out butter and raspberry jam. He made the coffee strong, because he remembered Freyja saying once that she couldn't stand weak coffee; he'd seen that she still made hers in a poki, a cloth filter sewn to thick copper wire. He thought it an affectation. It was the way his mother made her coffee. It was, he realized, one of her little rebellions. His father drank tea. Tom used a plastic cone and paper filters. He wet the filter first, added four heaping tablespoons for two cups, then poured the water slowly through the grounds. He wiped the picnic table and set it with paper plates. He used pieces of cardboard for placemats.

Freyja was familiar with the kitchen. She went to the cupboard beside the sink and took down two plastic glasses for the orange juice. He felt panic at her being in his space, a moment of déjà vu, a feeling that he'd made this breakfast before, that she'd gone to the cupboard for glasses before, that she'd turned toward him and smiled, as if this were a life he'd already lived.

He cut the frittata in half and set each half on a plate with three pieces of bacon and carried the food outside. He filled their cups, and then they sat across from each other.

The bottom of the frittata was overdone. In spite of that, she said, "You can cook breakfasts. Maybe you are a possibility after all. You've just gone closer to the top of my list of potential mates." She was watching him closely. "Do you think that you're a possibility? Could you support both of us?"

"I don't know," he said. "I have a son and daughter. How would you feel about being a stepmother to an eighteen-year-old son and a nineteen-year-old daughter?" They were joking, but at the same time, they were testing each other, seeing what possibilities there were, if any, and he felt the way he had when he was still a Mountie and one time in early winter he'd had to go out on the ice to rescue someone and was not sure the ice would hold him.

"Are they like you? Or are they like your wife?"

"They're like themselves," he said. "My daughter is goth. My son wants to be a stand-up comedian. He supports himself by working as a waiter. He plays too many computer games. Right now, we're not communicating much."

"Am I being serious enough for you?"

She was, he thought, beautiful. He wished he could tell her that, that he could just blurt out, "You're beautiful, so beautiful that I want to put my arms around you and hold you close, now and always," but he didn't know what he would want tomorrow, or the next day, and he wondered about what she wanted, if she wanted anything at all except to get a crazy ex-husband to leave her alone. The spray of freckles over her nose was charming and her green eyes this morning were emerald and her hair glowed in the sunlight like burnished copper.

"Yes," he said. "I'm sorry."

"That I'm being serious?"

"Yes. No. I don't know. I'm just sorry."

"More points for you. A man who can cook and say he's sorry. What next?"

He shifted uncomfortably. There were spruce trees between where they were sitting at the picnic table and the trail that went from the dock to the store, and two women were standing there, staring at them through the trees. He wondered if they could hear what he and Freyja were saying.

Freyja saw him looking at the two women. "Ignore them," she said. "They'll use any excuse to come over. Nosiness is an Olympic sport here. They turn everything into a soap opera."

She looked away from the women to the top of the spruce trees. "There's Huginn and Muninn," she said, pointing up at two ravens that were eyeing the remains of breakfast. "Ravens are smart. Some people get chicks and teach them to talk. Like a parrot. See if you can get them to sit on your shoulders and whisper in your ear."

As she ate, she studied him, until he said, "What is it?"

"Are you sensitive about your scar? Should I pretend it isn't there?"

"I was. Not so much now. I've gotten used to it."

"We've all got scars," she said. "It's just that most of them are hidden."

"All I cared about, once I was able to care about anything, was whether my eye would be okay."

"If you had lost it, like Odin, you might have become all wise."

He shook his head. "Does this cult really believe that Odin will return? That the world will end and they will rise to Viking heaven?"

"Do Christians believe that Christ will return?" Freyja replied. "Do Muslims think that they'll rise to heaven and have seventy-four virgins waiting for them? Make a list. Besides, Vikings are exciting. Great costumes. Have you seen Kirk Douglas and Tony what's his name being Vikings?"

"So you think the Godi are playing? Pretending?"

"There are over four hundred recognized religions in the world. Aren't they all just playing dress-up?"

"Maybe," he said, but he was uncomfortable with the question and his answer. He'd lost his faith somewhere among the blood and bodies, the crazy, demented people in slums where a job was petty theft, but he hung onto some shreds of his faith, some stubborn belief from confirmation class and hymns he enjoyed singing. "But isn't everybody guilty of playing a part, wearing a costume? My daughter is goth. Every day she looks like she is in a play. My son is a computer nerd and looks it. Mountie uniforms, nurse's uniforms, all of it. The world's a stage and we are merely players on it. Or something like that, but I don't remember the exact quote."

He pointed toward the road that led down to the dock, and through the trees they could see that two Odin women in their long, light brown Viking dresses were going to the dock.

"They buy fish off quota. You won't hear the local fishermen bad-mouthing them," Freyja said.

"Rituals," he said. "Karla says they had orgies. Sex is always mixed up in these things. Witches were supposed to cause men to go mad with desire."

"That was when the Odin group first came. I don't think they've had orgies for a long time. Now, it's more like a group hug."

"Do people really believe in this crazy story about Odin's hidden treasure?"

"People buy lottery tickets."

"But they know there's a prize. The winners are reported in the newspaper."

"Fourteen million to one. Not great odds."

"But there are no odds here. No one has found anything. It's all just rumour."

"That's not true. Years ago, McAra found a tobacco tin. It was rusted and when he broke it open, there were gold coins. Someone had been helping themselves, creating a private stash. At least that's what people thought. And three gold coins have been found on the beach. People have gone over the property with metal detectors. They still do. But over the years, the beach has eroded. Every northeast storm takes a bit of land."

"A lot?"

"Maybe fifty feet so far. Cottages have been put on skids and moved back more than once. Your house used to have fifty more feet of land in front of it. I've seen people going back and forth in canoes, one paddling, another holding a metal detector over the water. After a storm, people scour the beach. The believers don't like it when non-believers intrude, but they can't do anything about it. The beach and lake are public property."

"Crazy," he said.

He offered her more bread, butter and raspberry jam, but she turned it down. If he'd had a chest of silver and gold, precious gems, he'd have offered them to her as well. Having none of those things, he said, "I could come over now and again and do some work at your place."

She looked pleased but replied, "That's very kind of you, but no. If I let you do that, people would say I was just leading you on to get my house finished."

"Now who's worried about what people might say?"

"I'll leave you with the dishes," she answered, handing him her paper plate.

"The Norns say there will be coffee and cake. You'll like that. They'll have lots of desserts. It's an Icelandic thing. I'll come by and pick you up."

After Freyja left, Tom looked up at the ravens. They were still watching the bread. "Huginn and Muninn," he said, "here's bread." He picked up a slice and held it up. He tore off a piece and threw it into the air. It fell and he caught it. He did it twice more, then on the fourth try, one of the ravens dropped from the tree, swooped down and caught the bread at its apex. The air from its wings beat on his face. He tore off another piece and threw it. The second raven launched itself and snatched the bread from the air. He tore the rest of the slice into pieces and scattered them on the table, then he got busy cleaning up. He went into the house, and when he looked out, both ravens were on the table eating the bread.

Tom went into the small bedroom and searched through the boxes until he found his pickle jar full of coins. He took out three dollars and thirty cents and took it to the emporium. Karla was still behind the counter. He put the money down and said, "I want to see you write paid. Either that or give me a receipt."

Karla behaved as if his request was perfectly normal. She opened the book and said, "Oh, yes. I'd forgotten about that. One can of milk, three dollars and thirty cents. The bill is due in thirty days. If you pay before the end of the thirty days, there's no interest charge. You know, you didn't need to rush away from your date. Interest isn't charged by the day." She printed *Paid* behind the amount. "Did you have a pleasant breakfast?"

They were behaving like arguing lovers he realized. "Just looking," he'd said to Sarah. "There's no harm in just looking." But Karla had been looking back, and he knew it, and she knew it. He'd anticipated being given a key so he could slip upstairs some night. He'd even thought about taking an antihistamine to deal with her perfume. They'd been leading each other on, in a way. Neither of them had actually done anything, it wasn't like he'd been sliding his hand up her skirt, but both of them had been thinking that something might happen. He'd heard that Horst had to go into the city to the hospital every so often. Frenchie took him in, dropped him off and picked him up in a couple of days. Tom had half wondered if that would be a possible night, and he wasn't sure what he'd do if Karla did slip a key into his hand. *Shit*, he thought, he was just window-shopping.

Freyja came by that evening at 6:45. He was ready. He'd put on a clean pair of tan jeans and a long-sleeved white shirt. He put on a white panama that he hadn't worn in a long time.

"Nice," Freyja said. "Classy. Have you got something to take as a sacrificial offering? A gift of appreciation for the invitation?"

"I never thought of it," he said. "I didn't ask to be invited. I don't know them."

"That's not the point. They know you. They're giving you an audience. One of them knows everything about the past. One knows about the present. One plans for the future."

"You're mocking them."

"A little. They're okay. It's just they take themselves a bit too seriously. You know, the we're-one-hundred-per-cent-Icelandic thing. We can trace our ancestral line back to 894. We're of royal blood. We have seven bishops, eight goði and one hundred and eleven poets in our lineage. We are related to Erik the Red, Leif the Lucky and Snorri Sturluson."

"My father was a direct descendent of King Arthur and Canute," he said, replying to her exaggeration with his own, but his voice still had an annoyed edge to it. "My great-great-whatever sat on Shakespeare's lap. William Wordsworth wrote his poems on their kitchen table. Ancestors are not an accomplishment. You don't get to choose your parents. You don't get credit or blame for your parents. My kids aren't responsible for me."

"Shhh," she said, putting her finger to her lips. "Your genetic inheritance is the reason for the invitation. Not everyone is called into their presence."

"A gift?"

"Yes, have you something sweet?"

He thought for a moment and said, "Peanut butter cookies."

"We'll have to divide them into three packages. One package for each. They'll squabble over them if we just bring a dozen in one package."

She went to a closet in the smallest bedroom and came back with Christmas paper, a bag of coloured ribbons and a paper bag with Santa Claus on it. Santa had bright red cheeks and an enormous white beard, but someone had drawn spectacles around his eyes with a dark pen.

"Is it necessary?"

"When in Rome," she said. She made three tidy packages and tied one with red ribbon, another with green and the third with blue. She put them all into the Santa Claus gift bag.

"Christmas?" he said.

"Every day."

"The Norns," he said. "What do they do?"

"They don't just weave our destinies. They know all the days that are important. Þorláksmessa, when Icelanders eat skate. Dagur íslenskrar tungu. Jónsmessunótt, midsummer night. Þrottándinn, the old Christmas, when cows can talk and seals take on human form." She counted them on her fingers. "Even the Odin group depends on them for explanations. They are our pride and our memory. They demand that we remember. If it weren't for them, we wouldn't know any of these things anymore. You'll like Þorrablót. It's a feast in March to celebrate the end of winter. In honour of the god Thor. Everybody goes. We even have visitors from civilization."

"Do Odin followers celebrate it?"

"Brokkr stays through the winter. He's sort of their caretaker. Sometimes there might be four or five others who overwinter. They'll come, make up a table, but they don't have a celebration of their own. It's not Viking. It's recent. The Norns can tell you about it chapter and verse."

He was going to take his truck, but Freyja said no, they'd walk. Their home wasn't far, just north of the Odin group's property.

He thought they would follow the same cut in the bush that he'd followed the night he went to see the huts. Instead, Freyja led him to a footpath. The bush grew thickly on both sides of the trail, but branches and small bushes had been cleared away. Where there were trees of any size, the path curved around them and wound back and forth. There were hazel bushes, highbush cranberry. In places, the ground was boggy, with a few white birch, clusters of spruce, the occasional wild rose, and chokecherry bushes here and there. Freyja pointed out and named each one. "City boys need to learn all they can about their environment," she said, mocking him a little.

"There are trees in the city," he said.

"Elm trees, oak, ash. Nothing that'll feed you, fill your jars with jelly and jam, your containers with nuts. We're hunter-gatherers here."

"Anna used to take me to pick chokecherries and saskatoons. There's lots of wilderness areas in Winnipeg. Along the river. We picked raspberries, mushrooms. You have to know where to look. Tanya and I helped her make jam and jelly."

"I'm impressed. The urban pioneer."

As they walked, they constantly waved away mosquitoes.

"We should have worn netting," he said, smacking himself on the forehead. His hand came away with the black remains of a mosquito and a spot of blood.

"This is why I told you to wear a long shirt, long pants and a hat, remember?"

She waved her hands around her head, turned around and started to walk more quickly. Although he feared that the pins in his leg might snap, he hurried to keep up. The difference in the length of his legs made him hold his weight to one side. It threw him slightly off balance and sometimes made him feel like he might stumble and fall. In school he'd been on the track team. It hadn't cost much. Shorts and shoes. He'd sometimes won the hundred-yard dash and the hurdles. He missed running.

The Norns lived in a simple cedar cottage. He was surprised. Because people treated them as if they were important, he'd expected their place to be elegant. A path curved away from the trail toward the front, where a veranda overlooked the lake. Large mountain ash sat on each side of the doorway. Before Freyja climbed the steps and knocked on the screen door, she pointed toward the trunk of one ash. Runes were carved in lines down the trunk.

Someone from inside the house called, "Enter."

Freyja opened the door, and they made one last attempt to brush off the mosquitoes before ducking inside the screened veranda and quickly shutting the door behind them. Across from them was an open doorway. There were two looms, one to either side of the door, each with a partly finished weaving.

Freyja led the way. Their hosts were waiting for them, seated, with the twins on either side of their older sister. A weak ceiling light with a cone-shaped shade cast a circle of light. Leaning back, the three women were in shadow; leaning forward, they were in the light. Their faces were veneered with makeup, their mouths red gashes, their eyes darkened so they looked unnaturally deep set, their blonde hair stiff, identical, shimmering as they moved in and out of the light.

The eldest reached out a withered hand to greet Tom and Freyja and to indicate that they should sit on two chairs facing their hosts.

Tom sat, but Freyja knelt on one knee, reached into the Santa Claus bag and said, "I've something you might like." She took out the red package and set it on the low table in front of Skuld, then set the blue package in front of Urdh and the green in front of Verthandi. She folded up the bag and sat down.

The three women leaned forward. Their eyes glittered. They smiled without opening their mouths. The bones of their foreheads and cheeks stood out prominently. Their ears, because of the emaciated condition of their faces, looked disproportionately large. They were all dressed in the same dresses they'd worn at Angel's funeral. A white blouse, a coloured vest and long black skirts that covered everything but their leather slippers. Skuld's vest was red, Urdh's blue and Verthandi's green. They wore black caps with a tail.

It took Tom a moment to realize that there was something odd about the way they were seated. He finally realized that the legs of the Norns' chairs were taller than the legs of the chairs where he and Freyja sat.

"Thank you for coming," Skuld said to Tom. "We met you at the funeral for that poor young girl."

"Your mother's name?" Urdh asked.

"She took my father's name. Parsons."

"Her real name," Skuld insisted.

"Runa," he said, "Gudrun Einarsdóttir. "

"What was the name of the farm from which your mother came?" Skuld asked.

"I don't know," he said. "She didn't talk about her family very much."

"Her grandfathers' names?"

"Her father was Einar. One of her grandfathers may have been Ketill. Maybe not. Her parents rented a small croft. I really don't know anything about it. When she met my father, the family was living in Reykjavik."

"Many farms have been long abandoned," Urdh said. "But the Icelanders kept close parish records, and Iceland was never bombed. Icelanders can always find out who they are. If they want to know."

Tom squirmed. What she was suggesting threatened to open doors he had long ago closed, and he wished that his resentment at the funeral luncheon hadn't pried open this one. He thought of the endless hallways and doors of the apartment blocks managed by Anna and her mother. When he'd been little, the hallways had intimidated him. They'd been filled with foreign sounds and smells, and the sudden appearances and disappearances of strangers. His mother's warnings about not taking candy from anyone or going into anyone's apartment had made him even more nervous, but it hadn't stopped him from creeping up stairwells, hiding in corners behind large potted plants and, sometimes, even in unlocked closets with mops and pails, spying on all who came and went.

Verthandi picked up a small brass bell that was sitting beside her. She rang it once.

Dolly appeared with a silver coffee pot, sugar bowl and cream jug on a silver tray. She smiled broadly at Tom and said, "I've got about half of your meals in the freezer."

"Meals?" Freyja said.

"I ordered thirty meals."

Freyja rolled her eyes, but the Norns beamed in approval. "Dolly," Urdh said, "comes every Tuesday to make a week's meals for us. She's an excellent cook."

Dolly set the tray on the table, left, then came back with two oval glass trays, one with an array of sweets, the other with slices of brown bread cut diagonally. On the bread sat slices of meat, heavily marbled with fat. She smiled at Tom and ignored Freyja.

"Rúllupylsa," Dolly said. "Rolled and pickled lamb flank. Have you had it? It's very good. I made it myself."

Dolly put a dessert plate and a paper napkin in front of each of them, but no one made any attempt to pour the coffee, so he sat waiting.

Dolly returned to the kitchen and came back with five shot glasses full of a clear liquid and a small plate of white cubes with toothpicks inserted in them.

Dolly said, "Brennivín. It's a kind of schnapps with caraway."

"Hákarl. From Iceland," Urdh added proudly.

Freyja took a piece and pointedly said, "Thank you, Dolly." She pulled the cube off the toothpick with her teeth, chewed, then picked up the glass and drank it in one gulp.

The Norns watched Tom intently. Dolly held the plate up to him. He took a cube and put it in his mouth, stopped before he had taken out the toothpick, as his mouth filled with the taste and smell of urine. He pulled out the toothpick, bit down twice, then shot the brennivín into his mouth and felt it go instantly numb. He gulped down the hákarl and the brennivín.

Dolly lifted up both plates, first to Skuld, then to Urdh, then to Verthandi. They smiled and nodded their thanks, then chewed with apparent relish and drank their brennivín without flinching. That done, Dolly poured coffee for all of them.

As they tried the desserts, Urdh said, "I am interested in genealogy. If you can tell me the farm from which your mother came, I can trace your family line back to the beginning of Iceland. You may be related to poets and bishops and goði."

"Snæfellsnes," he said. "That's all I know. I've never been there."

"Under the mountain," Urdh replied. "Snæfellsnes has many wizards. Magic was practised there. Good and bad."

Skuld, her chin slightly tilted, her mouth pursed, miffed by the attention her sister had drawn to herself, said, "You used to be a policeman, but now you have decided to live here. There are many other places. Why Valhalla?"

He put down his coffee cup. "You are here."

Skuld tittered, lifted her hand with its withered fingers to cover her mouth. "So you came to be here with us. You couldn't resist."

"I grew up in the city. I thought I'd try the country."

"And what are your plans for the future?" Urdh asked.

"Jack of all trades. Do you need some carpentering, plumbing, drywalling, plastering? I'm your man."

"A simple life, like Thoreau," Urdh added. "A cabin in the woods. Have you read Thoreau? Yes, you know his life was not simple. His diary shows that he was involved in his community. There is no escaping complications. Know where you came from to know what you are."

"You always want to talk about the past," Skuld said, her voice stiffening a bit. "Everything isn't governed by the past. We have to live in the present. We have to make decisions now. As a psychologist, I may discuss the past, but people have to live in the present."

They both looked at Verthandi. It was obviously an argument that had gone on for years, perhaps for a lifetime. The psychologist against the genealogist.

"Everything affects the future. Kill a butterfly and you may change the path of history. Isn't that right, Constable Parsons? Sometimes the most innocent decision can change a life," Verthandi said in a barely audible whisper. They all leaned forward to catch every word. Although her face was stiff and she barely moved her head, her eyes shifted back and forth from Tom to Freyja.

"Yes," Tom replied. Sadness washed over him. "The best intentions can destroy lives."

"Dolly tells me that a casting of the runes might help you with your future," Skuld said.

Tom looked toward the kitchen. Dolly was standing just at the edge of the door. She nodded for him to agree. Tom said, "Yes, of course. That would be great," and Skuld said, "Bring your chairs closer. But don't drag them. You might scratch the floor."

Tom and Freyja stood up, moved their tables aside and shifted their chairs closer to Skuld. Urdh and Verthandi turned their chairs inward.

As they sat closer, the difference in the height of the chairs became more apparent. The light was weak, and outside their little circle the room was filled with shadows. Dolly appeared and set aside Verthandi's cup and saucer and plate. Urdh reached into a drawer and took out a blue cloth bag that Tom thought was the same colour as the bag in which his father's ashes were buried. The bag he'd thought was a Crown Royal bag. Urdh spread the cloth, smoothed it with the palms of her hands. Skuld reached into another drawer and drew out a small leather bag and placed it on the cloth.

"Your question of the oracle?" Verthandi whispered. Her eyes glittered in the light.

He had not come for this. His father would have mocked it as mumbo-jumbo, witch-doctor stuff. His father had no time for folk tales or superstitions, would have derided his wife's beliefs in huldufolk, in elves and dwarves, in ghosts who fought battles with the living. Henry thought it absurd that Icelanders believed in giants and trolls. He laughed at Anna's Ukrainian belief in planting by the stages of the moon, her warning him when he was going fishing of the water dwellers who marry young drowned maidens and eat fishermen.

"My question? How am I to proceed?" Tom replied.

The Norns did not move but watched him intently. Then Verthandi's skeletal fingers disappeared into the bag and drew out one tile. She placed it onto the cloth.

"You must understand, Constable Parsons, this is not a telling of the future. It is not what is ordained, only what is possible if you continue on your present path," Skuld said.

"This is the past. Eihwaz," Verthandi said in a harsh whisper, "a rune sacred to Odin, who gathered the dead souls for their journey to Valhalla. There is death. These deaths may have been both physical and spiritual. But this is a death that can be followed by regeneration and rebirth. Patience is needed."

Verthandi drew forth a second rune. "This is the present. Partho, sacred to Frigg, the wife of Odin." It is reversed, so now there are hidden things that may be revealed and cast out into the open."

She pulled the third rune out of the bag with her middle finger. "This is the rune of the future," she said. Although her face appeared frozen, emotionless, her eyes glittered with reflected light. But she looked at no one, only into the darkness. "Sowulu, a rune sacred to Baldur, the son of Odin and Frigg. It is not ordained, but if you continue on the path you have chosen, what is hidden will be revealed, though what is revealed will not necessarily be what you seek. There is a place in life for dark corners and caves. Secrets and the pain they hold are sometimes best left where they are hidden."

They had all been focused on the tiles and the words, but now that they were silent, Tom could hear large moths fumbling against the screens.

Mumbo-jumbo, he thought to himself, Norns and fortune-telling and warnings of consequences. But a girl with a wide smile and large dark eyes was buried in a nearly abandoned graveyard. She'd drowned, and it didn't matter whether it had been in three inches of water or thirty feet. He thought, perhaps, that was right, that secrets had their own place, the way the garter snakes and mice and rats had their own place beneath the soil, in cracks and crevices, in caves in the limestone. And he thought of Angel's foot sticking out from under the blue tarp, obscene and vulnerable, and Mindi Miner striking the ground with one of his canes, and a snake disappearing in a flash into a hole, and Mindi laughing out loud at his power.

He tried to catch Freyja's eye and would have indicated that they should leave, but Dolly came with the coffee pot and topped up their cups, and the twins pressed baked desserts on him. Verthandi, exhausted by speaking, closed her eyes and was still. Tom wondered if he already had a reputation in the village for having a sweet tooth. They remained sitting close, knees separated by the small table at their centre. He could smell the talcum powder they used and hear the creaking of their joints.

The Norns asked him about his house, and he detailed what needed to be done and how he would go about doing it. It was, he thought, an opportunity to sell his services, to let them know how careful he was about his work.

"Are the people in Valhalla really so dedicated to their heritage?" he asked. "Do they know their history and language?"

Skuld and Urdh leaned toward him, and Verthandi's mouth pulled tight in disapproval.

"They think that the essence of their identity is vinarterta," Skuld said. "You saw how Vidar ate it at the funeral reception. He must have gobbled up a quarter of a cake."

"They spend their time debating whether vinarterta should be iced or not. Or how many layers it should have. That is their intellectual exercise," Urdh broke in. "Ask them to recite verses from *Hávamál*, the wisdom of the Vikings, and they can't say anything because their mouths are full of dessert."

"What about the Odin group?" he asked.

There was complete silence, and he knew that he'd said something wrong. Dolly craned around the kitchen door to stare at him.

"Óðinn," Verthandi said, correcting his pronounciation, emphasizing the "th" sound of the ð.

Urdh explained, "In Icelandic there are five extra letters in the alphabet. The ð looks like a d, and in being adapted to English, writers have conveniently dropped the crossbar at the top. You don't speak Icelandic, so it is understandable that you would say O-din rather than Othin, but people who should know better say it. It drives us crazy." And she unexpectedly broke into a mocking song to the tune of "Camptown Races": "Oh din to run all night, oh din to run all day, Camptown ladies sing this song, doo dah, doo dah day." Her bony chest rose and fell with indignation. "They don't even spell the word properly."

"Sorry," Tom said.

"The Óðinn may be pretenders, but at least they are honest pretenders. They try to get their Viking history right," Urdh said. "They study the sagas."

"Not one of them is Icelandic," Skuld objected. "They're not even Scandinavian."

"That may be," Urdh replied, "but they're better than the locals. Joseph Brandsson marrying that slip of a girl and calling their child Jesus! And he has the nerve to call himself a Lutheran." She was so incensed her body jerked like she'd had a shock.

"You'll hear them," Urdh said to Tom. "The Óðinn telling people that there is gold buried here. We're all going to be rich. Valhalla has been going to be rich for nearly a hundred years. People are afraid to leave because they might miss out." She turned toward where Dolly was peering around the kitchen door and shouted, "Isn't that right, Dolly?" Dolly's head jerked out of sight. "Dolly wouldn't leave Valhalla for anything. She knows she has a lottery ticket that's going to win."

Tom thought he'd move the conversation to a safer topic and asked, "Has Pastor Jon been here a long time?"

"If Pastor Jon was as good at saving souls as he is at saving tractors, we'd be a community of saints," Skuld retorted. Talking about the foibles of the community had got her all worked up. The calm of the runes had been shattered.

Verthandi had shut her eyes again. It was all too much for her.

Skuld said, "Our people have been here since just after 1875. Five generations. It's no wonder that people forget or don't learn. We get frustrated with them. We have a noble history. We don't want them to forget it."

"I don't think the Óðinn are so bad, either," Urdh said. "At least they ask for advice. They do research about Viking times. You can have an intelligent conversation with some of them. They try to be authentic. They make excellent copies of Viking jewellery."

"You have been taken in by Godi-4," Skuld said. "He's a smooth talker, asking you to explain how a sunstone works. Don't you think he knows about using Icelandic spar to get his direction when it's foggy? He uses flattery to get your approval." She abruptly changed the subject. "The local people make things up," Skuld complained. She squirmed on her chair, her hands clenching and moving in circles over her lap. She looked like she might be churning butter. Tom hoped she wouldn't have a heart attack. "I heard one of them telling a tourist that Icelanders rode on reindeer."

"That's because Laxness created that fool of a farmer, Bjartur of Summerhouses, in *Independent People*. He rides a reindeer across a river. Have you ever heard anything so ridiculous?" Urdh said in exasperation. "The rantings of a communist Catholic. And the Swedes gave him the Nobel Prize for it! Whose fault is that?"

"You must have read Laxness, Constable Parsons," Urdh insisted, and when Tom said no, he hadn't, she looked pleased and said, "Good. Don't waste your time. Icelanders have a noble heritage. You won't find it there. Read the sagas, instead. We have complete copies in English. If you would like, you could borrow them over the winter."

Tom was watching Verthandi's chest to see if it was moving. He thanked Urdh for her offer, then asked her what she could tell him about the history of the Óðinn, careful to pronounce it correctly.

"For that," she replied, "you should talk to Helgi History. I think he is writing a book on them."

Tom and Freyja stood up, but before they could leave, Verthandi opened her eyes and said, "Constable Parsons, we are a small ethnic community." Because she barely moved her lips, her voice was weak, and they had to lean close to hear it. The air was still hot from the day. The humming of mosquitoes seeking blood and the moths rubbing against the screens as they sought light combined to sound like distant waves on a beach. "Our reputation is important to us. I don't expect that you know *Hávamál*. It is a collection of the sayings of the Vikings. It says that we all die, but that what lives on is our reputation. It is true. If someone is a buffoon or a philanderer or a thief or a murderer, that remains after they are dead. It is the same with a group. We hope nothing damages our reputation. Because of your mother, our reputation is your reputation, too."

"My mother had me read *Hávamál*, but I didn't memorize the poems. She never told me anything about Iceland except how beautiful it was. Freyja says that there were executions at," and he tried to remember how she pronounced the word, "Þingvellir, where the parliament was held."

The Norns were silent, and he wondered if he'd crossed some boundary into unacceptable history.

"Yes," Verthandi replied. "Thieves were hanged. Male adulterers were beheaded. Sorcerers were burned at the stake. One of those was an ancestor of ours. He was accused of making someone ill and causing his sheep to die in mysterious ways."

"Women," Skuld added, "were tied up in a sack and drowned in Drekkingarhylur, the Drowning Pool."

"For what crimes?" Tom asked.

"Incest, adultery, breaking vows," Skuld answered. She hastened to add defensively, "It wasn't just the Icelanders. The Scots had drowning pits."

"It was the Reformation," Urdh said. "The old religion wasn't so cruel. The new religion was very cruel. Everything was about the punishment of sin."

The Norns remained sitting on their slightly raised dais while Tom and Freyja backed out of the room. The small circle of light enclosed them, and he felt for a moment that they should have both bowed.

When Tom and Freyja were on their way back, the sun was below the tree-line. Shadows had flooded the forest.

"Are they always like that?" he asked.

"They were well behaved tonight. No one mentioned the kreppa and the bankers. They lost some money in that. Six per cent on bank deposits, fifteen per cent on bonds was what the Icelanders promised. They couldn't resist. Didn't you know, Icelanders are so honest that they never had any police? You used to hear that all the time. You don't hear it anymore."

"Was it true?"

"No," she said and laughed. "Icelandic Canadians didn't understand how the legal system worked. People were locked up on farms. If their crimes were serious, they were shipped to prison in Denmark. Conditions were so terrible that most died there."

"They disagree on some things."

Freyja laughed again. "When they were young, they used to duke it out in the yard, pulling hair, screaming and yelling. Tonight, they were on their best behaviour."

"What was that we ate that tasted like an outdoor toilet smells on a hot day?"

"Hákarl," she said, amused at his discomfort. "Rotted shark. Eat it fresh and you'll bleed to death. After it's been buried in the sand for six months and dug up, the urine in its flesh has dissipated enough that it's safe to eat."

"They eat that?" And then: a vague memory of his mother objecting to eating laverbread and his father saying, "How can you complain about laverbread when you used to eat rotten shark?"

"During the Móðuharðindin, they boiled and ate their leather shoes."

He tried to say Móðuharðindin, stumbled over it, gave up.

"This was the mist after the Laki volcano erupted in 1783. It spread ash and fog that killed a quarter of the population."

"I don't know anything about this stuff. I shouldn't have let myself be goaded into saying anything about my Icelandic background," he said petulantly.

"You came to a place called Valhalla," she answered. "What did you expect? If you wanted to live among the Brits, you should have chosen some place with an English name."

"And you? Are you one hundred per cent Icelandic?"

"Yes," she answered. "Is it a crime? I don't think I'm a member of a master race, and I don't think I'm inferior, though if you want to talk English prejudice toward the Icelanders in Canada, we can talk about that. The English hockey teams wouldn't let the Icelanders in Winnipeg play in their league. But in 1920, the Falcons went on to win the first Olympic medal. All Icelanders on the team except for one player."

Before he could think of an answer, Freyja took out a whistle and blew on it. "Bears have been seen around lately," she explained. "You don't want to surprise them."

"What was that visit about?" he asked.

"Cattle die, kinsmen die, the self must also die. I know one thing that never dies is the reputation of each dead man," Freyja said. "That's from *Hávamál*. Reputation is everything to them."

He kept running his tongue over his lips, trying to get rid of the taste of the rotted shark. "Why didn't you warn me about the rotted shark?"

"How was I to know that they had hákarl brought from Iceland on one of the charters? Besides, we both ate it. We can kiss goodnight. Just like if one eats garlic, the other has to eat garlic."

"Did you arrange this visit?"

"No," she replied. "Dolly housecleans for the Norns. She cooks for them. She knows they love to have an excuse to read the runes. Besides, she got to cater the evening. She'll get well paid for that. Her prick of a husband hardly ever sends a cheque."

"They're very strange," he said, thinking of the painted faces grouped together, pressed toward him.

"They spoke Icelandic at home. No English until they went to school."

"Mumbo-jumbo. Hocus-pocus."

"Yes." she answered. "But they try to get the hocus-pocus right. Skuld said she wasn't predicting the future. She knows her mythology. She got a master's degree in it. She knows that predicting is supposed to be left to the völva. The völva is a shaman, a seeress. Even Odin so valued her knowledge that he chanted her out of her grave to answer his questions about the future. Would you like to go to the graveyard at midnight and chant the völva out of her grave?"

"Do the locals go to the graveyard at midnight?"

"When they're drunk. To prove how brave they are they sit on a tombstone to drink their beer. Some, I've heard, have got pregnant on a grave under a full moon."

He snorted in derision but remembered what he'd said to Anna about his parents' ghosts refusing to leave the apartment, though he didn't know if his mother was dead. At times, it had been as if his parents were standing nearby, watching him, still stern and disapproving.

"Who is this Helgi they mentioned? Sarah talked about someone called Helgi History to me at bingo. He needed a haircut."

"Helgi History," Freyja said. "The local historian."

"Where does he live?"

"North," Freyja answered vaguely. "He's a terrible drinker. When he's drinking, he's friendly. When he's sober, he's grouchy and bad-tempered. When he's sober he's mostly silent, but when he's had a few drinks it's nearly impossible to shut him up. He'll lecture you on any topic you mention."

"Reliable?"

"He knows his stuff.

"Do I need an introduction?"

"A bottle of whisky will do. I'll draw you a map. There's a sign. You can't miss it. I'd walk. It's about half an hour."

"Why not drive?"

"He talks best when people drink with him. You may come home the worse for wear. If you want him to take you seriously, you have to wear a tie. Do you own a tie?"

He thought about it. In a box of clothes that was currently stored in the guest bedroom there were two ties. Or he thought there might be two ties. It was possible. He wasn't sure if he'd thrown them out or packed them. His father always wore a tie, even when he went fly-fishing. He dressed like an English gentleman. His father insisted that Tom wear a tie to school, even though it was a public school and no one except the principal wore a tie. When he left in the morning, Tom wore a tie, but once he was safely away from the apartment, he took it off and put it in his pocket. He put the tie back on before he returned home. If he had turned up at the school wearing a tie, he would have been made fun of by everyone there.

"It wouldn't hurt to press your shirt. Short sleeves are all right in this heat. Wrinkles are a sign of a careless, inferior mind. And polish your shoes."

"How do I get inside his door?"

"You said you used to play chess with your father. Helgi tried to start a chess club here. No luck. Boys like to play hockey and kill aliens. So he plays mostly against himself. Mention chess to him."

"What does he do for a living?"

"This and that," Freyja said. "He's brilliant. PhD in economics of small nations. People avoid him unless they've got an hour to spend and don't mind listening to his ranting about what's wrong with the way politicians, business people, the church, the administration, everyone is doing their job. He's got the answers to all the world's problems. He comes to Valhalla to live in his winter-ized cottage, to drink and to do research and to write undisturbed. He supports himself doing translation, genealogical research and government contracts. He fills in for professors on sabbatical."

"Urdh said he was the expert on Odin. Othin," he corrected himself. He was going to get the pronunciation right so he didn't have to listen to another version of "Camptown Races."

"He's the expert on everything. Last winter he offered two lectures in the community hall. The first one was on the effect of temperature changes on harbour ice in Iceland in the eighteenth century and its consequences for trade. Two people came. I stayed. I'm a loyal fan."

She skipped ahead of him, partly hurrying to escape the mosquitoes, he thought, but also partly because she liked hurrying, always just out of reach, teasing him, tempting him to chase her. Her red hair was loose and swung as she moved, sometimes obscuring her face, then revealing it. He reached out to her and she danced away. She laughed and tagged him with her fingertips, then darted away. For a moment, he forgot about his leg and its multitude of pins and screws and plates. He felt young, younger, a teenager again, and he followed her along the forest path with her saying, "Come on, come on, come on." He favoured his leg as he followed her, and she didn't run fast enough to outdistance him, but she was laughing and flirting, always staying just out of reach, and he forgot his annoyance and began to laugh at the game she was playing with him.

When they reached her place, they were both running slowly for the fun of it, enjoying themselves, and he thought she might invite him in, thought he might want her to invite him in, but when they reached the steps, Ramses was lying on the porch, dead. Freyja clasped her hands to her face and screamed a high-pitched scream of despair.

When he knelt to look at the cat, he saw that it had been strangled. There was a copper wire tight around its neck.

CHAPTER 25

RAMSES

Tom got a shovel from Freyja's garage, went to the edge of her property where her garden ended and began to dig.

He dug a grave six shovels long and three shovels wide, and deep enough that no wild animal would dig up the cat's body.

When he was finished, he went to the porch. Freyja was sitting on the top step with Ramses's body in her lap. He reached down, pushed the copper wire through the loop and eased it away from the cat's neck.

"Come on," he said. "It's better to get this done." His father had been like that—get the pieces picked up, buried, say a few words, move on. In war, there had been no time for grief. The dead were dead.

She held Ramses close, pressing him to her. She cried silently, her head bent. Tom helped her stand, put his arm around her and walked with her to where he'd dug the grave. Freyja slipped to her knees, then sat on the ground, Ramses in her lap. She rocked back and forth. Finally, when her rocking slowed, then stopped, Tom lifted Ramses from her and put him in the grave.

"Wait," Freyja said, got up and ran back to the house. She returned in a few minutes with Ramses's favorite catnip mouse. "He can't go anywhere without it," she said. "He'd be lonely."

She sat there as Tom filled the grave with soil.

"Stay here," she said. "I can't be by myself."

Freyja fell asleep on the couch in the living room. He got undressed in the guest bedroom, lay down on the foamy and went to sleep.

When he woke in the morning, he could smell coffee. He got up and went into the kitchen. She hadn't changed clothes.

"I'll kill him," she said. Her voice was determined, certain.

He said nothing, let her pour him coffee.

"He wants me to stay married to him because he thinks as long as we're married, I can't testify against him."

"Wife beating?"

"That and other things. When you're scared, you make bad decisions."

"Cream?" he asked, and Freyja went to the fridge.

"It may be sour," she said after handing it to him and reached down a package of Carnation powdered milk. He sniffed the container and handed it back to her. He sifted Carnation into his coffee, stirring it with a knife that was on the table.

"Divorces are messy."

"It will be more than messy. He is out of control."

"A winner."

She sat down and looked to one side, waiting for Ramses to come and pat her leg with his paw to be lifted into her lap. Then her face tightened, but it didn't stop the tears.

"I'm not a winner," she said, misunderstanding him. "I'm a two-time loser." Tears ran down her cheeks. She wiped them away with the side of her hand. "I got married at sixteen. Sixteen. Nobody in their right mind gets married at sixteen. He was twenty-one. My parents tried to talk me out of it. His parents thought it was fine. He had a good job welding. It lasted six months." Tom wasn't sure whether she meant the job or the marriage. He handed her a Kleenex. "I got a divorce. I went back to school. Kept going. Got a teaching degree. It wasn't easy." She gulped down air. "Then three years ago I came back here. Things hadn't been going well with my life. Siggi came along. I was lonely, bored, stupid."

Ramses's ghost ran around the kitchen, ate from his dish, drank his water, lay down on his blanket, got up, came to Freyja's side and sat waiting for her to pull her chair away from the table so he could jump into her lap.

Tom didn't know whether he should touch her, should put his hand on her shoulder, should put his arms around her, pull her to him, make things better with the closeness of his body.

"He isn't worth spending years in jail for," he said. As he said it, he was thinking he needed to get hold of Sarah, needed her to reason with Freyja, needed a woman to watch over her for the next day or two. She would need comforting and understanding.

He stayed with her until she said she felt better, then got her to go with him to his place, where he made a cross from a piece of scrap two-by-four.

"Was Ramses a Christian?" he asked, and Freyja smiled at his attempt at humour and put her hand on his arm. Where her hand touched him, his arm felt hot. She tightened her fingers, and then pulled her hand away.

"Better than many," Freyja answered. "He never did any of the things people who go to church have done."

They walked back together and he pounded the cross into the ground.

"You can paint it and paint his name on it," he said, thinking that keeping busy was good for dealing with grief and anger.

They stopped at her front steps. "Thank you," she said. "For everything."

"Don't shoot anybody," he said. "Prisons are no place to spend your time." He had hoped she'd agree or nod, but instead, she just looked directly into his eyes for a long moment, then turned and went inside. He wondered, then, if he should have taken her rifle, thought that she could easily borrow another and that if Siggi appeared and harmed her because she wasn't armed, he would have to live with the guilt.

He went to Sarah's. She wasn't home. He remembered that she often went to Dolly's to visit. He knocked on the door and Dolly said no, she wasn't there but she might be at Ben's.

There was no one outside at Ben's, but the door was open so he leaned in and yelled, "Anybody home?"

"We're in here," Sarah called back. "You looking for me?" She came to the door.

"Freyja's cat, Ramses, is dead," he said.

"Ben found him." She turned in the doorway and called, "Ben, you come here. He's asking about Ramses."

"He was caught in a rabbit snare. One of the kids didn't clean up their rabbit snares when the season was over," Ben said.

"She thinks Siggi did it," Tom said.

"I was going to come back and tell her, but then I saw that you were there and I didn't want to intrude, if you know what I mean?"

"She slept on the couch," Tom said.

"That so," Sarah said.

Ben stood behind Sarah. He obviously wasn't going to invite Tom in, and Tom wondered if Ben still thought he had something to do with Angel's death.

"Yes," Tom replied, his voice edgy with the lack of sleep, the sorrow of Freyja, his own turbulent emotions, the hammering in his head of his parents saying, "Don't want anything" and his thinking not of Freyja but of her first husband and what his story would be, of him wanting Freyja and how it had all ended in tears and anger, and of Siggi, choosing Freyja even though guys with big trucks, big salaries, hundred-dollar bills to throw on the floor of the bar usually had lots of choices. There were always lots of young women, women like Sally, who would take off their shoes and everything else in the hope of striking it rich.

"I'll go tell her," Tom said.

When he got to Freyja's, her red Jeep was gone. People in Valhalla seldom locked their doors when they went out. He opened the door and looked inside. Freyja's rifle was gone. *Oh shit*, he said to himself, then turned and ran to his truck. He backed up, spun his wheels in the gravel as he raced away. He wished he'd paid more attention when she described where the embassy was, but he had some idea.

The road wound and twisted through tamarack forest and swamp. The gravel that had been pushed from the crown of the road onto the sides was dangerous. He knew a vehicle was ahead of him because dust hung in the air. He pressed on the accelerator and felt the truck slew in the gravel. He straightened out, slowed for the next curve and accelerated into it. The plume of dust was thicker, whiter. Even with the windows closed, it settled over his face, got in his eyes and mouth. The road snaked around hogbacks. Built by following a cow drunk on fermented mash, the locals said. He swung wide on a curve and saw Freyja's car nose down in muskeg. The back wheels were still on the road.

He pulled up behind her, and a cloud of his own dust enveloped his and Freyja's car. He waited until most of it had settled. He got out and went to the driver's side. He knocked on the back window. Freyja ignored him. He knocked again, harder.

When she put the window down he said, "You are damn lucky you didn't roll over and end upside down. You'd be a candidate for a body bag." He struggled not to shout.

"I'm fine," she said. Her cheeks were stained with tears.

Her words were lies—she was not fine. Perhaps they were the truth in that she was uninjured from the accident, but he had seen her this way before, when he had first come to Valhalla searching for a place where he could heal his pain, and he wondered if it would become his role in life to rescue her from her impetuousness, her inability to see the danger that lurked around her. He held tight to the car radio antenna as the sun bore down upon them like a great furious weight, and the landscape around them shrunk and hardened, the stunted tamarack now like a million dark spears against the sky and the muskeg underfoot, dark green and softly dangerous. Beneath his feet the road was silently sinking, providing briefly a place where he might stand with solid footing, and he felt that everything, like his heart, was on the edge of speeding up, and the road and the car might sink before his very eyes, and he would sink with them, disappear without leaving a trace of where they had gone.

He felt that they were suspended on the edge of disaster, saved by the inconsequential gravel on the road, their lives only moments from what could have been. The dust was still slowly settling over him, over the red Jeep, over the muskeg, making no sound, although if his hearing were acute enough, he would have heard a thousand thousand boulders crashing onto the moss and over the trees. When he spoke it was as if he were announcing a reprieve to the condemned.

"Your ex didn't do it. Ben found Ramses in a rabbit snare. He put him on the porch because you weren't home. If you are going to shoot someone, you'd better be sure you've got the right person." He said the last sentence harshly as he struggled to contain his anger.

Freyja rested her forehead on the steering wheel.

"We'd better get your car out or it will disappear. This stuff is bottomless."

He moved aside and she struggled out, hung onto the side of the car because the muskeg provided no firm footing. He took her hand and pulled her onto solid ground. Then he went to his truck, got a chain and hooked it to Freyja's Jeep and onto his trailer hitch. She stood well back as he pulled the Jeep out.

"No damage done," he said, "but it needs washing." There was moss stuck in places and dirt all over the front of the car. "Where's your rifle?"

"Inside," she said. She started shaking, closed her eyes and leaned against the fender. He opened the front passenger door, took out the rifle, ejected the bullet from the chamber, kicked it into the muskeg and put the rifle into his truck.

He wanted to shout at her, tell her how stupid she had nearly been, but there didn't seem to be any point. "Get back in. Turn it over," he said. "See if it runs all right."

She started her car. When he'd pulled it out, he'd made sure it was facing back to Valhalla. "I'll follow you," he said and got into his truck. He wasn't taking any chances on her turning around. *Stupid*, he said to himself, *stupid, stupid*. No idea what fifteen years in prison would be like. Shooting an innocent person and having to live with it. He'd seen the devastation caused by hunting accidents, drunken brawls, family arguments. As Freyja drove ahead of him and she couldn't hear what he had to say, he shouted, "Stupid!" repeatedly, until he got it out of his system.

When they got back to Freyja's, he followed her into the house. He put the rifle back beside the door.

"I'm sorry," she said. Her shoulders drooped, and her hair was a mess—it was white with dust—and tears had made white channels down her cheeks. With her whitened hair and her tear-stained cheeks, he thought that she looked like a lost waif.

"You've got a bad temper," he said. He was still angry.

"Siggi knows how important Ramses is to me."

"An irresponsible kid was snaring rabbits and didn't pick up his snares when the season was over. Are you going to shoot him?

"No," she said, "of course not. It was an accident. Stupid but an accident. Kids don't think."

"You had the intent and the means to kill. You set out to commit murder. Do you understand that is a crime? You could go to prison?"

She sat down at the table. "I couldn't do it. I was going too fast. I was crying. I couldn't have done it. I hit gravel and spun out."

"My hair," he said, "is so thick with dust that it feels like it has plaster in it. I'm going for a swim. I'm going to be coughing up this crap for days."

He went out but didn't go straight back to his trailer. He went to Sarah's first.

"Well?" Sarah said. He told her what had happened. "If you've got time, I think it would be good if you went over to Freyja's."

"You're angry."

"Angry? What makes you think I'm angry?" He could hear his voice rising. "I'm furious. I hate stupidity. She never gave one thought to the consequences."

"She's got red hair. What do you expect?"

"That's an excuse."

"You sound like you care."

"No," he answered back. "I don't care. I refuse to care. She can shoot the whole damn village for all I care." He would have slammed the door on his way out, but it was on a spring and slowly eased shut behind him. It infuriated him.

"I'm taking pönnukökur out of the freezer for coffee," Sarah called after him. "Come back in an hour, after you've cooled down."

It was so damn hot that it was like he was suffocating. The heat lay over everything like a blanket, he thought, trying to come up with clichés that would explain the weight of the air, the thickness of it, the feeling that it was pressing down. It was like being in an oven. It was. But he was too upset to keep searching his memory for clichés. Mrs. Galecian had been good at clichés; she never ran out of them, her apartment was crammed full of them, she kept the cliché business in business. If she were still alive, she'd give him a list.

The questions of the Norns plagued him. They were like a swarm of wasps that he was constantly waving away. He didn't know the name of the farm from which his mother's family came. However, there had been letters. He'd found them, a wooden box of them and what he assumed was a diary, but they were in Icelandic, and not being wanted, he refused to want in return, and he'd thrown the box into the garbage.

Anna had rescued them, said she'd put them away, and if, some day, he wanted them, he could have them.

He'd followed his father to Valhalla, or thought he had, but now it was his mother's voice he heard behind the doors in the endless hallways, and he wished, for the first time, that he could open a door and ask her questions, but the thought was so painful that he slammed shut the door that had opened. There were things better left alone, forgotten.

He would feel better after swimming. The water close to shore was shallow and warm, but if he swam farther out, dove down, down into the darkness, to where he could grab a stone from the bottom and bring it to the surface, a stone that had been hidden for centuries, down there, the water would be cool.

CHAPTER 26

HELGI
HISTORY

"You're sure I have to wear a tie?" Tom asked.

When Freyja had come by to say she was sorry about the day before, he'd told her that he was going to Helgi History's, so she stayed to inspect him.

"A light summer sports jacket would help."

"In this heat?" he said. The armpits of his shirt were stained, and there was a line of sweat running down the centre of his back.

Tom rummaged in a box, found three ties, picked out the string tie, thought it would be regarded as frivolous, and put on a blue silk one with polka dots that Sally had given him one Christmas. She liked it when he was dressed up. He ironed a short-sleeved cotton shirt, polished his shoes but then decided he couldn't wear them in the heat and brushed his sandals instead. He touched up a pair of tan slacks that were tight in the waist, taking out some creases, put on a straw hat and his sunglasses, and put a pen and a notebook and his mickey of Scotch into a grocery bag.

"You'll have to come by and tell me how your meeting goes," Freyja said. "I'll have something cold to drink. He has dogs. Do you like dogs?"

"No," he said, thinking of the dogs in the apartment block. "Are they German shepherds?"

"No," she answered. "They bark a lot, but I've never known them to bite anyone."

Dogs, bloody dogs, he thought. He'd once had a Rottweiler lunge at him when he went to clean an apartment. The owners had left it behind, and it was crazy with thirst and hunger. A wiener dog had bitten him just above the ankle and Anna had to take him to the doctor.

The forest trail was motionless except for the bees. High grass leaned inward. He stopped to pull his socks over his pants. There was a sign at the store to check for ticks. He was soaked with sweat by the time he came across a wooden sign that said *Helgi Helgason, Independent Scholar*. The name was carved and the letters highlighted with black paint. A university graduate's cap was carved on one side of Helgi's name and a book on the other. It looked like Jumpy Albert's work. There was no gate and no sign of a house.

The driveway was just a single lane, barely wide enough for a car. It curved into the trees. It obviously wasn't used a lot, because grass was growing over it and small saplings sprouted here and there like weeds. There were two shallow ruts made by a vehicle's tires.

By the time Tom could finally see a house through the bush, a dog began to bark and a second started baying. A moment later, a brown mastiff with a square head and crazed eyes came sprinting toward him. A beagle followed, baying all the while. Tom stood absolutely still. He wished he still had his service pistol or a shotgun. The mastiff skidded to a stop, coming so close that when he shook his head, saliva sprayed on Tom's shirt. The beagle circled around to cut off Tom's escape.

Just then there was a sharp whistle and a man's voice called, "Dogs, here!" in a commanding tone. The mastiff's head turned toward the voice. He gave Tom a threatening glare and a low growl, then raced back the way he'd come. The beagle followed.

When Tom reached the house, Helgi was standing in the doorway with the dogs on either side of him. His black hair and beard were long, and his hair stood out stiffly from his head and face. He wore half-frame glasses, and with his face buried in hair, not much showed except his nose—it might have been a mouse hiding in a haystack.

"What business have you with me?" Helgi asked.

"Freyja says you are a chess expert."

"Freyja," Helgi said her name with delight. He might have been given a small but precious gift. "A bloom in the desert. A flower in any man's life." He studied Tom suspiciously. "Are you investigating a chess crime? A villain stole a pawn? Or kidnapped a queen?

Tom ignored the sarcasm. "I had a question for you about the Icelandic chess club in Winnipeg."

"You know about that? Isn't it rather obscure?" The question had gotten his attention. He stopped rubbing the mastiff's head and looked more closely at Tom.

"My father played chess. He heard about it at the Jewish chess club." His father, wanting to play the best players, went to the Jewish chess club. Although he was Anglican, he was always welcome, only his skills at the game mattered, but Gudrun didn't approve. In Iceland, the prejudice against Jews was so great that the few Jews who lived there concealed their religion, practised it in secret, their deception helped by the fact that Icelanders were lax Lutherans. During the war, Jews who escaped to Iceland were often sent back to Europe, to certain death.

Tom could feel sweat running down his sides. The air was absolutely still. The leaves on the trees were limp and curled at the edges. *Shorts*, he thought. *I should have worn shorts.* His legs felt like they were enveloped in steam.

They stood there awkwardly, held in place by a gossamer fragment of history. The mastiff seemed to be studying Tom's throat, the beagle his ankles.

Helgi was wearing a white short-sleeved shirt and a blue tie with a repeated gold pattern. *It must be a school tie*, Tom thought.

"You play?" Helgi History asked.

"A little," Tom replied. "But I'm out of practice. I played with my father and was in the university chess club."

"Dogs, go!" Helgi History commanded, waving them away. They reluctantly shuffled a few feet from the door.

"Come in," Helgi said to Tom. "Shut the door behind you." He turned abruptly and went down the hallway. Tom followed him. The walls on both sides were fitted with bookshelves from floor to ceiling and every shelf was filled. They went into a living room that took up the entire front of the cottage and overlooked the lake. The wall facing the lake was glass from floor to ceiling. The other three walls were bookshelves, and stacks of books of various heights were piled here and there about the room. There were a half dozen chess sets with the chessmen in various configurations of unfinished games. A leather couch stood behind a table, the top of which was a chessboard with a game in progress and a chair opposite. The chess pieces were copies of figures from Viking times. Helgi History sat on the chair and told Tom to sit on the couch.

"What's white's next move?" he demanded.

Tom studied the board and finally said, "Knight to queen five."

"Good enough," Helgi History answered. "Make the move."

"Whose game am I playing?" Tom asked.

"My other self," Helgi History replied. "My light, virtuous side against my evil, dark side."

"Jekyll and Hyde," Tom answered.

"Or Heckle and Jeckle. Or Mutt and Jeff. Or Martin and Lewis."

"Antony and Cleopatra. Sherlock Holmes and Dr. Watson," Tom replied. It was a game of pairs he'd often played by himself.

"Too obvious," Helgi History said, his eyes shifting rapidly from side to side behind his glasses. He looked like he was sorting through invisible files.

Tom reached into the grocery bag and took out his nearly full mickey of Scotch.

"You know the way to a man's heart," Helgi History said, and he leapt up and collected two glasses from a table covered in papers. "Ice?"

"An inch of water," Tom said. "Cold."

Helgi History went into the kitchen and washed the glasses. "Pawn to rook four," he yelled, and Tom made the move for him.

Helgi History came back into the room with two glasses, one empty and one with a faint line of water on the bottom. Tom poured them each an ounce of whisky.

"You had a question?"

"Was there an Icelandic chess club in Winnipeg?"

Helgi History had a single ice cube in his glass. He swirled the whisky around, held it up to the sunlight to admire the colour, then drank it in one gulp.

"Through the 1920s, 1930s. They were among the best."

"Did the Cuban come to Winnipeg?"

"The Human Chess Machine? You know about him, then you know more than anyone else."

"Capablanca. I remember his name because it's similar to the movie *Casablanca*."

Tom hadn't thought about these things in a long time—names, games, end games, strategy, moves, countermoves—had forgotten this basement room in his mind that contained all the things his father had talked about, the people he had admired, the books that he'd told Tom to read, while, at the same time, with his tone of voice, or the way he held his head, making a subtle suggestion that Tom wasn't up to chess. And when he went out to the chess club, he left Tom at home. For a long time, it was chess, and only chess, that would cause him to set aside everything else he was doing. Later, bridge began to take over his life, and the fierceness of the competition, the desire to be the best, to be a grand master, may have led to his gambling. No game was so hard fought as one in which one's paycheque was at stake.

"Don't you find players among the Odin?"

"They're more interested in less demanding pleasures."

"Chess is the Icelandic game, I've been told." It may have been an Icelandic game, but it was his father who had given him his own chess set.

"In the golden past, it was," Helgi replied. "Now, our culture is reduced to eating Icelandic sweets and wearing costumes on special occasions. Our people brought their Bibles and chess sets in their wooden chests." It was obvious to Tom that he'd struck a nerve, because Helgi History's attention had strayed from the board. "There's a folk story in which a boy and girl, waiting in a cave for a giant to return, play chess to pass the time. In the 1500s, German trader Gories Peers said that Icelanders spent the winter lying in bed playing chess. Here, here in Valhalla, the tradition has died out. There are chess sets, but no one knows how to use them. It's like the spinning wheels and the Icelandic books. They are decorations. I collect the chess sets. I collect the books so they don't go to the garbage dump. Lost, lost, all lost," he said dramatically. "It's your move."

Tom had seen players like Helgi in the chess club he'd belonged to. Brilliant, focused, able to play numerous others at the same time and defeat them. Tom studied his move and was glad they weren't playing against the clock.

"In the days before the Odin, Valhalla was very Icelandic. Everyone spoke the language. You hardly heard a word of English. It was their own world. Those people had the true Viking spirit but no money. Money destroys everything.

"They came to find Baldur's palace—Breiðablik—and instead got hunger and cold and disease. But they survived the winter playing chess, spinning and weaving, waiting for the sun. Dr. Ford, the builder of your house, turned up looking to catch big fish. He stayed with the Frederickssons. Paid cash. There wasn't much of that around. The Frederickssons always had an eye for money," he said with contempt. His eyes swivelled from the board to the bottle that glowed amber with the sunlight streaming through it. Tom poured out another ounce.

"I don't like to drink alone," Helgi History said, and Tom poured himself half an ounce. "You are miserly with yourself."

"Dr. Ford," Tom said and moved his rook.

"He had that place built that you live in now. It was unimaginable. To build a house just for the summer. Our people had come from rock and turf huts. They'd lived and died in shanties here the first years. In Iceland they never built with wood. Here, at least, there were houses with stoves. Stoves! You don't know what that means. There were no stoves in Iceland. What would have been the point? There was hardly any fuel. Driftwood for those who had shore rights. Brown coal for a few in the right location. People were so desperate they burned fish bones and seaweed. Body heat, animal heat, in that climate. Ten to a bed, head to foot, to keep warm. There was injustice everywhere.

"But we had books." He leapt out of his chair and held up his empty glass and described an arc around the room with it. "Precious books. No kings in palaces, but we had palaces built with books."

The shelves from floor to ceiling were crammed with books, with books set flat on top of those shelved with their spines out, with piles of books towering up like high-rises in a city made of books, so that a person had to be careful moving about the room, for if one tower fell, it would bring down another. Tom could imagine the chaos that would ensue. A stumble, a careless reaching out, a shivering of the house in a violent storm, even the pounding of the waves against the shore, and one dislodged book would bring chaos, with the chessboards toppling, scattering chessmen through the tumbled books. It was a room jammed full of delicately balanced knowledge, and he wondered about the mind that had created it.

"What does each pillar represent?" Tom asked.

"Projects," Helgi answered. "Every one is a research project. An independent scholar has to have many irons in the fire."

He went to a shelf and selected four books. *The Elder Edda*, poetry," he declared, holding up a book with a green cover. "Here, the *Passíusálmar*, the

Passion Hymns, written by Hallgrímur Pétursson. He held up a blue book. Here, a history of Iceland. Here, *Njáls saga*. It's all there. Know these books and you know Iceland."

He put three of the books back, kept the *Passion Hymns*, sat down and moved a chess piece. "We had our own ways. Then Dr. Ford came with his modern ideas. And Ingibjorg, the beautiful, dangerous Ingibjorg. He fell under her spell." Helgi History went to a cabinet and took out pictures in old-fashioned frames and sorted through them. He selected one and handed it to Tom. It was a sepia picture of a beautiful young woman with long flowing hair. She was wearing a traditional Icelandic dress.

"A heart-stopper," Tom said.

"A heart stealer," Helgi History replied. "She had a fantastical mind. To her, dreams were a path to another world, a world as real as this one, the one we are in right now. We enter this other world through dreams, but every morning we have to return. She sought ways to enter this dream world while awake, to join the two together.

"She took Ford as her lover. He took her back to Michigan with him. He introduced her to people in New York. Took her to meet artists, playwrights, actors, producers, philosophers. He took her to Iceland on a rented yacht. They came back with Godi-1." Helgi History rummaged excitedly through the drawer again. "Here is the great Rune Master, the knower of all things, the guide to the portal to the other world.

"Godi-1 became her lover. There was conflict between him and Ford, so Ingibjorg came up with the idea that they were all One, that what one did was like all doing it. There could be no separation. Everyone shared themselves with everyone else. There was no sin, for they were all one and the same."

He thrust a studio portrait at Tom. It was of a man with a prominent forehead, deep-set eyes, sunken cheeks and long hair. He was wearing a floor-length robe and held a large book to his chest with one hand above the other. His fingers were long. On every finger there was a ring.

"Godi-1 was charismatic. He soon had a following. Imagine living out your wildest fantasies. Not just given permission but encouraged to engage in sex and drugs. Why wouldn't people give donations?

"Valhalla. The name was propitious. It was, he said, a portal to this other world, Valhalla to Valhalla, the world we live in for a third of our lives as we sleep and are vaguely aware of its terrors and pleasures." He held out his glass. Tom poured another ounce into it. Poured another half ounce into his own glass. Helgi History raised his glass in a salute, and they both drank.

"That other world could have been a bunch of uptight Lutherans flagellating themselves with guilt." He laughed. "Ingibjorg's other world was much more attractive. She understood that religion and sex go together like ham and cheese, like hangikjöt and rúgbrauð, like..." but his attention wandered for a moment. "Queen to knight seven," he said. "Make my move for me. My hands are full." He was leafing through the *Passíusálmar*, humming to himself. "Do you sing?" He was waving his index finger as he read one of the passion hymns.

"I'm tone deaf," Tom replied.

"That's unfortunate. Pastor Jon is tone deaf as well. His predecessor could sing. He held Bible study classes. He read Latin, Hebrew and Aramaic. He also knew about bees."

"He left under awkward circumstances," Tom rejoined.

"Talent should excuse little peccadillos."

"He got a farmer's wife pregnant. Or so I heard. He was lucky he didn't become mink feed."

"Don't you think that Ingibjorg's solution is better? What harm was he doing? It's not like we can only have sex so many times and then are used up. Move my bishop to rook six."

"Crazy," Tom said.

"Yes, but Ingibjorg was no crazier than lots of others," Helgi said. "At least they didn't kill millions. They didn't destroy countries. They were too busy finding enlightenment. Be grateful for small mercies. If Hitler and Stalin had been as involved with finding truth through sex, millions would have survived. Those making love have no time to make war."

"And now?" Tom said. "What about now? What of Odin today?" Tom moved his queen.

"Everything changes," Helgi History said. "New truths emerge." He held out his glass and Tom filled it to the top this time. Helgi demanded he drink up too, and Tom poured the last of the whisky into his glass. They drank, and Helgi took the empty bottle and held it up to the light to be sure nothing was left. He threw the bottle out through the front door and disappeared into the kitchen. He came back with a green bottle. "Black Death," he announced. "At one time there was a skull on the label. They should have kept it. I'll repay your generosity."

He opened the brennivín and filled both their glasses. The liquor looked like water. He drank from his glass and Tom did the same, remembering what his mother told him: "Always look in the eyes of your drinking companions. Otherwise, they will think you dislike them or have an evil intention toward them."

His mouth went numb and he thought, *Thank God there's no rotted shark*.

Helgi opened a can of tobacco and filled his pipe. He tamped the tobacco into the bowl and fished a wooden match out of a box.

"I won't ask permission to smoke in my own house. You are free to leave if you object." He struck the match and there was the sharp smell of sulphur. "There are few enough pleasures in life. I don't intend to give up any of mine. These new puritans that would protect our health—do you think on their deathbed they'll proclaim they've had a good life because of all the things they haven't done?"

The sweet smell of tobacco filled the room. Tom did not bother to answer what was obviously a rhetorical question.

"So," Helgi History said, "you have come to find the portal, to see Valhalla?"

"No," Tom protested.

"Bottoms up," Helgi History cried. "You have already found one treasure. To Freyja," he said and drained his glass, and Tom felt compelled to do the same. "There are portals and portals. A beautiful woman is one."

"What of this treasure?"

"You already know of the hidden treasure! You are investigating our history, unravelling our secrets. Be careful—many secrets are benign, but a few are like old bear traps rusting in the bush. Step on them and they clamp tight on your leg." He started using his index finger to direct his humming of a hymn.

"Do you think it exists?"

"Many think it may be buried on your property. You have become its keeper. You will have to protect your property ferociously. Otherwise, there are those who will tear everything down, dig up every foot of land, dynamite the rock."

"The Whites," Tom said. His head was spinning from the whisky and Black Death.

"A house fallen into ruin," Helgi History declared.

"What about Siggi and Freyja," Tom managed. His tongue was thick and clumsy.

"Siggi," Helgi History said. "Freyja shouldn't have gotten involved with him. She's too smart. He's not stupid. I'm not saying that. He's like those bright students who won't study, won't do their assignments, because they are too busy playing sports, partying, making a buck. High energy."

"Sports hero," Tom added, trying to clarify.

"Hockey hero, mud-race hero, speed-skating hero, every kind of hero. Like he's on Red Bull twenty-four hours a day." He said it with a resentful tone.

"Not a chess hero?"

"Doesn't think ahead. Ideas of the moment. No thirteen moves figured out. If you're losing the hockey game, beat your opponent up. Lot of penalty time. High-sticking, tripping, checking from behind. Fighting."

"Bad guy?"

"Local hero. Generous. Loyal. Helps people out. Never grew up. Now playing a more dangerous game."

"Growing tomatoes and cucumbers."

"And lettuce," Helgi said. "Difficult place for it. Wrong climate."

"And Freyja? What's he likely to do about Freyja?"

Helgi was sitting with his back to the front windows. As Tom waited for him to make his next move, he saw the face of an elderly bald man appear. He had a long white beard and was holding a baby. Before Tom could react, Joseph rapped sharply on the glass with his knuckle.

Helgi turned just enough to see who was at the window, then turned back and said, "Baby Jesus has arrived. We'll have to finish this game another day."

He rose and Tom rose with him, uncertain what he should do.

"You can find your own way out. Here." He picked up a red rubber ball. "Throw this over the roof on your way out. Show it to the dogs first. They will chase it. Then scoot up the driveway. They never go farther than the end of the driveway. Nothing in their universe is more important than chasing this ball."

Tom staggered as far as Sarah's. She opened the door and he grinned foolishly, stumbled over the threshold. She pulled out a chair for him and he slumped into it. He ranted about Helgi History and chess, but his mind couldn't focus, and he told her he was going to meet with Siggi and have a discussion about his treatment of Freyja.

"Don't go there," Sarah said as she handed him a bowl of skyr. "Here. Food and coffee will help. Visiting Helgi History is dangerous. If he dislikes you, he'll sic his dogs on you. If he likes you, he'll drink you to death."

Tom sat with his head back and his eyes wide open. "I haven't felt like this since I got drunk as a teenager," he said. "The room keeps trying to spin like Albert's trees."

"If you need to puke, do it outside."

"I thought I might be able to talk to Siggi," he said stubbornly.

"His friends are Freemen on the Land. No rules apply to them. No laws. They think that by calling some place an embassy, the law can't touch them. That's no ordinary building. It's a survivalist bunker. Johnny Armstrong dug it down. He does blasting and concrete work. It's built with rock and steel. You want to get them out of there, you need to bomb them out."

"Freyja was going there with a twenty-two." He could hear that his words were slurred and slow.

"Into the Valley of Death rode the four hundred," Sarah declaimed. "They say they have pretty good parties. A lot of people like to go the embassy. Lots of liquor. It's all free. Especially if you're young and cute."

"Embassy?" he said, trying to catch hold of fragmented images and thoughts. "Edmonton," he said, but there were spaces between his sentences as the thoughts took a long time to get from his head to his tongue. "A guy rented. Wrecked the place. Wouldn't leave. Claimed it was an embassy."

He struggled to keep the room from spinning. He focused on a cuckoo clock. He felt that if he just looked at it and nothing else, the floor and tables and chairs, the walls, would remain still. What he couldn't still were the memories—liquor was bad for memories; it let them loose like zombies, like ghosts, like an insane mob from the asylum. He'd tried to bury them. Some of his former colleagues buried them with booze. They started drinking as soon as their shift was over. The rule was never to admit the maimed, the dead, the screaming, the crying that sounded like it was ripping out a mother's soul. It seemed to work, but then someone would shoot himself, or force someone else to shoot him, or shut himself in a garage and turn on the car, or have an inexplicable accident after the zombies rose up and swarmed him and he couldn't fight them off any longer.

Tom rubbed his head with his right hand. He hated that term: "male vio-lence"—he protested against people who used the term as if it was only men who were violent—but it was dead girlfriends, dead wives, dead rape victims that had to be put in body bags, and men raging, justifying what they'd done, yelling out the women's faults as if jealousy, disappointment, imperfection were to be punished with death. He could only remember two cases of wives having killed their husbands. Girlfriends never killed their boyfriends. Boyfriends killed their girlfriends all the time. *But not me*, he thought, *not me, not Henry, not...* but the room began to spin like a carousel. He staggered up from his chair and into the yard, where he leaned against a tree and threw up until all he had were dry heaves.

When he went back inside, Sarah gave him a glass of water to wash out his mouth. He leaned out the door, rinsed his mouth and spit. He came back inside and sat down, and Sarah poured him a fresh cup of coffee.

"Valhalla is the end of the world," Sarah said. "Nothing from here to Hudson Bay, then there's Siberia. This is as far as people can run. Why are you here?"

An image of Valhalla in winter appeared, and he stared at it as if it were on a screen. "It was like a postcard. A Christmas card," he said, correcting himself. "Snow," he lifted his right hand and described a curve with it, "drifts." He put down his hand. "Everything covered in snow. Quiet. Perfect. No noise."

It was like he had forgotten she was there and he was talking to himself. He was remembering the constant noise of the traffic that passed by his parents' apartment. The sirens. Ambulances. Fire trucks. The noise of the buses. The noise in his head that wouldn't go away. He thought that in the silence of the country, the silence of the snow, the noise would recede, and for a moment, he was distracted by the word "recede," pleased with it. It was a good word. The noise would recede so he couldn't hear the sound of cars racing, tires squealing, the harsh sounds of vehicles colliding. He broke into a cold sweat when he heard them. People he'd worked with killed themselves to stop the noise. Now, he sat in Sarah's kitchen staring into space, trying to smother the sounds, and Sarah watched him as his eyes moved back and forth, seeing images she could not see.

"I shouldn't have drunk Black Death," he declared. "It let all the devils out." He thought he would get up and go. And because Sarah was a literary-type person, he would say, "I will arise and go now, and go to Innisfree, to a house, or something made of clay and wattles, daub," the word coming to him through the confusion of his drunkenness, "and wattles." *What*, he wondered, *are wattles? Nine bean rows and a hive for the honeybee.* He couldn't remember the rest of it. He'd memorized it in grade ten. Instead of saying anything, he licked his lips. They felt dry and cracked.

"People wash up here," Sarah said. "They've run out of places to go. We all become a little strange, but everyone just wants to be treated like they're normal."

He went to get up, and then felt the room move and sat down before he fell down. He remembered Helgi turning and saying that Baby Jesus had arrived, and there was Joseph with his long white beard at the window, and he was carrying a child.

"Baby Jesus came," he said. "I saw him. In the window in his father's arms."

"Joseph's an old fool and his wife is a young fool. She didn't have an immaculate conception. She wanted to get pregnant so she'd have his pension and welfare. He thinks they're a living crèche."

Tom licked his lips. He pulled the skin of his forehead together in an attempt to keep the room from spinning.

"Horst and Karla," he said. "A house fallen into ruin. That's what Helgi said." Everything was fragmented. Baby Jesus, a ruined house, a crèche.

"They're not the only ones," Sarah said. "That could describe a lot of people."

"Siggi," he said, veering back to a random thought. "Survivalists."

"I don't know what they want to survive for if everybody else is dead. You hear Siggi and his friends talk, it's a kind of men in the wilderness. When they talk about women, it's not by any name. It's 'my woman,' or 'Come here, woman.' Women will just be in the background, keeping the place clean, making meals, providing sex on demand. I heard they've got five hundred pounds of dried beans. The same of rice. Rooms full of freeze-dried stuff."

"Beans," he said, as if the word was filled with meaning.

"Siggi has a lot of fans. When he has money, he spreads it around. He hires local. A local is having a bad time, he might drop off a few dollars. Anybody comes to Valhalla who looks suspicious, people let Siggi know."

The door opened and Freyja came in.

"You were planning on starting World War III, I hear," Sarah said.

Freyja looked at Tom and his silly grin and said, "What happened to him?"

"Ossified. Helgi History. They played chess."

"I wish Ben had left me a note."

328 ~ W.D. VALGARDSON

"He's sorry. He didn't think you'd think what you did, if you know what I mean."

"You're a portal," Tom said loudly. "Helgi History said so. You will transport me to a better world." He might have been making an announcement to an audience.

"I think I'll transport you home and put you to bed." She put her hand under his arm. "Come on. Helgi probably thinks this is a big joke."

To Sarah, she said, "Have you heard the latest? Helgi is helping Joseph write a book on the meaning of life. In a language they're inventing. No one else will be able to read their great revelation."

"No worse than having the Bible in Latin and nobody but the priests can read Latin," Sarah said. "I'm sure it's a great idea discovered at the bottom of a green bottle."

"Do you want to call Mary and tell her to go get Jesus? They'll lay him down behind a pile of books and forget him, or, if he cries, they'll give him a shot of brennivín . I know those two."

"Mary," Tom said as he swayed a bit in his chair.

"She wears pink lamb slippers. I'm sure you've seen her around."

There was a fly buzzing around the table. Tom tried to grab it. Freyja put her arm on his shoulder before he fell.

"How long will Siggi hang around this time?" Sarah asked.

"He can't risk leaving before he's got his debts paid. Tom has complicated things. Siggi thinks Tom's still a cop, here because he's undercover."

"What does he want from you?"

"I don't know. He has his moods. There are days when he can't live without me. Other days he thinks I'm a rabid bitch that should be put down. I never know from one day to the next what he's going to do. Siggi is completely paranoid since the Freemen turned up. They've gotten him to cut up his driver's licence, his health card, his birth certificate. He was a nervous wreck anyway."

"We'll reason with him together," Tom said. He kept squinting to try to get the cuckoo clock into focus.

"Come on," Freyja said and pulled on his arm. "You can reason with your bed."

"I hope he's got painkillers," Sarah said.

CHAPTER 27

WORK

During the night, he woke up terribly thirsty. There was a glass of water beside his couch and two Tylenol. Sally wouldn't have done that. She didn't believe in mollycoddling. His mother never believed in mollycoddling, either. Unless he had double pneumonia and a confirmed brain tumour, he was expected to look after himself. After he took the pills, he drank the water, grateful for Freyja's thoughtfulness.

When he woke up in the morning, the room no longer thought it was a carousel. He lay there, wondering if he dared lift his head.

"You're alive," Freyja said. He raised his head slightly to look, then laid it down again. She was standing in the doorway to the porch with a glass of orange juice. "Drink this. I'll make you coffee. What were you drinking?"

He eased up, rested his back against the wall, sipped the orange juice and leaned back. He had moved the wolf from the living room to the top of a pile of chairs, so he was staring into its snarling face.

"Black Death," he said. It felt like during the night, his mouth had been lined with shag carpet. He rubbed his tongue against his teeth. Shag carpet that hadn't been vacuumed for a year.

"Really?" Freyja said. "Helgi must really like you. Sharing his favourite drink."

"I was holding my own with the chess game."

"He usually wins in three moves. Did you survive more than three moves? He can be so drunk he falls off his chair and has to have help getting back, and he still wins. If he doesn't win right away, he likes getting his opponents drunk. You don't usually get drunk, do you?"

He refused to move his head. "No," he said, studying the ceiling the way he might in the Sistine Chapel. He promised himself that as soon as possible he'd pull off the wallpaper. "I saw Baby Jesus and his father."

"That's Joseph. He's always looking for a free drink."

Tom kept his head absolutely still and shut his eyes. "You can't do that." His voice sounded like a frog croaking. He ran his tongue over his lips. They were cracked and sore.

"Do what?"

"Call a person Baby Jesus and name his parents Mary and Joseph. It's sacrilegious."

"Nowadays, you can call people anything you want. I've had students called Edsel, Seven Up, Rover. Anyway, his real name is Joseph, and he married Mary because she was called Mary. He has delusions of grandeur about his destiny. They're going to set up a living crèche at the annual Christmas party. You can donate a few dollars to Jesus. It'll pay for baby food and disposables."

"I've a rather large drum pounding in my head."

She got two pills out of her purse, and he struggled up and took them with a sip of orange juice. When she brought coffee he sat up straighter and said, "I thought the liquor would make me welcome and loosen him up."

"Helgi? Really? How much liquor do you think it would take to loosen him up? He has brennivín in his morning coffee."

She made him scrambled eggs and toast, and by the time he'd finished eating, he was feeling better. The pain in his head had been reduced to a dull throb.

"Since you're mollycoddling me anyway, would you be willing to pack up Jessie's personal things? I haven't done anything with her bedroom."

"I'm mollycoddling you because I feel partly responsible for the condition you're in. I shouldn't have let you go there alone."

"Yes," he agreed. "You would have been a distraction for him. He lit up like a Roman candle when I mentioned your name. He's obviously an ardent admirer."

"He's an ardent admirer of old Icelandic books and chess sets. When Dolly was single, he invited her to his place one afternoon. They made it as far as the bed. He got her down to her panties. Then he went to top up his drink, and she waited and waited and finally got dressed. When she went into the living room, he was sitting in his undershorts studying a chess move. He'd forgotten she was there. She was so insulted that she knocked over a pile of his books. And it knocked over another pile. She said it looked like an earthquake had hit. She threw that red ball of his into a burr patch. It must have taken him hours to get the burrs out of his dogs' fur. Do you think he's a hot prospect?"

"Chess is an absorbing game," he said, and then thought that wasn't what she expected to hear, so he added, rather lamely, "That wouldn't have happened if it was you. He says your name with reverence."

She glared at him but was a bit mollified by his compliment.

"When you went to see the Godi did you hear anything about Angel?"

"She may have gone to visit the group on the beach. What's his name's group. Jason."

"Could she have committed suicide? Lots of kids commit suicide when they feel hopeless. I've taken some short courses on suicide prevention."

He thought about the way Angel was lying on the beach. She was too far up from the waterline. There had been no waves, and even if there had been, there wouldn't have been any in the harbour, not enough to carry her that far up the beach. And there'd been the smell of whisky.

"Can't you ask your Mountie friends to help?"

The coffee turned bitter in his mouth. He thought of the talk that went on in the station, in the cars, the way the cops talked about anyone with any Aboriginal blood, like some of his colleagues saying, "Indian girls are all going to be whores anyway, so it's not doing any harm to get a piece before they get ruined." Complaints about rape or disappearances were shoved into a bottom drawer, men who were known to hire prostitutes often provided party places for cops, requisitions for help in finding missing Aboriginal women were laughed off. Not worth anyone's time or the taxpayer's dollar. No one was going to look at Angel's file. Ben didn't know anyone important, didn't live in the right neighbourhood, didn't have an important job. "Throwaway people," a journalist had said. "These people exist to be used." He'd heard the snickering laughter. It was like a Force-wide conspiracy by people who knew that society didn't care enough to object, the same way that police in the USA were able to pick up black teenagers and have sex with them in return for not charging them with crimes they hadn't committed.

"Siggi and friends," he said, "they're survivalists? Freemen on the Land? End-of-the-world stuff? Kill-your-neighbours-and-eat-them kind of stuff? What about them?"

"Maybe. They're crazy, but Siggi keeps them under control. Lots of sex at the embassy parties but no gang bangs. They know they've got to keep on the good side of the community. Siggi spreads his money around to create goodwill. He doesn't want anyone destroying it."

"He thinks I'm undercover. I think you or Sarah said that. Will that keep him away?"

"It's hard to know how he thinks. It depends on what he and his friends are up to. They're always up to something. If there's a straight way to do a job and a crooked way, they'll choose the crooked way. They believe no one should have to pay income tax. The government is a criminal organization because it's stealing their hard-earned money."

"Hard-earned like how?"

"Liquor on dry reserves. Cigarette smuggling. Marijuana grow ops."

"There are people buying young girls from the Inuit communities up north. They're paying fifteen to twenty thousand for them. Flying them into Montreal or Toronto and putting them to work."

"No," Freyja said. "None of that. Not that I know of."

"Bikers?"

"Connections, distribution. Look," Freyja put her hand over his, "stay out of it. They've got weapons. Automatic rifles, land mines, dynamite, crossbows. You'd think they were preparing for a war."

"You've seen them?"

"Siggi used to take me there. That was when we had just started going out. He wasn't always so crazy. At least, he didn't seem to be until he got involved with these guys. They are out of control at times. They set up targets on the lake. One of them trapped a wolf. They froze it standing up and set it out on the ice with the feet frozen in, then they shot at it until there was nothing left."

"That's crazy," Tom said. "Crazy as in dangerous. We need a war, a place where we can send people like this. Cannon fodder. They could be killed-in-action heroes."

"It didn't happen all at once. Just a little at a time. Siggi didn't set out to be a dealer. He did a friend a favour by bringing him a bottle of whisky. His friend gave him a few dollars in appreciation. Then if you're bringing a few bottles, it's as easy to bring a lot of bottles. And then if a friend wants a little weed, it doesn't take up any space, but you've got to get an introduction to have a regular supplier. Like it keeps getting bigger and bigger."

"You married him."

"You married your ex."

"You split and got his house."

"No," she said. "It was more complicated than that. I didn't tell you all of it. He was bringing booze in for the local reserve. It's supposed to be dry. He'd bring it and transfer it to a guy who lived on the reserve. Thomas Moose. Moose would sell it and give the money to Siggi when they met for the next swap. Siggi would send the money to Winnipeg to pay his suppliers. It was a lot of money. His suppliers would pay their suppliers across the border. One time, Moose didn't have the money, but Siggi let him have the next load on credit. It was too dangerous to take the stuff back. Besides, Moose didn't have it anymore. He'd distributed it. Moose didn't turn up for their next meeting, and Siggi went looking for him. He went for Siggi with a skinning knife. Siggi beat him up and left him outside. He froze to death. Siggi didn't intend to kill him.

"The Mounties were sniffing around Siggi, so his suppliers demanded their money. He thought he'd lose his house—that it would be considered proceeds from crime. So he turned it over to me. I borrowed against it and took out a big loan against my line of credit as well. He was to pay me back right away, like in a couple of months. He paid off part of his debts to his suppliers. He still owes lots. He still owes me. That's all I had. Now, I've got no savings and a house mortgaged to the hilt. These guys charge huge interest."

She hesitated, and he could see that she was unsure of what else to say but then burst out, "Look, he's an idiot. But he's our idiot. This is a small place. Nobody is a stranger. Siggi's not very good at what he does. He's not organized enough. He's not ruthless enough. He gets distracted. He loses his temper and does dumb things, and then regrets it. He started dealing drugs as a sideline. He wasn't looking for business. Helgi would say this was demand driven. People started putting in orders. 'Hey man, I hear you're bringing weed. Bring me an ounce.' The whole thing got out of hand. Then this Freemen on the Land stuff started. He needed them for protection. Or thinks he does. He just needs .

to get his bills paid, go back to working in the oil fields, driving his big truck, partying and being dumb on a normal scale."

"Oh," Tom said. He put his hand on his forehead. As long as he didn't make a sudden move, the throbbing faded into the background. "Life was too boring. You needed to add a little excitement."

"I didn't know. I'd been away. I came back. Siggi and I went to school together. He was a couple of grades ahead of me. He was the school's top athlete."

"How long were you seeing each other?"

"Three months. Maybe a bit more. He courted me. Assiduously. He paid a bush pilot to fly us to Winnipeg for Rock on the Range. Then we were married for nine months. We split close to two years ago."

"Would he have involved Angel? Would he have used her as a mule?"

"No." Freyja's voice was certain. "Ben would have gone berserk."

"Her brother deals."

"He lives with Wanda in the city. He only comes back on business. Angel lived mostly with Ben and Betty until she started grade nine. Siggi listens to Ben, at least now and again. Ben was good to Siggi when Siggi was a kid. Young girls like going to parties at the embassy. They don't have to kidnap anyone. Girls like a good time. Free food. All you can drink. Lots to smoke. Music. Dancing. Siggi's big on pinball machines. He's got three old ones. Everybody loves to play them."

Tom handed Freyja his plate and cup and eased himself forward. Outside, the sun had already burned the sky white.

"Nobody objects to these parties?" he said, aggravated.

"Do you think it would matter? Do your kids jump when you bark?"

His head was too fragile for an argument. He could feel his brain inside his skull. It was like a delicate glass ball that could shatter at any moment.

Freyja was standing in front of him holding the plate and cup, and he realized she was wearing green nail polish. Fortunately, she wasn't wearing green lipstick to go with it. If it were Myrna, she'd have green lipstick, green eyeliner, green hair. Myrna liked colour coordination.

"You need to get rid of this stuff," Freyja said. She was staring into the glassy eye of the wolf. A patch of fur was missing from his head. The porch was piled high with furniture that Jessie hadn't wanted to throw out. "Some things become antiques but most are junk."

Jessie had stacked the eight extra chairs in the corner. They needed clean-ing, but they were early American maple. He pressed his hand to his head. "I've promised Arlene Sigurdsson that I'd look at two rooms that need drywall. I'd better get over there."

Freyja was amused. "You aren't a drinker," she said. "You don't have to struggle with it. My father had to struggle with it. You're lucky."

"I'm just taking measurements. Thank God I don't have to hammer nails."

By the time he got to the Sigurdssons', the pounding in his head was down to a dull throb.

Vidar and Arlene's house was purple with white trim and the yard was a conflict zone, with flower beds made from large tires painted white, a patch of mowed lawn, a sidewalk lined with ceramic animals that guarded the house from an aluminum boat, a Bombardier, a Ski-Doo, and piled-up plastic fish tubs. A foot-high fence of black plastic edging guarded the grass.

Vidar opened the door but didn't step aside.

"Come in, come in," Arlene called from inside the house. "Vidar, get out of the way and let the man get inside out of the sun."

Vidar reluctantly backed up. Arlene was standing at the far end of the hall-way with her shoulders hunched forward and a grim look on her face like she was ready for a brawl, but once Tom was inside, she turned and went to one of the rooms that needed to be finished.

"There's nothing wrong with the rooms the way they are. The kids don't mind," Vidar said defensively.

The rooms had bare insulation between the studs. Tom wondered how long they'd been like that. "We added on because the kids were getting bigger and wanted their own rooms," Arlene explained. "Boy and girl. Hard to keep them from fighting. They wanted different things."

"You want me to put up drywall?" Tom asked.

Arlene was standing in the middle of the room. Vidar stayed at the door-way. "And mud it and sand it and paint it." From the tone of her voice, she wasn't going to put up with an argument.

"I can paint it," Vidar objected, but it was an argument he'd already lost, and his voice sounded like he knew it.

"He paints it," Arlene said. "The kids will be grown up and moved out before you get around to it."

Vidar shook his head and sighed. "I heard you tied one on with Helgi."

"Yes," Tom admitted. He wasn't sure if it should be a mark of shame or pride.

"He's a genius," Vidar declared. "He was a genius in school. Spent his whole life in school. Read every book he could get his hands on. Went to university. Knows all this stuff, but he can't keep a job. He's always getting a new job, but then he drinks, and when he drinks he writes letters. He can't stop writing letters." Vidar stood on the hallway side of the bedroom and leaned into the room but didn't cross the threshold. He made Tom think of a scolded dog.

"Letters?" Tom said. He was measuring the room and writing down the dimensions. Whoever had added on the rooms hadn't got them quite square. He'd have to do a bit of filling.

"Letters," Vidar said. "He gets a job teaching and after he's there for a while, he gets depressed because nobody is doing their job perfectly right. He's an idealist. He writes letters describing what they're doing wrong and how to change it. A lot of people don't take it well. Being criticized. He was teaching at a university, and he wrote to the president's wife saying that she needed to see that her husband was better dressed in public."

"He's a cousin," Arlene said. "He was going to do big things. We figured he'd become prime minister or an ambassador." Arlene was a tall woman with long arms and legs and a determined set to her jaw. She kept shifting her eyes between Tom and her husband, trying to catch them in a male conspiracy against her plans. At the same time, she tugged at the bedcovers to straighten them out. Tom assumed they were in the son's room because there was a poster of Sidney Crosby in action.

"He's fine when he's not drinking," Vidar added. "It's when he gets depressed by life and drinks. If he writes to you, remember that. It's nothing personal."

"He needs a wife," Arlene interjected and gave the quilt such a hard tug that it went askew on the bed and revealed a magazine with a picture of a large-breasted naked woman on the cover. Arlene snatched it, rolled it up and glared at Vidar.

"Too smart," Vidar said, then clarified what he meant. "You can't be that smart and be a fisherman. You've got to be willing to take what the Lord provides and not complain."

"When can you start?" Arlene asked.

"As soon as Ben brings the drywall and the screws. If he can bring the mud and the tape at the same time, it would be good. What colour do you want?" It was just a job, but he felt like he was agreeing to an anti-husband conspiracy.

"Blue for the boy's room. Pink for the girl's," Vidar said. "That way they'll grow up knowing what they are. No confusion."

As he was leaving, Tom told Vidar that he needed a screw jack to lift the corner of his house. Vidar didn't have one, but he said Johnny Armstrong had a few. According to Vidar, no one else had them. It wasn't the sort of thing that most people kept around. Johnny was good at moving buildings or lifting them so you could put a foundation underneath. He also did excavating and could dynamite.

Tom got directions to Johnny Armstrong's and walked over. The yard was obviously more of a parking lot being used for business. There were a couple of trucks, a flatbed, a large Cat, a pile of tires of various sizes, stacks of old railway ties.

When Tom arrived, Johnny Armstrong was hooking his tractor onto a small flatbed trailer.

He was tall, wiry and slightly stooped. His hands were covered with oil. He wiped them on a rag hanging from his pants pocket. He said nothing, but his eyes travelled up and down Tom, assessing him the way he might a wild animal that had unexpectedly appeared from the swamp.

"I heard you've got a screw jack," Tom said. Making a deal, Tom realized, might be difficult, because of the way Johnny stood, his knees slightly bent, his arms tensed, his body ready to spring forward or back across the hard-packed gravel.

"Could be," Johnny said, giving nothing away.

"I need to lift the southeast corner of my house. It's down a bit. You know what it looks like. I think Jessie had asked you about raising it."

Johnny ran his tongue over his upper lip. The tension in his body eased and he lifted his shoulders a bit. "You willing to pay a couple of dollars for it?"

"How much?" They were in a standoff, Tom realized, even though there was little at stake. The blasted, destroyed ground where nothing grew anymore and the accumulation of vehicles that looked prehistoric were all part of some small desperate kingdom. He had learned early in his career that the closer to

338 ~ W.D. VALGARDSON

the edge a person lived, the more dangerous to them was any threat or opportunity, for the one could bring a devastating loss and the other a lost possibility.

Beside Johnny, the tractor gave a steady beat, but every so often it
coughed and sounded for a moment like it might stop. The sun bore down
on them, staining their shirts with sweat. The air smelled bitter with the tar
from the piles of used railway ties and the old rubber stink of the mountain
of tires. Tom's mouth was dry, and he was so thirsty he kept wishing he had
a bottle of water with him. He just wanted to get the negotiation over with
and get a drink.

"Would you pay five dollars a day?"

"Seems steep, but okay."

"Would you pay seven?"

"That's not neighbourly." It was an old trap and he'd fallen into it, a clever
little pawn move before he knew he was even playing the game. His stomach muscles tightened and he clenched his left hand. It was the game of the
used car salesman, of the smart-alecky huckster and, once in a while, to their
discredit, of the landlord assessing how desperate their prospective tenant
might be.

"It's just business. I've got it. You want it. Besides, I heard you don't quib-
ble over prices."

"Ben sets a fair price. He doesn't try to gouge me."

"It's a long trip to Winnipeg, then you'd have to buy one. It wouldn't pay
to rent it." Johnny smiled the way he would if he'd caught an animal in a trap,
a slight turning up of his lips. It was the attitude of a long-time resident to
an outsider, Tom realized, to a newcomer not yet connected to the intricate
web of having lived for decades in the small community where there was
a sense of mutual obligations and past favours. He and Sally had lived in
places like that. His paycheque had been nibbled away by people who saw an
opportunity to charge more to an outsider who wasn't going to be around
permanently anyway.

Tom shifted his weight off his bad leg. When he stood too long, it began to
hurt. Walking was fine, but standing could become agony. "You've been here a
long time," Tom said, "but you've still got an accent. What kind is it?"

"Nothing really." The shift in subject had caught Johnny by surprise, and
he jerked back slightly, puzzled. A raven flew overhead and they both looked

up, for it was the only moving thing above the trees. They watched until it settled at the top of a large spruce. From there, it could observe them in their gravel arena.

"I had a friend who sort of sounded like that. He grew up in Boston." *Pawn to pawn*, Tom thought, now that he knew what game they were playing. He hadn't chosen to set out the board or to move the first man, but he wasn't going to lose the game. It was games like this that were going to determine how the community saw him.

Johnny had on a well-worn Stetson that had once been white. The brim was down all around except in front of his face where it was turned up. He reached up and tugged at the brim to settle it more tightly on his head.

"I grew up in Saskatchewan. Moose Jaw. Went to high school there." The words had come quickly, practised. They were part of an old story, but Johnny's feet had started to move, and the gravel made a soft crunching sound. *The liar's small dance*, Tom thought. He'd seen it lots of times, at the side of the road, in back alleys, in parking lots, in houses where women were supposed to have accidently fallen down the stairs.

"What years were those? I was stationed there for a while. Maybe we have mutual friends."

"Why do you want to know? What business is it of yours?" The superior tone had gone out of Johnny's voice; the words were sharp-edged. He turned toward the hitch to assure himself that it was still there and to let Tom know that his question and answer were of no importance, but his voice and his eyes had already betrayed him.

"None. None at all. Just being friendly. It's nice to get to know my neighbours. Most people don't mind talking about where they come from. I come from Winnipeg."

"I wouldn't brag about that."

"Most Americans up here are running from their past. I heard it mentioned that you had a thing going with Ben's daughter at one time."

"So did lots of guys."

"Any chance you're Angel's dad?"

"No," he said. "Look, we all make mistakes. We all do dumb things when we're young. Okay. I'm married. I've got two kids. I don't need this."

"I heard that Wanda hits you up for money now and again."

"That was a long time ago. She's wasn't doing well and she asked for a couple of small loans. That fucking Sarah. She can't keep her mouth shut."

"Not Angel?" Tom said. "How about Derk? Does she hit you up for the occasional loan because of Derk?"

Johnny's feet moved more quickly for a moment, and his eyes darted away, then darted back. "Where are you going to take this?"

"No place. Just you and me. I want to know about Angel. Do you like young girls? Mother and daughter? A hat trick?"

"I never did anything with Angel. Let this drop before you do real harm. I came up here during the Vietnam War. Guys were being killed every day. They were dead fifteen minutes after getting off a plane. We thought we were going to be sent to invade the north. We were cannon fodder. I split. I got a new name. I got a new life. I work and I take care of my family. Christ, leave me alone. My wife's got cancer."

The sun was merciless. Tom pulled off his hat and wiped the sweat off his forehead with his hand, then wiped his hand on his pants. He put his hat back on. The top of the spruce tree was bent over under the weight of the raven. They stood awkwardly, no longer quite facing each other, as Johnny had shifted slightly to one side to see what was moving in the bush on the other side of the road. The raven suddenly launched itself, its wings spread, unmoving except for the tips of its feathers, dropped into the ditch but didn't land. It rose up with a frog in its talons. When they both looked back, Tom said, "I heard you were saying I might have been responsible for Angel's death."

"We were just talking. Speculating. It doesn't mean anything. A couple of beers and we flip our lips."

"You weren't just dodging? You deserted?"

"That goddamned Sarah. You're thick as thieves with her. She's got secrets of her own, you know. Her husband disappeared and was never found." He was angry, and the anger made his face turn red. Each time the tractor's motor paused it was like a dying man's heart threatening to quit.

"Got into an airplane and went to the West Coast I heard."

"That's one story," Johnny said.

"Went through the ice."

"There'd been this Odin woman who'd been hot for him. Gossip had it that people thought he was going to leave with her. Everybody was talking about it. Like she'd turn up in a plane and he'd hop aboard. Sarah might have heard the rumours, went to confront him. She always carried her three-oh-three."

"But what of the dog and sleigh?"

"He loved that dog. It was half-wolf. He never went anywhere without it. He'd raised it from a pup. He'd never have left it behind."

"All the more reason to think he went under the ice."

"It was shot. By the time it washed up on the shore and was found, there wasn't much left but bones and skin. The skull had a bloody big bullet hole in it."

Their shadows were faint and small. The tamarack forest on the far side of the road was dark, thick, impenetrable. They heard a truck approach, then it passed and the driver honked his horn once to acknowledge them, then disappeared into the village.

"He could have shot it if he couldn't have got it on the plane. Rather than leave it."

"He'd rather have shot his wife and kids than that dog."

"You're sure about the skull? You saw it yourself?"

"No, but a friend of mine saw it. Sarah took what was left and buried it. Maybe in the graveyard where her husband's tombstone is. You could always dig it up if you're interested enough."

"No," Tom said. "It wouldn't prove anything. How would anyone prove that it wasn't just a wolf skull? Lots of wolves killed by trappers."

Johnny laughed out loud, and the sound was bitter, disillusioned. "That's the way it is, isn't it? There's what we know and what the law knows. You just have to keep under the radar. Don't have anything to do with those top folks. Frag an incompetent officer and they throw you into the brig for life. But incompetent officers can send you off to be slaughtered and it's just fine. They say it's for country and democracy. It's all crap. It's for oil and business. Little people like us don't matter."

"Some of the time," Tom said. "Some of the time little people matter." But he was trying to think of an instance where a person from Tuxedo or River Heights in Winnipeg did harm to a street person or even a working-class stiff and felt the full weight of the law, and he couldn't. Money hired high-priced lawyers. Money smoothed out anything. The question always was: How much do they want? Tom often thought that the whole legal system was a version of *The Price Is Right*.

"I'm not running anymore," Johnny said. "I'm tired. I'm too old. Turn me in and my wife and kids will be on their own. Will you be real proud of that?"

"No," Tom said, "I wouldn't be real proud of that. I just want to know about Angel so guys like you can't make me out to be a child molester and murderer."

"Ask Wanda. Maybe she was using her for bait. There are women who do that. They start to fade. They aren't so popular anymore. They take their daughter to the bar. They want to keep the party going. Fuck the mother. Get on her good side. Maybe she'll set you up with the daughter."

"That's bad."

"There are worse things. I don't do them. I take care of my wife and kids. I drive carefully. I live carefully. I don't want to draw attention to myself. I don't do stupid things anymore."

"You don't like Sarah."

"She bulldozes people. You think you're her friend? You get between her and whatever she wants and she'll run right over you. You aren't special."

"The American military has a long memory. Even deserters got amnesty but you're still here. Any chance you helped burn down a recruiting office, did some serious harm during a protest? Something like that?"

"You don't need to tell me. I keep track."

"Three dollars a day for the screw jack," Tom said, "and you and I won't do any more speculating."

"You're a prick. This is blackmail." Johnny's voice had a sense of injustice, not just now but built up over the years, culminating in a deal gone wrong.

Tom had first heard that tone of voice when he was a teenager. He'd secretly given some of the people who slept in the alley behind their apartment sandwiches or leftover food, sat down to hear what they had to say. Their stories were litanies of injustice, of lives gone wrong, but always running through the story was that it was someone else's fault. There was a whining that lay beneath the tales, and after a time, he quit being sympathetic. But when he mentioned it to Anna, she said, "Don't be so superior. You're father hasn't abused you, he hasn't kicked you out. You can come here nearly anytime you want." That had softened Tom's judgment, but his father had no sympathy for "riff-raff." He said, "I made my own way in the world." "Respect," Anna said. "Do what you need to do to get respect." Henry said, "Nobody owes you anything. You have to earn it." One time, he'd seen Tom looking out the hallway window into the alley and come to see what he was looking at. There were two young men and a young woman doing drugs. "Make the wrong choices and you end up there," he said with contempt. "Make the right choices and you end up here." Henry slammed the window shut.

And after he'd started working as a Mountie, what he'd seen occasionally before, he now saw every day. The unkempt pushing grocery carts full of their belongings. The overdoses. The violence fuelled by drugs and desperation. But the stories hadn't changed. There were constantly changing haggard faces with matted hair. Everyone had a sad story, except it was the same story told and retold. After a while, he quit listening to the excuses, and he quit caring about why the perp had shoplifted, done a B and E or mugged a senior citizen, and people quit being individuals and turned into reports. And when he went to court, they were there, like pieces from a terrible shipwreck, but he had to quit caring, couldn't rescue them all, just a few now and again. When there was hope, he made an exception, but as often as not the exceptions were just better con artists, had better-practised stories, turned out like Morning Dawn. And he thought about his father and his rigidity, his making no exceptions for anyone, and he wanted him not to be right. One of Tom's colleagues had said early on, "You should have become a preacher." It wasn't a compliment but a warning about weakness.

"It's just business," Tom said. "It's what I can afford. I'll come back with my truck and pick up the jack."

There was a movement at the house, and Tom saw it was a woman come to see who Johnny was talking to. She watched them for a moment and they both watched her, and then she went inside.

"She worries all the time," Johnny said. "About money. About the kids. About what is going to happen to me after she's dead."

"That's too bad," Tom answered. "There are times when people go into remission."

"You think you're smarter than us," Johnny said. "You stay here, you're going to find you've got to get along. You're going to need people to do you favours and help you out."

"I don't think I'm smarter than anyone."

"Of course you do. I thought I was when I arrived. You don't know yet what you don't know. I came up here from the big city to nowhere and thought I knew more than these hicks. I didn't know nothing." As he leaned forward to stare into Tom's face, the tips of the trees looked like they were catching fire from the sun and would burn up the earth. He clenched his left hand, but it wasn't to make a fist so he could fight. It was like he was trying to hold everything tight and not let it go.

"You're friends with Siggi," Tom said.

"Better to be friends than enemies."

"His tomato business hasn't been doing too well lately."

"You'd need to ask him about that. You want me to dig you a basement, blast out rock or tree stumps, I can do that. I can haul rock and gravel for you. You leave Siggi alone. He hires local. He pays decent. Are you going to hire anyone? Are you going to pay good wages? When my wife got sick, Siggi paid the hotel bill for me to stay in Winnipeg with her when she had chemo. Are you going to do that?"

"No," Tom replied. "I can't do that."

He'd got his screw jack, but Johnny had let him know his position in the community vis-à-vis Siggi. Tom wouldn't be hiring. He'd be looking to be hired. And he had no money to give away.

Tom turned on his heel and went to Sarah's to apologize. Sarah was cleaning and splitting small pickerel and saugers outside when he arrived.

"That's all right," Sarah said, cutting the head off a sauger. "You didn't puke on the floor. You didn't want to fight. You didn't break anything. You're a better drunk than most." She was working on a board with a diamond-shaped hole in it. The board was set over an old oil drum that had the lid cut out. She flipped the sauger onto its back, slit its white belly and scraped out the insides, pushed the guts and head through the hole, scraped the blood off the board and pressed the blade against the edge of the hole to clean it.

He told her about his visit with Johnny but left out the part about her and her husband's dog.

"Johnny can be difficult," she said. "Don't be too hard on him. While he's been up here, his mom and dad and his sister have all died and he's not been able to go home. It's sort of like he sentenced himself to prison."

"Me too. You too, I guess."

"We can leave. He can't. Lots of things he can't do. Can't take his kids to Disneyland. Can't get on a plane that lands in the US." She held down the sauger, ran the stubby-bladed knife along the spine, flipped the fish over, repeated the motion, severed the backbone and left the two sides attached at the tail. She threw the fish into a plastic tub of salt water.

"Ingvar drove by, said you two looked like an old dog and a new dog trying to decide who was top dog. That right?"

"Sort of," he agreed.

He hadn't thought about it that way. Being exiled. The Vikings had practised outlawry. Once you were declared an outlaw for a set number of years, if you didn't leave the country, anyone could kill you without penalty. There was nothing romantic or chivalrous about it. People you'd offended would gather up servants and relatives and ride en masse to kill you as you worked in your fields or slept in your bed. The outlawry was usually for a set term, maybe three years. But for Johnny, it was for a lifetime.

"We didn't have to stay here. McAra was good with engines. We could have moved to Pine Falls," she said grimly. "He could have got a job at the pulp mill. No, he couldn't do that. Having to report to work every day at the same time. Not going hunting when the spirit moved him. Being ordered around. Too much like the armed forces."

He thought about that as she cut off the heads of more fish and scooped their guts into the barrel. The heads made him think of severed arms and legs and ripped-open stomachs in mangled vehicles, and he pushed away the images that had crowded forward.

When Sarah was finished, she scraped off the board with the edge of her knife and pushed blood and scales into the barrel. She brought a hose over to wash the board and used a stiff bristle brush to clean it, finishing off with Javex.

"Three days in salt water, then I hang them out to dry. Makes good hard-fish to chew on in the winter."

"No tapeworm?" he asked.

"The salt and drying kills them. People have been known to get worms deliberately to lose weight, then take a pill to kill them off."

He didn't know if she was making it up, so he didn't reply.

"I've done thousands of these. At one time, we depended on them during the winter. Now, it's just habit. Help me with this." He took one side of the barrel, and they lifted it onto the back of her truck. "I'll take it out to the gut pile. The maggots and the bears will clean it up."

He watched drops of sweat gather on Sarah's forehead. It was too hot to be working. He wiped his face with his hand and wiped his hand on his pants.

"Do you lend out your books?" Tom asked, thinking about the long winter ahead.

"Yes, but I take your first child as a hostage until the books are returned."

"Deal," he replied. "But you'll have to feed her, put up with her, listen to her. Do you speak French?"

"A little. Why?"

"If she's annoyed, she'll only speak French to me. When I started learning French, she switched to Mandarin."

"A clever child. Communication with an intelligent child is always difficult. Usually, though, it's adults that choose to speak their native tongue so kids can't understand. She sounds like she might be worth knowing."

"What would you do with her?" And he wondered if salvation could be found in the middle of nowhere, if whatever he'd done wrong as a father could be washed away, along with the metal studs, the hair dye and the chains, and for a moment he tried to imagine what she'd look like without them. The tattoos and the scars would always be there. If she came to Valhalla, she'd probably have all the kids in town in the community hall practising kick-boxing, and they'd all be wearing black and metal and sporting tattoos.

Sarah used the hose to wash the blood and fish scales off her hands. The scales flashed rainbow colours as they spiralled to the ground.

"Teach her a skill she doesn't know anything about. Shoot a rifle, hunt moose, anything that would allow her to compete with you."

"You're supposed to be on my side," he said.

"Often kids' problems get solved by parents sorting out their own lives." With that, she drove away to put the brined fish into the ice shed and the guts in the swamp.

He wondered if she'd read that in some self-help book. His shrink had said the same thing. "If you won't do the hard work of therapy for yourself, do it for your kids." "I don't have my face covered in studs, I don't spend all my time playing computer games," he'd replied defensively. But, now, away from it all, his heart lurched as he asked himself if his wife and kids had become perps to him, had become no different than the people he confronted, handcuffed, pushed into the back of a patrol car, wrote reports, endless reports about, and he didn't want to think about it, so he pushed it away, pushed it away and locked it up.

He went to the store to get a can of fruit cocktail. After searching through the cans, he went over to Karla and said, "Everything is past its due date. Haven't you got any stock in the back that is newer?"

"We've got what we've got," she said.

"This stuff should be off the shelf."

"Nobody's forcing you to buy it," she said. "Best-by date doesn't mean food's gone bad." She pressed her lips together, narrowed her eyes at him and gave her blouse a hitch.

"I've seen the girls get supplies from the back room."

"Those are special orders. You want to give me an order, Frenchie will shop for you. Cash only, in advance. There's a fee for the service."

"In advance?" he asked.

"We don't want people ordering lobster and then changing their mind."

"I wasn't asking for credit."

"That's good. You want to see our accounts? Overdue. Overdue. Thirty days. Ninety days. A year. The Odin group sells vegetables and fruit for cash. People run out of cash and then they come to us." Her voice was stiff with the injustice of the situation.

He put the can of fruit cocktail on the counter and rummaged for cash to pay for it.

"I heard," Karla said, "that the Odin has offered you a deal on your property."

"Millions," he said. "They want to build a golden temple on it."

She didn't appreciate his sense of humour. "They think that property belongs to them. They don't have millions. Not unless they find their treasure. We know how they operate. They'll do you a favour and get you obligated. Like they've already sent over an attractive young lady to offer you fresh produce. Straight from the garden. Just so you can try it out. And they'll suggest you go there to pick out what you want. And there goes another of our customers for fresh produce. They don't have a licence. No expenses. They work for board and room and anything they need. Not want. Need. We bring in produce and it sits on the shelf. We need to cook with it or throw it out. People want us to stock canned goods, but they drive four hours to the city, load up at a case sale and don't buy what we've got."

"Make a deal with them," he said.

"They won't sell to us. We've tried."

"Do they ever have visitors? They've got extra huts."

It was like the skin on her face shrank, tightened over the bones of her skull. As if all the injustices she had ever suffered had come like a swarm of wasps to sting her. Normally, Karla filled up the store with herself, with her energy, her broad smile that had long ago become automatic, her cheerful greetings to those she thought might benefit her, her bustling about, but now he was seeing everything that wasn't in the emporium: the customers who weren't in the chairs, the metal framework no longer new, the ice cream window with no one on the other side of the screen, the yellow real estate sign rusted on one edge, the rough planks of the walls and the shelves haphazard with empty spaces.

"Visitors?" She said the word so that it sounded angry and hopeless at the same time. "They're One, didn't you know? And there's no way of knowing if their visitors are One or not. Maybe they pay with cash, but how would anyone know? They have guests and our cabins aren't always full."

Her face seemed desperate with the unfairness of it all. "They don't follow the rules," she said. "We pay our licences and our taxes. We hire local. They hire nobody. They just take and take and take." She shut her eyes for a moment and clenched her hands. "They wanted Jessie's property, and I heard that they're going to start a Viking theme park. Compete with us for sports fishing. There's the tall guy with the beard—Jason. He's got plans. They've got connections. They'll push us out of business."

Horst had appeared and stood just behind his wife. His face clouded over as he stared at Tom. "Communists!" he declared. "Lousy communists. It shouldn't be allowed in a free country."

Tom was going out the door as Linda Olafson was coming in.

"I've got a message for you," she said. "The kids have summer complaint, so I forgot about it. Bob phoned. That girl you got him to take with him. Morning what's her name. She took off. They got to Winnipeg. He stopped to gas up, and she said she was going to use the washroom and she never came back. You owe him twenty bucks.

"Sorry," he said. "I thought she was in trouble. I'll pay you at the end of the month when I get my disability cheque."

"Cash," she said. "I don't want to drive all the way to town, take the kids or find a babysitter, just so I can cash a cheque."

"Okay," he said. He wished he hadn't made a fuss about the fruit cocktail. Karla cashed cheques for people she liked, and Frenchie took the cheques to town to deposit. She charged 5 per cent. He'd ask Ben.

He walked down to the dock and wandered along it looking at the sailboats, nodding to the boaters who were suntanning. He watched three kids climbing onto the top of a boat and jumping into the water. There was a lot of squealing as they cannonballed to see who could make the biggest splash. At the end of the dock, Jumpy Albert was sitting on a canvas stool, with a line in the water and an umbrella to keep off the sun. He had on a Tilley hat, a short-sleeved khaki shirt and shorts. Tom stopped to look at Albert's catch. He had four good-sized perch on a line attached to the dock, a string run through one side of their gills as they lay near the surface, slowly waving their tails.

"A good catch," Tom said.

"Good enough," Albert replied. His rod was jiggling in his hand. Beside him was a minnow net, a child's red plastic pail with water and minnows in it. "I hear you went to visit the headmistress."

"Who's that?" Tom asked.

"Verthandi, the Icelandic queen," Albert replied. "She was a headmistress at a fancy schmantzy private girls' school. Used to having everyone do as she says."

"A schoolmarm?"

"Nose in the air. Better than you and me. Always teaching us inferior creatures a lesson. Came by one day and gave me a lecture on what was wrong with my birdhouses. She's never made a birdhouse in her life."

"Bossy?"

"A know-it-all. Knows your business better than you do. What'd she want? She never invites you unless she wants information or a favour."

"She wanted to know about my mother."

"Are you one of them?"

"Half," Tom said. "My father was from London."

Albert looked up sharply. "What do you think? Are the sagas more important than Shakespeare?"

"Is it a competition?" Tom asked.

"She thinks so," Albert said. "Skuld's in our reading club. Starts in September. She stays most of the year. You going to join?"

"Probably," Tom said. It was the first he'd heard of it. "Verthandi is here in the summer?"

"Now that she's retired, she stays until the first snow flies. It's Skuld who stays for six months and a day. They're not going to miss out when the Odin's gold is found. Verthandi isn't here during the winter, but she's on the committee that picks the books. She always wants them to be Scandinavian writers. You'd think nobody else had any writers." He sounded petulant. "You'd think she'd never heard of Swift or Defoe or Austen."

"Good writers," Tom agreed.

"She and Mrs. White got into it at the last meeting. That's because Mrs. White's Danish. She wanted a novel by Blixen. Two wildcats in a burlap sack."

"It should be entertaining," Tom said. He hesitated, then asked, "Do you know if Angel swam?

"Like a fish," Albert said. "Not here. Too many boaters. They take over the dock. She and Mary swam off the shore."

"Mary? Baby Jesus's mother?"

"She's a few years old than Angel. She used to babysit her. Nice girl until she got caught up in the craziness." Albert stopped to pull in his line. A fish had stolen the minnow without biting on the hook. He re-baited his hook and cast his line.

"Craziness?" Tom said.

"She got pregnant. Said she'd never had sex with any man. Swore up and down. I saw her standing on the dock crying and I worried that she was going to throw herself in. She'd always been polite when she brought Angel over. They liked to watch me carve. I carved whistles and birds for them. I think they had a flock of them. They'd come by and say, "Make me a robin. Make me an oriole.'"

"What's crazy about that?"

"Nothing about that. Joseph has always had this religious streak. Doesn't really know much about religion. He likes Westerns better than the Bible. Hides them in those black Bible covers." Albert jiggled his line, pulled it gently to see if he had a bite. "He probably doesn't know more than the stories in those pasteboard books for kids. Or maybe not. I don't know. Anyway, he said his name was Joseph and her name was Mary and he believed her, and when she had her baby it was going to be a virgin birth. Her parents had kicked her out and she was staying with this person and that. Joseph married her. She moved into his winter cottage with him. I don't know what she'd have done if he hadn't taken her in. Went to the city and lived on the street?"

"Oh, shit," Tom said.

"You never know, do you?" Albert said. His body looked like it was having an earthquake. "Maybe I'd have asked her to stay with me until she got sorted out. But I couldn't. People would have talked. They'd have said all sorts of things that weren't true."

"If Mary had thrown herself off the dock, where do you think her body would have ended up?"

"If she did it inside the harbour, hard to say." Albert pressed his elbows against his sides as he tried to stop the shaking. "Not much wave action in the harbour. If she didn't come up against anything, she'd have drifted onto the shore."

"At the waterline?"

Albert turned to look at Tom as he realized what Tom was implying. "Remember where she was when we found her?" Albert looked back at the water, then toward shore, but the boats were moored in the way. "If she fell in," Tom continued, "how did she get from the edge of the water up that extra five or six feet?"

"I didn't see anything. Not until I saw you move. You were against the horizon. I could just barely make you out. I wondered if someone was stealing fishing equipment. I thought maybe she'd taken drugs. Kids passing out."

"No drugs," Tom said. "She'd made a promise."

A silence fell between them and Tom watched as Albert's line tugged. He jerked it to set the hook, then pulled in another golden perch. He took out the hook, slid his catch line through the fish's gills, then eased the fish back into the water, where they lay close to the surface, slowly waving their tails back and forth.

"I heard," Tom said, "you get a remittance."

"That's me," Albert admitted. "A remittance man. They were ashamed of me back home. Sent me away. Send me a cheque every year to stay away. Bunch of hypocritical snobs. If Marcel Proust turned up, they'd have offered him tea."

"Your carving is just a hobby?"

"Not anymore," Albert said. "When I came out, the cheque was substantial. I was able to do lots of things. I didn't live like a lord, but it was pretty good. The trouble is that the cheque has stayed the same and the cost of things hasn't. I need to make money from my hobby now."

"You invest anything with Siggi? It's not a professional question, just personal. I've heard a lot of people have."

"They're going to be making marijuana legal pretty soon. Get in on the ground floor. Besides, when I use some, the shaking isn't so bad."

Later that evening, Tom had eaten supper and was sitting at the picnic table when two children appeared at the edge of his trees. They moved silently, not there and then there, magical, mysterious. He wasn't sure if they were watching him or if they were watching the two ravens at the picnic table. The ravens were bold, cheeky, even demanding, walking up and down the bench. He put a piece of potato on his shoulder and waited for one of them to jump up for it. Instead, the other one grabbed a spoon and flew off with it. "Thieves," he said to the remaining raven. He'd moved and the potato had fallen onto the table. The remaining raven pounced on it. "You will sit on my shoulders," he whispered to it, but it was ignoring him and staring at a piece of carrot. Would greed and familiarity be enough to train them? And would they whisper into his ears all that they had seen during their travels the previous day? Not that they travelled far. They seemed to spend most of their time in the spruce trees around Valhalla. He'd seen them on the beach, turning over stones as they looked for crayfish and clams. They rummaged on the dock, looking for bait left behind or leftover barbecue. They probably also mooched at the cottages.

Still, he mused, it would not be a bad thing if they came each day to tell him what they'd seen and heard.

The children hadn't moved. The way they were dressed made him think they might be part of Odin. The girl wore a long dress with short sleeves, and her hair, caught at the back, fell between her shoulders. The boy wore brown shorts and a loose tan shirt. They both wore straw hats with wide brims.

The girl was taller than the boy and he wondered how old they were—maybe seven and five. He tried to remember his own children when they were very young, but his children had been noisy, argumentative, boisterous, constantly fighting. They would never have stood like this, silent, unmoving, watching.

Since they had come to his property and now were standing about fifteen feet from him, he thought he'd wait for them to say what they wanted. He wondered if they'd been told that he was RCMP and they'd come expecting to see him in full dress uniform. He didn't know the Odin group's etiquette. He wished Freyja were with him. She would have known what to do. He didn't want to do anything that would bring the whirling dervishes—nice tits or not.

"Hi," he finally said, "my name's Tom. What's yours?"

It was if his voice had broken a spell the girl was under. She immediately came forward until she was about three feet away. She had hold of the boy's hand and pulled him with her. The girl said, "Samantha," loud and clear. "And my brother's name is Gabriel."

"Is there something I can do for you?"

"We are messengers. We have been sent to invite you for supper on Sunday with the Godar. We will have a musical afterwards. If you will share with us, we will be sent to get you."

"Godi?" Tom said questioningly.

"Godar," Samantha replied. "It's plural and applies to all of us."

"I see," he replied. "I didn't know that."

"We'll be here at five o'clock." Samantha sounded quite precise and as archly proper as it was possible for a seven-year-old to be. Tom was charmed.

The Norns and Karla had warned him about attractive young women with flowers in their hair wearing diaphanous gowns. They hadn't said anything about charming children. The two should have had wings on their feet instead of sandals. Cherubs meant to melt the heart. He couldn't imagine saying no to them. "Yes," he said, "I accept."

With that, Samantha and Gabriel smiled, looked at each other and ran away holding hands through the trees, their mission accomplished.

He went to the emporium for an ice cream float and was sitting at an outside table when Freyja came to the store. When she saw him, she joined him. "I ran out of salt," she said. He could see that she was annoyed. He knew that she bought staples from the Whites as seldom as possible, making lists of everything she needed, paying Ben to shop for her, occasionally driving into the city to load up on groceries.

"There's a box of Jessie's salt in the kitchen cupboard," he said. "You're welcome to it. I've got my own." She beamed and relaxed. He wanted to prolong the visit, so he offered to buy her a Coke float. She insisted on having it made with diet soda.

He told her about the two emissaries from the Godar. "How can anyone say no to a couple of cute kids?"

"You have a tender heart," she said.

"Could you have said no?"

"No," she admitted. "They know the best messengers to send. Small angels. I've seen them around. They're very huggable. Especially Gabriel. He's got a smile that would melt any heart or get any passerby to drop money into his hat when he plays his recorder on the street. His sister plays the violin."

"I've been had," he said. "They're con artists."

"How come I can't pull on your heartstrings like that? I'm cute." She adopted a pose and he laughed.

"When you asked me for supper, I came right away."

"The way to a man's heart is through his stomach, Sarah says."

He looked down at his stomach. It was tight against his pants. "Big heart, big stomach."

Freyja looked pensive. Finally, she blurted out, "I've got a kitten."

He was surprised but said, "Good. Where did it come from?"

She didn't answer right away, and as he waited, a shadow fell over them. Tom looked out across the lake and saw clouds like white islands drifting by so that light and shadow changed intermittently. Tracy brought the soda in its tall glass with the straw already in place. She set it on the table. Freyja said thanks but ignored the drink.

"Siggi," she replied. Her voice was tight, frustrated. "I don't want his kitten. I don't want his gifts. It'll give him an excuse to drop by, to say he's sorry about Ramses. He'll want to know about the kitten and we'll talk through the screen door and I won't let him in, and then he'll get angry and abusive because I won't let him into his own house."

"Give the kitten away," Tom said.

"Then he'll be angry because he was being kind and thoughtful and I'm an ungrateful bitch."

In her anger, she flung her right hand out, caught the straw with her arm and knocked over the tall glass with its bevelled sides. The drink spilled across the table. Tom jerked his chair back, grabbed a handful of napkins from the metal dispenser on the table and mopped up the soda and ice cream. He took the napkins to the garbage can at the far end of the veranda. He asked Tracy to bring Freyja another soda.

Freyja said, "Bad luck. Spilling a drink. It means that a drunk will come to visit me shortly. Are you wet?"

He looked at the front of his shirt, his shorts, and shook his head. "The kitten," he reminded her. "Let it run away."

"I can't do that. Siggi knows that. And he knows I don't want him giving me anything."

"Maybe he was just trying to be kind. I thought about trying to find a kitten for you."

"You haven't threatened to kill me. You haven't broken into my house when I'm away and pissed on my floor. Then he called and apologized and offered to come and clean it up. He's that bloody devious." Her voice had gone tight with frustration and anger.

There were a half dozen tables on the veranda. Customers eating fried pickerel fillets and french fries out of pink plastic baskets sat at two of them. A motorboat was pulling up to the shore. Its bow wave made a soft hushing noise. One of the men jumped into the water and pulled the boat forward.

Tom said, "There's a poster in the window. It says, 'Come to the White's Friday Night Jamboree.' That's tomorrow. You interested?"

"Yes. It's the first one of the summer. I wanted to go, but I wasn't going to go alone. Siggi will be there. His friends will be there and they'll snub me and make snide remarks. I need some support." She reached out and put her hand over his for a brief moment. "I'm sorry. I don't mean to drag you into my problems, but sometimes it's like clan warfare and he's got the biggest clan. How could I be so stupid as to get myself involved in this?"

"The hardest person to forgive is yourself," he said. He was repeating something the shrink had said to him many times.

"I was pretty and school was easy. Everything was a joke."

"Yes," he said, and he thought of all the teenagers he'd helped put in body bags. All the kids on the street with a guitar and a dog. All the angry couples with bills they couldn't pay and disappointment they couldn't bear who blamed each other. All a joke until it wasn't.

"Is that a yes?" he asked. "To the jamboree? I think we both need some fun."

Just then Tracy brought the soda and put it on the table.

Freyja stood up and crossed her arms over her chest, and her face was dark from the feelings she was having. "I'm sorry," she said, looking at the soda. "You'll have to drink two." She didn't quite manage a smile and said, "I'll meet you there."

He began to think about insulation—how much he would need and what it would cost. He was just starting to jot numbers down on a napkin when he noticed Mary. She was standing about six feet from the veranda, but she was obviously staring at Freyja's soda. He picked up the glass and waved for Mary to come and get it. She hurried over and would have taken the soda away, but he pulled it back.

"Sit down," he said. "Keep me company."

Mary looked nervously around, bit her lip, hesitated, then climbed onto the veranda and sat down. He handed her the drink. She grabbed it with both hands and began to suck on the straw.

"Where's Baby Jesus?" he asked.

"With Joseph," she replied as she took a breath.

All at once, Karla appeared and in a quiet but accusatory voice said, "Mary, what are you doing here? Have you forgotten our agreement?"

Mary would have jumped and run away, but Karla had her hand on her shoulder, keeping her in her chair.

"What's the matter?" Tom asked.

"Mary and I have an agreement, don't we, Mary?" Mary nodded. She'd quit sucking on her straw. "Mary was hanging around the veranda and eating food that customers left on their plates. Isn't that right, Mary?"

Mary's head jerked up and down, but she still had a tight grip on Freyja's soda.

"Mary and I agreed that if she didn't come here and bother the guests or cause any kind of a fuss, no selling crosses or begging, that at the end of the day she could come to the back door and I'd give her any food that was left over. There's often some hot dogs, hamburgers, french fries. There's always some salad. More than Horst and I can eat."

"It's my fault," Tom said. "I wanted to talk to Mary and when I saw her, I invited her to come and drink the soda that Freyja had to leave behind." He turned to Mary and said, "I'm sorry, Mary. I didn't mean to get you into trouble.

It's just that I'm new here and I don't know all the rules. Bring your drink and we'll go for a walk and you can tell me all about Baby Jesus."

As they walked toward the shore's edge, Mary said, "This is where you found her. I know. I came to look and to say a prayer. She went to heaven."

"Are you sure of that?" Tom asked. "She had committed a sin. She was pregnant."

"Maybe it was a virgin birth. Just like me." She noisily sucked the last of the drink out of the glass. "She'd started going to church in the city. Her music teacher took her there and she sang in the choir. She even had a solo. She told me that when she came at Christmas. She said she never wanted to have sex with any man. She didn't want any man grunting on top of her."

"I'm sorry I got you into trouble," Tom said.

"Joseph doesn't have much money. Just some old age money. We live in a tent in the summer. He says that Jesus lived in a tent when he was a baby." She had finished the drink and didn't know what to do with the glass. Tom took it from her. She said, "Thank you. That was very kind of you." A shadow seemed to fall over her face for a moment, but then she smiled and said, "Karla gives us good things. Sometimes there are desserts left over. Joseph says we have to be grateful for the good things in our lives."

CHAPTER 28

FRIDAY NIGHT
JAMBOREE

The next day Tom quit work early, got cleaned up and went over to the café. The grocery shelves had been curtained off. The counter had been pushed against the back wall and a small foot-high platform had been placed in front of it. More tables and chairs had been added to the café area, and the open floor space between the entrance and the counter was filled with folding tables and chairs. Karla was busy supervising the setup of sound equipment. Tom sipped on his float to electronic squealing and squawking and Karla's voice repeating, "Testing, testing, one, two, three."

Tracy was hostess for the evening. She'd changed out of the usual waitress' skirt and blouse into a short pink dress with a plunging neckline. Like Karla, she had a silk rose behind her left ear. Her long hair was tied back with a ribbon that matched her dress, and she was holding a stack of menus that she handed to people as they came through the door. Normally people found their own tables, but when there was a Friday night musical or another special occasion, they were led to their tables in the café area where meals were served. If people didn't want a meal, as most of the locals didn't, then they were simply pointed toward the tables on the other side of a yellow rope that separated the two sections. It was nearly all summer people who sat in the meal area.

A sign said, *Please wait to be seated.* It was obvious from the way Tracy stood with her head up that she was enjoying her position of authority. She barely paid any attention to the locals, holding out a menu and, when they refused it, sending them to their location with a flick of her fingers. Tom noticed that her fingernails were bright red and so were her toenails.

There was a lot of noise as people came in and got settled: chairs being dragged over the plank floors, people greeting each other, excited chattering. Four waitresses were edging through the café area. Only Barbara was taking orders in the area where Tom was sitting. A customer came in and wanted to appropriate the second chair at Tom's table. He waved him away, then leaned the chair against the table to indicate that it was taken.

Four men came in wearing gold plastic Viking helmets and seated themselves at a table with a *Reserved* sign. Siggi and friends, Tom realized. He recognized Siggi, with his blond hair tied back with a leather band. He was wearing a sleeveless T-shirt with a picture of a snarling bear on the back and the words *Siggi and the Bears* on the front. In spite of the heat, he wore jeans and short black boots. At one time, he'd lifted weights every day, run on the spot, tried to keep up the exercise regimen of his hockey days, but Freyja said that had slipped away. Now, his shirt showed that he was a bit overweight. He had a gym at the embassy but used it only sporadically. Tom wished that they could have been friends. He would have liked the use of the gym. And the satellite TV. Especially during football season.

Tom had to admit that Siggi was handsome—Nordic, just slightly rugged looking. His Viking helmet suited him. He didn't walk so much as swagger. He had a tattoo of a heart with a knife through it on his left bicep, with the word MOM in block letters underneath. His slightly skewed nose was obvious and, seeing it, Tom touched the scar on his forehead. *On the ice or in a bar*, Tom wondered. Siggi would have been a brawler on the ice, the kind who'd go after a star player, making hits when the ref wasn't looking, using his stick to trip him, pushing him until there was a fight, gloves off.

His swagger, Tom realized, had a lot to do with his success with women. No female on hand was too old or too young for a moment of his undivided attention. He engulfed them in his smile, if only for a few seconds, making them, for that moment, the centre of his universe.

Tom wondered if he'd be able to hold his own with Siggi and doubted it. Before his accident and his depression, he could have. Tom's arms were longer and he was an inch taller. The extra inch would be an advantage, but now a fight would have to be quick—a couple of well-placed punches or a head butt. Real fist fights weren't like in the movies. One broken nose, one smashed sinus, one broken jaw and it was over. Guys in bar fights fell down and died after one punch to the head. Chairs swung or thrown didn't fall apart like Hollywood chairs. The people they hit ended up in Emergency. He pressed his palm to his stomach. In spite of Myrna chiding him, he didn't have a potbelly, but his stomach muscles were slack. He needed to clean the garage to get the dust out of it and, once the heat eased, start using his weights. He would, he promised himself, quit eating so much ice cream and start drinking diet soda.

Siggi's friends were nondescript—full beards, bulging stomachs under their T-shirts. They wore the same shirts as Siggi. Two of them had full sleeve tattoos. They shifted their chairs around to get a better view of the stage.

Tom kept an eye on the door. Freyja appeared. Although she must have seen Siggi, she made like he and his friends weren't there. She stopped at a couple of tables to say hello to people, waved at others, then came and joined Tom. She set her chair so she could see the stage without looking at Siggi.

There was a lot of shout-talking. The noise of the voices and the shuffling of chairs and tables made it hard for them to hear each other. Tom leaned toward Freyja and asked, ""Siggi and the Bears?"

"Same name as his high school band," Freyja said. "Different players."

Arlene Sigurdsson went by, stopped for a moment, leaned toward Freyja and said, "I see that the berserkers are here."

Without watching any of them directly, Tom kept his eye on Siggi's group. When they noticed Freyja, they started talking among themselves and pointing and poking Siggi, obviously razzing him. He wasn't amused. He brushed away their hands and scowled. Then their attention was caught by Amanda, who was waiting on their table, and they immediately started teasing her. One of them tried to get her to sit on his knee. She kept shaking her head, and they kept laughing. One of them undid her apron, and they threw it back and forth a few times as she tried to retrieve it.

"Comedians," Freyja said.

"Do they like little girls?" Tom asked

"I don't think they're fussy eaters."

Barbara came to take Tom and Freyja's order. He remembered her from the conversation they'd had when he ordered an ice cream cone. Tonight, she'd been elevated to waitress, but she had the least lucrative tables to serve. Locals didn't order big or tip big. They'd be just as likely to sneak in a tin of pop and popcorn from home.

Barbara wore the same outfit as all the other girls, but on her it looked out of place rather than sexy. She should have been in a plainer, more severe outfit. She wasn't unattractive, but with her glasses and her hair pulled into a bun, if she had been appropriately dressed, she would have looked serious, dignified. With her flat chest in a low-cut white blouse and her flat hips in a too-short skirt, she just looked like a child wearing an adult's clothes.

Siggi and his friends were sitting near a table of young women, and they turned their attention to them.

"A laugh a minute," Freyja said. "Everything's a big joke."

"They're having a good time," Tom said.

"It changes very fast," Freyja said. "From laughs to violence. Just like that. Flick, flick." She flicked her thumb and forefinger.

"They have good parties, I've heard. Lots of food. Lots of booze."

"The best. No expense spared. They all play musical instruments," Freyja said. "Keyboard, guitar, banjo, violin, trumpet. They jam, playing hard, trying to outdo each other. It's like they're competing, but they're still playing together."

"Lots of music in Valhalla," Tom said. He wished he could play, could be part of a group sharing an experience instead of always just an outsider in the audience.

"There's hope in music," Freyja said. "You can dream about being onstage and everyone admiring you. How many kids in Valhalla dream about being an astrophysicist or an archeologist? They probably don't know what those are. They know about singers, musicians. The good hockey players dream of being in the NHL."

Tom had asked Karla about the Friday night soiree and she said the regular menu was cancelled. They only served pizzas and salads and drinks. There were four kinds of pizza for sale: pepperoni, ham, vegetarian and Greek. There was Greek salad, Mediterranean salad, taco salad and Caesar salad, but the salads seemed more for the weight-conscious yachters than the locals. The patrons could order a whole, half or slice of pizza. This was their first pizza night. Karla had stumbled on the idea of selling pizza. She'd been at a salvage place that had recently acquired equipment from a bankruptcy, so she got the ovens cheap.

She figured that once they were ready to sell pizzas to go, the boaters would take pizza out sailing. The cottagers would order pizza to avoid cooking in the heat, and the locals, though they didn't usually eat in the café or buy coffee, would buy pizza. "Everybody," she said enthusiastically, "loves pizza." Horst thought she was crazy and had wanted her to take the equipment back. "You'll see," she'd insisted. "Everybody loves pizza." Tom didn't bother to tell her that his father wouldn't let pizza past his lips.

Tonight, Karla was in one of her Western outfits. She blew into the mike a couple of times. The café was nearly full. People were still coming to the door and standing on tiptoe to see where there might be a free chair. Tracy wasn't letting anyone into the dining area except people from the summer crowd who were responding to a wave inviting them to empty chairs. The windows to the veranda were open and newcomers were sitting there. Karla tapped her fingernail on the mike to get attention. The conversation slowed down and everyone started turning toward the stage.

"Mike time is all taken up," Karla said. "We've got a great evening ahead of us. We've got our local talent. We've got visitors from out of town. I'll start off the evening with a fast number." The fiddler started "Hey, Good Lookin'," the guitarist joined in and the drummer picked up the beat. Karla wiggled and sashayed but kept it short. Then she introduced Tracy, who got a round of enthusiastic applause. She grabbed the mike and launched into "Crazy." She just about had Patsy Cline down pat. She did three songs, then there was a jig, and a couple of the locals got up and jigged in front of the stage. Tom saw people in the audience with spoons, Jew's harps and penny whistles playing along during the instrumentals. There was a lot of whistling and shouting. Amanda followed with a couple of sad love songs. A guy from the sailboats played two tunes on a banjo. Tracy got up to sing again. It was obvious Karla was pushing Tracy. She introduced Amanda and Louise effusively but saved her greatest praise for Tracy.

Just before the set was over, Barbara came to the mike. Karla kept the introduction short. "This is Barbara. You all know her. She is going to sing three folk songs a cappella."

Tom was expecting it to be a disaster. Barbara stood at the mike, closed her eyes and began to sing, "Oh, Danny boy, the pipes, the pipes are calling." Her voice was sweet and full of emotion. She followed it with "Early One Morning" and finished with "Foggy Dew." She never missed a note and never opened her eyes until the songs were finished. She got a warm round of applause, stamping of feet and whistling. Karla said, "Thank you, Barbara. That was very nice." Tom was expecting her to add, "And now go wait on your tables." If Barbara had expected any praise, she didn't get it.

"Cripes," Tom whispered in Freyja's ear. "My father used to listen to the old ballads. She sang them just right." He'd applauded vigorously. He was going to say more, but a fast fiddle tune had started, every instrument in the café joined in and two couples were jigging in the open space in front of the band. It was obviously a wild night in Valhalla.

Siggi and his friends went out. They came back with their instruments, except they were hillbilly down-home pieces: a washtub and broomstick tied together with rope, a saw and bow, a fiddle and a banjo.

Freyja grimaced. "Don't let them fool you. They've got a fortune in instruments. Next time they'll turn up electronic. They're full of surprises."

Siggi and the Bears hee-hawed and yahooed through three tunes. Ten people clogged. Siggi's three friends with their full beards might have come from the Ozarks, except for the gold-coloured Viking helmets with horns.

When the set was over and the intermission started, Tom leaned close to Freyja and said, "Barbara's got the best voice of the lot. What's with Karla?"

"It's not country and western."

Karla had taken Tracy and Amanda over to a table where two men dressed in whites were sitting. She was talking enthusiastically, putting her hand alternately on Tracy and on Amanda's shoulders.

Tom waved at Barbara to get her attention. Even with the doors and windows open, the café was stifling. A lot of people were going outside, where it was slightly cooler. There was a lot of talking, someone playing a tune on a mouth organ, chairs being pulled back and pushed forward. Barbara looked flustered from having too many tables to serve.

Tom and Freyja each ordered a large lemonade with ice, and Barbara jotted it down on her notepad. "You have a beautiful voice," Tom said. "I love the old ballads. My father used to listen to them." Barbara's cheeks turned pink, and she looked away. "Do you know one that has parsley, sage, rosemary and thyme?"

Barbara said, "Scarborough Fair."

"Maybe one of these Fridays you can sing it for me," Tom said. Barbara blushed again, then fled.

"That was very good of you," Freyja said.

"If us outsiders aren't good to other outsiders, who will be good to us?" he asked. "When I was in school I never belonged. I was always on the outside looking at others who had friends and were popular."

"You've got friends now. Here comes one." Freyja slipped her hand under Tom's arm as Sarah came up to them.

"Having fun?" Sarah asked.

"Yes," Tom said. "You must have enjoyed the ballads."

"I gave her the recordings," Sarah said.

"But where did she learn to sing like that? She must have had lessons."

Sarah stared at him balefully. "She has a perfect ear. She played the tapes over and over. I helped her a bit." To Freyja, she said, "I see Siggi is here."

"How could I miss him?" Freyja said. "It's too bad he can't go back to the oil fields. If he gets his business straightened out, maybe he'll get work in Newfoundland or Dubai. Some place far away. Maybe his greenhouse business will pick up and he can pay back everyone he owes."

One of Siggi's group had brought in a five-gallon wooden basket loaded with cucumbers and tomatoes. He carried it from table to table, handing out the produce. Siggi took two tomatoes, put a cucumber between them and turned in a nearly full circle showing them to the crowd. It got a lot of laughs. He offered his art piece to a woman at one of the tables and she shook her head in embarrassment but then put out her hands and took the gift.

"Cucumbers and tomatoes," Tom said, taken aback by the incongruity of Siggi and his Bears distributing vegetables.

"You're seeing the results of another great government-funded project," Freyja said. "Too bad the grants aren't available anymore. You could fix up the old barn in your meadow. Free money."

The porch was crowded, and the crowd, invigorated by the music, was noisy. The harmonica player started "Home on the Range." The waitresses were bringing out trays of drinks. The sweet smell of marijuana mixed with the more pungent smell of tobacco drifted over the crowd.

"I think he's expecting you to go over and thank him for the kitten. At least I think that's what I heard him say," Sarah said.

"Just how did he say it? You think that dumb bitch would come over here and thank me for that bloody kitten?"

"Something like that," Sarah admitted.

"I'd like to meet him," Tom said.

"I don't think so," Freyja replied. "Let's go stand out on the porch. There's a bit of a breeze there."

They went onto the porch and Freyja introduced him to a number of people. He said hello to Ingvar and Pearl and Dolly. Ben and Wanda and Derk were at the far end of the porch. Tom raised his hand and gave them a wave and Wanda waved back. He walked through the crowd, keeping his eye open for Albert Scutter. He had something he wanted to ask him. There was no sign of him, but Tom realized that about halfway down the veranda Rose was sitting at a table with her husband and her two children. She'd dressed up for the occasion, a yellow dress with a bright print. Her baby was in her lap. With her free hand, she was holding a paper cup so her daughter could drink through a straw. *One of the girls who fell for the "Come and have a beer with me in the back of my truck,"* he thought, and it dredged up his memory of the young woman who had come to his father's door because her boyfriend had kicked her out. *It never ends,* he thought, and the thought made him feel crazy, like the way he imagined the woman who had been able to see the future but couldn't get anyone to believe her must have felt. Her name eluded him, but his father mentioned her sometimes when his advice wasn't followed at work. Cassandra and her curse, he remembered. He had protested when his father said the outcome of many situations is obvious. It will end badly. But he sometimes found himself saying the same thing to his kids and to the people he dealt with on the street.

Rose's husband—he assumed it was her husband—had turned his chair sideways, away from his wife, and was sprawled back, laughing at what a couple of his friends were saying. He held his empty beer bottle upside down, then went into the emporium. Tom took the opportunity to go over to her.

"Hi," he said, "Remember me? I was looking for Pearl."

She nodded, looked away, then looked down at the baby to avoid looking at him.

"You live next door to Albert Scutter. I don't see him here. Do you know if he's at home?"

"He's away. He's always away on weekends in summer. He goes to celebrations and craft fairs to sell his carvings."

He thanked her, and as he left he caught the eye of one of the Norns. He couldn't tell which one, but he nodded to her and smiled and she came over.

"I'm Urdh," she said. "We really should wear name tags. It's been this way all our lives. I heard that Freyja's cat died."

"Yes," he replied. "It's been difficult for her."

"It may not be such a bad thing," Urdh said. "It just appeared. Scratched at her door until she let it in."

"An abandoned kitten," he answered. "It happens all the time."

"Perhaps," Urdh said. "Do you know what a sending is?"

He shook his head.

"Someone who wishes you evil seeks an animal from the dead and sends it to do you harm. Did Freyja tell you that just after Ramses came, he scratched her and she got a very bad infection? She ended up in the regional hospital."

"A sending?" he said, uncertain how to reply.

"Of course," Urdh said, "you wouldn't believe in those old religion things. Superstition. But it wasn't necessarily a sending. It could have been a stefnivargur. That doesn't include raising the dead." She saw his look of skepticism. "Surely, as a police officer you've seen the depravity caused by jealousy, envy, resentment, all those sins the new religion talks about?"

"Yes," Tom agreed. "I saw the results every day. But why would anyone wish Freyja harm?"

"Those who have more are envied. Is that not so, Constable Parsons? A man with only one dollar can envy a man with two dollars. What is that old Greek saying? 'Dear Lord, give me a goat and kill my neighbours.'"

"A cat is sometimes just a cat," Tom said.

Tom rejoined Freyja just as Siggi came up to her and said, "I thought you might have said thank you for the kitten." He ignored Tom.

Freyja froze, then she put her hand under Tom's arm and gripped it tightly. "Thank you for the kitten. That was very thoughtful of you. This is Tom Parsons. He's a Mountie."

"We've met. I know who he is. Ex-Mountie. Unprofessional conduct or something."

"That wasn't thoughtful," Freyja said. Her voice had gone cold, her words clipped. The conversation on the veranda had quieted as people watched and listened. "You just cancelled out your Brownie points. You're back to zip."

"I wanted to talk to you in private," Tom said to Siggi.

"Sure," Siggi said. "Anytime. I'm quite willing to discuss how hot she is in bed. You want a blow-by-blow description?" He emphasized the word blow.

Freyja didn't say anything for a moment, but she didn't look away from Siggi either, and Tom thought they were experienced fighters. When Freyja did reply, her voice was low, emotionless, threatening. "Don't push it, Siggi. You want to talk in public about business?" Freyja said.

"Fuck you," Siggi snarled and turned on his heel and went back to his friends. More people had stopped talking and were watching the encounter. As Siggi went back to his table, he smacked the vegetable basket with his open hand. There were no vegetables left and the basket simply flipped off the table onto the floor.

"That didn't go well," Tom said.

"Shut up," Freyja said. "Shut up, shut up." But she said it quietly, and he wasn't sure if she was saying it to him or to herself or to Siggi. She held tightly onto his arm, leaned her head against his shoulder and briefly closed her eyes.

Two women who'd watched the confrontation waved at Freyja, and she left Tom to go over to them. Vidar was nearby, standing by himself. Tom joined him.

"Siggi's not the friendliest guy when it comes to his possessions," Vidar said. "He wasn't any good at sharing even in elementary school. He was always getting into wrestling matches. We'd call three strikes and he'd start yelling they weren't strikes, or he'd swing and miss and then say it didn't count."

Just then Karla came by with her arm through the arm of one of the yachters dressed in whites. He was fat, and his belt separated his stomach into two parts. His face was bright pink from the heat.

"What do you think?" Tom asked, tipping his head toward Karla.

Vidar shrugged. "The Danish songbird?"

"Danish? Her last name's Kerr. It doesn't sound Danish."

"People change their names to get ahead. Kerr was Kjærgaard. Too long."

"You don't seem to approve." As they were talking he saw Dolly go over to Siggi, and he put his arm around her and hugged her. She was laughing at something he said. He let her go, but she stayed close beside him.

"It's nothing. Just that the Danes ruled Iceland," Vidar held up his clenched hand, "with an iron fist. They controlled everything. They said who you could trade with. How much you got for your wool and meat and fish. They set the prices they would pay for nails, horseshoes, tobacco, sugar. Everything. They sold the Icelanders mouldy grain and cheap brandy. Shiploads of cheap brandy." He smiled briefly. "It's history now, but we don't forget. Nothing changes, does it? People come here and the system follows. The Icelanders catch the fish and the Danes are the merchants."

"She had a good career, I heard."

Vidar gave a twisted grin. "Motels, bars, that sort of career. Won the weekly prize on some radio station once. That was the top. Successful from here to Winnipeg."

"How did they end up here?"

"She's from here. Horst had got sick from asbestos. He has a pension. Not much. He was trying to be a promoter. Going to make all these people famous. She didn't become famous. He didn't make anyone famous. They were in a bad way until they got the store from her parents."

"They look like they've got a good business."

"You thinking of buying?"

Tom laughed. "I'd rather clean toilets." Tom went back inside. Barbara was clearing tables. He got her attention and she came over. He told her again what a good voice she had and how well she'd sung the ballads. He asked her if she'd been a friend of Angel's. Barbara said yes and looked downcast.

"Were you going to be in Angel's band?"

"Maybe," Barbara said. The tub she was carrying held dirty cutlery and plates. She looked exhausted. The skin under her eyes was dark, and her face was slack. "We were thinking different music, you know? Not C&W.

He asked if she wanted to be a singer, but Barbara shook her head. "Miss Karla doesn't think I've got the looks. Or the right kind of voice."

"There are lots of different kinds of music. It's not just country and western." Since they'd started talking, she'd never looked directly at him. He tried to catch her eye, but her gaze was fixed on the table.

"She's got her favourites," Barbara added, and her voice was full of hurt. He wanted to tell her that being excluded by some people was of no account; their worlds were small and narrow. But he remembered what it had been like at school, and he knew that telling her being popular wasn't important would be a lie. "They get the best tables. They get to cater the parties on the boats and at the cottages. They're the ones with talent. It's important for them to meet the right people."

"Catering?" he said. That was a new twist, but it made sense. It would be pretty hard to cook for a party on the yachts and sailboats. Even in the cottages, catering would be the way to go.

Suddenly, Barbara started piling dishes into her tub. Tom turned to see that Karla was watching them. He waved at her, but she didn't wave back. Barbara scuttled away, her head down and her body pulled tight. Freyja came in just then and joined Tom at their table.

The confrontation with Siggi had taken a lot of fun out of the evening, but Freyja was determined not to let him chase her away. If she did that, she said, he'd chase her away from every event and she'd be totally isolated. There were already enough people who kept their distance from her for fear of being drawn into the conflict.

The evening was noisy, with more of the crowd joining in the singing, playing the instruments they had brought, clapping, dancing in the small space in front of the band and out on the veranda. It was obvious that some people's drinks had more in them than lemonade or cola.

When the evening was over, Tom walked back to Freyja's with her, and she asked him to come in. Just in case Siggi wanted to keep the argument going, she said.

"You and him fighting," he said. "Is that what you were expecting?"

"No," she said. "I don't want any fighting."

"I saw lots of that—in bars, outside bars, at weddings. You'd be surprised at the number of brawls at weddings. They aren't happy events for a lot of people—too much jockeying, too much jealousy, too much power tripping and hurt feelings. We had to break up a fight once between the groom and the best man. Apparently, the best man and the bride had been getting it on before the wedding. You and Siggi fight. It's a kind of power trip."

"I don't know why I like you," Freyja said. In the distance, people were shouting good night and vehicles were starting up and driving away. "You analyze stuff too much. Can't you just live in the moment?"

"My father started showing me how to play chess when I was two."

"I'm not a chess game. If Siggi was here, he'd be ripping my clothes off."

"Give him a call," Tom said. "I'm doing my best not to rip your clothes off. You're beautiful. You're gorgeous. I'm thinking about consequences."

"Are you worried that I'll move into your house? That I'll quit teaching and claim half your pension? Do I look like I'm dependent?" When he didn't reply, she moved over to the couch and sat beside him. She used her toes to push off a running shoe, then changed feet and pushed off her other shoe. "There," she said, "I'm partly undressed." She pulled off her blue sports socks with a happy face on them. She held up her feet. "Aren't feet ridiculous things? Still, as feet go, don't I have beautiful feet?" She wiggled her toes and he wanted to hold her feet, with their feeling of life, and hear her laugh in anticipation, as they would both know where holding her feet would lead.

"Consequences," he said. His father's face was stiff and his mother's mouth was pursed with disapproval.

Freyja slipped her arms inside her blouse, reached behind her and undid her bra, pulled it out one sleeve. "Nice, eh?" she said and held it up. It was pale blue.

"Are you worried about money?" she asked. "You're a financial mess. I'm a financial mess. I've got a teacher's pension plan of sorts when I retire. You've got a government pension of sorts. Or are you afraid of Siggi?"

"No, I'm not afraid of Siggi." Tom said, but he was distracted by the scent of her, the way her red hair fell over the side of her face, the fullness of her lips and the soft way her breasts now moved under her blouse. "I shouldn't have said that about you wanting him and me to fight. You didn't do anything to provoke him."

Just as he leaned over to kiss her there was the roaring of truck motors, and suddenly there were two lifted trucks circling the house. The drivers were leaning on their horns. Freyja and Tom jumped up and ran to the back door. Tom shoved the door open and stepped out onto the landing, and Freyja came out behind him and threw something at one of the trucks. The trucks raced back to the road and disappeared.

When the noise of the trucks had faded Tom said, "Did you see who that was?"

"I don't need to see who it was. I know who it was." Tears of frustration and anger ran down Freyja's cheeks. "Shit," she said. "That was one of my good mugs. An Amara. It cost me thirty dollars."

"You missed the truck. Maybe it didn't break."

Freyja got a flashlight and they went searching. The mug was sitting handle up. Freyja picked it up and held it to her chest.

"Maybe you should make a formal complaint."

She laughed hysterically. "The last time one of our local girls made a formal complaint, two Mounties picked her up to take her back to the station for questioning. Do you want to hear what happened on the way there?"

He refused to be distracted. "Can't you talk to Siggi? Make a deal? Dolly says he's not so bad."

"Dolly? Dolly! Her husband left for work up North two years ago and hasn't come back. He sends her a cheque now and again. She's got the hots for Siggi, but any guy who's willing to pay the bills will do. Do you think she's selling donuts and making meals because she's got nothing better to do? She hates my guts because she wants Siggi to forget about me. Her dream is for Siggi to get his house back and ask her to move in with him."

"Oh, God," Tom said. "What next?"

"Yes," Freyja said angrily, "what next?"

"Why don't we go for a late-night swim? The lake is calm. The moon's out. Do you like swimming?"

"Yes, fine, I love swimming." She was on the verge of shouting. She caught hold of his arm with one hand and gripped it tightly. She leaned her forehead against his shoulder, took a couple of deep breaths and said, "I love swimming, but I never go at night. It's too spooky. I'd be scared to go alone."

She went into her bedroom and came out in a green bikini, flip-flops and a short white robe that came just past her hips. She put a towel and a blanket into a cloth bag, then got a bottle of wine out of the fridge and two wine glasses from the cupboard. She gave him the glasses and a corkscrew. She put the wine in her bag.

White's was dark by then, but a couple of the boats in the harbour had lights on. In the silence, the occasional sound of metal on metal or glass on metal carried. There were muffled bursts of laughter and the faint sound of voices. People were keeping the party going.

"Swimming after midnight," Freyja said. "Who would have thought? Siggi would never go swimming. He's terrified of the water. When he was a kid, he got thrown off the dock once and didn't know how to swim. Somebody jumped in and dragged him off the bottom. Ingvar maybe. He won't even go wading."

"The beach in front of my place is rocky. Is there a better place?"

"Over a bit to the south there's a bit of sand. Sometimes, I go there during the day. No tourists."

The moon filled up the sky, a great golden disc so close it felt like Tom could reach up and touch it. He lifted his right hand with his fingers spread to hold the moon and Freyja laughed. He went into his house, pulled on his swim trunks and found a towel. Put a package of condoms into the pocket of his swim trunks. Freyja waited for him at the picnic table and he didn't encourage her to come in, because he knew that if she did, they'd never make it to the lake, and he wanted that, swimming together in the moonlight.

Tom took Freyja's hand as they silently threaded their way through the trees like conspirators with a secret until they came to a small patch of sand guarded by two projections of limestone, looking in the darkness like they might be the fallen walls of an ancient fortress. Freyja spread out the blanket and set the wine bottle in the water with the glasses beside it. She took off her short robe and in the light of the moon she was touched with silver.

"There's rocks for a bit. Keep your sandals on until we get past them," she said. They waded into the water that had been so warmed by the sun that there was no shock to it. He threw his sandals onto the shore and Freyja threw her flip-flops. "There are bits of current that run along the shore," she said. "They're not strong. If you get caught in one, don't fight it. Just swim with it. It'll peter out."

The bottom had dipped then risen with the sandbar so that they were knee deep. "It drops steeply away from here," Freyja said, "There's another sandbar farther out."

She dove into the water and he dove after her. They swam together along the moon's path. The water, as it was flung off their arms, turned to drops of silver in the moonlight. The second sandbar was wide and two feet under the surface. They stood up and shook the water out of their hair. Then Tom put his arms around Freyja and kissed her, and as he kissed her, he pushed the straps of her bikini top off her shoulders and pulled it down so it fell around her waist. They sat down on the sandbar and, with the water around them, they kissed and he ran his hands over her breasts and her back. He pulled off her bikini bottom and she tugged at his swim trunks until they came off.

"Not here," she said suddenly and plunged into the water to swim to shore. He felt the sandbar for his swim trunks but couldn't find them. She reached shore ahead of him and was drying herself by the time he reached the blanket. She gave him a quick once-over with the towel. He put his arms around her and pulled her down beside him. "Have you got a condom?" she said. "I'm not on the pill."

"Not here," he said, wishing that he'd had a vasectomy after Joel was born.

"In the house?"

"In my swim trunks."

"Oh, shit," she said. "How good are you with your tongue? I'll return the favour."

The limestone cliffs were ragged, with indentations and projections, not more than a few feet high but high enough to provide privacy. And then the clouds drifted across the brilliant face of the moon so that the small indentation in which they lay was in deep shadow.

Afterwards, Tom went to the lakeshore to retrieve the bottle of wine, and he pulled out the cork with the corkscrew, careful not to pull back too soon and break up the cork. Freyja held up the two wine glasses. The clouds had uncovered the moon and light reflected from the rims of the glasses. He set the bottle aside, they touched their wine glasses together and the sound was a precise musical note. They drank the wine in silence. That surprised him, because he had thought that when this happened they'd have a lot to talk about, that they'd need to share their entire lives, that there would be a waterfall, a raging torrent of words, but instead, there was no need to say anything.

After they had emptied their glasses, they lay on the blanket with their arms around each other and kissed over and over again, as the clouds hid them from each other and then revealed them, and he wished that he could see in the dark, that the water was transparent and he could swim out and find his swim trunks. He told her this, and she laughed quietly and said, "If wishes were horses, beggars would ride. That's what Sarah says."

They lay there with her head on his shoulder and his arm around her, and he said, "When Verthandi asked me why I'd come, I should have told the

truth. My world ended. I didn't know who I was anymore. I'd never been anything but a Mountie. It was my community. I got up in the morning and I
knew what I had to do. I knew my purpose in life. It was all gone. Identity,
community, purpose. Just like that. One bad decision." He paused, then added,
"Mindi Miner—I think it was him—said flotsam and jetsam wash up here
after storms."

Behind them, the spruce trees rose up as a solid wall. They were made of
forged iron and filled with lurking beasts. A late-night breeze came off the lake,
and Tom wished that they had brought a second blanket so they could have
slept there on the very edge of land and water, falling asleep and then waking
up to the sound of small waves on the shore.

Freyja leaned over and kissed him, then said, "Time to go."

He wrapped himself in the blanket and Freyja made a skirt from a towel
and put on her short robe. They stopped at his place so he could put on a shirt
and trousers, and he walked back with her to her place. "Do you think you can
find more condoms?" she asked when they got to her doorstep.

"I'll try," he said. "Can I buy a package from White's?"

"Don't you dare," she said. "It'll be all over town. People buy condoms there
and everyone knows when they bought them, how many they bought, when
they came back for more. They keep track. It's a hot topic at coffee time. Go to
Ben's in the morning. Ask him to get a box for us. He keeps his mouth shut."

He kissed her slowly, wrapped his arms around her and felt her towel start
to slip. She grabbed it, pulled it tight and said, "Don't get me started again. I
don't want to be a mommy." She opened the door, stepped inside and locked
it behind her.

The next morning, he pulled apart the boxes until everything was spread
around the living room. No condoms. He walked over to Ben's and when he
asked for Ben, Wanda said he hadn't been feeling well. He'd been having chest
pains. Derk had driven him into town to see a doctor.

He went back to the beach, took off his clothes except for his black undershorts and waded to the first sandbar, then swam to the second. The water was
fairly clear. He crawled along the sandbar and found Freyja's bikini top but no
sign of her bottoms. He tied it around his left arm and dove on either side of
the bar. He could feel the current pulling against him. Freyja had warned him
about it. It ran along the sandbar. He remembered what Freyja had said and

he swam with it, using as little energy as possible, and when it weakened, he broke free of it. It flowed north toward the dock.

He swam back to where he had entered the water, got dressed and went to White's. He handed Horst two dollars and said he was renting a punt for an hour max. Horst called to Tracy and sent her to the storeroom. She came back with two oars and oarlocks.

He went down to the shore, flipped over a punt, remembered how the one he'd used before had leaked, searched for a bailing can, then rowed out of the harbour, turned and rowed back on the south side. The water wasn't deep and he could see the bottom as he rowed. He thought he should have brought a rake, but he'd have a hard time explaining what he was searching for. He eased the punt under the dock. The shadows darkened the water so he couldn't see. He was dragging one of the oars over the sandy bottom when he saw a flash of colour where a shaft of light came through the boards of the dock. The space was too tight to use the oars, so he pulled himself over by grasping the pilings. There was a pink flip-flop caught on a spike end that stuck out from one of the pilings. When he pulled it loose and held it into a shaft of light, he realized it was a match for the one the large poodle had found.

He pushed his way back into the sunlight and rowed around the dock and into the harbour. He beached the boat. *Angel's*, he kept thinking, *Angel's*, but when he got to the Whites' porch to return the oars and oarlocks, he looked into the galvanized tub that was full of flip-flops for people to wear into the store and many of them were exactly the same as the one he thought was Angel's.

He took the flip-flop with him to the picnic table. He thought the first one would be on the ground under the picnic table, but it wasn't there. He'd raked up the leaves and debris, so he went to search the piles he had made. He'd taken two loads to the dump. It could have been in one of them. He studied the flip-flop. It was the same colour, and it looked like it was the same size, but he couldn't be sure.

CHAPTER 29

SIGGI AND THE BEARS

Around ten o'clock, he walked over to Freyja's to tell her about his failed search for his swim trunks and to return her bikini top, but she wasn't home. In case she was gardening, he went around to the backyard. Her red Jeep was gone. He went back to the front door to see if her rifle was beside the door, but the screen door and the inside door were both locked.

He thought about the night before, the trucks circling the house, Freyja's reaction and Sarah's warnings about the embassy, and he got his truck and drove over to see Sarah. She wasn't there, but the door was unlocked. He let himself in, picked up her rifle, rummaged in the cutlery drawer for six cartridges and drove home. Freyja had told him that the driveway to Siggi's embassy was half a mile long and had two gates that were kept locked all the time. There was no way he could drive in or walk in from the road. The land alongside the road to the embassy was swamp—impassable except in winter. Too marshy to walk, too mossy to canoe, with patches of bulrushes and pools of open water.

The lakeshore was a possibility. From the lakeshore, the ground gradually rose to form a slight ridge parallel to the lake, its crest a quarter mile from the water. The embassy was built on the eastern slope of the ridge. The land immediately in front of the embassy was cleared, but after that there was a fringe of underbrush and thick tangled forest. The trees along the lake were higher than the ridge, so no one with a rifle and a scope could get a clear shot at anyone in front of the building or spy from the lake with binoculars. Between the bush and the building was a hundred feet of sloping yard. They held barbecues and parties there and, according to Freyja, brawls. When she was last there, they were saving all their liquor bottles to build a glass shed. They were greatly amused by the idea and determined to do their share to increase the supply of building blocks.

Tom was grateful that the breeze was offshore because it exposed more of the beach. The broken limestone meant he had to pick his way carefully, but without the water covering it, there was less danger of slipping or his foot dropping into a space between the rocks.

Bush grew to the water's edge in places, and because of erosion from high water and storms he had to climb over trees that had toppled. Willows grew thickly in the swampy areas, creating patches of sand infested with sand fleas. Rather than try to force his way through the thickets, he waded into the lake. Occasionally, small streams drained the swamps. In early spring, the streams would be large, the water difficult to wade through, but now, with the melt-water having run off, the water was turgid, stained brown by rotting vegetation. He hated these slow sediment-filled streams because wire-thin bloodsuckers twisted about in the water. Even though fish often gathered near where the streams entered the lake, he never fished near them. Bloodsuckers were often clinging to their gills, and, inside, when he slit the fish open, there were long flat tapeworms. After he'd waded through each of the streams, he stopped to check his legs.

The bush along the shore was made up of larger trees, and beneath them was thick tangled undergrowth of dead wood and low bushes, the kind of forest you'd have to push your way through, breaking branches, forcing shrubs down, watching for holes and crevices in the limestone. The ground was uneven and treacherous from the eroding limestone, covered in moss and thick layers of leaves. On the other side of the beach was the lake, a vast expanse of silver-blue water, with no land in sight. Two distant sailboats made precise white triangles against the horizon.

The day was perfect, warm, sunny, the slight breeze taking away the intensity of the heat, the sky clear. A heron, disturbed by his appearance, rose up, its wings pumping hard, and a flock of terns ran ahead of him. Five pelicans swooped down and landed on the lake not far from shore. A soft, sweet smell wafted from the forest. *This is crazy*, he thought. *Nothing bad should happen on a day like this.* But he knew from experience that human craziness paid no attention to beauty or goodness but was tangled up in its own dark forest. Terrible crimes occurred on the finest of days.

When he joined the Mounties, he'd had an idea that he'd be stopping people like the Nazis, that he'd be joining with a force dedicated to justice, organized around mutual loyalty, that he'd become part of an extended family. Instead, when he'd gone to his first posting there had been a reserve nearby. His sergeant had taken Tom's pistol and locked it up—"No arms allowed on a reserve," he said. He drove him to the community centre, dropped him off and said, "I'll pick you up in two hours." Tom had been in three fights before his ride came back.

He learned to fend for himself, to ignore a host of small crimes, to know when he would be on the losing end of a fight and avoid it. The people he dealt with, he realized, didn't have to hate him personally. They had lots to hate, and he was just the representative of whatever they happened to be angry about at the moment. When he moved to other small towns, nothing improved much. In the surrounding countryside there'd be shrinking villages with a church, a graveyard and a closed store, and five houses with outbuildings, some of which were being used as grow ops and gun shops.

The limestone formed a white line separating the green of the forest and the blue of the water. The slight lapping of the water could have lulled him to sleep. He sat on a piece of driftwood large enough to make a comfortable seat, with a stub of a branch providing support for his back. He wondered if everything would be all right if he just stayed where he was, if the craziness of the world would stop, if his craziness would stop. He should have brought a fishing rod instead of a rifle, caught perch or bass, made a fire with driftwood, sat here in the silence, cooking the fish, eating it, no sound except the noise of his feet on the rock. And for a moment he thought about McAra, about Sarah resentfully saying he could have had a job at the pulp mill but couldn't accept living by a clock. *But that wasn't it, that wasn't it*, Tom thought. *It was more than that*. In the pulp mill there would never be silence. There was the incessant noise of the machines overriding everything else, shutting out everything else. For Tom it had been the car radio, the voices, the static, the motor, the car doors slamming, the siren wailing, sidling up to the driver's window of a car he'd pulled over, waiting for the sound of a pistol, the sound of a bullet tearing through flesh and muscle and bone. Life was never so good, no day so beautiful that it would stop the noise and the craziness.

He stood, hefted the rifle in his left hand, feeling its weight. There was no reason for it to be loaded yet. He felt the two shells in his shirt pocket and the other four in the pocket of his shorts. The pockets of his shorts were large, could have taken a dozen shells, but he knew from experience that seldom were more than one or two shells needed.

He picked his way along the broken slabs until he came to an area where the limestone cliffs were high, reaching into the lake, and, holding Sarah's rifle with his left hand, steadied himself with his right by gripping the rough surface of the rock. He was grateful that here there were no snakes on the ledges. He faced the rock and worked his way sideways like a crab. The lake bottom was sand mixed with pieces of limestone that had been forced loose from the cliff by water and ice. *Why*, he wondered, *why can't people behave sensibly?* Why can't they just behave themselves, show a little self-control? Why have they got to get into conflicts all the time? Why have they got to want stuff so badly that they do crazy things to get it? Why can't Siggi just screw Dolly? And why can't Freyja give Siggi back his house? Why have people got to want things they can't have and be unhappy with what they do have?

He was in hip-deep water, grumbling to himself, when he stepped into one of the many holes created by erosion in the lake bed. As he plunged straight down, the water closed over his head. The hole was narrow as a chimney and he banged against projections. He had his left hand down with the rifle and right hand up. He tried to lift his left arm, but the rifle caught on the rough edge of the limestone. The noise of the water from his thrashing filled his head. He let go of the rifle, caught the edge of the chimney with his right hand and pulled himself up. He shot to the surface, heaved himself free of the hole and stood on the rocky bed. He leaned against the cliff, gasping, and fought back the panic of nearly being trapped in the hole.

Once he was breathing normally again and his heart had slowed, he thought about having lost Sarah's rifle. *Shit, shit, shit.* There was nothing philosophical or profound about it. He just leaned against the cliff and said, "Shit," thinking about having to tell her that her rifle was at the bottom of the lake. He hoped she wasn't emotionally attached to it. He could come back with a rope and hooks and drag for it. The pocked, shattered face of the cliff in front of him was dangerous with eroded rock. He took a pencil stub out of his shirt pocket and jammed it into a crack to mark the spot.

His arms were sore. He held up his left arm, then the right and saw that in thrashing his way out of the hole, he'd banged and scraped them on the rock. He looked at his legs. They were both scraped, and he could see that there were going to be bruises shortly. Blood thinned with water ran down his arms and dripped into the lake. *Thank God there are no piranhas*, he thought, then wondered if the blood would draw bloodsuckers.

Freyja, he thought, as he worked his way along the beach. Why couldn't she just shrug off Siggi and his jealous behaviour? If she'd gone to confront him with her peashooter, they'd turn her into a rag doll and use her for target practice. He remembered what Mindi Miner had said about the fate of Billy Begood and the Jones boys. Or Siggi might profess his undying love and, if she played along, treat her like a princess.

Freyja had told him about the sandy beach and wooden steps up to a path that led to the embassy. As he came around a corner of limestone, he saw the beach—twenty feet of sand in a tiny cove. At one time the four steps were painted grey. Wind and rain had stripped away most of the paint, but bits of it still clung to rough spots on the wood. There was a floating dock, with a jet boat tied up to it. Tom had seen one like it that had been seized in a bust in Ontario. Someone said it was worth US$78,000 and could go ninety-eight miles an hour. Beside it were two Sea-Doo Speedsters. Tom waited at the edge of the cliff until he was sure no one was around, then picked his way along the shore. The boat and the Sea-Doos were chained to the dock.

He climbed the steps so he could look down the path. It was grassy, narrow and turned to the left. The trees spread over it, blocking out the sun. To follow the path was to risk traps or cameras or Siggi and his friends walking to the beach. He crossed over the small cove, made his way along the beach for another fifty feet, got down on his knees and forced his way into the bush. The forest floor was thick with moss and decaying leaves, the smell of the ground heavy with the soft scent of rotting wood. A woodpecker startled him by suddenly tapping at a tree, then stopped. He could turn back to the beach, he thought, to the open sky and water, slip away unseen. After all, Freyja had never asked him to rescue her. She might be there, in bed with Siggi, and if he appeared like Sir Galahad, she might say, "What are you doing here? Are you crazy?" Saying, "Whoops, sorry, my mistake" and backing out discreetly wouldn't really rectify the situation.

He lay there, trying to decide what to do, trying not to think about the thin-stemmed wild rosebushes that were covered in hair-like thorns. He regretted wearing shorts. Even when he was in the chimney, his sandals had stayed on. His hat had floated away, but he'd managed to retrieve it. He wiggled forward now. A branch caught his hat, and it stayed behind. He reached up, felt that it was gone, rolled onto his side and snatched it back. When he'd plunged into the hole, his sunglasses had pulled up but managed to stay, slightly askew, on his head. He took them off now, folded them and went to put them in his shirt pocket, saw that the useless bullets were there, took the bullets out and put them into his shorts pocket. He slipped his sunglasses into the pocket and pulled a twig out of his hatband. He lay there for a moment, wondered if he just stayed there long enough, would Freyja come find him and drag him home.

"Things don't always work out," Anna often told him, "but you just keep going. No matter how bad it feels, nothing lasts forever." He'd been disheartened after he'd left Anna's apartment block; his sense of aloneness had increased, nearly overwhelming him, and when she'd called him to come and help her clean apartments and do maintenance work, he'd quickly agreed. "One foot," she would say and show him by putting one foot in front of the other, "then the other foot. You don't feel like walking, it doesn't matter. Don't think too much. You can think later."

He rolled over onto his knees and searched for a way through the underbrush. There could be no rushing, no straight path. Dead wood littered the ground, and he tried not to break any of it. It was so quiet that sound would draw attention. Branches slapped against his face; broken bits stuck in his shirt. A piece of dead branch got stuck between his shirt and his neck. He stopped and fished it out. The woodpecker startled him again with its staccato rapping against a tree. The noise, sharp, precise, stopped as suddenly as it had started and was replaced by the sound of his own breathing, the slight movement of his hands and knees in the forest debris.

He was at the edge of the forest when he saw the roof of the greenhouse—three greenhouses side by side, mounds of soil, plastic bales of peat moss, piles of wooden pallets, a small front-end loader. As he watched, one of Siggi's companions appeared carrying a sack of fertilizer, but instead of going into the greenhouse, he put the fertilizer down, started the front-end loader, moved it forward ten feet, then lifted a door that was disguised to look like turf. He picked up the sack of fertilizer and descended, pulling the door shut after him.

Tom crawled back into the bush, then sideways to where he thought the embassy might be.

He didn't have a plan, couldn't make a plan until he saw the embassy and the layout and whether or not Freyja's Jeep was there. If it wasn't there, he'd slip away unseen. No one would ever know he'd been there.

He finally came to a partially built structure that he recognized as the house of bottles Freyja had told him about. The bottles were stacked sideways, layered in concrete, forming walls of green, blue, brown, transparent glass. So far the highest wall was about six feet. There were stacks of empty bottles inside the walls, along with a wheelbarrow and a couple of shovels, a stack of cement bags with a tarp thrown over the top. Judging from the leaves and twigs on the tarp, it hadn't been moved for a long time. Enthusiasm for the project had obviously waned.

He eased past the bottle house and was so focused on what was ahead that he didn't notice the movement around him. Then he heard a stick snap, looked back and froze. There was a black bear not six feet behind him, watching him as intently as he was now watching it. He backed away and hadn't gone more than a few feet when he saw a flash of movement, and when he looked, there was another bear. Neither bear charged. He backed farther away and realized he was on the path from the lake, stopped and stood still. As he watched, he realized that there were other bears. One stood up on its hind legs, then got down. *What the hell, what the hell? What the hell?* And he backed out into an area where a circle of underbrush had been cleared away.

Siggi was lying in a blue canvas chair with an aluminum frame, scooping dog food out of a fifty-pound bag. There were empty bags on the ground, two bears sitting and lying down, and two more gobbling up dog food.

Siggi looked startled, stopped scooping and said, "What the hell do you want?"

"You said I could drop by anytime to talk to you."

"So talk," Siggi said.

The forest surrounded them on three sides and the embassy sat behind a screen of small planted spruce at the other side of the yard. The building was long and made of stone, then wood siding, with windows up high to let in light but to keep anyone on the ground from seeing inside. There were skylights in the roof. Most of the building was below ground. *Johnny Armstrong's work*, Tom thought.

"Freyja?" Tom said it tentatively, as a question. There were ten feet separating them, and Siggi might have been a pagan king in the midst of his personal zoo. The ground was littered with empty dog food bags.

"She's not here. I thought she'd be with you, lover boy."

"What the hell are you doing?"

"Feeding my security guards. Do you object?"

"No," Tom said. "Whatever."

"A full bear is a happy bear," Siggi said. "Most people aren't stupid enough to come here when there's an army of bears protecting the place." A slight breeze lifted the leaves of the moose maples and, for a moment, the trees lost their limp, defeated look.

"Nobody told me." There were bears here, there and everywhere. He wondered if they were trained to attack, like Rottweilers.

"You should leave other men's wives alone."

Tom felt his exasperation rise. People who weren't logical had always distressed him, but since his accident, people's refusal to acknowledge reality infuriated him, at times drove him to shouting.

"You need to read up on the law. Nowadays, wives can testify against their husbands. Trying to make her stay married to you so she can't testify is nuts."

"If I say m-e-a-t," Siggi spelled out the word, "these guys will see you as a meal. They'll eat everything except your shoes." His face had turned dark red and Tom wondered if he had high blood pressure.

"I didn't just come to ask about Freyja."

"What?" Siggi asked sharply and started scooping dog food for a bear that was staring at the bag.

"Angel. She was seen in your truck the night she died."

"The night before," Siggi said. "So what? Her death was an accident."

"Maybe not," Tom said stubbornly. One of the bears had come up to sniff him. It pushed its nose against his leg. He hoped he didn't smell good.

"Do you like bears?" Siggi asked.

"I grew up in the city."

Siggi laughed. "That's Bruno who's seeing if you've got anything delicious in your pockets. I often have treats for him in my pockets. He loves peanut butter sandwiches."

"I'm allergic," Tom said.

The sun, which had been hiding behind a cloud, appeared and the relief from the momentary breeze was replaced by a suffocating heat.

"You're a prick," Siggi said. "A city prick. The kind that comes on a fancy boat and lords it over everyone." The unfairness of the accusation offended Tom. Living in the city hadn't bestowed any benefits on him.

"I've never owned a boat. I can't afford it. I'm mortgaged to the hilt."

"You're a cop. A prick cop. You suck up our taxes to persecute us."

"Angel," Tom persisted. "She was in your truck the night before she died. Do you like fifteen-year-olds?"

"You should mind your own business," Siggi said. "She might have been my daughter."

"Might?"

"Wanda says she was, but she wouldn't do a DNA. If she was, I'd have given support. Has Freyja been telling you how I never pay her the money I owe her? I'm supporting two other kids. When the bears aren't hibernating, it costs me around five thousand a month to feed them. I've got big debts to pay."

"Illegitimate kids?"

"They are not illegitimate. You're a prick. They're just as legitimate as you or anybody else."

"Did Angel know?"

"I don't think so. I hardly ever got to see her. I'm always away working. Wanda's always moving. When I was here and Angel was here, I tried to be good to her. I took her for rides on my snowmobile. I bought her treats at the store. I help Ben out when I can. What the hell do people like you want?"

"Did she say anything about being pregnant?" The woodpecker started tapping on a tree again. Sunlight reflected from the discarded bags, and Tom shuffled to the side to get the glare out of his eyes.

"No. She was crying. I thought maybe boyfriend problems."

"Any idea who it was?"

"I don't know anything about her life in the city." Siggi said it in a loud voice, offended, unfairly accused.

"You're a survivalist."

"So are you. Why did you come to Valhalla if you aren't? You're just not as prepared."

"Is Freyja here?"

"She's not here. What do you want me to do, go inside and drag her out by her hair? You think she's such hot stuff? Maybe in a while you might change your mind."

"What about Wanda?"

"Wanda is a party girl. She doesn't know how to do anything else. Lots of guys would have married her. She was beautiful. Hot in bed. But she can't lay off the booze, and when she boozes, she forgets what she's been doing and wanders away. She's living with you and you think everything is hunky-dory and you're going to be together for life, and then she goes to the bar and has a few drinks and it's like there's nothing there. No brains. She goes off with a guy, might remember you in a week or a month. 'Oh, hi, how have you been? I haven't seen you for a while.' She needs a dog collar and a chain."

By the time he was finished, he was shouting. His words were bitter. He opened and closed his mouth a few times after he spoke, and Tom thought he saw the young man who had started out to be a rock star, a hockey hero, certain of his success. Siggi sat there looking surprised at what he'd said.

Tom thought it best not to get into a discussion of a subject he knew nothing about.

"What happened to Angel?"

"You're the cop. You go figure out what happened. Fuck off before I sick Bruno on you." His voice had lost its force and sounded like a riff of sadness.

Another bear had come up and was staring intently at Tom. Tom stepped back, but there were bears in front of him, to the right of him, to the left of him, behind him.

"Don't run," Siggi said. "They'll chase you." Bruno went up to Siggi, who rubbed the heels of his hands between the bear's eyes.

"Why don't you just pay Freyja the money you owe her and she'll give you your house back?"

"I pay my employees first. I have creditors." He pushed over the bag of dog food, grabbed the bottom corners and emptied it onto the ground.

"Just speaking hypothetically, but what if a person knew that you had an underground grow op and said he wouldn't report it so you could cash in and pay your debts—at least he wouldn't if you started paying Freyja back, say five thousand a month, and you quit harassing her?"

"Fuck you, you son of a bitch!" Siggi yelled. "Don't tell me what to do!"

"You guys can kill each other off and no one gives a shit. As a matter of fact, most people figure, 'Good, another dealer gone.' You kill me and there's going to be a fuss. Even those of us who have left the Force getting killed bring lots of heat. They'll come and search, and they'll find your underground grow op just as easily as I found it. And if your name isn't on the property, it won't matter. It's you who owes the money, and your bankers aren't known for giving easy credit. If they realize you can't pay, they'll make an example of you."

"Shut your mouth," Siggi said, and his face twisted with anger and fear, because he knew what Tom was saying was true. It was not the law that he needed to fear but those others with real rules and penalties. There would be no meeting to discuss his childhood, to hear the pleas of his friends as they extolled his many virtues. No one to listen to his excuses.

"You don't dare leave here. You go to jail and you know how that works. You'd be a dead man walking. All it takes is a mug filled with wet paper towels in a plastic bag. You know the Iranian from the West Coast? He tried to muscle into Winnipeg. He was up on murder charges. His bankers didn't want to wait for the courts. Three guys beat the crap out of him. He's got so much brain damage that he's an imbecile. You wouldn't last six months in Stony Mountain."

"Shut the fuck up!" Siggi shouted. "Shut up!"

"You're trapped," Tom said. "You can't leave. Do you know how many guys like you I helped put into body bags?"

"I've got a deal," Siggi said stubbornly. "I'll pay my bills."

"One road in and out. You've got people watching it. Do you think your creditors don't have people watching it? You and your friends aren't going to turn up for a few days and one of the locals is going to come to see why. They're going to find you with your head blown off."

"Not a chance," Siggi replied.

"How about a couple of kayaks coming in at night? Not a sound. Or three or four snowmobiles over the ice in winter? Or four or five guys on snowshoes? They want you, they'll get you."

"My friends will look out for me."

"Friends," Tom said. "You're short of money. You think people love you because you were a high school hockey hero? You haven't got money, they'll work for whoever will pay them."

"Shut up!" Siggi screamed. "Shut the fuck up!"

The bears were not used to Siggi yelling, and they all began to look at him uncertainly.

"You're in the wrong business," Tom said. "Everybody says so."

"Meat, meat!" Siggi yelled. "Meat!" He twisted in his seat to reach behind and when his hand came up, it held a bang stick.

Tom spun around and began to run. The canvas of the chair Siggi was in hung down so low that he had to struggle to get out of it. Then he had to get past Bruno, who was still hoping for a peanut butter sandwich. Tom ran, swinging his gimpy leg slightly to the side. It threw him off balance, and as he raced past startled bears, past the glass house, around a sharp curve, he slipped on the grass, skidded, tumbled, rolled onto his feet and kept running. Siggi skidded in the same place, held the bang stick up so it didn't touch anything and crashed into a tree. He rebounded and ran full tilt.

The bang stick had to be pressed against its target to work—a shark, a bear, a man. Tom had seen what happened when they were pressed against a watermelon at a party. The watermelon disintegrated, sweet pulp instead of blood and brains over everyone. He knew if Siggi managed to get close enough to jam the end against his back, it would blow a hole so large that Siggi could put an arm through his chest. The bears would gobble up the evidence. Siggi was right. There wouldn't be much left except his shoes.

He hoped the metal pins holding his leg together wouldn't snap, that they'd keep his leg in one piece. He skidded around a tight corner, and there was the lake, shining pale blue ahead. Tom ran now in a shaded tunnel created by thick bush and overhanging branches.

He ran along the float, felt himself start to trip, threw his weight forward and dove. He pulled himself down as deep as he could and swam along the bottom.

Siggi had been gaining, close to driving the bang stick into Tom's back. He leapt after Tom over the steps onto the beach, onto the float, staggered, stopped at the water's edge and screamed. Behind him, curious bears that had followed them stood in the bush, watching.

Tom surfaced, rolled over to look back at the shore. Siggi was standing on the float, holding the bang stick in the air. When he saw Tom's head appear he flung the bang stick at him. As Tom tread water, he watched the weapon make lazy circles as it arced up then began to descend, passed over him and splashed into the water.

Siggi looked back at the bears, yelled, "Meat, meat, meat!" and pointed frantically at Tom. "Meat, you stupid bastards, meat."

Siggi raised his arms in the air, yelled one more time, then turned around and ran to where the jet boat and Sea-Doos were docked. He grabbed first one chain, then another and screamed in frustration. He raced back toward the embassy.

Tom could see his hat floating on the water close to the dock. There was no time to retrieve it. Remembering what Freyja had told him about the cache of weapons, he swam as hard as he could toward the first point of land that blocked a clear shot. He reached it, waded ashore and picked his way over the rock, worked his way past the next point, then heard a motor start, so he turned into the forest and swamp. Bloodsuckers or not, he was going to have to cross stinking brown streams. He lay in the bush and watched. Siggi was riding on a Sea-Doo with an AK-47 in one hand. As he rode parallel to the shore, he fired bursts into the bush. After he'd passed, Tom began to pick his way over rocks and through the bush. He could hear Siggi firing in the distance.

He hoped that Siggi would run out of ammunition and return. Instead, the sound of the motor stopped and there was silence.

Oh, crap, was all that Tom could think. *Oh, crap. Oh, crap.* He backed deeper into the bush. Siggi would be waiting for him.

He could hear his father saying that most people have no common sense, no ability to understand consequences, no understanding of cause and effect. He wished he could get his father to have a chat with Siggi. No wonder Siggi liked bears. If they were hungry, they ate. If they were angry, they killed. Living in the moment.

The successful dealers were perfect psychopaths. He'd had to deal with people like that. They were never anxious or worried. They lived completely in the moment. Often charming, always manipulative and completely ruthless. They killed each other without any agonizing, dumping bodies into shallow graves or rivers. Their weakness was that they were so self-confident that they made mistakes, and because they had little if any anxiety about the future, they seldom planned well. They never became chess masters. The successful ones were cool and calm, never impulsive. *Freyja was right*, he thought. Siggi was in the wrong kind of work. He was too emotional, too impulsive, too sensitive.

He edged forward, waded into swamp where the bulrushes were over his head. He found an open lead, and careful to make no sound, frog-kicked across the open water, then pulled his way through the rushes.

Siggi was impatient, Freyja had said. What he wanted, he wanted now. He was given to fits of rage, like a child having a tantrum. But his attention span was short. He was easily distracted. There was nothing calm or robot-like about him. He was unpredictable, and unpredictable made people nervous. Sorry afterwards, even apologetic, falling into a kind of torpor in which he sat and did nothing for days, hardly speaking. "He's not a bad person," Freyja had said. "He can be lots of fun; he's just crazy. He doesn't think."

With Siggi to the north of him, it was too dangerous to go that way. There was nothing but wilderness and swamp to the south. The lake lay to the east. He remembered when he went to Angel's funeral that the road had stopped just beyond the church. There'd been large limestone blocks at the end. Beyond that the bush had been cleared for a road, but nothing had been done to finish it. Weeds and small plants had grown up, yet the path was obvious. There had been tire tracks around the limestone boulders that blocked the way. The trail, it was hardly a road, was usable, and from what he had learned from Freyja, Siggi had built a private road from it east through the marsh to the embassy.

He only knew that if he didn't find the cut in the bush, he'd have to turn back to the beach, wade and swim his way to the lake, wait until dark and swim until he figured he was past wherever Siggi might be waiting. He came to a muskrat house and stood on it. He could see that the bulrushes and pipe grass were being replaced by willow and then by trees. Red-winged blackbirds hung onto bulrushes, making their sour cry. After he'd rested, he eased himself back into the water and swam toward the line of trees. When he was free of the swamp, Tom checked his legs. His Nikes were covered in mud and there was a bloodsucker clamped to his left leg just above his knee. He shivered, slid his thumbnail under the head end, and when it pulled its head back, he flicked it away. It left a round red mark.

He sat there, listening, but there was no sound. Siggi was still waiting at some choke point.

He pushed his way through the bush, keeping low, cursing the fact that he'd lost Sarah's rifle that he'd worn shorts. His legs were covered in a thousand scratches. Given the crap he was wading through, he wondered if he'd die of blood poisoning.

Eventually, he found the cut in the bush for the road, where the trees were smaller and the shrubs lower. He turned north and limped along, slapping at mosquitoes.

He was marooned in the wilderness but not lost, and when the unfinished road ended, there would be water to slake his thirst, and the blinding forest that pressed in upon him would be replaced by a gravel road. At the end of the overgrown trail, there would be the church on one side and the graveyard on the other. He'd been told that the church door was never locked. He could find shelter there, go inside and lie down on a bench. He wished that there was a breeze, even if it were momentary, to cool him. There was the buzzing of bees. A few of them flew about his head but quickly disappeared.

He was not prepared for this. The streets of his childhood had been paved, controlled by traffic lights, lit by streetlamps, awash in the steady noise of traffic. Even when he couldn't sleep and sat in the window at 3 a.m., there were vehicles appearing and disappearing and the sound of sirens from time to time as ambulances rushed through the city.

He licked his lips to moisten them, but they dried right away and he could feel that they were chapped. He would have sat down to see if there was a splinter in his foot, but there was nothing to sit on and no place on the ground that was open, because the forest had grown with a fierce determination to reclaim the land that had been stripped bare. He wondered what it was that had been planned. Perhaps a summer resort, cottage lots, a scheme that would make friends of the local MLA rich. He blew out his breath and grimaced, wished he'd been able to return along the lake and could cool off by swimming part of the way.

With no hat, he squinted against the sun that pressed down, trying to set the world on fire. There was a faint smell of wild roses, roses that had grown tall where the bush had been cleared. He ripped a flower off and put the petals in his mouth, chewed on them, then spit them out. He thought about how, in spite of his father's warnings, Tom had, from time to time, given food to people he found sleeping in the back alley. He was desperately thirsty, and now that he wasn't scrambling to escape, he was hungry. He wished he could magically have one of the sandwiches he'd given away. He scavenged food from the apartments he cleaned, and when his father was at work or out playing bridge or chess, Tom cooked up beans or pasta or made sandwiches, took them out. No matter how hungry they looked, if they had a dog with them, they'd share whatever he gave them. Right now he would have been hard pressed to share a sandwich with a dog.

He followed the trail until it came to where the road started, and standing in the shelter of the bush, he studied the graveyard and manse. It was a dangerous location. Although the land rose up from the lake so that anyone standing on the beach couldn't see anything but the very tip of the church spire, it was a choke point, and if Siggi were sitting on the slope where he could see both the church and the beach, he could watch two hundred feet of cleared ground. Anyone trying to cross it in daylight would be a dead man. Tom waited, watching for any movement. He didn't want to go into the bush and work his way toward the beach to see if Siggi was there. A movement in the bush might draw a burst of shooting. He slapped at a mosquito and looked to see if he had any wood ticks. They were often thick in the tall grass.

From where Tom stood, he could see the graveyard, the church opposite it. On the south side of the church, in front of the manse garage, Pastor Jon was working on a car.

The rear wheel was off and he was studying the brake. He was wearing white coveralls, a cap blackened by years of grease and oil, and heavy work boots. Tom waited, watching the pastor as he worked, couldn't keep his eyes off the black pump with the red handle that he'd seen at the funeral. Ice-cold water. He ran his tongue over his lips. When he was certain that Siggi was not watching, he limped to the car. Pastor Jon was a bit deaf and didn't notice Tom.

Tom went to the pump and began to work the handle. It creaked and squealed. Pastor Jon looked up. Tom waved at him, but a drink of water was more important than good manners at the moment, and Tom wondered if he could even manage to speak with his throat so dry. The well coughed, and cold water gushed out all at once. He put his left hand over the spout to hold the water back, then bent down and began to drink. The water was so cold that it took his breath away and made his forehead ache. He took a deep breath, then bent down and drank again. When he'd had enough to drink, he put his leg under the spout. His skin went numb. He rubbed his leg, and the mud thinned out and ran onto the ground. He rinsed off his right leg, then the left one. When he finished, he turned to the minister.

"A Jew by the side of the road," Pastor Jon said, clearly searching for an experience in his past that would explain the present. There was a double out-house with a moon cut in the top of one door and a star in the other, and beside it a small greenhouse and garden. Past that was a barbed-wire enclosure with sheep lying down and beyond that the marsh. There were ten beehives, and the humming of the bees entering and leaving the hives was a steady low murmur.

"Tom Parsons," Tom replied. "I live in Valhalla. I bought Jessie Olason's house." As they stood there, Tom wondered if it were really possible that Siggi had been trying to kill him, that he had been running and swimming for his life. Here, everything was quiet, the only sound that of the bees that flew by while the sun hung in the sky, a huge lemon disc watching over a landscape where everything was at peace.

Pastor Jon rubbed the side of his face and got a streak of dirt on it. "Jessie was my most faithful servant. She never came without peanut butter cookies."

"I was here for Angel's funeral. I was better dressed then. I came with Sarah McAra.

Do you think I could get a ride into town?"

Pastor Jon hesitated—not because he would have said no, but rather he had to take time to figure out how he would do it. He pushed his glasses up on his nose to get a better look at Tom's condition. "I can do no less than a Samaritan," he said, "but would you mind riding in the back of my truck? The seat covers are new."

Just in case Siggi had worked his way west to the road, Tom lay flat in the back of the truck. The truck bumped in and out of ruts, and Tom had to brace himself sideways to keep from being thrown in the air. There was an old blue tarp in the truck box. The dust was so thick that Tom pulled the tarp over himself to protect his eyes and lungs. The limestone dust rose up in a cloud and settled over the tarp.

There was a place where the road curved nearly to the shore, an open piece of ground on the lake side of the road, and on the other side, swamp. Siggi had decided to wait here. He had the lake, the lakeshore and the road covered. Tom heard Siggi yelling, felt the truck slow then stop, and he wondered if Siggi would shoot him while he was lying in the back of the truck or if, out of consideration for Pastor Jon, he'd make Tom get out first. The dust caught up with the truck, swept over it. Pastor Jon climbed out of the truck, and Tom heard him walk to the far side of the road and Siggi yell, asking if he'd seen anyone on the road, and Pastor Jon yell back that no, he hadn't seen anyone on the road. He could hear Pastor Jon's footsteps on the gravel, then the truck door open and close, the truck shift into gear and roll forward, and Tom realized that he'd been holding his breath, tensing, ready to leap from the truck at Siggi. There was no point in trying to run from a man with an AK-47. It would have been charge and maybe survive. He'd done it before with a domestic dispute in which a husband with a shotgun was just inside a door. Tom, seeing through a crack in the back edge of the door that the husband lowered the shotgun so it was aimed at the floor, slammed the door hard so it knocked him off balance, and then Tom was on him, taking him down hard. He didn't get any medals for it. The consensus at the station was that he should have shot the guy, never mind the distraught wife and two kids. "She's still good lookin'," one of his colleagues had said. "She can get another guy next week."

After they were out of Siggi's sight, Pastor Jon stopped the truck, leaned out of the window and told Tom to get into the truck.

"You and Siggi don't get along," Pastor Jon said as he put the truck into gear. "Money?" Tom shook his head. "Drugs?" Tom shook his head again. "Women?" Tom nodded. "Centuries go by. Nothing really changes. Samson and Delilah. Bathsheba and David.

"Look at me. Harvard. Oxford. Living in the midst of—" he took one hand off the steering wheel and swung it in a small arc indicating the passing swamp and forest. "Taking care of bees and cattle. I'm going to buy a breeding pair of goats from Albert Scutter. I hunt and fish a few nets. I spend more time fixing motors than I do preaching.

"I'm not complaining, though. In Iceland, ever since the Vikings became Christianized, it was never assumed that a minister should derive his entire living from taxing his parishioners. Instead, he was given land and a few sheep and maybe a cow or two, and he was expected to mow his own hay, milk his sheep and cows, or have his wife milk them, and even join the yearly exodus to the coast to fish from an open boat at peril of his life, then walk back five days to his farm and church when the winter's fishing was over. There were no trees and no grain grown, and hardly any vegetables struggled to life in Iceland. The way of the preacher could be hard."

"Harder than Mindi Miner's life? Or Ben's?"

"No, no harder than their lives. It's just that some people think that the clergy should all make a vow of poverty. And so should teachers and doctors. People want things but don't want to pay for them."

"Like the Freemen on the Land?"

"Yes, but they are extreme. They are searching for false solutions. We are all searching for answers. We think if we find them, we will be free of pain. If you came to church, it might help heal your soul and you'd get to meet people who might hire you. Sarah said you would fix the cross on the church. She thinks highly of your skills."

"Does my soul need healing?" Tom asked.

"If it didn't, you wouldn't be here," Pastor Jon replied.

They rode in silence for a time, then Pastor Jon said, "Siggi is a conundrum. But so is the devil. The devil is a fallen angel. Most people don't know that. What Siggi does with drugs is destructive. But he is also generous. What he has he often gives away. He paid for a new roof for the manse. Unasked. A half dozen locals turned up. Ben delivered the shingles. Said Siggi had paid for them. It is hard to live in a small village where everyone believes that you will be in the NHL or lead a famous band and become rich and successful and for it to come to nothing but a job in the oil fields. He is violent, and then he is sorrowful. Will you," he said, turning his head to the side to look at Tom, "take Uriah's wife?"

"She's getting a divorce," Tom replied.

"I pass no judgment," Pastor Jon said, and he quoted from Romans: "Let not the one who eats despise the one who abstains, and let not the one who abstains pass judgment on the one who eats."

They were within a mile of the village, so Pastor Jon, not wanting to have it seen that he had given Tom a ride, and that news getting back to Siggi, stopped at the side of the road.

"I will drop you off here," he said, "but I will continue on my way to buy a pound of bacon that I lust after. The Israelites would not eat pork because the pig has a cloven hoof. I don't eat its trotters, but I like bacon sandwiches with fresh garden lettuce and tomatoes, a bit of cheese. Besides, it will be clear to everyone why I drove into town. That which is unknown is speculated upon."

When Tom stepped onto the road, he spit three times to try to get the dust out of his mouth. His nose felt plugged and his eyes gritty.

"You could get your road graded," he said.

"Barnabas and I have ecclesiastical differences," Pastor Jon replied. "He says that if you believe, that is all you have to do. It doesn't matter how you live. I say you have to live the Bible."

"Thank you for the ride. It would have been a long walk."

"Are you going to come to church?"

"I lost my faith on my job. God never turned up when I needed him."

"I'm not sure about God, either, but I believe in goodness and fellowship."

Pastor Jon put his truck in gear but didn't pull away. Instead, he leaned out the window and said, "I heard you might sell Jessie's property to the Whites."

Tom said no, he wasn't planning on it.

"If you decide to sell," Pastor Jon said. He pulled out a business card and handed it to Tom. "I've my real estate licence. I get some business because Horst is difficult to deal with."

As they talked, a truck appeared from a dead-end road that led to the swamp where the fishermen dumped their fish guts. If Pastor Jon had wanted to keep Tom's ride a secret, it wasn't likely to be anymore.

"I told no lie," Pastor Jon said. "He asked if I'd seen anyone on the road. I never saw you on the road. I saw you in my yard. There are times when being precise is important."

"I'll come by one day and fix your cross," Tom said. "I'll see if I can borrow a ladder."

"Johnny Armstrong," Pastor Jon said. "He's the only one who's got a ladder tall enough." Pastor Jon reached behind the seat, pulled out a jar of honey and handed it to Tom. "Take this. You can pay me later."

Pastor Jon pulled away before the truck reached them. It was a beat-up Toyota half ton, covered in rust. The back was filled with empty gut barrels. As the truck passed Tom, he saw Ingvar and Larry inside. Ingvar didn't slow down, and a cloud of dust enveloped Tom.

When Tom arrived home, he got a bar of soap and a bottle of shampoo. He went to the lakeshore, lay in the shallow water, took off his runners and washed them. He pulled off his shorts and scrubbed them with his hands. He took off his shirt. The pocket was torn and two buttons were missing. His sunglasses were still in the pocket. He lifted them out. One of the arms was bent. The scratches and scrapes on his legs stung, and there were numerous fine thorns sticking into them from the wild rosebushes.

When he'd finished bathing, he went inside, looked in the mirror and realized that his face was stinging because of the scratches and gouges on his forehead and cheeks. Scabs were starting to form. "I hope that son of a bitch waits there all night and the mosquitoes suck him dry," he said out loud.

He found a pair of tweezers and picked out the thorns. It was too painful to wear jeans, so he put on another pair of shorts.

He was going to the Emporium to see if Karla had an antibiotic ointment when Larry and Ingvar were coming back from the dock. "I seen you had a chat with the preacher," Larry said. His tone implied that the conversation must have been of great significance.

"I got lost," Tom said.

"You been in the bush," Ingvar said, studying his face and legs.

"Tried to take a shortcut," Tom said. "Wasn't a good idea. I wish I'd met Pastor Jon earlier. It would have saved me a long walk."

"He stopped to sell you honey," Ingvar said. "It's pretty hard to get away without a jar of honey."

"I said I'd take two jars the next time I saw him," Tom answered. "I heard that it's good."

"You know Biblio Braggi lived there before," Larry said. "He came here selling Bibles, saw the place was empty and set up the hives. He talked to God and he talked to bees."

"He had good honey," Ingvar broke in. "He took good care of his bees. He was always trying to sell you a Bible. You can't get to heaven without a Bible on your chest when you're in your coffin. When he left, Pastor Jon bought the place, and people who were there saw him put the bees into mourning and court them."

"I was there," Larry said. "You shoulda seen it. He took strips of black cloth and wrapped them around the hives for a week, then he took them off and brought food from his table."

"This was at his housewarming," Ingvar explained. "A lot of people came. He carried a bit of every kind of food out on a tray, held it in front of each hive and said, 'Braggi is gone now. I have brought you a piece of everything I have served. It is yours to do with as you will, and I hope you will accept me as the new master of this house.'"

"But I thought the church had been long abandoned," Tom said.

"Not totally abandoned," Ingvar replied. "Braggi liked selling Bibles. He had study groups—a men's study group and a women's. You wanted to be in one of those groups, you needed to have a Bible."

"The house was lived in," Larry said. "Braggi kept his cow in the church in the winter. You couldn't use the church in the winter anyway. It was Pastor Jon who cleaned it out, tossed out stuff, washed everything, painted everything."

"You should have heard Pastor Jon," Ingvar added. "'Help me do God's work.' He shamed us all into helping, and we did it for him, not God, and maybe because if we didn't, when a tractor or truck broke down, he wouldn't be there to fix it."

"You could say that," Larry added.

"He'd like more people here so he can have a proper congregation. He's got plans."

"More in the collection plate," Larry said. "He wouldn't have to fix so many cars and trucks and toasters."

"He's smart," Ingvar said.

"Smart, smart," Larry added. "He always prays over anything he's fixing, doesn't matter if it's a cow or a tractor. He says, 'A little prayer never hurts.'"

The praying fixer-upper and his acolytes, Tom thought, as he watched them shamble away. A quote of his father's came to him, but he didn't remember where it was from: "They've known every sin but live in innocence." Henry often said it about the men with whom he'd been in the army.

When Tom got to Sarah's, she was ironing clothes. "What?" she said when she saw his face and legs.

"I lost your rifle."

"Where have you been?" she asked.

"Siggi's," he said.

"Are you nuts?" She went to the closet to be sure the rifle was gone. "Where'd you lose it?"

"In the lake. I stepped in a hole and let go of it. I couldn't hold on to it and get out. If you come with me in your skiff, I can drag for it. I marked where I lost it. Freyja was missing. There was an incident last night. I thought..." He let the sentence trail away.

"There are lots of holes. You're lucky to be alive. You drop a net anchor into them and it can keep going down until it's dragged everything with it. No bottom in places. You try to drag the nets up, and they catch on the sides."

"I was going along the shore." He hesitated, embarrassed, then added, "Later, things didn't go so well. There were bears."

"That so?" Sarah said, raising her eyebrows and tipping her head to the side. "Quite a few bears?"

"Yeah," he said. "More bears than I've seen in my entire life. Siggi was feeding them dog food."

"Six thousand a month, they cost," Sarah said. "At least that's what I've been told. You guys talk?"

"He says he might be Angel's father."

She'd forgotten about the iron until the smell of scorched cloth made her jerk it away. She'd been ironing a shirt. The shape of the iron was clearly visible. She held it up and said, "I'll wear it under a sweater."

"If I can't drag your rifle up and make it good as new, I'll get you another one."

"Before deer hunting season," she said. She was scraping the burn with her thumbnail, trying to see if the charred top part would come off. "Could be," she said, going back to his earlier statement. "Possibly. Probably. He and Wanda were pretty hot about fifteen years ago. They couldn't keep their hands off each other. Sort of like a person I know."

"He's prolific. He gets around."

"I heard you went swimming after midnight. Skinny-dipping."

"It was dark," he said.

"If you sit on a sandbar in water up to your waist and there's moonlight, what you're doing from the waist up is public. Good thing you're not a member of the royal family. Your pictures would be all over the front pages of the newspapers."

"He has a bear called Bruno who likes peanut butter sandwiches."

"He wrestles with Bruno. Friendly like. No claws. It's sort of like they're dancing. He puts his head in Bruno's mouth. Bruno likes riding in the back of his truck. Siggi brings him to town for ice cream cones. He likes strawberry."

For a moment Tom felt confused. He wasn't sure whether it was Siggi or Bruno who liked strawberry ice cream, then decided it must be Bruno. "He shouldn't do that. He's supporting two kids."

"Two? Is that all? I think it's more."

"Oh, God," Tom said and put his head in his hands.

"What are you Oh, Godding about? You've got two kids. You could have one with Freyja. You quit chasing her all over the place and hook up with someone else and you could have four kids with three women just like that. Good thing you don't drink much. You could have half a dozen whoopsies in no time. Siggi had four women pregnant at one time when he was twenty. Back when he first had his band, the girls were taking their underpants off and throwing them onto the stage."

"Four at once?"

"Variety is the spice of life. Didn't you know? He's just lucky that Wanda never could get her act together enough to sue him. That would have made five we know of."

"It might not be him."

"Maybe. Maybe not. Anyway, that was later. When he was supposed to be grown up. He helps Ben out if he needs work done. When Siggi's not working or going to National Rifle Association meetings in Idaho with his Freeman friends to make plans for creating a city where everyone has to carry a weapon. Their motto is Life is war."

"He should have joined the army and gone to Afghanistan. If he thinks war is so great, he should try the real thing."

"He tried. They wouldn't take him. He's got a hockey injury. Somebody high-sticked him."

"What about Angel?"

"You can't bring back the dead. Done's done." She picked up another shirt by the tails and snapped it like a whip, then fitted it over the end of the ironing board.

"Justice." He coughed out the word. "What about justice?"

The iron looked too small, like a toy in her large hands with their swollen knuckles. She drove the iron back and forth in a sharp motion.

"Justice? Who gets justice? People don't get justice. They get the law. You start getting the cops involved, and they start poking around in people's lives, and people end up having to go to court, having to pay fines, maybe spend time in jail. How is anybody's life in Valhalla made any better? If Siggi gets hauled away for growing marijuana, does it make things better for the kids he's supporting? Who benefits?"

"What can be done about Freyja?"

"Tell her to give him back his house."

"He needs to pay her back the money he borrowed from her."

"He's trying to raise the money. Things haven't gone well. He just ran his business himself, but then things went wrong and he needed help. Those Freemen liked his embassy, so they moved in. One of them used to live here, moved to Edmonton, heard Siggi was having problems. He brought his two friends with him. It just used to be Siggi and the guys he worked with. The Freemen have changed all that."

"You're defending him."

"I'm not defending him. I'm just explaining the way things are. Nothing is ever as simple as it seems." She attacked the shirt furiously, jerking it this way and that.

Tom nearly blurted out what Freyja had told him about how Thomas Moose had died. He caught himself just in time.

"You were going to say something," Sarah said.

"Bees," Tom replied. "Ingvar and Larry told me about Pastor Jon feeding the bees."

Sarah looked disgusted, sighed. "When Pastor Jon was young, he went to England for a few years. He had a country parish. He learned a lot of foolish things from the locals. I'm surprised he didn't take up witchcraft. He's addled. Thank goodness he didn't go to the southern US. He'd be yelling, 'Hosanna!' and holding up poisonous snakes."

Sarah grabbed a hanger and draped the ironed shirt over it. "You might not be able to get the rifle back," she said, picking up another shirt. "Those holes in the limestone can go more than a hundred feet. Who knows what's at the bottom? You never know which way they erode. A diver from the city tried to go down one. It narrowed and there was no way he could get back up. Good thing he had a rope tied to his feet or he'd have died head down."

"It's worth a try," he said. "You put a ball of small hooks on a weight, drag it on the bottom. There's the strap holders, there's the trigger guard. The hooks could catch on the bolt."

"Ask Ben if you can borrow his canoe. Go on a calm day. You're sure you know where the hole is?"

"Yes," he said, "I marked it. I'll go as soon as I can. I don't want a storm to come and the hole to fill up with sand."

"You go to Asta Palsson's. Her husband died a while ago. He had a three-oh-three. I've never heard she sold it. She can use the money. It's the house with the rooster weather vane. You give me that. You find my rifle, I'll swap you back. You need a rifle for hunting season."

"There's no way I could get out of that hole with the rifle. I'm sorry. I feel terrible about this."

"I said you could borrow it. Lending things has risks."

"With any luck that hole is shallow."

He reached into his pocket, took out the six shells and put them on the table. "These got wet, but they're fine." He was going to leave but stopped and said, "I heard that it was McAra who found the tobacco tin of gold coins."

Sarah sighed and set down the iron. "I curse the day that happened," she said, and her voice was touched with anger and sorrow. "We thought it was wonderful at the time, but it didn't turn out wonderful. McAra got completely paranoid about the coins. He didn't want to declare them as income to the government. He was afraid to leave the tin in the house when we went away trapping and hunting. He took it everywhere with him."

"People knew that?"

"How could they not know it?"

"He had it on him the day he disappeared?"

"He never turned up, and the gold never turned up."

"The sleigh and the dog's body turned up."

"The dog's skull had a bloody big hole in it. Probably a shotgun slug."

"Did anyone come to investigate?

She nodded. "Disappeared. No body. A hole in the ice. He'd never have gone there. That spot never freezes to any depth because of the current. He knew that." She crossed her arms, closed her eyes and sighed. "Have they told you I shot him?"

"Implied."

"Implied? Did someone imply that he ran off with some rich broad from Odin? If he did, he's never been in touch with any of his sons."

"I knew of a case where a rich man fell in love with a poorer man's wife. He offered her everything. He could afford everything. But he said that she could never again have any contact with her husband or children."

"Did she stick with it?"

"Yes. Money does strange things to people."

"It does," she agreed.

He went to Freyja's. Her Jeep was parked at the back of the house. When she answered the door, he asked, "Where have you been?"

"Where have you been?" she replied. "Good God! What happened to your face? And your legs? You're covered in scratches. I drove to Stefansson's fish camp. They hire a lot of fishermen during the fall and winter. They stock stuff for their fishermen and always have stock left over. Inga had something we want. I stayed to visit." He followed her into the kitchen.

"Bears," he said. "You didn't say Siggi feeds bears."

"He's nuts," Freyja said. "He has this thing about bears. He figures they'll keep the Mounties away from his marijuana crop." She stared at him. "You were at Siggi's?"

"I didn't see your car here and I thought..."

"You went to rescue me?"

"Sort of."

"Superman," she said. "Batman. Which are you?"

"Dudley Do-Right," he said.

"What did you learn?"

"He loves bears."

"He must have been in a good mood. In a bad mood, he'd have smeared you with peanut butter and honey and set you loose among them."

"You fell in love with him."

"He can be incredibly charming. He's good-looking. He's crazy enough to be exciting. At certain stages of women's lives, they like bad boys. If they're lucky, they survive it. They get their head together and they marry a banker or a dentist. A sensible, sane, dependable guy, the kind of guy who will be a good father to their children."

He stood there sort of stunned, not quite sure what to make of the conversation. Then Freyja, remembering that she was holding a package of condoms, said, "Do you want to try these out, or not?"

Her bedroom, with its bed covered in brightly coloured pillows, ruffled shams, the tidiness of it all, intimidated him, so he took her hand and led her to the spare bedroom with its subfloor and futon. She started to protest, but he pointed to his legs and said he didn't want to get blood all over her good sheets.

They made love too quickly, and his lovemaking was darkened by fear that whatever had destroyed his desire and his ability to have sex would suddenly reappear, and he'd be left stranded on an island of humiliation.

They were on the verge of falling asleep when the phone rang. Freyja picked it up. She listened for a while and then said, "The next time I see him, I'll tell him. All right. You know what's best. You're the expert. No, he shouldn't have tried to tell you what to do."

"Siggi," she said after she hung up. "He's at the emporium buying Bruno an ice cream. He says to tell you it's a deal. If the tomato crop is good, he'll pay his bills and he'll start making payments on the money he owes me."

"Siggi!" He rolled onto his side to face her. "He tried to kill me."

"He's impulsive. If you don't tell him what to do, he usually comes around. He can't stand people giving him orders. You've got to let him think things are his idea. He's got claustrophobia. He'd go insane in solitary. That's why he's afraid of prison. What did you say to him?"

"I explained his responsibilities."

"Are you going to turn him in?"

"If his crop doesn't work out, he's done. He can't stay in the embassy or Valhalla forever. If his creditors lose faith in his ability to repay them, he's done. Maybe not today or tomorrow but soon. They'll kill him as an example. You won't get your money back. You'll end up with a house you can't unload. Your savings will not be returned."

"Kiss me," she said and pressed herself against him.

"How's he going to ship it?"

"You don't want to know," she said. "If your friend Travis and his buddies decide to give you the third degree, you don't want to let anything slip."

"What's he got in his underground grow op besides marijuana? Methamphetamine, shatter, cocaine, hash?"

"He didn't when I was with him. But he was being pressured. His suppliers wanted him to sell whatever they had, and his customers wanted him to provide it."

"He's got a cement mixer, but that one's too big. Did he have a small one, the kind you can pick up and carry down a set of stairs? Fentanyl producers are using cement mixers to mix the powder and coat the pills. Did he have pill presses?"

"I don't think so."

"You were underground, saw the operation?"

"There were a lot of plants. What does it matter? I wasn't growing. It wasn't my op."

"You helped finance it."

Freyja went rigid and pulled away from him. "I financed it?"

"You loaned him the money to keep the operation going."

"That's not the way it was. It was crazy romance. Do you love me? Will you help me out? It was a personal loan."

"Were you smoking the product?"

"Yes," she said, but she said it cautiously. "Are you a prosecutor? Or are you going to arrest me? Send me to prison?"

"No," he said. "Just old habits. I'm thinking about Angel. If someone killed her—why? If it was another teenager, there's probably no logic to it. Teenagers kill each other for the craziest reasons. They live in their own little worlds. But they're not subtle. They come to school with a rifle and shoot someone who has bullied them or a teacher they don't like. It's not like they work out an intricate plot. If it had been a teenager, she'd have been stabbed or beaten with something."

"Someone held her head underwater?"

"Possible, but there would have been bruises. People who are held underwater fight for air. How did she get so far up the beach?"

Freyja had not moved back to snuggle against him. To calm her down, he said, "Whose life is most like that of a drug dealer?"

"I dunno," she said.

"Guys on the drug squad," Tom said. "They know the same people, they hang around the same places, they think about the same things, they have been known to share the same girlfriends."

"This isn't sharesies," Freyja said.

"I'm glad to hear it. But it's not unknown for a cop or a politician to have a wife who used to be the girlfriend of a dealer. You marry who you know."

"What about Anna's daughter? You knew her."

"Pretty, pretty," he said. "Tanya. Dark eyes, dark brunette hair, big smile. Her mother taught her to make killer perohy and holopchi. But I didn't want to spend the rest of my life being a maintenance man and cleaning apartments. The Galecians are formidable. Yeah, she was nice, but I couldn't have spent the rest of my life looking at the crucifixes and the plaques. Every Sunday, church in the morning; every Thursday, bingo in the evening. What about you?"

"Ingolfur was twenty-one. He was five years older than me. We were necking a lot. We were on the beach one night. I said I didn't want to go all the way. He wouldn't listen. I got pregnant. My parents said they didn't want the kid to be a bastard. So we got married. We moved to Thompson. Two months later, I had a miscarriage. That often happens with first pregnancies. My parents paid for the divorce. Ingolfur got married again just about right away. His mother wanted grandkids. He's a welder for the mine. He makes good money. They come back now and again in the summer. Big truck, thirty-two-foot trailer. Three kids."

"Any regrets?" he asked.

She sighed. "That I got married at sixteen? Yeah. That I got divorced? No. Nice to have a thirty-two-foot trailer, though. Last time they came to Valhalla for a week, he told me he'd bought an eighty-inch TV. I got the message that if I'd stayed married to him, I would have an eighty-inch TV. Do you want an eighty-inch TV?"

"No," he said. "I'd rather read. Play chess with Helgi, if he'll play without my having to drink."

"Make love with Freyja," she said.

He laughed, and she let him put his arms around her. "That too," he said.

They made love again. Now they were able to take their time. There was no rush. His leg ached, so after he'd entered her, he held her close and rolled over so she was on top. Her red, curly hair fell over her face when she leaned over, making her seem mysterious. He reached up to stroke and hold her breasts, then she sat up straight and he shut his eyes.

On his way home he realized that the Stefansson's camp store had supplied one package of three condoms. They'd used two. He would have to go to town or get Ben to buy him a box once he was feeling all right and doing his usual run.

CHAPTER 30

ODIN

The next day, Tom went looking for the house with the rooster weather vane. Asta Palsson was a tall woman with white hair tied in a bun. She had a long face and tired eyes. She was shovelling gravel into a trench that ran from her house to the ditch. Pieces of turf and a ridge of soil lined one side of the trench.

When she noticed Tom, she stopped shovelling and leaned on her shovel. "Doesn't do much good when the ditch is full of water, but the rest of the time it'll drain off the puddles. You'd think when they settled this place they'd have had the good sense to pick a high spot of land, wouldn't you?"

"I thought it was because it was the only place there could be a harbour," Tom replied. He held out his hand. "I'm Tom Parsons."

She took the leather glove off her right hand and shook hands with him. There had been, he noticed, a slight hesitation, and he wondered what that was about. She held herself quite stiffly, her chin tipped up just a little. Anna would have described her as shrewd and a bit standoffish. Her grip was firm, the skin on her hand calloused. She put her hand back into her glove, and he took it as a sign that she had work to do.

"They could have driven back and forth. There's higher land five miles north of here. Men always want to live on top of their work."

"I've come to ask about your husband's rifle," he said, getting right to the point. "I borrowed Sarah's and lost it. I need to replace it."

"I lost my husband to cancer," she said, and sounded like she was blaming herself. She wasn't the kind of person who lost things. Tom expected she kept everything under control and wasn't pleased when she was helpless in the face of the uncontrollable.

"It's an ugly disease," he said. He remembered Mrs. Galecian. She'd been a hearty, heavy-set woman, the kind who could make dozens of perohy, a pot of borshch, feed everyone, fill up the kitchen with her energy and still be ready to dance. She'd gone to see the doctor about a lump on her leg. At first, it had seemed like nothing. Mrs. Galecian had made light of it. When anyone mentioned it, she flicked her fingers, dismissing it. Gradually, though, the visits to the doctor became more frequent, longer, with bouts of radiation and then surgery. They all talked about how good treatments were nowadays, but everyone could see that she was failing. The treatments, each of which was going to work, didn't, and they went from hopeful to fearful to resigned. Toward the end, she sat in a wheelchair, her hands in her lap, busy with her rosary. She'd had to give up teaching cross-stitch and making pysanka, intricately detailed Easter eggs, at the Ukrainian Centre. The last time he saw Mrs. Galecian, Anna was taking her to a hospice. He bent down and hugged her one last time, thanked her for everything and told her he loved her. "Tommy," she whispered, "you take care of yourself. Skinny is no good."

"Come in," Mrs. Palsson said. "I'll get it from the attic."

They went in and she went back out and returned with a wooden stepladder stained with many colours of paint. He'd have offered to get the rifle, but she obviously didn't want help and probably didn't want a stranger rummaging in her attic. Attics were private places, filled with people's past lives, objects that might lead to questions. She set the ladder up, climbed it and pushed open a square door in the ceiling. She caught hold of the sides of the opening and heaved herself up. She disappeared and he could hear her walking about on the studs. She came back, knelt at the entrance and handed him the rifle. She backed down the ladder, pulled the door into place and brushed herself off.

"Dusty," she said. "I haven't been up there in years. Spider webs everywhere."

"How much do you want?" he asked.

"Five hundred dollars," she said and handed him the key for the trigger lock. He turned the rifle over, inspecting it. It was covered in Cosmoline, and because it hadn't been wrapped in plastic, the wax had solidified. He wondered if it had been dipped but doubted it. That meant there wouldn't be any wax in the bore. It still would be a lot of work to clean it up so it could be used. He turned it over, took it to the window. He could spray it with WD-40 to soften the Cosmoline, then wipe it off. He might have to get mineral spirits. It would be tedious work. He unlocked the trigger, then took out the bolt and the magazine and put them on the kitchen table. The stock was clean, and the sights were in good shape. He aimed through the window with it, then looked down the barrel, and the barrel seemed okay. He put the bolt and the magazine back in place.

"It's going to be a lot of work to clean it up. It has to be taken completely apart and all the wax scraped out. It's kept the rust off, so that's good. The stock needs to be cleaned and lightly sanded, then finished."

"How much?" she said, and he knew she was re-evaluating him.

"There's the price a dealer asks. There's the price if you're selling it privately, all cleaned up and ready to go. With the work needed, three fifty. That's top dollar."

"Three fifty?" She was weighing the words, weighing him.

"I'd have to pay you fifty dollars a month."

She pulled a long face and her brow furrowed.

"If you've got work you need done, we could trade. Your back steps need replacing. We could work out a price. No need for cash."

"The rifle's for Sarah?"

"Yes, if I can't find hers."

"If you do, will you want to bring this one back?"

He shook his head. "No, I need a rifle for hunting season."

"It's not hunting season now."

"No, but I heard there were bears around. That made me nervous. If you let me have it so I can clean it up for Sarah, I'll pay you fifty now, then we can negotiate any work you want done. Otherwise, cash payments."

"I'll trust you for it while I decide," she said.

"I might do like Jessie and die."

"It happens," she agreed. "She always thought her sister would go first, being older."

"One minute older," Tom said.

"Older is older. You come first, you go first. That's the proper order of things."

"Life isn't that organized."

"You going to arrest some of these people?"

"I'm not a policeman anymore. It's not my job."

"That's too bad. People get away with little crimes, it just encourages them to do big crimes. Lot of stuff goes on that shouldn't. You going to do stuff you shouldn't?"

"I hope not." What, he wondered, were the things that he might do that he shouldn't? If her husband had been doing anything he shouldn't, it hadn't paid well. The floor had a bit of a slope to it and the floor tiles were chipped in places. Her kitchen counter was covered in worn brown linoleum. A lifetime of living and hard work that never returned much except meals and clothes and a place that kept off the weather. She'd had to work hard at preserving her dignity.

As he went to leave, she caught his sleeve. "That Johnny Armstrong is all right. He's good to his wife and kids. He works hard. Blasting. Cement. My Hjalmar worked for him when there were jobs. He paid fair. You can't criticize him for who he works for. You live here, you got to take work where you can get it."

On the way home with the rifle, he thought that Asta Palsson must have coffee regularly with Johnny Armstrong's wife.

Tom mulled over Valhalla. There were, as far as he could see, no gods, fallen or otherwise, no figures larger than life, just flotsam and jetsam, shipwrecked survivors scattered on the shore. *I wonder which I am*, he thought. *Flotsam or jetsam?*

He rolled four old oil barrels from the back of the property to the driveway. There was going to be a lot more junk than he'd expected. He'd thought he'd sell Oli's one-ton Chevy for whatever he could get for it, maybe trade it, but now he was reconsidering. He didn't really want to take a lot of this garbage in his own truck. Rough metal edges, rusted nails, broken glass were better in the wooden box of Oli's truck. It wouldn't cost much to license it for three months. Jessie had never mentioned the truck. He'd assumed she'd sell it before she left to join her sister. Josie didn't mention it either. He'd need to get a signature transferring the truck over to him. Josie had said she was going on a cruise, but not when. She said there wasn't anything she wanted and that everything left there went with the house. She just wanted shut of it so she could cruise and holiday. She said that she liked to dance with the men in white coats the cruise ship provided for the older ladies. "When you get to be my age," she said, "you don't get to hold a man very often. When you're young, it's different. They want to get their hands on you. When you get old and scrawny, you have to pay them."

When he'd mentioned Jessie's mission, Josie had spluttered and said, "Spent her life chasing God. Didn't do her much good. She never had much luck with those heathens. She taught Sunday school, she helped with confirmation, she washed vestments, she made sandwiches, she organized a ladies' aid society. Look around. See if you can find much evidence of them. She should have come back home and found a man with a good job, a lawyer or a doctor or a businessman. There was a jeweller who was interested in her. He was all set to give her a ring. No, oh no, what did she do? Married a fisherman in the wilderness and gave up a civilized life."

Perhaps that had been the bond between Sarah and Jessie. Tweedledum and Tweedledee; physically different but sisters at heart, Freyja had called them. Women travelling into the heart of darkness; he vaguely remembered reading a book by that name in one of his English courses. Sarah and Jessie had come north, left civilization behind, travelled into the wilderness and the unknown, but the main character in the novel had returned to England. They had stayed. They had found, he thought, their own heart of darkness, but they had stayed in it, survived in it, not been defeated by it. The main character—he searched his memory for the name—a journalist gone rogue, had disappeared into Africa, become godlike. Marlow, he remembered. But Jessie and Sarah had stood against the elements, faced the worst that could come, the loss of their husbands, and held on to what they believed. Here, in Valhalla, there was just individual craziness bouncing off each other. Unless the Godi were into pagan rituals. With cults, he thought, anything was possible.

He studied the shed. He wasn't sure what to do with the contents. He could haul everything to the dump on the edge of town. He'd ask Ben about whether anyone might want old traps and antique Evinrude motors. He still hadn't looked into the fish boxes and expected they'd be filled with nets. They'd hardly weighed anything when he'd picked them up. The lids were nailed on, but the wood was so old and dry that all it took was lifting one end with his hand for one lid to come off.

Inside the box, there was oilcloth—bright yellow with red poppies—the kind that at one time was used to cover kitchen tables. It would have cheered up a house on a winter day. It was folded over at the top, and he pulled the folds loose. There were items wrapped in brown butcher's paper. He unwrapped one. It contained a white knitted baby's bonnet. He carefully set it aside. The next package held a baby's blue knitted sweater. He was kneeling amid the debris of a life. The gasoline drums, the rusted traps, the nets, bits of harness for long-forgotten horses and the two wooden fish boxes. Rough cut but unstained, they'd never been used for fish. They'd been brand new when Jessie had packed away her dead child's belongings.

Following the original creases, Tom folded the wrapping back around the bonnet and sweater. He pressed the nails back into the original holes, then knelt there, unsure of what to do. *This child was wanted*, he thought, this child under the cement pad, with his name cut into the concrete, coloured stones set into the wet concrete; he wondered by whose hands: Jessie's, Oli's, both of them? A child anticipated, desired, and he imagined Jessie, young, excited, knitting, knitting, delighted, showing Oli what she'd done. The crib might have come by freight boat from Winnipeg, perhaps, or on a Cat train, pulled on a freighter's sleigh across the ice by tractor. He imagined the crib in the small bedroom. Wanted, wanted, and he put one box on top of the other, then picked them up and took them inside.

It was not for a man to decide, he thought. He'd ask Freyja or Sarah or maybe both of them. And he thought of Myrna and Joel; they'd not been planned, but they'd been welcome, and he and Sally had prepared a place for both of them, shopped for clothes and toys, before their lives had started to come apart. He'd wanted both of them to know that they were welcome, and he was sure Sally did, too, but that was in the beginning. He'd never wanted them to sit alone like he had at a window, looking out at the people passing by and wishing he had a place to go where he would be welcome. But now Sally's door was shut against them, and he was here, in this distant place, and they were... he wasn't sure where. And he thought about all the times he'd heard about how his bassinette and then his crib sat in his parent's living room, and he was an unexpected guest who wouldn't leave, and, finally, his presence forced his father out of his office, down the hall, dispossessing him, intruding, and the shocked look on his father's face the time that he'd put on his father's shoes, monstrously large and come clumping into the living room, a harbinger of doom. He put his hand on the top box, rested it there and thought about Jessie, the little woman with the sharp nose, no nonsense. What had she wanted from him? What had she hoped he would do?

He left the stifling air of the bedroom and went outside and replaced shingles.

He'd forgotten about the invitation to Odin until he saw the two children waiting for him at the edge of the spruce trees. He hurried to change and went to join them.

"Am I expected to bring anything?" he asked.

They looked at each other, and then looked back at him and both shook their heads. They turned and walked ahead of him, taking their task of leading him seriously. Gabriel's sandals looked a bit too big for him. Tom assumed they were hand-me-downs he hadn't quite grown into. Gabriel stubbed the toe of his right sandal on a tree root and stumbled. Samantha caught him.

They crossed the open harbour area to the beach.

"I thought we might have gone on the path," he said to the backs of their heads.

They both looked back, and Samantha said with the superior tone of experience, "No wind. Lots of mosquitoes."

Ahead, he could see a plume of smoke rising like a white pillar into the sky.

"What's that?" he asked, pointing.

"Smudge," Samantha informed him. "Mosquitoes don't like smoke."

Over the lake there were clouds like small islands.

Samantha turned to him and said, "Frigg is spinning."

"Frigg?" he replied. "Who is Frigg?"

Samantha looked at him like he had just declared himself illiterate. "Frigg is Odin's wife. Don't you know that? She spins clouds."

Reeds and driftwood were caught in the branches of the bushes along the high-water mark. The circles of stone and ashes from campfires were gone. The lake was the colour of unpolished silver, so flat and solid-looking that it seemed like it would be safe to walk on. They made their way along the edge of the water where the sand was soft, free of rocks, but gradually, even this sand gave way to broken slabs of limestone. Gabriel was looking over his shoulder at Tom when his sandal caught on the edge of a limestone block. He pitched forward on his knees and cried out in pain. He sat up and, holding his right knee, rocked back and forth. Tears ran down his cheeks.

Tom knelt down, looked at Gabriel's knee. The skin was scraped deep enough for there to be blood. A bruise was already forming.

"The healer will fix that," Samantha declared.

Tom bent down so Gabriel could climb onto his back, wrapping his legs around Tom's hips and his arms around Tom's neck. Tom carried him the rest of the way while Samantha ran ahead. At the trail that led from the beach to the commune's buildings, two women led by Samantha met them. Tom let Gabriel slide down. A young woman Tom assumed was Gabriel's mother hugged Gabriel, then got him to hold up his knee while he leaned on her.

"He wasn't watching where he was going and he wouldn't hold my hand," Samantha said stiffly, and Tom thought, as charming as she appeared, she was prissy and quick to absolve herself of blame.

"That's fine," said the woman who had examined Gabriel's knee. "We'll wash it and put a salve on it. It'll stop hurting soon enough."

The slightly bitter smell of burning green leaves permeated the air. A veil of smoke hung among the trees.

As they passed members of the commune, people nodded and smiled. When Tom saw the gardens, he stopped to admire them. They were Anna's dream come true. The raised beds formed a series of concentric circles with passageways from one circle to the next. Vegetables and flowers were mixed. Samantha waited for him as he walked along a path between two beds. Kale and spinach he recognized. Lettuce. Tomato plants. Farther on, he saw rows of corn. There were chairs and benches woven from willow set out so people could rest.

Samantha led him to a group of people standing together talking. Godi-4 left the group, thanked Samantha, shook Tom's hand and said he appreciated Tom's coming to join them for the evening.

There were a number of smudges. At the top of the trees, the smoke spread out, joined and drifted back down. The sun was moving to the west, its intensity softened by the haze.

"The gardens must be a lot of work," Tom said.

"What better way to spend your time than growing and harvesting the food you eat," Godi-4 replied, picking a young radish and offering it to Tom. He picked another for himself, brushed off the dirt and bit it off the stem. "You'll have to excuse the smoke. We don't believe in using insecticides.

Nothing has been invented that kills mosquitoes but doesn't harm butter-flies or bees."

The raised beds were made of old railway ties held together by iron rods fitted into holes at each corner. The ties were set six high so the gardens could be tended without anyone having to kneel.

Tom realized that he was being watched with great curiosity.

"We will walk over to the dining hall," Godi-4 said. "We eat communally. It is a way of being one."

The Godi had made good use of the limestone slabs from the beach. The areas around each circular garden were paved with them. The sidewalk led past two sets of huts and around the longhouse with its stone base and sod roof.

The Viking ship sat between the longhouse and the huts. Three men were busy using planes and a drawknife to make new pieces, but he couldn't see what was being shaped. They had a small wooden ladder so they could climb in and out of the long ship.

"It requires constant maintenance," Godi-4 said. "They are replacing two of the oarlocks. We are discussing building a shed in which to house it."

"Will you launch it soon?"

"As soon as the repairs are finished." He indicated logs that were piled to one side. "We will roll it down to the water on those logs. It will be a day of celebration. You should come and help. A strong back is always appreciated. We need a day with no wind to put it into the water."

The paved walk split at the end of the longhouse, and Tom thought they would go to the front entrance, but Godi-4 led him around the back where there were two square projections that Tom remembered from his earlier visit that housed a traditional food preparation area and washrooms. On the other side of the walk was a long low-frame building with a multitude of windows made up of small panes and wooden steps that led to open double doors. The building seemed so out of place that Tom looked at Godi-4 quizzically.

"We use this for our communal meals. It was a two-room school. We hauled it here. Simple prairie construction, but it's not suitable once the weather turns cold."

Godi-4 was called away for a moment, and Tom stood back watching the men and women cooking in the kitchen area while others set out dishes and cutlery on long plank tables. There was the pleasant clank of dishes and pots

and pans, and the smell of vegetables and fish and strawberries. Since his visit
to the longhouse, people obviously no longer considered him a stranger, and
as they passed, they smiled or said hello and nodded. One of the young men
brought him a glass of cold water.

When Godi-4 returned, Tom asked, "Why the invitation?"

Godi-4 smiled and patted a toddler on the head. "Many reasons. You were
a stranger, but now you live in Valhalla. Jessie Olason thought you should be
the owner of her house. You are, or you used to be, in the police. On the whole,
we try to avoid the police, not because we do anything to break the law, but the
police think in stereotypes. They usually have a very narrow view of the world."

"And I don't?"

"We do not know. We will find out. We've learned from your first visit
that you are curious about us. You must have heard stories from the people of
Valhalla. Perhaps some of the things they told you are true, perhaps not. You've
accepted our invitation. You are polite. When Gabriel fell, you picked him up
and carried him. You are kind."

"Perhaps I want the hidden treasure."

Godi-4 laughed out loud. "You have heard of that. Of course. What is the
most interesting thing about us? Our beliefs, the way we live, our goals? No, of
course not. That in our past there was gold hidden that has never been found.
The mysterious treasure of Valhalla."

"You don't search for it?"

"Of course we search for it. We are just as great a pack of fools as anyone else. Maybe greater, because we feel that since it is part of our history, we
should be more successful at finding it than anyone else. I wish we would
find it. We could make good use of the money, but more importantly, it would
stop the searching. Many have heard of this gold, of this treasure stored in
trunks and buried in the soil, in a cave, under the water. Do you know what
has been bought with this gold so far? No, of course not. Tragedy, greed, violence, pain, dishonour. People have come here, torn our buildings apart, ripped
up floors and walls, dug holes everywhere. People have joined us because of
greed, not because they want to be one with us. We've had people kidnapped,
tortured, beaten. Our belief is that the treasure will be found when our true
leader appears."

"And then?" Around them people were coming with their gardening tools and using two hoses to wash them. They dried the tools with what looked like bedsheet remnants and stacked the tools in two wheelbarrows. Then they dispersed to the huts.

"He will know the way. We will follow."

"The one-eyed man?" Tom asked.

Godi-4 paused, dipped his head in acknowledgement. Beside them a man threw an armload of green branches on a smudge and the smoke thickened. For a moment, a small flame rose up, but it quickly died away.

"I have both eyes." Self-consciously, Tom touched the scar that ran diagonally down his forehead to his eyebrow, then down his cheek.

"The mark is upon you."

"Odin gave his eye to gain knowledge. I nearly lost mine chasing a druggie who hijacked a car."

"And why did you chase this car? There are many cars. Too many cars. Insurance companies replace cars all the time."

"There was a baby in the back seat."

"You have a kind heart."

"I killed the child. I didn't stop the chase when I was told to. The car crashed and the carjacker and the child were decapitated."

Above them the sun struggled impotently to break through the smoke that clung to the tops of the trees. The top of the car had been sheared off. It looked like a grotesque convertible. His consolation was that it happened so quickly that the child's death would have been instantaneous. There would have been no suffering. People died all the time. One of the worst was a car with a mother and three children that rolled and burst into flames. Passing motorists had stopped and tried to get them out, but it was impossible. They never got free of their seatbelts. He reached into his pocket for the plastic piece of taillight and realized he'd forgotten it at the house.

"You feel guilt. You have a conscience. There are many who have no conscience. Do you think not having a conscience is necessary for success in this life?"

It was a question he'd asked himself many times, and having found no answer, he did not want to discuss it. "What do you want from me?"

"To share our supper. And then to watch our entertainment. Many others will come from the village to hear us. We have many fine performers."

With that, they came to the dining hall and went inside. Many of the places at the plank tables were already taken by older people. When the people in the kitchen saw Godi-4 and Tom, they started carrying out bowls of food. Tom and Godi-4 slid into their places.

Godi-4 stood up, and Tom thought he might give a benediction, but he simply said that there was a guest tonight from Valhalla, that his name was Tom Parsons, and he was here in response to their invitation. Then he sat down.

"Are you gypsies?" Tom asked.

"We are a mixed lot. But no, I wouldn't say we are gypsies. Some of us are transient, move from craft shows to fairs all year long. We have safe places here and there, sometimes just a house with a welcoming owner. Some places that can take in a dozen people. Like in pioneer days, we know of stopping places for travellers who need shelter. I've always thought it a strange failing of the churches that they don't have places of refuge for weary, distressed travellers, especially given the story of Joseph and Mary. Why is it that Lutherans or Catholics in need cannot go to any local church for help?

"Many of our people have their own resources. They are retired or have good jobs. A few are rich; they come here to renew themselves. However, in recent years we've attracted new people, younger people who have lost their way. Often they seek answers we cannot give. We are not a rescue operation any more than a monastery is. Others have tried to join us because of our reputation, because we are exotic. You just have to say 'Vikings' and people pay attention. Times change and people's circumstances change. They make new decisions. There are those among us who choose to travel from place to place selling the goods we make. They often entertain. There are those who have a lot of material wealth to contribute, but we no longer expect that individuals will give everything. There was a scandal when Godi-1 disappeared with the community's resources. We barely survived that. You have met Brokkr, who usually stays for the winter. He prepares this place for our return. It is hard to remain in the snow and cold while others travel to the sun. He lives a life of loneliness. If any of our people become ill, they return to rest and heal. They know they always have a place.

"Since you are determined to live in Valhalla, you will get to observe our Viking week. The public is welcome. If you want, you could choose a Viking name and people here would help you with your costume. Brokkr is our most skilled blacksmith, and he has apprentices who make chainmail and shields and swords and spears."

"Would I have to become One to participate?"

"No," Godi-4 said. "There was much travel in Viking times, and visitors frequented the longhouses."

"Should I arrive by boat or on a horse?"

"Either would be fine, but given the short distance, walking would probably do."

"I think," Tom rejoined, "I'll stick to being a guest the first time around."

"It always starts the first weekend in August. The Whites do not care for us, but they do not object to the business it creates for them. If the weather is good, many people come to be entertained and to learn. Their cabins are filled. The campground is filled. Their restaurant is busy."

"Karla complains that you compete unfairly."

"The diet in Valhalla is not good for many people. We sell what we can to get a return from our labour, but we also give healthy food to the local people at a price they can afford. We are not vegetarians, but we seldom eat meat because we cannot raise it ourselves. We eat a lot of fish." He handed Tom a platter of baked whitefish. "It is hard to get meat that is not suffused with chemicals."

Tom took a portion of fish and placed it on his plate. The person sitting on his left side handed him a bowl of vegetables and potatoes.

"You have five acres on the lake side of the road. Thirty-five on the other side, and that includes pasture," Godi-4 continued. "That is one of the things we wanted to talk to you about. Jessie would not allow us to use her property, and it sat fallow. We cannot pay you meaningful rent, but we can supply you with vegetables, berries, plums, even crab apples, delivered fresh to your door. We make preserves. A bachelor might appreciate these things."

Tom pulled the skin back from the whitefish and took a piece of the flesh on his fork. "If people offer you a favour," his father had always said, "it is because you have something they want. Do you want the favour? Do you want to pay the price? No favours are free." His father was used to keeping ledgers, and every asset had to be offset by a liability.

"There is no other pasture available close by. Besides, yours is already fenced. It is badly in need of repair, but you are one person. We are many. We can do that more easily than you can."

"Is there a great demand?" Tom asked. "Should I put it up for bids? Will there be competition?"

"You have a sense of humour," Godi-4 said. "Yes. Horst White covets the land. There may be others."

The fish had been stuffed with a bread dressing. Tom ate a piece of it as he thought about Horst White. "When I asked him if any place was for rent, he said no, there wasn't. It turned out he was telling the truth. Jessie didn't want to rent."

"If we had good pasture, we could promise you lamb and mutton, maybe beef and milk." A young man filled their glasses with cold lemonade. Others nearby had been listening to the conversation. They, too, were waiting for Tom's reply.

"Think on it," Godi-4 said. "It is not good to make a hurried decision."

They finished their dinner, then Godi-4 said it was the time for those who had been fed to serve those who had not yet eaten. He suggested they take their strawberry cobbler outside.

They sat in the shade of a green umbrella. There was a patch of snapdragons in a large ceramic pot on the step, and a hummingbird was hovering, feeding on the nectar. "This is what we seek," said Godi-4, indicating the flowers and the bird. "It is not always what we get."

Godi-4 lowered his voice and said, "You have been in the police. You know how to ferret out things. Morning Dawn, one of Jason's group, has disappeared. With the death of the village girl, we have reason to be concerned."

"Morning Dawn?" Tom repeated, giving himself time to think.

There was a rattle of dishes being washed in the kitchen area and quiet chatter at the tables as the second group ate. There was the scrape of benches being moved for the evening performance.

They sat in silence as they ate their dessert. Godi-4 put down his plate and fork. The sun was behind them now. A breeze had risen from the lake, driving the mosquitoes away, and Tom hoped that it would mean they no longer needed the smudges. Godi-4 said, "She had short blonde hair. Maybe more orange from a henna hair dye. Five foot one or two. Underweight, nearly anorexic. The last anyone saw her, she was wearing a brown-and-gold summer dress. I didn't see her in it. She and Jason's other companions have mostly stayed on the beach."

"She didn't tell anyone she was leaving? She didn't leave a note?"

"Nothing. She simply vanished."

Tom wondered what Godi-4 knew—if he knew anything more than he was saying, if he was fishing because he thought Tom might be hiding information—and his heart lurched because his name was already linked with Angel's death and could easily come to the forefront if another young girl was harmed. He put down his plate even though he hadn't finished his dessert.

"Did anyone else disappear at the same time? A young man?"

Godi-4 shook his head and looked away into the tangle of trees and underbrush. "There was money missing. Jason says two hundred dollars."

Godi-4 hesitated. He rubbed a bit of strawberry on his hand and stretched it out in hopes that the hummingbird would sit on it. The hummingbird lifted up and disappeared over the roof. Godi-4 licked his palm to clean it. "I would like to be like Saint Francis and have the birds flock to me. It has always been an image I've admired."

"The Vikings would have eaten them."

"They were not just warriors. They were great storytellers, poets, goldsmiths, boat builders. It is the violence that many people are attracted to, unfortunately."

The breeze was blowing the smoke away, but it was caught among the branches of the trees in places. With the sun behind them to the west, the shadows of everything lengthened. Daylight would linger until late, but the moon was visible, nearly transparent, looking like it might be made of ice. When he was alone, Tom hated the long passage from day to night, when human company meant everything, when the memories and thoughts that he had locked away with sunlight and work forced their way out and he had only himself to converse with.

He glanced through the door into the meeting room and envied the people who were working together, talking and singing snatches of songs. As he watched, a woman came up to a man and hugged him, then let him go and went to pick up one end of a bench. Tom would have given a lot for that spontaneous expression of friendship and affection. Others were standing outside. One woman was plucking the strings of a guitar, trying out a tune, while others stood around and made suggestions. Suddenly, they all laughed, delighted by what she had done.

Godi-4 was sitting, contemplating the snapdragons, his face pensive. At last, he sighed and said, "Jason was born here. That makes him One. However, after his birth his mother left, disappeared, and took him away. He came back when he was twenty. That was three years ago. He came back with five followers, but each year he has brought a larger group, a tribe, perhaps the beginning of a cult."

"That's why they live on the beach."

"They have the use of the huts. If they so choose. But then they have to live by the rules of One. They prefer their vehicles and tents."

"They don't seem to fit in."

"There is a great injustice in our country, and many would have us rescue those who are lost. That is not our task. We are not Mother Teresa."

"Men wait at bus stops watching for vulnerable girls who need a place to stay, who need a friend. I saw it every day."

"Yes," Godi-4 agreed. "But there are the poor of India, of Pakistan, of the world. There are governments for this, NGOs, charities. From time to time we find believers, and after a while they become One. Our way is not easy."

"Some of our people do go out and do street work, rescuing young people, mostly young women. We don't recruit them for Odin, however. A couple of our wealthy members have set up safe houses for young women where they can get counselling. Many are pregnant and ill."

"Angel was pregnant," Tom blurted out. "Did she come seeking refuge?"

Even as he spoke, the trees had become darker, closer together, so they hid more secrets. The horizon, what he could see of it through the gaps in the trees, turned purple with a slash of flaming red like an open wound. So far apart in most things, he and Godi-4 shared this, then—a harrowing, wandering stream of endless children with uncertain, haunted faces and frightened eyes.

"She spoke with one of the women who showed her how to play the dulcimer when she was here last summer. Angel had learned quickly. She was a natural musician. They had formed a bond. She told her she was pregnant. She was afraid of what her grandfather would do when he found out."

"Ben loved her."

"Yes, but what he loved more was her perfect image. Her grandfather's need for her to be virtuous was a heavy burden."

"Did she say who the father was?"

"She wouldn't say."

"Here? Or in Winnipeg?"

"She wouldn't say."

"This girl who disappeared. What was her real name?"

"Jane Smith."

"Not as romantic as Morning Dawn," Tom said, and he remembered that Jane Smith was not the name she had given him as she implored him for his help.

"Many want a new beginning. Is choosing a new name such a bad way to begin?"

Tom thought it was silly—or he thought his father would have thought it silly—this pretending to be something you weren't. But when he'd been a child, and even when he was a teenager, he'd often imagined being a character in the books he'd read or the movies he'd watched. When picking up severed limbs and bloody corpses had started to weigh down on him, he'd begun to fantasize about being a different person in a different place, where nothing bad ever happened, a place where there was nothing to do except those things he enjoyed doing. He'd even thought about going to a monastery, a place where everything was orderly, organized, with no sirens, no sudden moments of terror. He imagined learning hymns, learning responses in Latin, and he was glad he'd kept his father's Gregorian chants. They dissolved the images of dead children, of bloody wounds, of burned bodies. They filled up his head so he couldn't think, and he wondered then if that was why his father had listened to them, to block out images from his past.

"The local people won't tell us much. They take our produce, but they wait for news of the gold. It's like having a ticket in the lottery."

"Why would they care?"

"After he hid the treasure, Godi-1 wrote that when it was found, those families who had stayed in Valhalla should be given a share. There has to be an unbroken line."

"Can they go away and come back?"

"Yes, but they must be here when the treasure is found. Temporary absences are fine."

"You expect this treasure will be worth a lot?"

"Yes. At one time we had many wealthy patrons. Our friends will be rewarded. We do not forget those who have helped us. Our directive says that is to be. Too often in life, we go to great expense and trouble to punish wrong-doers but neglect to reward those who behave well."

"And your enemies?"

"We are not pacifists. We live in this world. The streets of many cities are dangerous."

"An eye for an eye, a tooth for a tooth?"

"We leave revenge to the Christians. We try to avoid situations that would tempt us to revenge."

The music that followed supper was enjoyable. Twenty or more village people had come to listen, and now they were all walking back to Valhalla. He'd told Sarah and Freyja about Godi-4 wanting the use of his pasture.

"So, they want your pasture," Sarah said as they walked home.

"I'm not surprised. They tried to have sheep and milk cows, but their land isn't suitable. One of their rented cows stepped into a crack in the rock and broke its leg. They had to pay the farmer for it. It was expensive, tough beef."

As they walked along the forest path, they slapped at the mosquitoes, but it was better than risking a fall on the limestone slabs on the beach.

"I'm just planning on using the uncleared part as a woodlot. Godi-4 said in a dry year, there might be thirty acres of hay. In a wet year, maybe twenty."

"So you'll say yes."

"I get fresh food. I just have to go pick it up whenever I want. They might even deliver."

"Oh," Freyja said suggestively, teasing him, "I saw those women eyeing you. They'll be happy to bring you a basket of carrots and beets and chard. I'll bet they'd even cook it for you and provide dessert."

The rich smell of the forest loam and the sweet smell of the trampled grass enveloped them. Shafts of moonlight slanted through the trees so that the forest seemed like intricate lace.

The evening had been fun. He'd particularly enjoyed the South American panpipes. The children had formed a band, and if they hit a sour note, it didn't matter. Cuteness overcame everything else. Gabriel was there, playing his recorder, his knee bandaged.

"Was that all they wanted?" Sarah asked, her voice sharp, suspicious. "They are great bargainers. Never accept a gift from them until you know what they want."

"They want to use the pasture. That's easy enough. I've no use for it. I'm not going to be raising any sheep or cattle."

It was the kind of evening when everything was soft—the air, the moonlight, the slight moan of the rippled waves on the beach, the sweet smell of wild strawberries crushed under their feet—and Tom thought, for a moment, of the basement apartment he had left and was grateful he had risked it.

CHAPTER 31

HORSES

There wasn't much wind from the northeast, but it was enough that areas of the beach that had been exposed were now underwater. Walking the beach to Siggi's like he'd done before wouldn't be possible.

Tom went to Ben's and asked if he could borrow his canoe. He explained that he'd dropped Sarah's rifle in the lake and needed to drag for it. "I'd dive for it, but it's down a hole. I don't know how deep it is."

"Don't go fooling around in no hole," Ben replied. "We'll be dragging for you." He was rubbing his jaw as he considered the situation. "With the water up, will you be able to stand and drag? How deep was the water when you dropped the rifle?"

Tom thought about it, trying to remember. The bottom was uneven, knee deep in places, deeper in others. "Crotch deep."

"Is it right up against the cliff?"

Tom said that it was.

"You can't use the canoe there. You'll get pushed into the cliff. A couple of whacks against the cliff and you'll be buying me a canoe to go with a rifle for Sarah. You'll need to beach the canoe, wade into the lake. Those waves are going to make you unsteady. You can't fight the waves and drag. Better to wait for tomorrow." Ben stepped out of the doorway to study the sky. There were small clouds scudding along. "You need to wait for it to calm down." He said calm as if were spelled cam. "Keep an eye on the water. It calms down and you come get the canoe. The paddle is in it."

Tom agreed, then went down to the harbour. The waves weren't high, not storm waves crashing into the shore but steady waves, maybe a foot or so. He kept imagining sand being pushed shoreward, dropping into the hole, filling it up, burying $350. If he cleaned up Asta Palsson's Enfield and gave it to Sarah, he still wouldn't have a hunting rifle. He and Sally had never been rich, they'd run an overdraft at times, but most of the time they had enough money to get the things they wanted—skates for both kids, computer games, the occasional night at a hotel by themselves. There'd usually been money in their savings account. He wished he'd insisted on a more even split, but when they were dividing things up, he'd been thinking about shooting himself, about having another car accident—this time, one that would be fatal, no turning the wheel at the last moment in an instinctive desire to survive. Their negotiation wasn't really negotiating. She'd say she wanted another piece of furniture, more money and he'd say fine, fine, whatever you want. He was a mental and emotional basket case, and he wasn't planning on living long enough for it to matter anyway.

The shrink had said, "Hang on and you'll come out the other side. All tunnels have two ends and you've got to plan for when you come out into the light." But Tom had been unable to hear that. There wasn't going to be an end to the tunnel where he was trapped; instead, it grew narrower and darker and lower, until he was suffocating. He'd wake up at night unable to breathe, and the pills didn't do any good, little blue pills that were supposed to bring him sleep. And when they did no good, he'd slip into the back lane and begin to walk past the parked cars, the garbage cans, the garages, the fences, the trees, wishing he could run until he was exhausted but terrified of slipping on the ice and snow, of the pins and plates wrenching loose and then having to crawl to safety.

The shrink had added, "Run, run. What does it matter if your leg comes apart and you crawl up beside a garbage can and you freeze to death? You're thinking about suicide anyway. You're thinking about making it look like an accident. Why not have a real accident? You see," he said, jabbing his index finger at Tom, "there is a light at the end of the tunnel. It may be very small, no more than a pinprick, but it is there. If it weren't there, you wouldn't worry about your leg or what would happen if it collapsed."

In a distant room in his mind, Tom knew the shrink was right. But it didn't stop what went on in his head any more than it would have for soldiers with shell shock who were told the war was over.

He realized that he'd been standing and staring at the waves for a long time. The repetition of them, their sound as they broke on the shore, had hypnotized him. He pulled his hand from the wall that ran along the outside of the dock. Without the wall, the storm waves would crash over the dock, sink open boats moored inside the harbor. The dock with its plank wall, set as it was against the great sweep of the lake jutting into the water, looked fragile, as if it might be cast up into a tangled, broken mess on the shore, but yet it held, protected people against the fury of the water.

Now he struggled to break free of the feeling that threatened to overwhelm him. He wanted to stay in the present, not fall down the rabbit hole into the past. "Five things," the shrink had said, when he felt like that, "name five things you can see." He named them. The dock, the boats, the lake, the shed where the fish were processed, the oil drums. "Four things that I can feel," Tom said to himself and ran his hand over the rough wood of the wall. He touched a mooring line, then an anchor. He reached out toward a seagull hovering overhead, but it slipped away, so he grasped the rusted head of a large bolt. "Three things," he repeated to himself, "three things that I can hear right now." There was the pounding of the waves on the dock, the cry of a tern, the rubbing of the mooring lines on the capstans. "Two things I can smell," he said and took a deep breath and let it out slowly. There was the pungent odour of old fish from the boards on the dock and the sharp smell of spilled gasoline. The last was the most difficult. Name one good thing about himself. For a long time, he hadn't been able to do that.

"I can work," he whispered. He held his hands in front of him and studied them. *I can work.* His father had said that in work is our salvation. Freyja had said that Karla and Horst needed work done. They'd probably want to trade for a credit in their ledger, but maybe he could do part credit and part cash. And he'd have to do serious negotiating with Asta Palsson. She needed a lot more than $350 of work, but she might not care about having things fixed up, she might not have the money. He'd go west, stop at a few farms and tell them he was available, talk to Pastor Jon. He was always travelling around fixing cars and tractors and lawnmowers. He'd know who needed work done and could afford to pay for it.

The white edges of the waves and their steady pounding on the dock had kept him from pulling back into himself, so he went back to the house. But before he could get started on anything, Freyja arrived.

"Remember," Freyja said, "I mentioned I wanted to ask you for a favour?"

"What?" Tom replied, not remembering. He was thinking about asking her for advice on finding work and admitting he was hard-pressed for cash. He'd taken a bigger loan than he needed for the house because he knew it needed a lot of work, but that money was earmarked.

"You have a small barn on your pasture. Have you looked at it?"

"No. Should I have? You can barely see it in the bush. I think it's falling down."

"Oli had a horse and a cow and some sheep at one time. He cut hay and kept it in the hayloft."

"Is this barn special? Derk thought it would make a great grow op. Godi-4 mentioned it. He wants to grow hay and keep animals."

"I've been planning on getting an Icelandic horse. Jessie had agreed that if I did, I could keep it there."

"Horse? One of those ponies? I've seen them on PBS."

"They're not ponies. They're horses. They're small but not as small as ponies. They're very good riding horses." She sounded indignant, as if he'd deliberately insulted her.

"This isn't riding country, unless your horse has gills and webbed hooves."

"Don't say it like that. I've always wanted a horse. I used to ride on Oli's horse when I was a kid."

He was having a hard time wrapping his head around the idea of a horse. Even a small one. Anna wouldn't let people have cats in their apartments. Or budgies. Still, people snuck them in. Little dogs and cats and birds and reptiles, hidden in their coats, in their grocery bags. They smuggled poodles in suitcases. The brought Dobermans in packing cases. People were crazy. When he was on the Force, he'd had a call one time from a motel. A customer had brought her horse into her unit because it was cold in its trailer. The customer couldn't understand why the horse couldn't spend the night as long as it didn't make any noise. First, Siggi with his bears. Now, a horse.

"I didn't want to mention it before because I didn't want you to feel that I was pressuring you. But now the Godi want the barn and pasture. You can say no to me. I can keep the horse in the garage."

"There's no heat in the garage," he said.

"That's all right. I can put in a couple of electric heaters."

"Are you going to toilet train it?"

"Can we go look at the barn?" He could tell she wasn't amused. When she got determined, she tilted her jaw up slightly and pressed her lips together. It was a look, he assumed, that warned her students to settle down.

They walked. The ravens followed them. They'd begun to think of Tom as the giver of all food. Tom wasn't sure what to think about horses. They hadn't kept any horses in the alleyway behind the apartment block. He'd seen horses in parades. There were horses at the RCMP school in Regina. He'd seen them on farms when he'd been posted to small towns, but he'd never gotten acquainted with any horses.

He and Freyja walked side by side. Small clouds were racing across the sky.

"Frigg is spinning," he said, trying to impress her.

"Good for her," Freyja said stiffly. He wondered whose idea it was that she should have a horse. She didn't look horsey. Horsey women had big square jaws and wore jodhpurs. He glanced at her. He had to admit she would be pretty attractive dressed in a Viking getup riding a small horse. He'd let her capture him.

"Where would this horse be coming from?"

"A farm in Ontario. I'd have it by now except for Siggi and the money. There are a lot of people who want Icelandic horses. They're thoroughbreds. Their bloodlines go right back to the Vikings. Once a horse leaves Iceland, it can never return. I put a down payment."

"Can't you just get your money back?"

"I don't want my money back. I want Snorri."

"Snorri?"

"That's what I'm going to name him."

Vidar was spreading nets in his yard. Tom waved. Vidar waved back. As soon as Ben brought the drywall, mud and tape, Tom promised himself he'd get started on Vidar's two rooms. Tom waved at Johnny Armstrong, but Johnny ignored him. It was too bad they'd disagreed over the screw jack. Johnny would know where there were jobs that needed doing. As much as Tom regretted it, he knew there had been no way to avoid the confrontation. If he'd given in, he'd have become known as a pushover. Maybe, maybe, he thought, there'd be a way to come to an understanding. Johnny would just need to see there was a mutual benefit. He'd have to ask him for the loan of his big ladder so he could fix the church steeple.

He and Freyja came to the corner where the lakefront road joined the main road out of town. Tom hadn't done much more than glance at this part of his property. A ditch overgrown with grass and bulrushes and the remnants of a barbed-wire fence ran along each side. There were a number of posts that had fallen sideways and were partially held up by the wire, then a few upright posts, then more that were tipped over. Godi-4 was right. Replacing that many fence posts would be a lot of work for one person. Tom and Freyja crossed over a metal culvert topped with gravel and grown over by weeds. They came to a rusted gate. Tom lifted the gate latch, and the hinges squealed as he pushed the gate open. Freyja knelt down and pulled her socks up over her slacks. "Ticks," she said. "You don't want to get Lyme disease."

Past the gate, off to one side, were three Bombardier snowmobiles—two yellow and one blue. They all needed a fresh coat of paint, and one had a cracked front window. They were curved at the front, the sides shaped like teardrops lying on their side, with a stovepipe sticking out of the roof and a series of small round windows from front to back. There was a door on both sides at the front. They had caterpillar tracks at the back and skis at the front. The fishermen used them for going to their nets and travelling to communities or homes along the lake in winter.

"Albert sometimes cuts hay and takes it for his goats," she explained. "A few others take hay as well. Pastor Jon takes hay, plus what he gets off the graveyard. He uses a scythe for the graveyard."

"Using dead people for fertilizer?"

"There's very little good pasture. They take what they can get. Even so, they have to buy quite a bit of hay."

They waded through the grass. "You want to be careful," Freyja warned him. "There are bits and pieces of equipment around. There's a mower over there. There's a hay rake. Oli never grew grain. Just hay. There's the old hay wagon. Watch out for holes people have dug. They get notions and dig." She pointed at a dilapidated wooden wagon. "There's rolls of barbed wire about. Watch you don't walk into them. I hope you've got your tetanus shot."

The barn was enclosed on three sides by small trees. It was small but had a loft. Freyja pushed open the side door. The air was hot and had the soft smell of old hay. He scraped his foot over the floor. Under the debris were pale grey planks. An alleyway led from the large double doors at the front. There were four stalls. A ladder was nailed to the end wall. It led to an opening in the loft. The first step of the ladder was missing. He led the way up, tugging at the railings before putting his entire weight onto them. There was a mound of hay in the loft. Light streamed through the cracks where the loft doors didn't quite fit. A wooden latch fitted into a wooden holder. He lifted it up and pushed open the doors. They were on ropes so they could easily be pulled back. The rope was rough, and when he rubbed it with his hand, pieces of it fell away.

He picked up a handful of the hay, then dropped it out the door and the slight breeze swept it away.

"Jessie didn't mind people using the barn but wouldn't let the Godi on the property."

"What did she get out of it? Anything?"

"Goat cheese from Albert and lamb from Pastor Jon."

"And the Bombardiers?"

"Palsson's, Stefansson's, Vigfusson's. They just leave them parked there. Out of the way. They'd give her a fish now and again."

"Pretty lonely for a horse during the winter," he said. "You'd have to come every day and see that he was all right and feed and water him. How are you going to keep his water from freezing?"

"There's electricity," she said, pointing at the wires coming in from the road. He looked up and saw a bare light bulb hanging from the ceiling. He found the switch and flipped it. The light came on. He flipped the switch off.

She stood there in a light beam streaming through the door. She was so enthusiastic that he was tempted to get carried away with her to that place where anything was possible no matter how impractical. The dust they had stirred up was golden as it floated through the sunbeam.

"Do you know what Snorri looks like? Have the breeders sent you pictures?"

"I want a grey," Freyja answered. "Do you disapprove?"

"Let's walk the property," he said, avoiding the question. Somewhere in the box of books about Iceland his mother had given him there was one on horses. He vaguely remembered them as variegated. "I haven't had time to see this ground that so many people desire."

"You're going to say no, or you're going to try to convince me that it's impractical." Freyja stood petulantly with her left fist on her hip like a defiant little kid, and he thought he saw what she must have looked like as a child, exasperated with people who didn't agree with her.

"No," he said. "I won't try to convince you of anything. This horse thing is your decision."

They opened the loft doors and stood at the edge looking out. "Would you want the hay as well as the barn?"

"Enough for the winter would be nice."

"How would you cut it? Dry it? Store it?"

"Maybe if you rent it to the Godi and they overwinter some animals, Snorri could stay with them. Maybe they could share the hay." It was obvious that she'd already given the question some thought.

"You don't think I should put in propane and set up an operation to supply Derk?"

"He was just joking. He's always been sarcastic. He's a bright kid."

"He may have been joking, but he's got a problem. You want to create pressure, teach a lesson, you could do it on a delivery boy."

"Oh God," Freyja said. "Everybody just wants the problem to go away. Just get the bills paid. Siggi gets the bills paid and life goes back to normal."

"You still infatuated with him?"

"No. It's more complicated than that. You live here for a few years, you'll understand. Nobody is just themselves. We're all part of everybody else. We don't even have to like each other. Somebody leaves. Somebody dies. It all shifts. Nobody is separate. You're already becoming part of it. Can't you feel it?"

"Should I take Dolly's advice and sell to the Whites, take you to live in the big city?"

"It would change everything. Like an earthquake. When you say that, it's like I can hear huge pieces of rock grinding and crashing upon each other." She momentarily put her hands over her ears, even though there was nothing but silence. "Don't you understand? Everything has gone wrong. Nobody meant for this to happen. It just grew, and then it got out of control. When you owe money how do you say no to your lenders?"

"Pastor Jon is hoping I'll sell and use him for a real estate agent."

"When he bought the church property, some land that goes on past the road came with it. It had already been subdivided. He has dreams of a cottage development. Johnny Armstrong wants a cottage development. All that land to clear. All those foundations to put in."

"I'm holding up progress."

"Or pipe dreams. Like the hidden fortune of the Godi that everyone is waiting to be discovered."

"Every girl should have a horse," Tom said. He was thinking of Myrna. She'd desperately wanted a horse at one time. They couldn't afford a horse. The best they managed were riding lessons from a local farmer's wife who rented out a couple of horses. Myrna had visions of herself on a noble steed. She got to ride on an old nag. Maybe she could be tempted to Valhalla with a chance to ride an Icelandic horse.

"Do you mean that?" Freyja asked.

"Yes. Of course. Why not? People want the strangest things. We'd need to see if we can get a deal with Godi-4."

She stood staring at him. She looked like she was trying to decide if he was telling the truth. In his basement apartment in the city, the only animals were the occasional mice, and once a baby rat had sat on the counter beside his toaster, eating crumbs. It wasn't the slightest bit afraid of him. He opened the fridge door and took out a beer and the rat continued to sit there eating crumbs. It wasn't a big complication. There was no water, and rats need water, so he knew it wouldn't stay. The problems were of his own making: the images in his head that drove him into the night to walk the streets, to drink coffee in twenty-four-hour gas stations, to prowl the city until the sun came up and he could sleep again. "Do you have any idea what might have happened to Angel?" he said and hoped she would have the answer he was seeking.

"I don't know. She was only here off and on. I hadn't seen her all winter or spring. I figured things must be going better for her. It was an accident. Let it go. Just enjoy having an old barn."

"Okay," he said, taking her advice. "How about making love in the hay?"

After, they stood again in the hayloft door, looking out across the land to the south. There wasn't a building to be seen. Trees and water and bulrushes, the white limestone surface of the road and the telephone poles disappearing behind the trees, reappearing, disappearing. They might have been the only two people on the planet. The church was too far away for them to see the spire. In spite of the heat, Tom had his arm around Freyja's shoulders and she had her arm around his waist. The hay and the tops of the trees, the tips of the bulrushes were moving gently.

Because of the emptiness of the land, the forest, the swamp, the silence, he felt how small they were and he wondered how the first explorers who had come this way could have borne the sense of emptiness and how the early immigrants, alone in a log shack with a sod roof, could have borne the loneliness. Husbands went away for months at a time to build railways or work on farms in more settled areas and left their wives alone with small children. The bears and wolves were an immediate danger, but the greater danger was the silence. Some people forgot how to talk, hallucinated, became so bushed they fled when another person did turn up. But he'd been like that in the city, and he remembered that the loneliest place could be in the midst of a crowd.

"It's really not the right area for a horse, is it?" she said, interrupting his reverie. "Swamp instead of prairie. Rocky outcrops."

"No. But it never is. It's like having kids. If you wait until you can afford them, you'll never have them." He momentarily tightened his grip on her shoulders, then eased it. "You could board your horse during the winter."

"Can't afford it," she said wistfully. "If I had my money back from Siggi, I could. Bad decisions."

"Yes. Me, too," he agreed.

In his despair, in the crazy, violent world of his head, he had given Sally everything she wanted, fought for nothing because nothing mattered, because there was no future, because the dying and the dead had taken over, because with no separation between the nightmares of the day and the nightmares of the night, when he'd sat with his service revolver in his mouth, trying to decide if he should pull the trigger and afraid that even that would not stop the images, he'd thought, *Perchance to dream*, remembering the phrase from his grade twelve literature class, and he could not remember the quote for certain, and he put down his pistol and searched frantically through his books, but the play wasn't there, a small blue book. And he'd gone out and walked until the stores opened, and he'd searched through a used bookstore before he found a copy and paid $1.50 for it and went to a sidewalk coffee shop and sat over a cappuccino and read until he came to: "To die, to sleep. / To sleep, perchance to dream—ay, there's the rub, / For in that sleep of death what dreams may come." He sat there with his cold cappuccino and thought, *What if death is that? What if death is not being able to stop the dreaming? What if all the doors come open all the time?* He had lurched up from the table, nearly knocking it over and with the book gripped tightly in one hand began to walk. He walked until he couldn't walk anymore, then found a place under a bridge where he fell asleep sitting up and slept until early afternoon, when he was able to walk home. His pistol was still on the table, but the bullets had been removed, and there was a scrap of paper underneath on which were printed just two words in capital letters: *YOUR DAUGHTER.*

He should not have been making financial decisions, any decisions, he thought. The wreckage of his life had become even more wrecked after he signed the separation papers.

He took one rope and she took the other, and they pulled the doors to the loft shut and he pushed the latch into place.

A horse, he thought, but he didn't say it out loud, didn't want his skepticism to ruin the moment, diminish whatever dream Freyja had.

He climbed down first, then helped her down. They went outside, and he saw that she had hay in her hair. She stood still as he picked it out, and she did the same for him.

"We're getting rid of the evidence, you realize."

"It won't matter," she answered. "Someone will have seen us, and whoever it was will tell someone, and someone will tell someone else, and someone will tell Siggi. Siggi won't believe we went to see if the barn was suitable for my horse."

"I worry about his craziness," Tom said. "I've seen too many women killed by jealous husbands and boyfriends." He pulled her tight, and they stood there in the tall grass, among the old farm equipment, the barn, the Bombardiers and the silence.

CHAPTER 32

OPPORTUNITIES

Frenchie was working on his outboard. Tom dropped off the dock into the boat.

"Bugger off," Frenchie said. He had a beard that was streaked with white, the eyes of a weasel and the nervous posture of a perp who feels there's someone watching him.

Tom pushed a toolbox out of the way.

"This is private property, you know. You're trespassing. Get off my boat," Frenchie barked.

Tom sat down. "How much does the compartment in the floor of your truck hold? Five hundred pounds of fillets when it's full?"

The commercial fishing boats were kept separate from the sailboats and the yachts, as if their presence might offend the finer senses of the tourists. It was an extension of the gated communities they came from. The privileges of the upper classes had infuriated Tom's father. The sons of the poor were slaughtered while the sons of the rich got nice safe positions far from the bullets and bombs.

"Go to hell," Frenchie replied. He picked up a wrench.

"Five hundred pounds a trip when the fishing is good. The back doors of restaurants, butcher shops. What's the back-door price? Three dollars a pound? Fifteen hundred a trip."

"Shut your mouth. You got no proof about nothing." He still had the wrench in his hand, but he'd lowered it.

"The income tax people come, they'll get a list right away. You think your buddies will keep a secret? Forget it. Scared people talk. Someone will cut a deal." Tom was thinking about how Sarah had said that cops were just enforcers for the tax collectors, and there was no modern Robin Hood to take back part of the money the rich stole. Ben had mentioned the tax people as well, so it was a subject they were all aware of, nervous about—sleeping on their money, Ben had said. Onshore, the tin fish shed's glare blinded anyone looking at it.

"What do you want?" Frenchie demanded. "A cut?"

"I don't care about the tax collectors. Let them do their own work." Frenchie eyed him suspiciously. "I want to know about Ben's granddaughter. I think she swam to shore. In her clothes. Why?"

"I dunno," Fenchie said. Now that the questions weren't about illegal fish sales, he no longer cared. "You gotta ask Karla. They're her girls. They're her parties. She provides the food. She sells stuff."

"Tupperware?" Tom said. "Girl Guide cookies?"

Frenchie didn't get it. "I don't know anything about Tupperware. I just hear that some of these guys who come are big shots. TV. Movies. They want pictures to take back with them. They show the right person the right picture and a girl gets to be a star. Karla creates opportunities."

"The American dream," Tom said.

"You gotta take your opportunities," Frenchie insisted. "It's not like we're forcing people to buy our fish. The restaurants, they get in touch. They want mariah. We can't get buyers because they don't have scales and the Bible says don't eat fish without scales. We get two cents a pound from the mink farms. The restaurants pay fifty and sell it to the suckers as cod or halibut. You wanna go after somebody, go after them."

"I don't work for Fisheries," Tom said, then went home.

Tom waited until the restaurant was closing. Karla was standing behind the counter. Horst wasn't in sight.

"We're closed," Karla said. "It'll have to wait until tomorrow." He could see that she was tired. Her smile was forced. She was studying a pile of money with disapproval, as if she might scold it.

"Let's go for a walk," Tom replied. "You and me."

"Won't Freyja be jealous if you take me swimming?"

"Then we won't go swimming."

Karla shifted nervously. "I'm busy," she said. "Maybe another time." She started counting bills into the cashbox to make up the next day's float. It was for cash sales that didn't go through the till.

"I think it would be good to talk to an ex-cop instead of a cop."

She eyed him suspiciously. Word had got around about him and Freyja, and now, if he had hope she would consider asking him up the back steps, it was dashed. "You're being a pain. Go back where you came from. And leave my girls alone. I pay them to work, not gossip with the customers."

"I hear you run a talent agency for the girls." The building was empty. The *Closed* sign was in the window, but the door was unlocked. Even though they were talking quietly, their voices echoed a bit.

"Barbara isn't pretty enough. Her hips are too big. It's like ballet. You got ambition but the wrong body, you don't get to be a prima ballerina." Her voice was harsh now, angry at the idea that anyone would interfere, would presume she didn't know what she was doing.

"Underage girls serving booze at private parties," he said. "That's illegal."

Karla shifted nervously. She lost track of counting her change and slammed a roll of quarters onto the counter. "Who says the girls serve liquor? You tell me who says they're serving liquor." She crossed her arms over her chest, and her words were angry and defiant.

"TV executives. Moviemakers. Looking for the next great star. The girls eat that up, don't they? A big boat, fancy clothes. Spend a little money. It doesn't take much to impress people."

"Everybody needs a chance," she said defiantly. "Everybody needs somebody from somewhere else to see them. You see any big chances in this dump? You think I want to see these girls end up here like me? Do you think this was my plan for my life? Does this look like Nashville?" She said these last words as if she were choking.

He'd touched a nerve, and the anger that lay just below the surface of forced smiles and exaggerated greetings made her face look hard and, at the same time, vulnerable. He'd dealt with people like that who had passed over opportunities for mundane jobs—teaching, civil service, banking—and then it hadn't worked out. They had gambled everything and lost. And the image Tom had from listening to his father when an artist of any kind was mentioned was that of a poor wretch standing on a street corner, trying to interest passersby in his poetry or CD or painting, instead of sitting in a comfortable apartment, warm and well fed, with money in the bank and the prospect of a pension. Although, after all his planning and anticipating, his avoidance of risk, his father had never gotten to enjoy much of his pension.

Just then Horst appeared from the store's living quarters. He was dragging his oxygen container behind him, and his shoulders were bent forward as if it were a great weight. "What do you want?" he demanded. "We're closed. Come back tomorrow."

Tom went back to tearing down the shed. There was a sense of privacy, of aloneness among the spruce trees. The ground was inches deep in needles from years past, a sort of reddish-brown soil that had little substance to it but that was so acidic nothing grew in it except here and there a dispirited thistle or a few strands of wiry grass that did not look like they would long survive. All the lower branches of the trees, deprived of sunlight, had died back and become dry and brittle, stunted, while branches higher up spread out, creating a canopy of sorts. He'd left the shed partly dismantled. Now that boards were missing, it had lost its romantic look with its moss-covered roof and sides weathered to silver.

He was methodically taking boards off and piling them to one side when Barbara appeared. She was crying and immediately burst out by saying, "I've been fired. It's your fault. Mrs. White didn't want me talking to you. She said I was causing trouble."

Tom hadn't heard her come up. He was startled and turned toward her with his crowbar partly raised. When he saw who it was, he lowered the crowbar and said, "I'm sorry. Talking to me shouldn't be a cause for being fired."

She put her hands to her cheeks, as if she were trying to keep her face from falling apart. Her glasses with their black plastic frames were too big for her, and as she held onto her cheeks, the glasses got pushed up and looked like they might fall off. Her eyes were red and swollen. "What am I going to do? There aren't any other jobs." Barbara sounded desperate.

"What about babysitting for the cottagers? Cleaning for them?"

Through tears, Barbara said, "She'll tell them she fired me. They won't hire me."

Tom wondered how many more things could go wrong. He thought about how much he had in his bank account. The house needed to be cleaned, but he couldn't afford to hire her. He'd need to ask Freyja for advice.

Locally, the two people who had money were Siggi and Helgi History. Maybe Freyja could get Siggi to hire her to clean the embassy after he and his friends went back to the oil fields. From the way she described it, they treated the embassy like a dorm room. The four guys and their friends partying meant that the place would be a shambles. It wouldn't work, he realized. Not unless she had an armed guard. It would be like throwing a rabbit into a den of wolves.

Helgi definitely needed his place cleaned. Windows washed, dishes washed, floors vacuumed, everything tidied up, but whether he would trust a teenage girl not to knock over his books was a question. *Money*, Tom thought. *Always easy to spend, hard to make. Shit*, he thought, here he was, already thinking about asking people for favours. Once he started getting more jobs, he wouldn't have to be so careful with his budget. He wished he had the twenty dollars he'd wasted on Morning Dawn.

"I'll talk to a couple of my friends," he said, trying to calm her down. "What was it you weren't supposed to talk to me about?"

"I told her I didn't tell you about the lingerie parties. There's all this fancy underwear, and Tracy and Amanda and Shirley, they get to go onto the yachts and serve food and put on a lingerie show. They do photo shoots to take back to the States to show people in TV and the movies. You've got to have a good shape. Mrs. White says I'm not built right."

"Would you really want to do that?"

"They get big tips. I've seen what Tracy got one time. She's got big boobs and she's pretty and she's got a good voice." Barbara held her forehead with both hands and leaned forward, and her face crumpled with the despair of not being good enough to be wanted and admired.

"Her voice isn't as good as yours. Not even close."

"My folks don't have money for me. I've got to pay for my own clothing and stuff. My dad hears that I've been fired, he'll kill me."

"Do the girls sometimes have sex with these men?"

Barbara looked scared and blushed furiously. "I don't know. They never told me anything like that."

"Did you tell her we just talked about your singing?"

"She wouldn't listen. She didn't like it that Angel and I were friends."

"Didn't she like Angel?"

"She just likes C&W. Angel wasn't going to sing C&W anymore. It's not fair."

"No, it's not. It's not fair at all." Many times he'd thought that, and the most unfair thing of all was discovering how unfair life is too soon. His father, instead of protecting him from unfairness, preached about its pervasiveness, about how life was rigged so that those who had more got more, and those who had little got less. Rich people got elected and got to make the laws that gave them more.

"Can you tell her I never told you anything?" Barbara said.

"I can try, but I don't think it'll do any good. I'll tell you what. I'll talk to people I know. Maybe we can find a job for you."

"What'll I tell my folks?"

"Tell them the truth. You didn't do anything wrong. Mrs. White is upset because you and Angel were friends."

"She keeps our tips for us so we won't spend them," she said in an aggrieved voice. "I said I wanted my tips because I was fired, but she said I'd have to wait and she'll give them to me at the end of the month when she does the books."

After Barbara left, Tom went to Freyja's to see if she had any advice.

"That bitch," Freyja said. "I know Barbara's dad. He's not an easy man to be around."

"How not easy?"

"He's got a temper. He may slap her around. I've seen her with bruises."

"What about the cottagers?"

Freyja said no, Barbara was right. Karla had an in with the summer people, and all she had to do was sound hesitant and give a lukewarm recommendation. That would be enough.

"She can outsing all of them. Karla included."

"That's part of the problem. There are people who don't like others around who are more talented than them."

"What about me?" Tom said, wondering about the power of gossip in Valhalla. "If she didn't want Barbara talking to me, then she didn't want me talking to Barbara. How about if she lets people know that she thinks I'm no good."

"You've got women making up lists of things that need fixing. Linda is already singing your praises for fixing her light. Arlene tells people that you're going to put in drywall. Karla has her own list. She's having trouble with one of the showers and the roof is leaking in one corner. The emporium is falling apart around her."

He thought about Horst's piercing stare and rude comments. "I don't think Horst likes having me around."

"She does put on a show for you, and you don't help by checking the inventory."

He went back to his place. *Not pretty*, he thought. It was the luck of the draw. Barbara wasn't ugly, but nothing quite fit. Her features were indistinguishable; her skin was pale. Her hair was mousy, and in a society obsessed with sex, she didn't have big breasts and hips. Makeup, a decent haircut, contact lenses and she'd be okay. What was it, he wondered, that tugged us toward one type of look and not others?

There had been girls in his school that attracted boys in packs. They weren't necessarily the best looking, but they triggered male hormones, jumped up testosterone levels. He thought of Freyja and wondered if she looked like Barbara, would he have been drawn to her like iron filings to a magnet, like a bee to a clump of brightly coloured flowers on the bald prairie? Why Freyja and not Dolly, for Dolly was certainly attractive. Maybe Dolly's being desperate seeped into her looks.

No breaks for Barbara, he thought, and he'd made it worse. All he'd done was praise her for her voice. She'd complained about Karla, but what teenager didn't complain about the boss, especially if she played favourites?

Myrna wouldn't win any beauty contest, but she was attractive, good-looking, striking. She had an attitude about her that brooked no nonsense. If anyone tried to bully her, she would see they didn't do it twice.

And Joel. Too thin, with his lopsided grin and his sense of helplessness. Sweet, charming, with a crazy sense of humour and a brain that never stopped working. If he was bullied, he'd slip sideways, out of reach, use sarcasm and logic like a razor.

Tom jumped the narrow ditch onto the main road, crossed the road, and then jumped the second ditch. There was no evidence that anything bad had happened. No one had put up a cross and festooned it with artificial flowers, as they would have if Angel had died in a car accident. All was as it had been— the sailboats, the fishermen's boats, two yachts, the lake barely moving. He knocked on Freyja's door and borrowed her phone.

When Anna answered, she said, "Thomas, is it really you? You need to come back to the city. The wild animals will eat you up if you stay there."

He reassured her that he wasn't going to be eaten; although when he thought about Siggi's bears, he wasn't so sure that was true. "I'm calling to ask a favour. Do you still need help cleaning apartments?"

"Do you want your old job back?"

"No, thank you. But I know a girl who needs work. She's a hard worker and dependable."

"You need to come by for tea more often," she complained.

He felt guilty because he had avoided her when his marriage was breaking up. If she had known what was happening, she'd have found him an apartment in one of her buildings, insisted he come for meals and, now that Tanya was divorced, invited her to join them. He might, he thought in retrospect, have been better off to have settled for perohy and borshch and bingo. He probably could have learned to ignore the plaques and the religious icons.

"Yes," he said. "The next time I'm in the city, I'll come for tea. Maybe I'll shoot rats for you."

She always liked it when he mentioned shooting rats. She'd never been able to find someone to replace him, someone willing to lie patiently on the fire escape landing waiting for a clear shot. She made him bring her the tails before she would pay him. One time, he had shot a rat with no tail, so he'd brought the entire rat, but she still wouldn't pay, saying how did she know that one of the tails didn't belong to the rat? He'd shown her that the stump of the tail was healed over and the cuts on the tails were fresh. She gave him his money.

"That's good," she said. "This girl? You think she would do a good job? Could she also babysit my grandkids?"

"Yes," Tom said. "She would be perfect for babysitting your grandkids. She's a good girl. There's just no work here in the bush. No apartment blocks."

"No apartment blocks? How can that be?"

Anna, as far as he knew, had never been outside the city limits. Wilderness, for her, was City Park. "Everybody lives in a house."

"Tanya needs help with the kids, and I need help with the apartments. I'm not so young anymore. Is this girl boy crazy?"

Boy crazy. He smiled at that. It was the greatest criticism. If a girl was labelled "boy crazy," she was beyond redemption. Unreliable, emotional, untrustworthy, the kind of girl who would leave an apartment uncleaned while she chased after a guy. Her daughter had not been allowed to be boy crazy. When young men came to take her out, Anna questioned them, evaluated them. If they were, in her opinion, girl crazy, they didn't get a second chance. She'd approved of a suitor who had been an altar boy. It hadn't done any good. The marriage foundered after ten years and two kids.

"No," he said. "Not boy crazy. She's a hard worker."

"You going to bring her and introduce her?"

He hadn't thought of that, but he needed to go to the city anyway. He agreed to bring her and introduce her. "We'll bring her with us when we come."

"We?" Anna said, her voice picking up. "Who's we?"

"You'll see. Maybe I'll introduce her, too. But we'll just be staying two nights in the city, then going back."

"You can stay longer. You can have supper with me one night. You don't need to go to no expensive hotel. I've got a nice furnished bachelor empty. You don't need nothing. Good kitchen. New mattress. Nice furniture. No bedbugs. No fleas. You can have a holiday."

After he hung up, he said, "The greatest sin a girl can commit is to be boy crazy. It's Anna's eleventh commandment."

"Maybe," Freyja said, "she'll think I'm boy crazy. Do you think she'll say I'm boy crazy? Maybe I shouldn't go with you. Maybe she wants you for her daughter." She thought about that for a moment. "Maybe I'd better go."

He ignored her. "We'll take her five pounds of pickerel fillets, two jars of honey and peanut butter cookies. She likes peanut butter."

After he left Freyja's house, he went back to tearing down the shed. He pulled away a corner support, and when the roof came crashing down, he jumped back to escape the dust. He got a flat shovel and slid it under the shingles. When the shingles were removed, he pulled apart the roof trusses. He threw everything into a pile. He would save it for the communal bonfire.

He'd been told there was a dance in the community hall on New Year's Eve. At midnight everyone went out on the lake where scrap wood had been piled high on ice four feet thick. They set the pile on fire, then danced around the fire, drank, sang. The ice surface was scraped clear of snow during the day so people could skate around the fire. Picnic tables were hauled onto the ice, and hot chocolate and apple cider were served. It was in memory of an old ritual. In the first terrible winter of 1875, when the Icelandic immigrants settled in New Iceland and thirty-four out of a hundred people died from scurvy, hunger and pneumonia, at New Year's they built a pyre on the lake, lit it and danced around it.

He wanted to be part of that. He wanted to watch the stars in the dark night, the light on the snow, the flames leaping into the darkness. He wanted more than a place out of the weather. More than an apartment in the city with neighbours who were constantly changing, neighbours he did not know. He wanted to be part of a community and share the beginning of the new year.

All that was left of the shed was the floor, and he used his pry bar to rip up the floorboards. He was about halfway across the floor when he saw there was a wooden box between two stringers. The box was covered in thick spider webs that were heavy with dust. He swept away the spider webs with his hand, and they clumped together and clung to his fingers, so he had to pull them off. Small black spiders raced around on the ground and disappeared. He lifted up the box. It was a pale, faded brown. On one side it said *Canadian Butter Saskatchewan 56 LBS NET*. The corners were neatly dovetailed. He took off the lid. There was a glass sealer with a metal screw-on rim. He picked it up. Inside there was a piece of rolled birch bark and a gold-coloured coin about the size of a silver dollar.

He looked around to be sure that no one was watching. He put the jar back into the box, put the lid back on and piled shingles to cover the box.

He went inside and washed off the dust and dirt, then went to Odin.

He found Godi-4 working in the garden and told him that he'd found something, and he needed him to come right away. Godi-4 put down his trowel and joined him.

"What is it?" Godi-4 asked.

"I'm not sure," Tom said.

They went back to the ruins of Tom's shed and Tom pulled the shingles away and lifted out the box and then the sealer. He handed it to Godi-4.

"Should we break the glass?" he asked, but Godi-4 said no, the jar itself would be worth keeping.

The metal rim wouldn't come off, so Tom got a hacksaw blade and pliers. While Goldi-4 held the jar, Tom cut the rim and eased it loose.

Godi-4 lifted the glass lid off, and Tom tipped the jar sideways so the rolled birch bark and the gold-coloured coin slipped to the mouth. Godi-4 carefully took out the two items. He turned the coin over in his palm. The coin had a runic symbol on it that looked like a capital *F*.

"Ansuz," Godi-4 said. "The sign of Odin." He gave the coin to Tom, then took the birch bark and set it on one of the boards from the shed. He pinned one end down with the fingers of his left hand and slowly pushed the roll open with his right thumb.

There was a message and it said, in neat printing, *Seek elsewhere*.

"No treasure map," Tom said.

"No treasure map," Godi-4 repeated. He handed Tom the coin. "It's yours."

Tom turned the coin over. "I'd rather have the money. I could pay some of my bills."

Godi-4 put his hand out. He weighed the coin in his hand. "We'll pay you for the coin. The price will be the market price of gold on the day it is valued. May I also have the sealer and the note?"

"Yes," Tom said. "When I finish tearing apart the shed, I'll dig up the ground just in case."

"We have suspected there was something buried on this property. It's been found. That mystery is solved. Now, if Jessie Olason could forgive us for unintentional sins committed."

Godi-4 went over to where the contents of the shed were piled. He put his hand on the crib with the picture of a rabbit and a baby duck. "She had a child. It wasn't well. It had a cough. There was no doctor and no way of getting help. The only person with any medical experience was a member of our group who had stayed for the winter. He was a homeopath. There'd been a conflict over the property, but she had no one else to turn to, so she asked for his help. He told her to bundle the child up warmly and put it outside for half an hour each day. It was the kind of treatment they used for TB. The weather became very cold, and one day when she brought the child in he didn't respond. She believed he'd died of hypothermia. It may have been true. A child has so little body mass. But it may have been the illness."

"His grave is on the property," Tom said.

"She believed our person had done it deliberately to drive her away and get the property. There was no such intent. Our healer committed suicide over it.

He walked out onto the lake and kept walking until he couldn't walk anymore. He meant no harm. It was a waste of two lives. We needed him. This is a burden on us, three burdens. The child, the practitioner, Jessie's sorrow."

"You didn't do it."

"We are One. We share the credit and the blame. Otherwise, our beliefs mean nothing."

"I, too, am atoning for a sin," Tom said. "We sound like Christians at Saint Peter's gate. I helped Morning Dawn leave." He told Godi-4 about what Morning Dawn had told him, and Bob and guaranteeing twenty dollars.

"I am sorry to hear that. But she was not One with us. She was with Jason. His return has not gone well. He would prefer to give up nothing and gain much."

"Angel sometimes joined Jason and his group. Would he have done her harm?"

"It is hard to say. If anything Morning Dawn said is true, then no possibility can be ruled out."

"The stories of enlightenment through sex are told and retold."

"Not with children. Not by force. Only from mutual desire. There are many portals. Sex is just one. One is music. Another is art. Meditation. We seek the entrance to our other world. There are many who would like their desires to be satisfied but do not want to give up anything for it. How much would you give up to be One with us?"

"I'd prefer a relationship with one person and to have friends."

There were, however, times when he'd been vulnerable, desperately lonely and lost. When he was a teenager, after his mother left, after his father died, when he joined the Force, desperate to belong. At those times he might have given everything and anything to belong, to have a place. Sally had six siblings and he thought he'd be part of an extended family, that he'd never be lonely again, but she was resentful of her siblings, alienated, jealous. They hardly ever saw any of them.

"This woman Freyja we have seen you with, she's had previous relationships, none have lasted. Yet you think she'll stay with you."

"I don't know. I hope so."

"Your previous relationship failed."

"Marriage," Tom corrected. "It was more than a relationship."

"Have you changed so much that whatever caused you to make an unfortu-nate choice doesn't exist anymore? Unless we change ourselves, we just keep making the same mistakes again."

"I'll try harder."

"She's very pretty, this Freyja. When she comes to our Viking week, she dresses in a Viking warrior costume. But what about when looks are not enough? What is it that she needs that her previous relationships didn't satisfy?"

With that, Tom thought of his mother and his father and never knowing for certain why his mother left, or why she left when she did, not a moment earlier or later, and he felt a moment of panic, as if Freyja was already leaving, and he was alone, and no matter how he tried to hold on to her she would slip away, like his mother, like Sally.

"I might be no more suitable to be One than Jason," he replied.

"Would you have done the things Morning Dawn said he did? Would you covet a piece of land so much that you'd destroy another person to get it? You did not hesitate to hand me the gold coin. You picked up Gabriel and carried him. There was no benefit to you in that."

Tom thought then of his basement apartment, with its green walls, its low ceiling, his cell-like bedroom, his loneliness, the emptiness of feeling there was no place for him. "Yes," he said. "I understand."

"Where is your mother?"

"I don't know," Tom said. "She left when I was young."

"Your father?"

"Dead."

"Your wife?"

"With someone else."

"Your children?"

"Gone."

"Life fragments," Godi-4 said. "We think it is solid, substantial, that it won't change, that it is as trustworthy as the earth under our feet, but earth-quakes happen, tidal waves appear and our world disintegrates. You will get to know us better. We will get to know you better." He half smiled and put his hand on Tom's shoulder. "Maybe we are a tribe, a cult. Maybe everything we believe is false. But then, what isn't? People came because there was an emptiness in their lives. Those who stayed found what they were looking for.

We belong to each other. We all have a place, a refuge. No one who is One is ever alone."

Sadness descended over Tom, and in spite of the heat, he was back in his parents' apartment, sitting in the window, looking down at the snow-blown street, the figures struggling against the wind, the other figures with shopping carts and bedrolls huddled in doorways across the road, and he thought of how flimsy the barrier between him and them was, how easily he could become One with them, a man with no place, and he was overcome with despair.

Godi-4 broke into his thoughts by saying, "You think that Angel did not die accidently?"

"I don't know," Tom said. "I know that there are people who think I am implicated. I need an answer to what happened, no matter how innocent it might be."

"Angel did come to us. Music was to be her portal to the rest of her life. Two or three times she stopped with Jason and his group on the beach. He is no longer satisfied with being One. He has been preaching a new vision. It is not one we share."

They walked around to the front of the house and stood at baby Oli's grave.

They were both looking at the concrete slab. It was tipped slightly and needed to be lifted so it was level. The concrete had darkened at the edges. Dirt was gathering once again around the coloured stones that had been pressed into the concrete.

They went back to Odin together and found Jason weaving a willow chair. He looked surprised and stood up as if to get ready for a confrontation.

Godi-4 put the question to him and Jason said yes, Angel had joined them, been with them three times, but what he had said was true; she had not been with them the night she died. "Her death had nothing to do with us. We said nothing because we didn't need any complications."

Godi-4 said, "Morning Dawn did not return to her parents' home. When she came to Mr. Parsons, she wanted him to let her into his house and hide her. She was afraid that you would do terrible things to her.

"Instead, Mr. Parsons helped her leave with a local person in the middle of the night. When they got to Winnipeg, she did not wait for him to find her a ride home, as she had said she wanted. If she was in no danger of being punished in the ways she said, why would she say so?"

"She has a vivid imagination."

"I don't doubt that," Godi-4 agreed. "However, perhaps her purpose was more devious. Mr. Parsons had found Angel. He's been under suspicion. If he let a young girl into his house and she then claimed he'd assaulted her, everyone would have believed it."

"The property belongs to Odin," Jason said stubbornly.

"I believe Morning Dawn is working in a café and waiting for you people to join up with her. She sought shelter with one of our members and hinted that a trap had been set. Would you destroy a reputation and a life for a piece of earth and an old building?" When Jason didn't reply, Godi-4 handed Tom the sealer, took the lid off and extracted the paper and the coin. He held up the coin so Jason could see it. He put it back in the jar and gave Jason the paper to read. When Jason had read the note, Godi-4 put it back in the sealer with the coin. "For this you would betray everything we believe in?"

"The property rightfully belongs to us."

"And the demonstration in front of White's? You did not bring this to One to discuss. You mistakenly believed that Morning Dawn had been assisted by Mrs. White."

"She hates us and wishes us harm, and I had heard she was going to help a follower leave. As for him," he edged closer to Tom so that he was staring directly into his eyes. "He wants to take what is ours. He knows it belongs to us. We have to defend ourselves. We can't just be passive and wait." He looked in that moment, his face darkening with anger, ready to kill, like an enraged participant in an old ethnic battle, in Ireland or Yugoslavia or Palestine or a thousand thousand other places where a sense of injustice excused any act.

"We cannot be One with such beliefs," Godi-4 said quietly. "I had hoped that this would not happen, but it is best that you leave and seek what you wish from life elsewhere."

Jason's face grew taut with anger. He turned back to the gardens and waved to those who were working. They all looked up, but most looked down again and kept working. His followers dropped their tools and joined him. They disappeared in the direction of the beach.

Tom and Godi-4 stood there for a time saying nothing. Then Godi-4 said, "The way is hard. He would be a leader but not for the One. He would lead to satisfy his own ambitions."

"I'm sorry," Tom said. "If I hadn't pushed it..."

"No," Godi-4 said, cutting him off. "This would have happened, instead of today perhaps tomorrow, or next week, or next year. It was inevitable."

"Do you know this man?" Tom asked and showed Godi-4 the picture of his father.

"I don't recognize him."

He opened his wallet and took out the paper with the name Valhalla on it. "I wondered if he might have come here."

"I've only been Godi-4 for the last ten years. When Godi-3 died, I took over. I had been elsewhere."

"My father died in 1979. He was a bookkeeper. He did pro bono work for a few charities."

"Brokkr might know. He's been here that long. He'll be working at the forge."

The forge was a trailer with an anvil set up under the canopy. Brokkr and his assistant were wearing leather aprons. The smell of burning coal was sharp. Brokkr was hammering a white-hot steel bar. Tom waited until the assistant put the bar back into the coals.

Brokkr came over to him with his hammer in his hand.

Tom showed him the paper and then the picture. "This was my father," he said. "Did you ever see him?"

Brokkr took the picture, held it up to get a better look. "We have had many visitors over the years."

"He was a bookkeeper," Tom added.

"There was someone who used to come. He always brought an army rucksack."

"Do you remember anything about him?"

"Vaguely," Brokkr said. "He did our books for us. Never charged. Instead, he came here for a week in the summer to fish. He never had much to say. He liked the music."

"Did he like anything else?" Tom asked.

"He'd fish every day and what he caught he would give to the kitchen. He had his meals with us. In the evening, he would listen to the music. He got up early, went to bed early."

"He had no car," Tom said.

"We would have arranged transportation."

Brokkr handed him back the picture. "It was a long time ago. Many people have come here and left. It's the army rucksack I remember. It was an odd sort of thing to have."

There was a rack with black metal hooks and trivets and silhouettes of metal cowboys in various poses all hanging on a series of crossbars. There was the soft *woof, woof* of the bellows and the heavy smell of the glowing coal. Brokkr's assistant pulled the metal bar out of the fire. Tom raised his hand in thanks, and as he was walking away, behind him, there was the steady pounding of Brokkr's hammer shaping the glowing metal into an object that would be sold at a fair or craft show, in a country store, or maybe at a roadside stand.

Tom walked to Freyja's. He told her about the gold coin and the note and Godi-4's story of Jessie's child.

"The smallest things can do harm," he said, feeling guilty in spite of Godi-4's words. "Even when we mean no harm." He felt a kind of agony, as if a knife were twisted inside him. He thought of Jessie's child, and the child in the car he had pursued. Distraught mothers. Decades apart, but both had their child wrenched from them by strangers. He hoped the woman in the parking lot would have another child. She was young, nineteen or twenty, and she was married. It would never replace the child she lost, but it would comfort her. He wanted to fall down and cover his head with his hands and cry until he couldn't cry anymore, and part of him wondered, a part not totally overwhelmed by grief, if that was such a bad thing, a weak thing, to feel pain for another person's loss, to grieve another's grief, to care about another's suffering.

"What are you going to do about Siggi?" she asked.

"Nothing," he said, and his words echoed in his head, as if it were an empty box. "I'm not a cop anymore. Maybe he'll stick to what he said. Maybe he'll have a good crop, pay his bills. Maybe his suppliers will be satisfied with just getting their money. Maybe he'll quit being stupid and go back to Fort McMurray and work on the rigs. A Valhalla solution."

CHAPTER 33

A HEART'S DESIRE

Tom left Freyja's and went to Ben's.

"Ben home?" he asked.

"No," Wanda said. She was lying in the sun face down on a foamy covered with a yellow blanket. She had on pink shorts and a matching top with a string tie at the back. The strings were undone so she wouldn't have a tan line. Her sandals were lying on the ground beside her. There was a child's yellow plastic bucket with a bottle of beer set in ice.

"You're going to get sunburnt," Tom said.

"Not if you rub this lotion on my back." She held out a tube of sunscreen. He sat down on the grass beside her and took the tube from her, opened it and squirted sunscreen onto his hand. He rubbed it onto her shoulders.

"That's quite the tattoo," he said. The dragon wrapped itself right around her leg and disappeared into her shorts.

"Big mistake," she said. "They seem like a good idea, but after a while they get boring, and it would be fun to have a different one. It's better to have the kind you wash off. Have a different one every month."

"Chinese?"

"It was love," she said, talking into the blanket. "He drove a Mercedes. It was going to be forever. We were going to live someplace fun."

He finished her back, put the cap back on the tube and tied her straps in a bow. She rolled over and looked at him.

"You still trying to figure out what happened to Angel?" Her face was full of sadness. She sat up and pulled her knees toward her. She rested her cheek on her knees. "Derk said maybe you would."

"He was upset about his sister."

"I told him not to deal, but he quit school after grade eleven. There aren't a lot of jobs. You can't live on welfare. He buys the groceries. He pays the rent. We've got a decent place. He says people like you look down on us."

"Everybody has to make a living," Tom said. "He seems smart. He should go back to school. Get a job as a salesman for a pharmaceutical company."

"Yeah," she agreed. "I've told him that. Ben has told him that. Angel was going to finish school, have her own band. Her music teacher said she was talented. She could go to college and become a music teacher."

"Ben says all she wanted was a good guitar. Too bad you were never able to get her one."

Wanda lifted her face off her knees and looked at Tom. "What do you mean she didn't get one? She got one. The best."

"Ben said she just had his old guitar and it's not up to much. It's tough when a kid dies and never gets her dream."

"She got a new guitar. She had her dream." Wanda bit her lip and used the back of her wrist to wipe her eyes.

"Where did she get it?" Her music teacher? Did he give it to her?" Tom asked and wondered if the music teacher had offered lessons in more than music.

Wanda lay face down again. ""She," Wanda said. "Miss Primrose. She didn't have no guitars to give away. Somebody thought Angel had a lot of talent. They gave her one."

In the sunlight, her back gleamed with the sunscreen Tom had rubbed on her. Her shoulder blades looked thin, sharp, like they could break through the skin. "Nobody thinks that somebody like me can love their kids. I love my kids. You leave Derk alone. You're not a cop anymore. You mind you own business. He pays the rent."

"Okay," he said.

"He's not using. He says if he uses, he'll end up with no profits. He says he's getting even. He has a few drinks when he gets depressed, that's all. He thinks too much. I tell him, 'Quit thinking so much.' He says it's war. Rich against poor."

Wanda sat up again, and Tom wondered if she'd get up and run into the house. Instead, she sat with her arms around her legs, her face on her knees, the folly of her dragon glowing like a neon sign in the harsh sunlight. Tom was sitting on the grass facing her. There were dark circles around her eyes and the black roots of her hair were starting to show.

"Derk says you think you're better than us. Big-shot cop with a pension and connections."

"No," Tom reassured her. "I don't think I'm better." He thought about his kids then as the heat weighed down on them. Myrna, in her black boots, her tattoos, her nose ring, eyebrow ring, her studded belt, leading her blonde girlfriend around on a leash. And Joel, out there with his crazy sense of humour and the possibility he had AIDS. "Not even a little bit. We all have our own problems."

He went back home and started building a set of stairs for the porch.

Ben came by later in the evening. "Wanda's sort of upset. She said you were looking for me. What did you want?"

"I don't know. I'm not sure. Angel, I guess. There's something just not right about it." He put down his chop saw. "Wanda said Angel got her guitar she wanted."

"I don't think so," Ben said. "When I picked her up, she was carrying my old case."

"Can I see your guitar?"

They got into Ben's truck and drove to his place. Wanda had moved onto the porch swing and was reading a romance novel.

"What's he doing here?" she asked.

"He wants to see my old guitar. That's all. I told him it was a good guitar at one time. Not electric, though. No electricity in the fish camps in those days."

"I don't think you should be showing it to him. What business is it of his?"

Ben waved her concerns away, and Tom followed him inside. They went into the living room and Tom sat down. Ben brought out a beat-up black guitar case. Wanda came in and sat uneasily on a wooden chair. Ben undid the clasp and opened the top. And there was a brand-new guitar. The three of them stared at it.

"Where did she get this?" Ben demanded.

"Karla," Wanda said. "Well, Karla didn't give it to her. One of the promoters was in Winnipeg and Karla told him about Angel and how talented she was.

Karla talked him into giving her an audition. He said that if she really was as talented as Karla said, he'd give her a guitar, but then she'd be under contract to him. It was okay. He was one of the regulars who come here in the summer."

Tom heard a car pull up and the motor shut off. Derk came into the room. "What's up?" he asked. In spite of the heat, he was back to wearing black. He looked at all of them and the guitar. "That's Angel's guitar."

"Where did this tryout take place?" Ben asked.

"I don't remember the name," Wanda said.

"The Sapphire," Derk snapped. "Big shots go there. When I make deliveries, I've got to give them to the concierge. We've got an understanding. He handles special deliveries and the girls. You've got to be dressed like you belong just to get past the doorman."

"It was okay," Wanda said. "She was with Karla."

"Yeah," Derk said. "Karla was in town for a week. Ordering stuff for the store, doing promos. She even had a couple of gigs. She dropped by to visit and took Angel to a show. She was really good to her. Took her to music stores. Took her to lunch."

This was, Tom thought, the girl whose name Karla said she could not remember, the girl she really didn't know, the girl that Barbara said Karla didn't care for because she wasn't interested in C&W.

There was a stiff, brittle silence. "It was okay," Wanda said. "Karla dropped by, that's all. She visited one day when she had time. She came back the next day and said she'd take Angel out for lunch, and they did window shopping." Wanda had clenched her right hand and began rubbing it with her left hand. "She said she might be able to set up an audition. The promo guy was in town on business, and she was talking to him about investing in their place here. Maybe build a real fishing lodge, new cabins."

"What was he called?" Tom asked.

"I don't know," Wanda said. "I wasn't paying attention."

"Merlin," Derk said. "Merlin the Magician. He makes magic happen. He's got connections"

Tom asked Derk, "How long was Angel gone?"

"I dunno. I had deliveries to do. Out of town. You remember, you're not a cop anymore."

Wanda had started fidgeting. She began shifting nervously on her chair. "I had met a guy. He took me out. I was away overnight. It was okay. Karla said Angel could stay with her."

"Did she?"

"Yeah. Two nights. Karla said the guy thought Angel was really talented, and he gave Karla a guitar for her. Karla paid for a taxi to bring Angel home. She was tied up seeing her suppliers."

Ben had sat down on the overstuffed chair. He was watching his grandson and daughter and not saying anything. Finally, he broke the silence. "That guitar cost a lot of money. That's no cheapo repo, no ninety-dollar special."

Wanda was getting frustrated. "What's the matter with you guys? Angel did her thing. Karla was with her. The guy and his business partners thought she was great. He said that when he came to Valhalla on his yacht this summer, he'd sign her up. He'd heard her sing last summer too."

"How was she?" Tom asked. "She must have been feeling really good after getting that guitar."

Derk said, "She had a sick stomach. She got the flu. She didn't go to school on Monday."

"It was nothing," Wanda said.

"She liked this school?" Tom asked. "Good music program?"

"Yeah," Wanda said. "They were practising for a big concert at the end of the year. She had a solo. We were going."

"She left before or after the concert?"

"Before, I guess. She musta found out..." They waited as Wanda struggled with what she had to say. "About being knocked up. She didn't tell me."

"Who was her boyfriend?"

Derk jumped in. "No boyfriend. Not like that. A couple of guys in their music group used to walk home with her. They practised together after school."

"Did she tell you everything?" Tom asked.

"No," he replied. "She didn't tell me about being pregnant."

"You don't know what kids are up to," Wanda said. "It's all a big secret. Like, we didn't talk much."

"Nice guitar," Tom said and picked it up. "What are you going to do with it?"

"I think Karla wants it back," Wanda said. "I was at the store buying cream for coffee and she said it wasn't a straight gift. It was more like on loan to help Angel."

"Possession is nine tenths of the law. You keep it," Tom said, putting the guitar back into the case. "You got a cellphone?" he asked Derk.

"Doesn't work. Lousy reception. Maybe if you drive south or paddle around out on the lake."

Tom said, "I'll call from Freyja's. Are you friends with anyone at the Sapphire? Would you be able to find out what room this Merlin and his friends were staying in?"

At Freyja's he called a friend who'd retired and was working for a private detective agency and asked him to run a credit check on the Whites. Derk called him with the names of Merlin and two other men. They'd stayed in a penthouse suite.

The next day he went to the dock while Karla was having her daily swim. When she went to climb up the loading chute, he put his hand down for her to grab. She shoved it away and took hold of the black metal spike that protruded. She pulled herself up. "Bugger off," she said. "Leave me alone."

"You're over ninety days behind on your bills. You're done. You can't get any more credit."

She picked up her towel and began to dry herself off. "I got an investor. He's interested in putting up a proper lodge. The kind of place hotshots will want to come."

"Merlin?" Tom said. He saw the surprise on her face. "I don't think he's coming back."

She gave a half laugh, as if to brush off his suggestion. "We've got a deal." She pulled off her bathing cap and shook out her hair. "We're going to build— log cabins, ten bedrooms, a proper dining room, a bar, a lounge with a stage and good sound equipment. We'll tear down the piece of crap we're in. It'll be all Western style."

"There's no deal," he said. "You want to talk privately?"

She wrapped herself in her beach towel and followed him down the dock. "Your place?" she asked.

Instead of going inside, he stopped at his picnic table and sat down. She sat down opposite him. Without her makeup, she looked her age, older than her age. The lines in her face showed and her skin was pale.

"You can't pay your bills and Merlin is going to magically fly away. He won't even come to say goodbye."

"Why are you doing this? What business is it of yours?"

"People have been blaming me for what you did. That made it my business. I don't want to wear that."

"What did I do?"

"You took a fifteen-year-old to the Sapphire Hotel. There were three men in the suite. I've got their names. Two of them had sex with her. She got pregnant. You're an accessory to rape, to corrupting a minor. I've got corroboration from her brother and mother."

"You can't blame me. Merlin saw her perform here. He was hot for her. He likes girls that look like her. Cute but sort of boyish. I wouldn't have hired her last summer, but he kept pressuring me. 'Give her a job.' So I hired her to scoop ice cream. He kept asking me if I could bring her to serve food."

"Or have a fashion show. I've got a witness for that, too. Underage girls serving liquor, doing drugs, being paid for sex. You can call it gifts, but it is still payment. You think that Tracy isn't going to blab when she's questioned?"

"Angel never did a show. Look, I don't know what happened. All I did was arrange an audition. One of them was interested in me. We went into a bedroom. We were there for quite a while. It wasn't wham bam thank you ma'am. When I came out, Angel was lying in the other bedroom. She had her clothes on, but they weren't on right. I got her to sit up and straightened things out. I helped her downstairs and got her into a taxi. I figured she'd had too much to drink. We went to my place. She threw up during the night. She didn't feel too good the next day, so I went and got the guitar for her. She said she couldn't remember what happened, and I told her she played real good, and there was the guitar to prove it."

"What did they give her?"

"I don't know. I was in the other room. I was busy."

"You left her alone with two men."'

"I didn't know there'd be two of them. I just figured it would be Merlin, and he'd make her an offer. Most of the girls would have jumped at a chance. That's an expensive guitar."

"They didn't use any protection?"

"I told you, I wasn't in the room. Maybe a condom broke. They do break."

"You should have given her the morning after pill."

"I should have done lots of things. I didn't do them. I feel bad about this. I try to create opportunities."

"What kind of pictures get taken at these parties?"

"Picture pictures. They're just pictures. Publicity photos for their portfolios."

He remembered the box from Frenchie's truck. Fancy lingerie. Supposed to be for women-only parties.

Karla went to get up, but he caught her wrist and held her there.

"It's a show. That's all. No touching. Just looking. The girls pose."

"The old guys must get pretty excited. You don't arrange any side deals in the cabins."

"I can't keep track of everybody. I'm busy hosting. I try to keep my eye on them. But you know what they can be like. Sometimes they get away on me. They're not all virgins, you know."

"And Angel? Was she a virgin? Was she worth more because she was?"

Karla's face twisted. Her mouth became a dark slash. "Merlin liked the way Angel looked. She turned him on. He kept asking me if I could arrange for her to come to one of the parties. I didn't think it was a good idea. I didn't know her well. He kept insisting."

"Was she an incentive for him and his friends to invest?"

"She wanted a good guitar. That's all she talked about. How was she going to get one? She had a good voice. I told her it was easy."

He waited. Karla's face was crumpling. "Nobody was getting hurt. I keep the girls' money for them. I'm not a crook. I've got it in the books. Every cent. How much each of them has earned."

"The night she died. You and Merlin drowned her to shut her up."

"We didn't. The little fool. She was hysterical. I took her to Merlin's boat. He said that he'd pay for an abortion, send her away to music camp, and she could go a few days early and have the procedure. She was scared shitless her grandfather would find out."

"You murdered her."

"We didn't. I told you, she was hysterical. It was raining. The deck was slippery. She was flailing at Merlin, and then she went running across the deck to get back into the punt. She was crying, and she slipped and she went over the side. We got into the punt, and she was floating face down. We couldn't get her into the boat. Merlin went back and got a bottle of whisky. We towed her to shore, dragged her up, Merlin poured whisky on her to make it look like she was drunk. I wanted to get help, but he wouldn't let me. He insisted we put her face down in the water."

"There was a bruise on her forehead."

"We heard a thump when she went over the side. She must have hit her head on the punt."

She twisted on the bench, as if sitting there was very painful.

"Look. I'm sorry, but there was nothing I could do. It was an accident. She fell off the boat. What good is making a fuss? You don't understand. You haven't lived here. What do you think is better? To take a chance, to get paid to get laid, or to get drunk and fucked by a local yokel for the price of a hamburger and a bottle of beer. Like Rose. You think she's going to have a good life?" Her voice rose. "Do you think it's better to get laid in the bed of some jerk's truck, and the next thing she's got a big belly, and she's living in a trailer with a kid, and she's seventeen, and then she's got another one because the guy is too stupid or lazy to use a condom? Why are you so goddamn pure, so righteous? Any risk is worth taking to get out of here and have a decent life."

"Why haven't you left?" he snapped back. "What are you doing here if you think this is a shithole?"

She looked like she would kill him if she had a gun handy. "Fuck you," she said, but there was a sob behind it, deep in her chest, like she was going to vomit pain. "I tried." It was short, sharp, hard as flint. She put her hands over her face and said nothing for a while. When she spoke, her voice was quieter, and she clenched her jaw. "Do you know what it takes to get up onstage night after night and wiggle your ass and tits and sing and listen to what the guys in the front tables are saying about you? Tonight this bar, tomorrow that bar. 'Come on, baby, sit in my lap and wiggle, so I can come in my pants.' Big laugh. And the bar owners wanting a feel or a blow job for a chance to sing in their crappy roadhouse. On the road, on the road, until you don't know what town you're in. Singing your heart out, hoping an agent is going to see you and say, 'You should be in Nashville' and mean it and help you get there."

After that she was quiet. "So," she said, "how do you want it? On top, underneath, behind?"

He didn't bother to answer.

"No. I'm too old, too ugly. Is that it?" She pulled her top lip in and clasped tight on it with her lower teeth. "People should have enough talent to make it or no talent. Hell is having just about enough talent. Just enough drags you out, wrecks your life. If you didn't have just about enough talent to make it, you could be happy being a secretary or a housewife or lots of things."

He found it difficult to look at her. She was crying now. Silently, her head forward, tears streaming down her face. "Do you know why I go swimming every day, why I have two and three showers a day, why I wear so much perfume? I can't get the stink of french fries out of my hair, off my skin. Everything I own stinks of french fries."

Karla took a deep breath, closed her eyes as she let it out. "Frenchie says you know about the pickerel fillets. People take the cash from Frenchie. When Siggi got in trouble, lots of them gave him loans. What are they going to do with the cash? They can't put it in a bank. He owes everybody money. He promised to pay it back with big interest. They won't lend Horst and me anything. They take the fish money, but they won't help us. I told them if we get the money and build a good place, the customers will come. You've got to have class to have classy customers. Business brings business. More work for everybody." Her voice was aggrieved, bitter at the perceived injustice.

"Angel's dead," he replied. "Sometimes the price of what you want is too high."

"You don't understand." She didn't look at him but at the table. "It was pouring rain. There was no moon."

"You saw her floating."

"Merlin got a flashlight. We couldn't get her into the punt. He rowed and I held onto her."

"And you dragged her up onto the beach. Merlin had the foresight to bring along a bottle of whisky."

"No, he went back for it." She shuddered at the memory. "She was lying on her back. He wouldn't let me turn her over because he wanted to pour whisky into her mouth."

"Her grandmother was Aboriginal. Ben says you 'don't like Indians.'"

"They're unreliable," she said. "They don't have to pay taxes. They can fish anytime they want."

"Is that why you took her to Merlin's hotel room? Why didn't you take Tracy?"

"He didn't want Tracy."

"I think you should close down the store pretty quick, start packing, get Frenchie to take you somewhere far away. Stay too long and I'll call my friends in Winnipeg."

"It was an accident," she repeated.

"It wasn't an accident when you took Angel to the hotel room. It wasn't an accident when you got your teenage waitresses to have underwear parties for the boaters."

She stopped and her face twisted in a grimace. "Why did you have to come here?" Her voice was tight and filled with pain. She moved her head from side to side, as if to shake off a nightmare. "Why have you got to interfere in things you don't understand?"

Tom left her then, sitting slumped at the picnic table. He was walking to Ben's when he saw Derk and waved him down. Derk pulled up beside him and he got into Derk's car. They sat there facing the harbour and the lake. Derk had the windows down and they could hear the shouting from the dock as kids pushed each other into the water. There were puffy island clouds sitting in a blue sky.

"We got business?" Derk asked. "Is this going to be a sermon on changing my life and becoming a preacher?"

"No," Tom said, and he told him about Angel, and Karla and Merlin.

"You going to call your friends and have them haul them away?"

"No point. There's no evidence. He's got lots of important friends. He's got money. Karla is scared shitless about losing her place and going to jail. He'll hire a hotshot lawyer for himself, another for her. Karla will suffer a memory lapse. They'll delay, delay, delay. Who's got the clout? An ex-cop with a bad leg and a bad attitude and a kid with a rep for dealing drugs? You and me, we've got a credibility problem."

"I'll take care of it. He's a client. He's anchored at Gull Harbour right now."

"It isn't worth twenty-five years."

"Accidents happen. There's new stuff in Winnipeg. Too pure. People are dying from it every day. The Magician likes nothing but the best."

"I don't want to know about it. If he knows people know, he'll leave. He won't be coming back. He goes back where he came from and the Whites don't get their financing. They're done. They're hanging on by a thread. Suppliers won't give them any more credit, and the salvage places deal in cash."

"No store? There's got to be a store."

"Bankruptcies happen all the time. They're over ninety days late. No more credit for them. You said you're dealing but not using. That means you must have lots of money stashed away. You could get the business cheap. Change professions."

"Me?" Derk exclaimed. "Groceries. A café. Rentals. There's no bling to it. Besides, I'm too young."

"Two dealers were found floating in the Red River just before my accident. Some guys shot up a house in retaliation."

"Look at this watch," Derk said, sticking his arm in front of Tom. "This is a Rado integral diamond ceramic bracelet watch."

"Pizza," Tom said.

"Yeah," Derk replied. "The pizza is a good idea, but you can't live on two months of business a year. People want my spices every month. Siggi could finance it after he gets his debts paid. Local hero." He hesitated, then said, "If your friends would stay away and I could sell spices out of the store, it might work. You pull some strings and make me a licensed dealer." He laughed out loud at the idea and clapped his hands, once.

"Siggi gets his debts paid and if he has any brains at all, he is going someplace like Saudi Arabia to drill wells. If he's smart, he'll stay there until his business associates forget his name or end up dead."

"You want me to sell creamed corn?"

"You're better dressed than Horst. You're a smart aleck, but you're much pleasanter than Horst. You could give Ben his contract back. He could help run the business."

Derk pointed at his watch, lifted up his necklace with its gold nugget. Waved it in front of Tom.

"The two guys in the river. They were wrapped in black plastic. It doesn't look like they were dead when they were thrown in. You like that idea, your ankles and wrists duct-taped together, then being wrapped in a couple of garbage bags and thrown in the water? There was air in the bags. They floated down the river for a couple of miles knowing they were going to die."

"You want to go for a ride?"

"No, I got a couple of phone calls to make. My kids. My daughter is two years younger than you. My son's a year younger than that."

"The red-headed chick with the great shape. She's got you on the hook."

"That, too," he said. He was going to take Freyja with him when he took Barbara to meet Anna, and without having to pay for a hotel room, he could take Freyja to listen to good live music, go to City Park. She had said she loved going to City Park; they could have lunch at the restaurant, and buy condoms in bulk. That's what a line of credit was for.

"What about Ben?"

"Later," Tom said. "After their place is shut down. After the Whites have gone. We don't want him taking his shotgun and blowing them away. He's too old for prison. They'll go away and live an unhappy life."

"Copper man," Derk said. "You're a wimp. Ain't you seen the movies? Going through the door with guns blazing. Bodies everywhere."

"It's just in the movies," Tom said. "They never show the consequences." He knew it was a waste of time, but he decided to say it anyway. They were just words, and they couldn't compete with an expensive car, gold chains, flashy clothes, a roll of money. What kind of work was grade eleven going to get? Esso, 7-Eleven, McDonald's? "I used to pick up the consequences. Siggi can't protect you anymore. He's hiding out because he can't protect himself. You get caught in his problem and my former colleagues will be pulling what's left of you out of your burned-out car or out of the river. Or somebody will punch you full of holes outside of a club. Your competition are assholes who can't think three moves ahead. They dial direct. Give it up. Ben's got enough grief."

When Tom got out of the car but hadn't yet closed the door, Derk leaned toward him and asked, "You gonna pay my mother's rent?"

CHAPTER 34

BARBARA

Tom took Freyja with him to see Barbara's parents. Freyja had been Barbara's teacher, and he knew that would carry weight. Tom emphasized that Barbara hadn't done anything wrong, that it was a misunderstanding. He ignored the ugly bruise on the side of Barbara's face. Tom explained about Anna Kolababa, who she was, what his relationship was to her, explained about her daughter, Tanya, and her need for a babysitter.

He'd seen a lot of houses like this—uncared for, unkempt, empty beer bottles on the table, kids a bit grimy—and he wondered how Barbara managed to keep herself tidy. She sat there, her hands clenched between her legs, staring at the floor, waiting for a verdict. He could smell urine, and he realized that it was from the youngest child who was wearing a soaking-wet diaper that hung nearly to the floor.

Barbara's mother whined, her voice high, irritating. She was concerned because she'd never lived in the city and feared that terrible things might happen to her daughter. Barbara's father was wearing an undershirt and kept pulling at hairs on his chest that stuck out from the shirt. He'd pull out a hair, examine it as if looking for something significant, then flick it onto the floor. What he wanted to know was how much Barbara would earn, how and when she would get paid, and if her employer would mail him her cheques for safe-keeping. He hadn't shaved for a few days, and his face was covered in dark stubble. There were clothes piled on chairs or hung over the backs of chairs, more dishes on the kitchen counter than in the cupboard. A summer with

Anna would be a relief. Maybe Anna and Tanya would need Barbara's services longer than the summer. If she worked out, it was at least a possibility.

"Why are you doing this for Barbara?" Freyja asked.

"I am partially responsible for her losing her job," he said, and he explained what had happened.

The next day, when Tom and Freyja pulled up to her parents' house, Barbara was sitting on the front step with a backpack. As Barbara got into the truck, her mother came to the door holding the baby. That may have been why she didn't wave goodbye. Tom got a glimpse of Barbara's father's face in the kitchen window. He was still in his undershirt.

The wind had died down during the night but had sprung up again with the dawn. Tom had gone to see Ben earlier to ask him about the wind. Should he wait to see if the wind died down so he could try to retrieve the rifle, or should he give up and go to Winnipeg? Ben had replied by searching in the shed for another paddle, picking up one end of the canoe while Tom took the other, and together they carried it down to the shore. They paddled to where Tom thought he'd dropped the rifle, but there was more than one place where the cliffs jutted into the water, and with the lake having risen with the wind, it was hard to pick the right spot. Ben held the canoe away from the cliff while Tom searched for the pencil stub he'd jammed into a crack. They looked at three places before he found it. The wind wasn't strong, but it was strong enough that the waves constantly pushed the canoe toward the cliffs.

"No good," Ben said. "You take the girls to Winnipeg. When it calms down, I'll go and drag." He was probing the lake bottom with his paddle while Tom kept them away from the cliff. He found the hole and went around the outside with the paddle. "Not a good place to go swimming," he said, and after a moment Tom understood it was a joke.

"You asked me one time if I knew where my kids were," Tom said. "I don't. I tried to call my daughter to get a phone number so I could talk to my son. No answer. I'll look for her when I get to Winnipeg. I'll try to track down my son."

As they paddled back to Valhalla, Tom tried to think of something to say that would help Ben, but every thought was a cliché. Ben's life had gone wrong and there was no point in searching for someone to blame. The loss of his wife couldn't be repaired. Wanda danced to a different band. Ben put everything

he had into supporting Angel and she, like so many, died because of the careless cruelty of others. They paddled strongly, holding the canoe away from the
sandbars. The roar of the waves meant there was no point in trying to have a
conversation. Derk, Tom, thought, was Ben's last hope. Henry would have said
Derk's life was doomed, the outcome predictable, but Tom hoped not.

After they carried the canoe back to Ben's, Tom said thank you, then, not
knowing what else to say, simply said, "I'm sorry about Angel." But it wasn't
just Angel he was thinking about, it was the girls he'd helped fish out of the
Red River, the girls he'd found with needles in their arms, the girls who'd disappeared, gone, never to be found, not just on the Highway of Tears but all
across the country. Reduced to photographs in files. Drawers of them. "I'm
sorry," he said, and they shook hands.

When he picked up Freyja, he mentioned that he'd talked to Karla and that
the Whites might be going out of business. Freyja said, "Oh, shit. I hope not.
No more pizza. I thought they were doing great. I love their pizza."

Barbara was sitting sideways on the small back seat, her backpack beside
her. Tom watched her in the mirror. He thought she might have turned to look
back at her mother, the house, Valhalla, but she looked straight ahead. She'd
never been to the city, knew it only from what Angel and others had told her,
small shared fragments, but she wasn't going to ask him to stop the truck so
she could jump out and rush back.

Barbara said nothing until they got to the road that turned south along
the lake. "Would it be all right to say goodbye to Angel?" she asked.

Tom slowed down, stopped and turned onto the lakeside road. He paused
to look at his land. The grass was bending in the breeze, and the tips of the
trees around the barn were fluttering slightly. Seagulls were riding the updrafts.
His land. He hadn't given it much thought—just a place to cut firewood, hunt
ducks and geese—but now it had possibilities.

"What are you thinking about?" Freyja asked.

"A horse," he replied. "Maybe lamb and fish in the freezer. Possibilities."

The crushed limestone surface was as dusty as ever. The roadside weeds
and trees looked bleached.

He pulled up in front of the church, and they waited for the dust to settle,
then climbed out and walked across the road. As they followed the path that

had been cut for the burial, grasshoppers made graceful arcs. The lake spread out before them, its surface endless points of reflected light. A hawk floated overhead. Having grown up in the city, on a street where traffic never really stopped, he was still astounded by the silence.

Angel's grave had no headstone. Ben had said he would buy one when he could afford it. Wanda wasn't sure that it was necessary, and Derk had rolled his eyes at their response and pointed to himself. The earth over the grave was no longer dark. Instead of a rich black, it had a greyish crust. Freyja had stopped to pick wild daisies. She laid them on the centre of the mound.

A raven called its clunky, wood-chopping cry, and Tom spotted it sitting on the arm of the church's broken cross. A second raven swung in a circle, dropped to the ridge of the church roof, flapped its wings twice, then settled to watch. Tom made a mental note to negotiate for a ladder from Johnny Armstrong, maybe hire him to cut down the big spruce around the house. Make amends. Tom would cut a new arm for the cross and screw it into place. A favour for Pastor Jon in return for a favour received.

He'd been here twice before—the first time for Angel's funeral, the second as he fled from Siggi. Now, the churchyard had a feeling of familiarity about it. The weathered headstones showing above the grass, the lake to the east, a broad swath of pale blue to the horizon, the overgrown road he'd followed, the manse and church with the well; he could feel the cold water again as it numbed his mouth and throat. Pastor Jon's truck was gone, but the equipment lying around the yard, the small greenhouse and the beehives all kept it from looking abandoned. The sheep were lying in the shade of some moose maple trees. He turned slightly, picked out McAra's grave and wondered where his bones might be. Lying on the bottom of Lake Winnipeg, buried in shifting sand or mud, or walking around a wealthy neighbourhood in California. And gold, tins of it, boxes of it, in a cave or crevice, or like the bones, on the bottom of the lake or perhaps buried on one of the local islands, a fortune for the finder.

Barbara stood at the side of the grave, staring at the bouquet of white daisies. Her head was tipped forward, tears trickling down her cheeks. Finally, she put her hand on Freyja's arm and said, "We were practising this. We were going to sing it together on a Friday night. I wanted to sing it at the funeral, but Mrs. White said no." Barbara shut her eyes, and still holding Freyja's arm, she began to sing, her voice sweet, rich, her words precise.

All in the merry month of May,
When green buds they were swelling,
Young Jemmy Grove on his death-bed lay
For love o' Barbara Allen.

Freyja took Tom's hand. For a while, the silence was filled with Barbara's voice. When she had finished, Barbara turned to Freyja, and Freyja put her arms around her and held her, then Barbara stepped back, attempted a smile and licked a tear off her upper lip.

A grasshopper jumped up and landed on Freyja. Tom reached out and gently took it off her shoulder and flipped it into the grass.

"It's a long drive," he said. "We'd best get started."